BLACK WOLF

"I suppose it is time we met. I am Ian Blackstone, and I assume I have the pleasure of meeting Kolyn MacGregor. Am I right?"

"I assure you, Blackstone, there is no pleasure."

"I thought so."

"What exactly is it you're thinking? Are you wondering what to do with me?"

"Yes. You've been causing me a lot of trouble lately."

"And I'll cause you more before it's over."

"Damn you, woman. What do you want from me?"

"I want you to pay for what you have done to me."

Ian looked at her for a long moment. "Nothing I have can ever replace your family."

"No, nothing can do that."

"Then what is it you want? What will you get out of my life?"

Kolyn moved closer, standing toe to toe with him. She craned her neck to look into his disturbing eyes. "I want your life, Ian Blackstone. I want you dead!"

Other *Leisure Books* by Fela Dawson Scott:
THE TIGER SLEEPS
GHOST DANCER

BLACK WOLF

FELA DAWSON SCOTT

LEISURE BOOKS NEW YORK CITY

A LEISURE BOOK®

April 1994

Published by

Dorchester Publishing Co., Inc.
276 Fifth Avenue
New York, NY 10001

Copyright © 1994 by Fela Dawson Scott

The name "Leisure Books" and the stylized "L" with design are trademarks of Dorchester Publishing Co., Inc.

Printed in the United States of America.

To Lesley Kellas Payne—
Thanks for helping my dreams come true.

BLACK WOLF

Somewhere in the far north of the Highlands,
where mountains shear the sky and dense
forests darken in the full light of day,
they tell of the Black Wolf, known
by his golden eyes.

Some say he is a man—as any other.

Yet, when the full moon's pale light
shadows the night and howls carry
from the woods across mottled
moors on the wind's raspy tongue, they say
the Black Wolf roams free—

and the man and the wolf are one.

Chapter One

1512

It was over. Kolyn MacGregor understood that. No more clash of steel on steel. No shrill battle cries. All was silent, though she could sense an eerie song, the notes of sadness where time meets death.

Kolyn took a deep breath. Then she stepped into the tiny hut where her father had been taken. When her eyes adjusted to the dim interior, she saw her father's men gathered about the pallet where he lay, his death bed a blood-soaked straw mattress on the dirt floor.

She thought it sad that her father should die in such a dismal place, that the dead and dying were in a shack unfit to shelter pigs.

She wanted to cry. No, she *needed* to cry, to ease the tightness in her throat and the pain in her heart. Her gaze moved to her brother's body, his plaid covering him. Neither tears nor begging had convinced Gilles of his foolishness, or that of their father.

She regretted not watching the challenge. Her own stubbornness had kept her at Gregor Castle. She was unwilling to watch another brother die needlessly. If she had been there, perhaps she could have stopped the MacGregor from attacking the Black Wolf after Gilles had fallen. Then her father would not be dying as well. Kolyn forced herself to turn away, to stop torturing herself and give her attention to Douglas MacGregor while he still lived.

"Father."

All eyes turned to her.

"Kolyn."

Dwight MacDougal, her uncle, crossed the hut and took her hand in his. She noticed how small her hand felt enclosed in his massive one.

"Come, Douglas has not long t' live. We dared not take him t' the keep."

Licking the dryness from her lips, Kolyn raised her gaze to meet her uncle's, his hazel eyes filled with sadness and pain. Still, he squared his shoulders, and his courage helped Kolyn step forward.

"Father." She took the MacGregor's bloodied hand and held it to her heart. "I'm here."

12

The MacGregor's eyes fluttered open, his faded green gaze meeting hers. For the briefest moment, something flickered in them, like memories of long ago. "Katherine," he mumbled, barely loud enough for Kolyn to hear.

"Father, it's Kolyn."

Recognition showed on his pale face. "Kolyn." He drew a shaky breath. "'Tis damned uncanny how much you look like your mother. All that red hair . . . those emerald eyes."

Kolyn tried to smile, but failed. She bit her lip to stop it from quivering. "We will get you well, then—"

He raised his hand, pressing his fingers to her lips and silencing her. "I'll not be gettin' well this time, daughter. Death, 'tis near."

He waved his hand to his men. "Leave us. I wish a moment in private with my daughter." Then MacGregor called to his half-brother, who was following the men outside. "Dwight, you and Father McCloud will stay. You shall bear witness to my daughter's oath."

"No," Kolyn cried out in surprise. She turned back to her father and whispered. "I'll not be a part of this."

For five years she had struggled to remain apart from the madness, the hate, the feud. The MacGregor had no more sons—there could be no more challenges. This must be the end.

The MacGregor's face became a stern mask, anger bringing a temporary fire to his eyes.

Fela Dawson Scott

"You are my daughter. You will do as honor demands."

Most would not dare to oppose the man, but Kolyn understood only the fierceness inside her that overrode her qualms. "Honor?"

"Aye." The MacGregor's tone spoke his fury. He struggled to raise up, but weakness held him down. "Aye, honor. You *are* just like your mother."

"Aye, I am." Kolyn stood firm. "And I'll not let you touch me with your madness, Father. I won't let you."

"Madness, you say. What do women ken of revenge?"

"Revenge." The disgust she felt colored her voice, years of violence and grief crystallized within the single word. "It's hatred that has driven you."

"Aye, lass. Hatred does fill me. Hatred for a single man who has killed and crippled my sons, and now I be dyin' from his sword. He has seen to it the MacGregor Clan will not live on. Your words are blasphemous. The clan's honor has not been regained, and revenge must be taken by the last of my kin."

The blood drained from her face. This would not be the end. Her father meant for her to continue in his place. "You cannot ask this of me."

Kolyn had never felt such desperation. She thought she could not breathe again, the air remaining still within her chest. The

14

MacGregor just watched her, and she knew he was thinking. It wasn't until a sudden pain seemed to shoot through him that he turned away.

Finally, when he was able to speak, he asked, "How can you deny me, daughter? To dishonor the clan means banishment, child. Would you risk this? Would you let me die with shame in my heart?"

These questions did not come out so fiercely as the previous words he had bellowed at her. Still, she did not back down. But neither would the MacGregor.

"Dwight," the MacGregor called out. "Get my men."

Once they had gathered within, the MacGregor spoke for all to hear, but his eyes remained on Kolyn. "You're the last of my children. All before you are dead, excepting Emmett, who lies dead inside a crippled body."

The impact of his words left her silent, grief returning to attack her bravado and strength.

The MacGregor went on. "You will take my place, lead the clan. You are the MacGregor now, Kolyn."

Shock replaced sadness. A woman had never been named MacGregor. "Father! I cannot. 'Tis not done."

"It matters little to me what has been done or not. You will obey my decision. 'Tis your duty,

Kolyn. I will not hear denials of who you are again."

Feelings of shame swept through her. "I understand, and I'll not fail you." Kolyn prayed it be all he asked.

Contentment flooded his expression before another grimace twisted his features. "I must be askin' for a promise, a promise you'll keep or die."

Fear pricked the back of her mind, but Kolyn ignored it.

"The Black Wolf, he must die . . ." Pain snatched his words. He moaned. Then he grabbed her hand. "He is the Devil, and he must die. Promise me," he demanded, his voice shaking.

Emotions warred within her. She couldn't. She wouldn't. She opened her mouth, but no words came.

Her father pushed his bloodied sword at her, his eyes telling her more than his words. "Swear it, upon my sword."

She could not move. Her father's eyes widened from his exertion, his disappointment in her hesitation apparent in their depths.

He leaned forward and whispered, "You cannot shame me, daughter. Will you kill this man for the sake of your clan? Is your love for your people strong enough?"

Again she tried, but no words formed in her dry mouth. She felt the eyes of her father's men bearing down upon her, questioning her sense of honor. How could she promise such a thing? It went against everything she believed in. She abhorred the hate, the killing, and now this was expected of her. This was her duty as the chief of the clan MacGregor.

The promise lay unspoken in her mouth. But, how could she deny him? To deny her father, the MacGregor, would mean banishment. No one would take in someone who brought shame upon her clan. And what of Andrew? She must take care of her son.

Out of all the conflicting emotions rising like a whirlpool inside her, one dominated. The desire to protect and provide for her son rushed forth so fiercely, her decision was made without distinct thought.

Kolyn drew her shoulders back and stood proud, stilling the terror and apprehension she felt. She placed her hand upon the hilt of the claymore. The words fell from her tongue, empty of the feelings she carried within her heart.

"Upon all that is holy, I shall see the Black Wolf dead. That I promise you, my father."

"You have your mother's blood, but mine as well."

The MacGregor motioned for his brother to come close, his words for his ears only. "Kolyn cannot fail . . ."

His words trailed off, choked by weakness and the tears that suddenly gathered in his eyes. "'Tis Kolyn who must regain the honor of the

MacGregor clan. Watch over her, Dwight, as I cannot."

Dwight nodded, then stepped away. He did not meet Kolyn's gaze. Once again, fear rested heavy upon her heart. When she looked back to her father, it was too late. No more was to be said.

The weakest of smiles curved the Mac-Gregor's mouth, then stilled, as did the rise and fall of his chest. With a strange calmness, Kolyn closed his eyes and laid his hand down. She removed the ring from his littlest finger and placed it upon her own. When she turned to leave, her father's men dropped down onto one knee, showing respect to their new chieftain. Kolyn turned to her uncle, but he bowed his head before she could read the message in his eyes. As brief as the contact was, it made her uneasy.

Kolyn left the dimness of the old hut and walked out into the sunshine. She crossed the field where the challenge had taken place, but pushed the event from her mind. The men who saw her knew instinctively the MacGregor was dead. None offered her sympathy. She would grieve alone.

Kolyn was numb. Soon the smell of death and the taste of battle were left behind. She continued on toward the castle, neither thinking nor feeling. The grounds were quiet, too quiet. The knife grinder's wheel was silent, as was the bellows at the forge. No one drew water from the well. No one milled about at all.

She continued on to the equally deserted village. Shops were closed. The vendors were silent. Only the occasional sound of a barking dog drifted to her ears. When she came to a quiet meadow, beyond the village and just before the wall of forest, she stopped.

Heather bloomed in the knee-high grass, and a gentle breeze caused it to sway rhythmically. She knew it was beautiful, but its glory was lost to her, its sweet smell only faintly noted.

Dry-eyed, she looked down at her father's ring, heavy and strange on her hand. She touched it, as if reading its meaning with her fingertips and memorizing its form. She felt a great pain rip her heart, allowing her grief to flow.

"Why?" she asked the emptiness about her.

She was alone now, except for Emmett and Andrew. And she couldn't understand why. For five years they had been fighting, the MacGregors and Blackstone. Her father's hatred had possessed him, causing him to send his sons to challenge the Black Wolf. Gilles had fallen beneath Blackstone's sword this day. In disbelief and anger, her father had attacked and been struck down, leaving her now the clan's leader. She was the MacGregor.

She felt the great weight of her father's hatred descend upon her. She had accepted the cross of the MacGregor and she must serve the clan. Still, deep inside, Kolyn knew she had sacrificed her own beliefs and conscience upon this cross.

"Why?" Kolyn screamed to the darkening sky, raising her hands up, as if reaching for an answer. Slowly, she sank down to her knees. Finally, the tears came.

The Black Wolf sat upon his giant steed, watching the woman in the meadow. A plaid covered her head and face so he could not see her clearly. Nor could he hear her cries, the wind carrying them in the opposite direction. But he understood her grief.

Ian Blackstone allowed the coolness of the oncoming night to steal away the heat of battle that still ran through his blood. In time, it eased from him. The freshness of the air relieved the smell of death that clung in his nostrils, and the quietness about him calmed the clamor of broadswords that echoed in his head.

Yet he could not rid himself so easily of the pain that lingered within his heart.

The forest's lengthening shadows kept him well hidden from any probing eyes. He knew he should go, but something kept him in place, watching the woman.

His gaze never left her as she slumped down in the tall grass, almost disappearing in its lush greenness. Absently, he massaged his wounded shoulder, the pain no longer a concern. He thought of other things.

Darkness fell. Still, he remained.

"Why," he asked himself. Ian looked down at the blood on his hand. Some of his own stained his flesh, but mostly it was that of others, of his enemy. He recalled the image of the MacGregor as his own hand dealt the wound that felled the big man from his mount. He'd known the chieftain would not survive. This had been his last battle.

Ian clenched his open palm into a fist. *When would the MacGregor clan stop this madness?* It was another question he had no answer to. There was no one left to lead the clan. *Perhaps,* he dared to hope, this would be the end of it.

Ian shook his head to rid himself of the strange melancholy mood that had descended upon him. Then, with something akin to a growl, he spurred his mount and rode straight into the blackness of the dense forest. Only the slightest rustle of the trees marked his passing.

Ian paused when the wolf suddenly appeared. The animal's ebony coat blended into the dark shadows as the glimmer of golden eyes reflected the moon's light. Then it turned and vanished into the trees, swallowed by the night. Ian moved on and, faithfully, the wolf followed its master along the thickly wooded path, never far off.

Stonehaven castle towered above the cluster of cottages like a giant guardian. Ian rode his black war-horse down the cobblestone streets, the clopping of hooves against stone echoing in the quiet night. The tavern snuggled into the edge of the village. The sign that bore the name of the tavern swung back and forth in the breeze, rusty hinges calling out, much like the sound of the raven carved upon it.

Ian dismounted and ducked to get under the door jamb, closing the door behind him. He stepped into the crowded room, filled mostly by his own men. The smells of strong ale, smoke, and bodies welcomed Ian, just as the warm greetings did.

"Ian, I was beginnin' to think you would not be comin'."

The man who spoke rose from a table near the fire, then crossed the room to where Ian stood. Geoffrey's frame was as large as Ian's, but his height did not measure up to Ian's six feet, five inches.

"I've not much to celebrate, Geoff."

Geoffrey slapped Ian on the back and led him to his seat.

"I dinna ken your thinkin', Ian. The last of the MacGregors fell today. You're free of their cursed feud."

Geoffrey put a mug in Ian's hand and sat. "'Tis a drink you're needin'."

"Aye." Ian drank the dark ale down, then sat on the rough-hewn bench across from his friend. The fire snapped, spewing hot embers out onto the wood floor, where the red glow faded, then died, leaving only black soot. His empty flagon was filled, by whom he didn't notice, his mind on the day's events.

Ian felt Geoffrey's gaze and turned his attention to him.

"The old man was a fool to attack after his son fell. Served no purpose but to kill himself as well," Geoffrey offered.

"He carried a lot of hatred in his heart."

Geoffrey nodded. "Aye. His hatred drove him to his end."

"The MacGregor men died honorably. I faced them in challenge, and they fought bravely. It's not their ghosts that haunt me."

"'Tis time you laid the child's ghost to rest, Ian. 'Tis time to put the past behind you."

Ian growled in answer.

Geoffrey did not seem put off by it. "You dinna ken Blair was with child. You cannot go through life blamin' yourself."

"'Tis none of your business, Geoff."

Just as Geoffrey started to reply, the tavern maid leaned over the table between them, her posture allowing Ian full view of her ample bosom.

"Will you be needin' anythin' else, Ian?"

Ian tried to still his reflex, wincing at Leslie's use of his name. It wasn't so much the familiarity of his Christian name, but the way she said it, suggesting more intimacy between them than existed.

"Will you see that a room is fixed for me, Leslie. A bath would be appreciated too."

Leslie smiled, a seductive look lighting her pale blue eyes. She tossed back her long, blond hair. "I'll tend to it myself, Ian."

Again she leaned low, her lips almost touching Ian's ear as she whispered, "I'll wash your back, my Lord. An' whatever—"

Ian stopped her. "The bath is all I need tonight, lass."

Her lower lip pouted out. "Whatever you say."

Geoffrey pulled Leslie to him. "You can come to my bed when you're done, Leslie, my love." He brushed his lips over the roundness of her breast outlined by the fabric of her bodice pulled tightly against her. This caused her to giggle and pull away in pretended coyness, the swing of her hips as she walked away serving as her reply to Geoffrey.

Geoffrey laughed warmly, his gaze admiring her ample curves. When he turned his attention back to Ian he shook his head and gave another short chuckle. "You'd think the lass would ken by now that you prefer to be alone than with her."

"It's not any fault of hers. She's quite lovely."

"'Tis bonnie enough, Ian, but I know what lies in your heart. You long for a wife to love, a woman to mother your children and be beside you till death. Not just a warm body to ease your longings for a night."

It surprised Ian that his life-long friend knew his hidden desires so well. Perhaps even better than he understood them himself.

"Your arm is strong," Ian said. "Your strength guards and protects my back. But it's your friendship I value, Geoff. I could not have endured these past years without you standing by me."

Geoffrey turned away from Ian's praise. "'Tis your English blood that makes you sentimental." He turned dark eyes back to Ian's, a look of faith and trust lighting them. "But I'd give my life for the Scotsman in you. 'Tis him I follow."

Chapter Two

The sadness of the music vibrated through Kolyn. Each strangled note of the bagpipes reflected her sorrow, her fear. As the music gathered momentum, so did the beat of her heart and the degree of her pain. Her father had been a hard man, filled with anger and hate, but she had loved him. As Kolyn looked upon his coffin, she realized how much she would miss him.

Grief. It was too much a part of her life. There had been years of loss. First her eldest brother, Emmett, crippled; then Malcolm lowered to his grave and covered with the dark earth; and now Gilles buried too. Kolyn had argued with Gilles the night before he was to meet the Black Wolf in challenge, but he would not be convinced that it was insane. She could do nothing to stop Gilles's actions, any more than she could stop her father's hatred.

Kolyn's gaze moved to her mother's head-stone. Memories flooded over her, comforting her in her time of grief. For the moment, sadness and pain drifted away as thoughts took her back.

She could almost feel her loving touch, hear her gentle laughter, smell the scent of heather she wore. Her mother had been so patient with her, the influence of three older brothers making it difficult for Kolyn to know whether to be a boy or a girl. In the end, her mother's counseling had won out.

To this day, Kolyn tried to be a lady, just as Katherine had taught her. But now she was the MacGregor—the men in her life still influencing her, still at war with what her mother wanted her to be, with what she wanted to be.

A chill wracked Kolyn from head to toe, a chill of dread and fear. What kind of madness had taken her?

She looked down at Andrew's small head of black hair and lovingly stroked the soft curls. A fierceness grabbed her, and she knew what had possessed her. Her father's question rolled across her mind . . . *Will you kill this man for the sake of your clan?* Another question followed: How far would she go?

Kolyn knew the answer. She would walk

through Hell and battle the Devil himself to keep Drew safe. And perhaps the Devil was Ian Blackstone, just as everyone said.

Dwight MacDougal stood a respectful distance behind Kolyn MacGregor, but his eyes never left her. He studied her delicate shoulders and wondered at the strength she possessed.

Anger muddled his thoughts and compromised his loyalties. All his life he had been his brother's right hand, his devotion to the MacGregor never faltering, until now. Guilt assaulted him. Hadn't his father and half brother's generosity provided him his place in life? Dwight and his mother might well have wasted away in poverty had it not been for the MacGregor. He was a bastard child, with no right to title or wealth. Yet he had lived with his brother, accepted as family, none shaming him.

Still, it angered him that the honor of the clan fell to Kolyn. He had expected revenge to be his, had wanted his brother to trust this deed to him. And another matter caused him grief. It was this very person he watched intently.

She was so very much like Katherine. She looked so much like her mother, Dwight could not remember any difference at all. She had the same fiery hair, cascading in abundant curls well below her waist. Her eyes were the same green, vivid and full of life. The same ivory skin, touched by roses on her cheeks, her lips . . .

Deliberately, Dwight stopped himself, not

trusting where his thoughts were going. He dabbed at the sweat that dampened his upper lip with the back of his hand, his lip curling in distaste at his own weakness.

Katherine was dead, and she had been his brother's wife, not his. Kolyn was not Katherine. He would do well to remember that.

Yet he found it difficult to bring his emotions under control. His heart seemed to have a will of its own, constricting painfully as he saw Kolyn step forward with Andrew's small hand in her own. She bent to cup a handful of the damp earth, sharing the contents with her son. Together they scattered it over the coffin of her father, then repeated the ritual over her brother, Gilles.

When she turned back, Dwight stepped forward and took her elbow. "Come, let's go home, lass."

Kolyn lifted the tray from the table and maneuvered around its great width. The smell of freshly baking bread filled the warm air, and the meat already sizzled as it roasted on the spit. Nellie walked from the pantry, her arms filled as she began preparing for the day's meals, a soft hum reaching Kolyn's ears.

"Now," Nellie called out as Kolyn slipped through the door, "just leave that tray upstairs, lass. No need for you t' lug it down as well."

"'Tis no trouble, Nellie."

The Great Hall seemed so large and empty, the great feasts she remembered as a child forgotten in the past few years. Each step echoed off the stone flooring, no belly-cheer warming its coldness. No fire burned in the huge fire-basket that claimed most of one wall, and the hie burde, the raised platform, was abandoned. The window seat cushions looked worn, as did the tapestry's faded artwork that graced the hall. The chambray stood empty, Kolyn's father having sold off their plate of pewter and silver years ago. This saddened Kolyn and she rushed through to the stairs.

Slowly, she climbed the long winding staircase, balancing the tray with each careful step. Huge portraits of ancestors long dead stared down at her. Painted eyes seemed to reflect the importance of family honor, sober faces reminded her of her duty to the clan. Everything around her haunted Kolyn, leaving her shaken and confused, filled with the grief and pain of all her losses—the loss of her own identity among them.

Kolyn stood for a moment in front of her brother's chamber door, pulling her mind from its turmoil to concentrate on what was to come. She eased open the heavy door with her elbow, keeping everything on the tray balanced. The squeak of the hinge announced her entrance, drawing her brother's gaze to her. She forced a smile and a note of cheerfulness in her voice.

"Good morning, Emmett." Kolyn looked at

Jacob, Emmett's manservant, and gave him a smile too. His expression remained a stony mask of indifference. Regardless of her feelings, Kolyn had always tried to be civil to him, though at times she wondered why she bothered. Since she was a child she had never trusted the hard, stiff man, and still didn't. And now, she trusted him even less, knowing he was her brother's source of information about all that went on in Gregor Castle. She turned her attention back to Emmett. "Did you sleep well?"

Green eyes, the same shape as her own, narrowed, the look in them one of anger. Emmett was still handsome, but Kolyn could see his disability had aged him beyond his 31 years. The MacGregor men had inherited the intense green of their mother's eyes, but none had her fiery red hair. Instead they all looked much like their father, with strong, square faces surrounded by thick, brown hair. Their temperament also matched the MacGregor's in quickness and intensity, this one trait making Emmett so difficult to deal with.

"I slept as I always do, dear sister, fitfully. It's a good thing I have nothing to do but lie around, so I can nap, like a babe in his crib."

She tried to ignore his bitter words, but could not keep the blush from heating her face. Emmett laughed, the sharpness making Kolyn wince as she placed the tray on a table near the window. Jacob moved to her side, preparing to take over.

"You may go, Jacob. I wish to visit with my brother a while."

Jacob merely nodded. His thin, chiseled features never revealed anything to Kolyn, yet she sensed his dislike of her. With a straight back and slow, deliberate stride, Jacob left them alone. Kolyn wondered if anything would ever make him break his constant, even pace.

"Did you bury them properly, Kolyn?"

Moving to the window, Kolyn pulled open the drapes to allow the sun to shine in.

Emmett moaned and pulled the bedcover over his eyes. "Are you trying to kill me! Close the damn things—I prefer the darkness!"

Kolyn didn't pay any heed to his tantrum. "You need some sunshine, Emmett. It's gloomy in here." Gloomy didn't seem to be the right word for Emmett's sparse, cold room. She suspected that he intentionally kept it that way, making his bedroom a prison of sorts, a reminder of his confinement.

"'Tis the way I like it. That devil of a man has plunged me into a living hell, and I prefer not to see it too clearly."

Heat rose inside Kolyn, as it always did when he was like this. "Feeling sorry for yourself will not help."

"Yes," Emmett barked. "It does. Do not deny

33

me this small bit of pleasure when I have no other."

Kolyn bit back her response and unfolded the napkin carefully. Then she picked up the bowl of porridge. She stepped over to the bed, pulled the chair beside it, and sat. "Here, you'd best eat while it's hot."

Neatly, she tucked the napkin into his nightshirt, fully aware he was studying her. She offered him the bowl, but he made no move to take it. She lifted a spoonful to his lips, treating him like the child he mimicked. He turned away.

"Please, Emmett. You must eat."

"Why? It would be best if I died."

Taking a deep breath, Kolyn placed the spoon back into the bowl. "Is that what you want? To die?"

Emmett didn't answer for a moment. "It should be what I want, to end my miserable existence. But I want to live. I want to live so I can see that bastard dead. I want to take the devil to hell with me."

"The Black Wolf is but a man, Emmett."

"No," he yelled, his arm sending the bowl across the room, the thick porridge marking the path it had taken before crashing against the wall. "He is not a man, and you would do well to remember that."

Kolyn started to stand, but Emmett stopped her, his grip on her arm strong and painful. "You have promised to see the Black Wolf dead, to kill the devil himself. 'Tis no easy task. Three have died trying, and I lay forever in this coffin of a bed because of his unnatural strength. He cannot be killed, not in a challenge."

"How then will I do what you could not?"

"Are you truly so innocent?" Emmett reached out and pushed back a stray curl, then caressed her cheek. "A woman has ways of getting close to a man, and you, dear sister, are too beautiful for any man to resist."

"I . . . I could not," Kolyn whispered.

The hand that had stroked her so gently grabbed her face cruelly. "You will do what you must! You are the MacGregor now."

Kolyn broke away and stood, facing her brother. "You ask too much."

"Too much!" he yelled. "He crippled me! Look!"

Emmett threw back the cover to show his lifeless legs to her. "Look what he did to me!"

Licking her dry lips, Kolyn fought to keep tears back. "He caught you with his wife."

"She was to be *my* wife, not his."

"Blair was in love with Blackstone. Had her father not forbidden her to marry him because of his English blood, you would not have been engaged to her at all."

"Damn you, Kolyn. He stole her away on my wedding day. He made a fool of me!"

Anger brought life to Kolyn. "You men make fools of each other, and then you kill each other in the name of honor. Where does it stop?"

"It stops only when he is dead."

"And I am the one who must kill him." Kolyn stepped closer. "I am the one you expect to spread my legs for him, so I can kill him as he sleeps. You *are* mad, just like Father was mad. I will not be a part of this sickness that claims your mind."

Emmett smiled a smile that sent chills down her spine. She turned away and took a step toward the door.

"You have no choice, Kolyn."

This stopped her. "Let the clan banish me. I'll not kill him for you." Kolyn didn't know where that had come from, only that she had said it. Hadn't she vowed to walk through Hell to keep Andrew safe? How could she care for him if they were shunned? They would starve.

"Banishment is not your worst fate, dear sister."

Something in his voice made her turn back. She waited to hear what he had to say.

"Do you think that because I am a cripple I no longer have full use of my brain? I know the secret you hide, Kolyn."

She swallowed hard. "I hide no secrets from you, Emmett."

He merely smiled—slowly, deliberately. "Do you think I do not see your secret each time I look at Drew?"

"What . . ." Her voice threatened to reveal her fear, but she stilled its tremor. "What do you mean?"

"I mean . . ." Emmett drew his words out, obviously taking delight in his cleverness. "I mean that Drew is Blackstone's son."

Kolyn felt the blood drain from her head and the strength leave her legs. Obviously Jacob was more thorough in his spying than she had dared think, and her brother even more devious. She sank to the floor.

"It wasn't so difficult for me to put it all together. Doesn't it worry you others may discover this fact too?"

"You wouldn't!" Horror swept over Kolyn, numbing her mind. "Emmett, please . . ."

Emmett laughed again; his callousness brought tears to her eyes.

"He is not Blackstone's son," she cried.

"You are lying. I know Blair was with child. She told me that night we were making love." His smile widened. "Do I shock you, little sister?"

Grasping at straws, Kolyn said, "Blair didn't know who the father was. Drew could be your son."

"Stop with your lies," he yelled. "Look at him. He's a little Black Wolf. She may not have known when she was carrying the child, but she knew when he was born."

"Stop it, stop it," Kolyn cried, putting her hands over her ears.

Emmett leaned over and pulled her hands away. "What do you think the villagers will think when they learn that you had Blackstone's son, that you betrayed your people to sleep with the Devil."

"They wouldn't believe you."

"Wouldn't they? You left for the summer right after my *accident*. You didn't return till fall when they brought the animals down from the mountain pastures. You brought back an abandoned babe to raise, but you never mentioned that it was Blair's child. Many assumed it was yours."

"You don't know that," she argued.

"Don't I?"

Kolyn wanted to say something, to dispute his accusations. She said nothing.

"Blair abandoned Drew when he was born. She spent the next three months working like the whore she was. Then she became ill. She sent for you when she knew she would die. Kind-hearted creature that you are, you went to her. You promised her never to reveal who Drew's father was, to keep him safe from Blackstone."

Tears flowed down her cheeks. "Everyone turned from Blair. Her family, her husband, her lover. She had no one."

"She was a whore!" Emmett shouted.

A dreadful feeling struck Kolyn as she stared at her brother. Saliva drooled from the corner of his mouth as he screamed at her, and a strange glimmer lit something frightening deep in his eyes.

"They would stone you, Kolyn, perhaps even burn you for being in league with the Devil. 'Tis a terrible way to die."

She opened her mouth, but she could not utter a sound.

"What do you think would happen to Drew? The son of the Devil—"

"He is an innocent, you cannot mean—" she gasped.

"I cannot predict what these superstitious fools might do. And what about Blackstone himself? What might he do when he learns Blair's child is not dead as everyone believes. One look at Drew will tell him the truth. Blackstone abandoned his wife when she was with child, sentencing them both to a cruel death. What might he do to the child if he discovered he lives?"

His meaning was clear, and it terrified her.

"I will kill him, Emmett. I will do whatever you say."

"Good," Emmett sneered, his gaze following her as she stood and walked to the door. "Send Jacob to clean me and change my bedding. Napping isn't the only child-like habit I have since being condemned to this bed."

"You cannot mean t' carry out your promise?"

Dwight MacDougal's words echoed about

the great chamber, the large room void of the family warmth that used to gather around the large stone fireplace. Even the quiet, loving times spent with Drew seemed slight in comparison to past memories.

Kolyn turned away from the window and let the worn draperies fall back over the rain-spattered panes. "Of course I do, Dwight."

Her uncle moved closer, disapproval plain on his square face. His hooded eyes drew together in worry, reminding her of her father. "Have all your senses left you, Kolyn? Two of your brothers and your father have died, while Emmett lays in the tower a cripple for life. The Black Wolf is not a joking matter."

A strange anger touched Kolyn, spreading slowly inside her. "I make no jokes. I will see Ian Blackstone dead."

Dwight threw up his hands in total frustration. "You're mad!"

"No, I'm not mad."

"You are! You cannot fight Blackstone. He'll kill you. Do you understand?"

Kolyn's anger increased, more from her hopelessness than from Dwight's argument. "Of course I understand. I'm not without my senses. I do know what *dead* is. I've known little but death the last five years. And I do realize I cannot fight him."

"At least you're talking sensibly now."

"I said I cannot fight him, but I *will* kill him."

This caused Dwight to stop his irritating pacing. He turned his tall frame to face her. "What is it you're thinking, lass? Has the Devil taken you t' his heart?"

Something seemed to snap in Kolyn, a red haze floating over her like a thin veil, blocking all caution. "I'll do anything, I mean *anything,* Uncle, to keep this ugliness that has claimed the MacGregor men from Andrew. I'll take the devil Blackstone himself to bed if that's what it requires. I'll not let my son suffer for this so-called honor of the clan."

"You go too far, Kolyn."

"No, I haven't gone far enough."

Dwight slapped her hard across the face, the sound loud in the sudden silence that engulfed them. She saw his face instantly register horror at what he had done, and the shame of it soon followed.

"Kolyn, I did not mean t' hurt you." Dwight placed the hand that had struck her on her reddened cheek. "I cannot bear t' hear you talking of death and killing so casually."

Kolyn placed her own hand over his large one and turned her head to kiss his palm. "You are family, and you are forgiven, Uncle Dwight."

Dwight pulled his hand away, her innocent touch undoing his composure. He focused his gaze on an object across the room, something less emotional, less painful. He felt his heart beat, the warmth that flooded him not from his anger, but from a more insistent feeling and

41

need. He swallowed hard. For the second time that day, he experienced overpowering desire. Anger was safer than this.

"What is it you plan t' do?"

Kolyn shrugged her shoulders, and Dwight turned away completely. Even such a slight movement from her caused his body to react.

"I don't know. For now, I think I need to let Blackstone know I am the clan chieftain . . . that the MacGregor isn't dead."

The dream came upon Ian, as it always did, sneaking into his slumber with the stealth of a thief.

Ian landed heavily upon the dirt floor of the stable, in a heap of twisted arms and legs with Emmett MacGregor. Together they rolled, over and over, dangerously moving under the hooves of their mounts. The horses stepped away, used to the noises of battle, trained to remain close enough to their masters should they be needed.

Breaking free, Ian scrambled to his feet. In one swift motion he drew his claymore, just in time to block the blow that fell from his enemy's sword. The clang of metal on metal rang out, shattering the stillness of night.

"The Devil take you, Blackstone."

The Scotsman's ferocity exploded at Ian, but he matched it with equal fervor. "Don't you know, MacGregor? I am the Devil."

Ian brought the shining edge of his sword around in a great circle, its weight and his thrust slicing the air in a grim arc of death. The tip struck MacGregor's arm, tearing muscled flesh away from bone. Dark stains marred the bright tartan, seeping across his chest and down his arm. The big Scot didn't suffer a moment's grief as he countered with a cry of outrage and a shattering stroke of his own.

Falling to his knees, Ian braced against the great weight and strength of MacGregor. Sweat trickled down the length of his neck and from his brow into his eyes, burning and itching. He heard the guttural growl coming from the man, his nostrils flaring, his teeth gritted. As the blade inched closer, he felt the heat of the man's breath on his own face. Hate burned like coals in MacGregor's eyes, as threatening as the man's broadsword.

With a great burst of energy, Blackstone threw MacGregor from him, sending him tumbling. In two long strides Ian was upon him, striking out, their claymores clashing, steel against steel. MacGregor fought his way back onto his feet, the Scot matching Ian stroke for stroke, his wounded arm hanging by his side.

The muscles in Ian's arm quivered from exertion, yet he gave no quarter to pain or tiredness. He could no longer feel the weapon he held, each strike threatening to break his hold.

Blair's scream called up turmoil within. The flush of emotion made him stumble, and this time the cold edge of MacGregor's sword sliced into his side, blood marking the path the metal had taken.

The pain was immense, the weariness hard to overcome. He drew in a sharp breath, to ease the agony in his lungs, then swung his broadsword up in an arc, the force of his swing pulling MacGregor's weapon with it. MacGregor's heavy weapon flew into the air, landing with its point buried deep in the ground.

MacGregor's face showed surprise, then anger. Ian had the advantage, but he hesitated one second too long.

With another Highlander's cry, MacGregor jumped at Ian, his entire body lifting from the ground before slamming into him. Ian felt more than saw the point of his sword bury itself in the Scot. Together, MacGregor now clutching Ian like an animal its prey, the two men stumbled back until the wall blocked their way.

When they hit, the force knocked the air from Ian's lungs. MacGregor stilled as the broadsword went deeper. It took a full moment before Ian realized he held a dead man.

Ian came awake. He threw his long legs over the side of the bed and laid his head in his hands.

Pain crawled over him, just as it had the last five years, ever since that night he thought he'd killed Emmett MacGregor.

The dream, the memories, and the hatred hung about him like fetid fog. The feelings came full circle, just as they always did. Ian stood and crossed to the window. Angrily, he pushed aside the hangings and studied the night sky. The rain had stopped and the clouds moved away to reveal the full moon. Even it mocked him, its golden light a reminder.

Dwight stood at the side of Kolyn's bed, watching her as she slept. The great amount of drink he had consumed had dulled the lust that burned within him, but could not keep him from seeking her out.

He reached out and picked up a soft curl from the mass of red hair spread out in wild disarray on her pillow. The fire that still burned in the fireplace cast enough light for him to see the vibrant color, bright against the whiteness of the linen. He smelled the scent of heather she always used in her bath.

"Katey," he mumbled, the liquor slurring his speech. "My bonnie Katey."

He sighed, long and heavy, and dropped the curl he caressed.

"Dwight?"

He stepped back, startled.

Kolyn sat up in bed, pulling the bedcover up to her chin. "Is something wrong? Is Drew all right?"

When Dwight did not move or answer, panic took Kolyn. "Drew!" She tossed the cover aside, swung her legs over the side of the bed.

Dwight held up his hand to stop her. "Drew is fine. He's sleeping."

45

"Then why . . ." Kolyn brushed back her hair in sleepy confusion. "Why are you here?"

Kolyn could smell the strong odor of wine upon his breath. He took another step backward, and his tall frame rocked from too much drink. She felt anxious.

"I . . . I thought I heard a noise. I came in t' see if you were all right."

"As you can see, I am fine," Kolyn mumbled, her nervousness slowly turning to fear under his open stare, a stare that was unguarded and clear in meaning.

"Forgive me for intruding, lass."

When Kolyn heard the door shut, she let out her held breath, ending in a sob. She crawled out of bed and went to the door to listen, fearing her uncle would return. The sound of slamming down the hall confirmed he had gone to his own chamber. The relief that flooded Kolyn was so great it left her weak and shaking. She climbed back into her bed and hugged herself, pulling her knees beneath her chin.

Confusion muddled her fear. She understood the look upon her uncle's face. Having grown up with three older brothers had not left her totally innocent of men. What she didn't understand was why it was so suddenly there. Since her father's death, Dwight had acted strangely toward her. Something was now different between them. When he looked at her, she saw . . .

Kolyn didn't want to put a word to this feeling, not yet, not until she was certain. Shaking off her unwanted thoughts, Kolyn slipped from her bed and walked to the door. She winced when the hinges squeaked, the sound loud in the tense silence. She peeked outside. The long corridor was empty. Quietly, Kolyn moved to the room next to her own and stepped inside. The moon's light filtered through the tall windows guiding her way to her son's bed.

Andrew slept hard and undisturbed. Kolyn brushed a lock of hair from his forehead and watched him sleep.

"I promise, little Drew, I'll not let this ugliness scar you."

Kolyn closed her eyes, but tears escaped beneath her lashes. A deep-seated fury grabbed her and shook her clear to her toes. She turned and fled. She ran down the hall and into the bedchamber that had been Duncan MacGregor's. Above the stone fireplace hung a portrait of her father. Standing before it, she studied the man.

Her gaze fell to the claymore that lay in its place on the mantel. The sword the MacGregor had fallen with—the sword she had sworn her oath upon. Slowly, Kolyn removed it.

It was heavy, but it wasn't unfamiliar. She'd played with swords with her brothers more often than she'd played with dolls by herself. She lifted it high in the air. Kolyn felt a chill run over her flesh, but it was the coldness that

47

settled in her heart that terrified her—a stoic indifference that cut her tender feelings off, leaving her empty.

"I'll do your dirty work, Father. And may you be damned to Hell for the sins I commit."

With an anguished cry, Kolyn swung the broadsword and slashed the painting, bringing it back around to complete her destruction.

"What's the matter, lass?"

Kolyn turned to face her uncle, her emotions running too high to pull back. "Nothing's the matter. Go back to your drinking, Dwight. But mind you, you'd best be sober tomorrow. We'll be taking a midnight ride."

She dropped the sword. It clattered on the stone floor, echoing the thunderous storm that churned inside her. Kolyn walked past her uncle, but he grabbed her arm, stopping her.

"What madness are you planning?"

She twisted free of his grip and turned on him, the fear she had felt only moments before gone, leaving only anger. "Are you questioning me?"

The surprise was clear on his face, and he took a step back in the face of her fury. "You're the MacGregor. 'Tis not my place t' question you. Again, I ask forgiveness."

Suddenly, Kolyn felt foolish, wondering if she had overreacted to his appearance in her private chamber. "Once again I forgive you, Dwight. But only if you promise to be just as forgiving. I'm not myself."

"Nothing you could ever do will distress me. I love you, Kolyn MacGregor."

He was her uncle and he had said those words before. Only this time, what she heard made her take a step back. Something *was* different, and she understood why. "Good night, Dwight."

Chapter Three

"I spoke with Kolyn last night. She's not thinking straight, lad, and it worries me."

Emmett MacGregor watched his uncle pace back and forth at the side of his bed. He pointed to the straight-backed chair near his bedside table. "Sit. And stop fretting like a mother, Dwight."

Dwight did as he was told, his frame overly large on the simple chair. "Kolyn's talking crazy."

"She's harmless. Let her be." The look on Dwight's face prompted Emmett to go on. "Kolyn will be doing us a great favor."

Dwight's confusion was apparent even before he expressed it. "I dinna ken your point, Emmett."

"My point is," Emmett drawled, a smile twisting his lips, "my sister will provide a distraction for us while we do our business."

"What business is that?"

"Killing the Black Wolf."

Dwight said nothing, his only movement to push back a graying strand of hair from his temples.

"Kolyn swore an oath to see him dead," Emmett said.

"Aye, she did," Dwight agreed. "But a woman cannot fight Blackstone."

Emmett's smile remained. "Of course not. What a woman can do is distract the Black Wolf, keep his mind on other things, and then *you* can kill him."

This made Dwight smile, years of sun-baked flesh wrinkling up around his hazel eyes, a small scar appearing as it whitened against tanned skin.

Suddenly, Emmett's own joy disappeared. "I should be the MacGregor, not Kolyn." He pointed to his legs, lying dead beneath him. "My legs are useless, not my mind! I could have led the clan. Instead my father declares a woman chieftain, denying his son because of his shame."

"The lass will need your help, Emmett."

"Don't patronize me, Dwight. I will not just help, I will be the MacGregor. But first, Ian Blackstone must die. I want you to bring me that bastard's head!"

Dwight shook his head. "I cannot interfere with the oath she swore t' my brother."

Emmett was undisturbed by his statement. "You will, and together we can rule the clan."

Dwight stood and moved to the window.

Emmett went on. "I know it is a desire you keep hidden in your heart—to be a MacGregor . . ."

"'Tis an impossibility, lad."

"No," Emmett yelled. "You will marry Kolyn and become the MacGregor. I will be the brains; you will be my legs."

Slowly, Dwight turned back to watch Emmett, his features carefully masked to hide the surge of emotion he was feeling.

"Dwight, my dear uncle. Do you think I do not know your dark secrets? Do you think I do not know of your love for Kolyn?"

"Of course I love her, just as I love you, lad."

Emmett's laughter caused Dwight to wince.

"The look in your eyes and the fire in your loins are not for your niece, but for a woman. You can have her, Dwight, with my blessings. But I'll have no more of your lies."

Dwight moved back to the side of the bed. "Aye, Emmett. No more lies."

Ian rode through the cool shade of the forest, the sun's light blocked by the thick overhang of leafy branches, stretched fingers of entwined wood creating a canopy above him. The smell of dampness and earth was stirred with each step of his war-horse, mildewed needles and leaves long ago fallen softening the sound. He had spent the night in the forest, as he had many times in the past years, seeking the peace it offered.

He stopped when the black wolf paused, its ears alert to some sound Ian couldn't yet hear. The animal held his head high, then moved toward the noise. Ian followed and, slowly, the wind brought children's laughter and song to him. Curious, he rode to the edge of the trees, careful to remain hidden.

A group of children ran in the tall meadow grass, some so young they were nearly hidden, the elder ones helping them along. Their innocence rang clear in joyous laughter, contagious among them. It touched Ian, drawing him to their playfulness. He made out a young woman who ran amidst the children, a full head taller than the rest. Her voice was softer, gentler, her own laughter drowned out by the shrill cries of the children. His gaze remained on her.

Envy washed over him, the force of it catching Ian off guard. He watched her lift one child and whirl him about, his cries of delight heard above the others. The other children gathered close, their arms lifted to the woman, calling out to her to let them too fly like birds. One by one, she caught them up, then circled about so they could fly. Finally, she fell upon the ground in exhaustion. All the children piled about her, hugging and kissing her gratefully.

Ian's heart constricted and his breath caught in his throat as it tightened. He wondered if he would ever know the delights of having a child. Was he deserving of such pleasures?

In his own mind, he thought not. God had given him a child, and he had turned away in anger. Even the knowledge that he had not done so intentionally did not relieve him of the guilt. What would he have done had he known Blair was with child? Would his fury at her betrayal have tainted his feelings for the baby?

"Drew!"

The woman's cry intruded on Ian's thoughts, breaking his cycle of self-inflicted torture. It took a moment for him to locate the woman, who was moving away from the group.

"Drew," she called again.

Ian glanced back to see the older children gathering up the younger ones and starting back to the village. Only the woman headed toward the forest, her pace showing her urgency.

The little boy's cry from within the forest rippled over Ian, causing him to react instantly. Fear spurred him into action, his war-horse responding to his command. As Ian reached the child, the boar charged.

Ian hung low off his saddle and swept up the boy in his arm just as the black wolf intercepted the wild hog, blocking its attack. The growl of the wolf and the grunts of the boar sounded as they clashed again. The boar retreated in face of the wolf's fierceness.

Golden eyes looked into Ian's, the color like dark honey. Rumpled black hair and dark skin made him think this might have been what his son would have looked like—had the child been a boy and lived.

"Drew," Ian heard the woman call out again, her voice closer.

"Are you all right, lad?" Ian asked.

The small head nodded.

Gently, Ian lowered him to the ground. The child pointed to the wolf. "Doggie not hurt?"

Ian smiled. "Doggie's all right, Drew. Go on now."

Again Kolyn called out for her son, her instincts telling her of the danger. "Drew."

"Mommie."

Tears blinded Kolyn as she ran toward his voice. When she saw him, relief flooded her. She knelt down and hugged Andrew to her.

"You scared me, Andrew. You know you aren't supposed to wander off alone."

"I see bunny and wanted to take home."

Kolyn gathered Andrew into her arms and stood. "Let's catch up with the others."

Andrew twisted about in her arms and looked behind her. "Take doggie home."

Slowly, Kolyn pivoted about; then she froze.

"Nice doggie," Andrew cried, squirming to get down from her arms.

"Ssshhh," Kolyn whispered in Andrew's ear, stilling his struggles. "Doggie wouldn't want to come home with us. He likes living in the forest."

She took a cautious step away from the wolf, her grip on Andrew tightening as she prepared to run.

"Look," Andrew squealed in delight. "Doggie go home."

Daring a glance back, Kolyn watched the wolf inch closer. Fear rushed forward as a dominant thought, yet instinct told her that the animal was not menacing. He sat back on his haunches and waited, his head cocked to the side, as if curious.

"Doggie help me."

She didn't see any fear in her son's eyes, and when she looked back to the wolf, he had stretched out on the ground, his head cradled on his front paws. His manner was submissive, even friendly.

Kolyn tossed that notion aside, chiding herself for being careless. "Listen to Mommie, Andrew."

Andrew turned inquisitive eyes to her and waited.

"Wave good-bye to the doggie. We must go."

Andrew waved his chubby hand in the air, and Kolyn walked away, glancing behind every

Fela Dawson Scott

few steps. Now the animal simply watched them, making no move to follow. It wasn't until they were out of the trees that Kolyn allowed herself to slow her pace.

Ian turned to leave only when he knew the young woman and her child were safely away. He had not been able to see the woman clearly, her head covered and her face turned away from his view. He knew only that she had a son named Andrew.

"Come on, doggie," Ian called out to the wolf, then laughed outright at the child's innocence. A sudden desire rushed forward, and he longed for a dozen just like that little tyke.

Kolyn walked into the small village church, its doors open wide to any who wished to enter. As always, a sense of peace touched her, the support welcome in her time of inner turmoil. She paused a moment, gathering to her the strength it gave, then walked past the worn, wooden pews and the simple altar to the back, where she knew she would find Father McCloud.

"Good morning, Father."

Father McCloud looked up from his book and smiled, his gray eyes lighting with joy.

"Kolyn, what a pleasant surprise. You've not been by as often as I've grown used to."

The priest rose and hugged Kolyn, the strength of his grip belying the gray hair of age that covered his head. He picked Andrew up and tousled his hair with affection.

"You grow an inch each time I see you, lad." He gently set Andrew back down.

"Good morning, Father McCloud," Andrew said properly, looking as grown-up as his small frame would allow. "We have some bread. I helped Mommie make it."

Andrew reached out and pulled on the handle of the basket Kolyn held.

"See," he pointed proudly.

"My, what beautiful bread! Andrew, you are such a good boy." Father McCloud accepted the gift. "I just happen to have some gooseberry jam in the kitchen. Should we try this out? To make certain it is good bread?"

Andrew took the basket and ran ahead to the kitchen, his burden nearly scraping the floor.

"You spoil him, Father." Kolyn tried to look stern, but a smile replaced her frown.

Father McCloud's look told her he would not allow her this point. "Nonsense. And what of you, Kolyn? A lady of the manor does not bake bread. And what is this you are teaching Andrew?"

She merely shrugged her shoulders in feigned nonchalance, pushing off his concerns as easily as he had hers. Kolyn relaxed in the good father's company, their banter loving and honest. "I enjoy baking, and Drew enjoys helping me in whatever I do."

Fela Dawson Scott

"Well," Father McCloud concluded as they reached the tiny kitchen at the back of the church, Andrew anxiously waiting there for his bread and jam, "the better for me."

Kolyn sat beside Andrew, the small table barely able to seat them both. She watched Father McCloud retrieve the jam from a small, battered cupboard, which served as a pantry and sideboard in one. Carefully, he cut the warm bread, then spread it generously with the sweetened gooseberries. Andrew licked his lips and took the slice offered him.

"Thank you," he muttered politely, then wasted no more time before taking a big bite, evidence of what he ate left on his mouth. "Good!" He beamed his approval.

"I'll warm us some wine, lass."

It took Andrew only a minute to devour his treat. "May I go play?"

As Father McCloud placed the kettle upon the fire, Kolyn wiped the red stain from Andrew's face. "Stay in the garden. I won't be long."

Feelings of love filled Kolyn as she watched Andrew skip out of the kitchen, so full of happy exuberance.

"You are truly blessed, Kolyn MacGregor."

"Aye, Drew is a blessing . . . he is my life."

Kolyn paused, and the love that filled her heart was overpowered by a fierceness that shook her both physically and mentally. "I don't understand why God has chosen to curse me on my father's death. Why has he done this to me, Father?"

Father McCloud walked over to the window, his back to Kolyn as he watched Andrew playing in the church's tiny garden. "'Tis not ours to ask why, my child."

He turned back to look at Kolyn, his face sympathetic. "You cannot question the path he has chosen for you to follow."

"'Tis the path to Hell," Kolyn whispered. "I'm afraid."

"Your father has been buried but a week, lass, and your grief creates this fear. Look to God. He will guide you."

Kolyn stood and moved to stand by Father McCloud. "Sometimes I'm not sure my faith is strong enough."

He took her hand into his, then covered it with his other. His touch was warm and comforting. She wished she could remain in his care forever.

"You have always believed in God and trusted in him, Kolyn. Why do you doubt your convictions?"

She was quiet for a moment, then asked, "Do you believe that he can turn into a wolf?" Kolyn knew she didn't need to define *he*. "Do you believe in such witchery?"

The priest took Kolyn's hand and placed it upon his arm, continuing to pat it as he walked with her. They left the kitchen and went back to the chapel.

"Men are driven to many things by their weaknesses. A weakness in faith can be fed by ignorance, greed, or shame, leaving those who grasp it grasping their own destruction."

They sat upon a pew, and Father McCloud gazed at the cross and the image of Jesus. "Ignorance drives the people of the village to embrace the idea of witchcraft and spells. What they do not understand they blame on witchery."

"I've always been secure in what I believed, or didn't believe." Kolyn looked down at her hands, confused, unhappy. "But I don't know what I think anymore, Father."

"In the end, you will know what is the truth and what is not. Look into your heart for the answers."

Andrew ran into the chapel, a touch of pink on his cheeks from his play.

"Mommie!" He stopped in front of her, taking in big gulps of air. "For you."

He presented his hand-picked bouquet of flowers, pride glowing on his dimpled face.

"They're beautiful, Drew."

She accepted his gift and leaned over to kiss her son on the cheek, then pulled him onto her lap. Andrew laid his head on Kolyn's shoulder. Within seconds his eyes drooped, then closed in sleep.

"He's a lucky boy, Kolyn."

"In what way, Father?"

"He has you," he said simply. "It took great

courage to raise another woman's child as your own, and to love him so completely, so unselfishly."

"'Tis easy to love him. There is nothing I wouldn't do for Andrew." Her own words brought back the argument she had had with Emmett, and a cold chill ran over her. Kolyn's hold on Andrew tightened.

"Lass."

Father McCloud drew Kolyn's attention back to him.

"Kolyn, are you all right?"

"Yes," she murmured. "I'm fine."

Her words didn't seem to convince Father McCloud. "You looked quite"—he struggled for the correct word—"fierce."

Kolyn tried to pull herself together and put a carefree smile on her face. "I am fine. And we must be going."

"But the wine should be warm."

Kolyn gathered up her sleeping bundle and stood. "Another time perhaps."

He nodded.

"Father, I have a favor to ask of you."

"Anything, my child."

"Should something happen to me," Kolyn said, drawing in a deep breath and quieting her emotions, "would you take Drew?"

Surprise filled Father McCloud's face. "Child, what of your family?"

Kolyn did not wait for him to go on. "No, I want you to promise to take him away from here. Away from my family, and"—she paused again and then plunged on—"away from his real family."

Father McCloud looked confused. Then his eyes told her he understood. "I promise, Kolyn MacGregor."

She smiled in relief. "Thank you, Father."

"May God bless you and keep you safe, my child."

Chapter Four

Kolyn pulled back on her horse's reins as the animal stomped impatiently to be off. "I don't want anyone injured," she called out to the men gathered about her. She was comforted by Father McCloud's promise given that very morning, knowing that should anything happen to her, Andrew would be taken away from all this hate and vengeance.

Dwight MacDougal looked at her, his scowl telling Kolyn he was not happy with her or what they were about. But he did not say anything. For that she was thankful.

"We shall show Blackstone the MacGregor is not dead, nor to be forgotten."

A shout went up among her men, and she

65

understood their excitement. Yet her own emotions remained numb. Their actions gave them
hope, while it crushed her own hope, killing
the ideas and convictions she had always held
dear. The wind that whipped her hair about in
tangles kept her cool, keeping her mind clear
about the chore ahead. Her mount reared, his
giant hooves pawing the air.

As soon as the beast's front feet struck the
earth he was off, his tremendous might carrying Kolyn with ease. They rode quite a distance,
but it seemed like only a few brief seconds
had passed. They slowed their breakneck pace,
then stopped altogether. A silence claimed the
group, which only the horses' heavy breathing
and occasional snorts broke.

Kolyn looked at the stone hut, the smoke
that drifted from the chimney telling her the
family was inside, the soft lowing of cattle
letting her know their ride in the night had
not been for nothing. For this she was grateful,
even though she found it difficult to breathe
as apprehension overran her mind.

"Are you sure you want t' do this, lass?"

Dwight's deep voice penetrated her raging
emotions, the sound familiar, somewhat comforting. She turned to her uncle, determination
bringing up her chin to a defiant angle. "Yes,
I'm sure. He owes me a debt, Dwight. And I
intend on taking payment."

"Aye, I can see that. I dinna ken your reasoning's all."

A sigh escaped before she could stop it. "Reasoning has little to do with it. It is merely a means to an end."

"'Tis the end that I'm fearing, Kolyn."

A full moment passed, and Kolyn experienced an odd feeling of sadness. If she plunged on, there would be no turning back, and Kolyn would be forever lost to the duties and honor of the MacGregor. "One way or the other, it will come to an end."

"Aye, that it will." Dwight seemed puzzled over something. "What is it you're thinking? I'd be grateful, lass, if you'd tell me."

"I want the Black Wolf to know I am the MacGregor. He has taken my family from me, and this cursed madness has left my home and lands in woeful disrepair. We haven't enough stores to get us through the winter, and Ian Blackstone has plenty in his possession. So that is where I will start. Something for each brother that lies cold in the earth, and even more for Emmett as he lies abed for all his time."

Kolyn turned to look directly into her uncle's eyes, her voice deepening with emotion.

"I will become a persistent thorn in his side. I want him to feel angry, as I do. With anger comes carelessness. Then, and only then, will I take final payment for my father's death. His life."

"You're a determined lass."

"Yes, I am. Shall we go?"

Dwight nodded, then followed Kolyn as she rode off. A strange pride overcame his other emotions. He admired her ingenuity. Much of the time she was more like her mother, gentle and kind. But at times like this, she reminded him of his brother—strong and stubborn.

Once in the courtyard of the small farm, Kolyn slid from her saddle, and Dwight did the same. He remained only a few steps behind her, his hand resting upon the hilt of his sword, ready to defend her should the need arise.

Dwight stepped forward to pound on the door, then backed away to let Kolyn tend to her business. A sleepy-eyed farmer answered, a wary look filtering past the haze of slumber.

"Aye, what is it you're wantin'?"

"I've come to collect your payment to Blackstone."

"Do you realize what time it is?" The aging Scot rubbed a calloused hand over his head, pushing back his tangled hair.

"Yes, I do," Kolyn answered, patience reflected in her voice. "Now, please tell me what number of cattle you owe."

He raised a suspicious eyebrow to her. "Lord Blackstone visits me an' the wife an' decides what rent I pay. What are you doin' here?" His eyes narrowed as he studied the men who still remained on their horses. Nervously, his fingers wiped at the sweat that appeared on his brow, at the graying stubble prickling through toughened skin.

"We have no intention of harming you or your family. I want only the cattle you owe Blackstone."

Fear finally settled in the man, and he stepped back. "I can no' do this, lass. 'Tis my payment to Lord Blackstone."

"And"—Kolyn's voice remained even and calm—"I shall take these cattle as *my* payment. Tell Blackstone if he wants them, he can come see me."

"And who might you be?"

"Kolyn MacGregor. I am the clan chief, the MacGregor."

"This canno' be," the farmer said, his eyes widening.

"I *am* the MacGregor, and you'd be wise to remember my words. I want the Black Wolf to know who has his cattle and why."

He nodded readily, his shaggy head bobbing up and down anxiously. "Aye, lass. Kolyn MacGregor."

"Tell Blackstone this is only the beginning. He owes me a great deal, and I intend for him to make amends."

Dwight watched the man's reaction, the meaning of Kolyn's words slowly sinking into his simple mind. Again the farmer nodded, even more vigorously than before. Dwight stepped forward and demanded, "The number for payment?"

The farmer held up his hand, giving them the number.

Kolyn smiled and motioned for Dwight and her men to collect them. "Blackstone is a very generous landlord."

"Aye, most generous," the old man agreed.

"Now, remember to tell Blackstone exactly what I've told you. You will remember?"

"Aye, every word. I will no' forget."

"You'd best go back to bed. My apologies for having disturbed you."

Without saying more, Kolyn walked back to her horse and mounted. She wasn't prepared for the guilt that engulfed her when she looked at the man standing in the doorway to his house, his mouth still agape in wonder. She pushed the feeling aside and gritted her teeth in anger. How she hated this war of wills that struggled inside her. Tonight she had proven she was the MacGregor to her men, to the Black Wolf, and to herself. She could not tolerate any weaknesses. She would not!

Ian Blackstone stood in the small cottage, listening to the story his tenant, Malcolm, was telling. A cold anger churned inside him, an old anger he had hoped could be buried with the MacGregor.

"This woman claimed to be the MacGregor?"

"Aye, said she was Kolyn MacGregor—the new clan chief."

"That's impossible!"

Ian regretted his show of temper, the old man cringing beneath his rising voice. "I don't mean

70

to dispute what you're saying, but . . ."

"A bonnie lass she was. Said if you're wantin' the cattle to go see her. Said she would be back."

"Well," Ian drawled, deciding it not worth his anger. "The witch is welcome to them. Perhaps she's worked out her tantrum."

"Perhaps," Malcolm agreed, but doubt crept in his voice. "I did no' do anythin' to stop them."

"You were wise not to fight over a few cattle. Do not worry about them. Just watch after your family, and I'll take care of this Ko . . . K . . ."

"Kolyn," Malcolm repeated as Ian stumbled over the name. "Kolyn MacGregor, Lord Blackstone."

"Aye," Ian mumbled. "I'll remember her name from now on, Malcolm. I'll remember."

It was true. He would not forget. Kolyn MacGregor's name was burned into his memory by a fire he foolishly thought had died with her father. Ian let his mount run, a fast, hard ride working the anger from him.

Over and over the scene played out in his mind, and each time he came up with the same solution: nothing. By the time Ian reached Stonehaven, he had convinced himself that she would not be so foolhardy again.

"Here's to our benefactor."

Kolyn lifted her drink to salute Blackstone, the man who generously, though unwillingly, had provided the meat for their feast. For two days the spits had turned over the stone fireplace in the great hall as well as in the kitchen, the staff happily preparing for the celebration. Meat juices dripped into the flames, sizzling, and aromatic smells filled the air. It had been much too long since Gregor Castle had known such joy. Everyone quieted to hear Kolyn speak.

"To Ian Blackstone!"

This time everyone joined her, lifting their mugs to him, their shouts ringing clear and echoing against the stone walls in the large room. The music began again, bringing many to their feet in dance.

As Kolyn joined in the gaiety, her laughter drifted to Dwight, distracting him from his conversation. Her hair was loose, the jubilant dancing causing it to fall from its plait. It spilled like fire about her delicate shoulders, the light of the torches giving it life. Her face was flushed, and a brightness sparkled deep in her green eyes. Never had she been more beautiful.

His gaze followed her as she was pulled back amongst the dancers. The young man who whirled her about seemed to have had too much to drink. Dwight scowled, not liking the way the lad looked at Kolyn.

Dwight drained his flagon of wine, then held it up for more. The more he drank, the less he would feel; he was sure of it. Enough wine and the burning inside him would be overcome with the numbness of drink. Again he emptied his cup.

A buzzing already invaded his mind, blurring his sight and slurring his thoughts. But still, he could not keep his eyes from Kolyn. She danced with the same Scotsman—his name escaped Dwight at that moment, but his name didn't matter. What did matter was the hand that slipped about her tiny waist, the fingers that slid down over the gentle swell of her hip.

Dwight's grip tightened about the pewter stem and he drank again, long and deep, wishing for it to cool the heat spreading from his loins. He ground his teeth in vexation, clamping harder as the man pulled Kolyn closer.

Jumping up, Dwight strode through the crowd like a bull, pushing aside and shoving those who stood in his way. His fierceness and bulk guaranteed no resistance as he reached for the man who danced with his niece.

"Get your hands off her, lad, or I'll be splitting your head in two."

"Dwight." Kolyn's smile faded, and she scowled. "You're drunk."

"Aye, my lady. That I am."

"Perhaps you'd best retire."

Dwight was familiar with that look and knew better than to go against her. But he wasn't in the frame of mind to take heed of her warning. "I'll not let the lad paw you in such a way. He owes you an apology."

Kolyn braced her feet apart and placed her hands upon her hips. The anger nearly leaped from her emerald eyes, and he would have sworn he saw flames of a fire within them. The persistent knot that lay in the pit of his stomach tightened, causing him great discomfort.

"He was doing no such thing, Dwight. Perhaps it is *you* who owes the apology."

This took Dwight totally by surprise. How in heaven's name did she come up with that? Women! He wanted to throttle her . . . no, he wanted . . .

"I will not stand by and let him . . ."

"Let him what? Dance with me? Are you going to split everybody's head in two, Uncle? And . . ." Kolyn stopped, lowering her voice for his ears only. "If I *were* being pawed, I do not need you charging in to rescue me."

"Hah," Dwight barked, making her flinch at his sharpness. "You're needing someone t' rescue you, lass. You're bent on finding trouble."

"Yes, I am," she replied, her eyes squinting up into his darkened ones. "If trouble has the name of Blackstone."

Suddenly, Dwight's look of anger changed into another, stranger one. "Let me take care of him, Kolyn. I'll kill the bastard for you, and for Douglas."

"You cannot. You know that. It is for a

MacGregor and no other." Kolyn's voice softened, but her words were firm, brooking no further disagreement.

"I'm half a MacGregor. Does that not count for something?"

Kolyn wished it did. But when it came to a Scotsman, his clan, his honor, his very way of life, it did not. "This is not for you to deal with, Dwight MacDougal, but for me and me alone."

He stood staring down at her, hurt and anger clearly reflected in his face. Kolyn feared to breathe, thinking he would explode at any moment. Instead, he turned and walked away.

Dwight didn't stop until he reached the door to his rooms. He stood in the hall, his hand poised upon the door handle, listening as the noises drifted up to him. His eyes closed when Kolyn's voice came to him. He quickly disappeared into his room to escape the torture. The fire in the fireplace had burned low, casting only shifting shadows and dim light about his room. At that, the gloom around him was bright compared to the despair he carried in his heart.

The wine had taken away the intensity, but the feeling was still inside, gnawing at his innards like a disease consuming muscle and flesh. He could no longer control it. It came at its own will, as if his passions had a mind of their own. He felt the wicked desire festering, turning into a monster of sort, taking his mind under its control.

"'Tis a wickedness you have awakened in me, Kolyn. I dinna ken what t' do."

Carefully, Kolyn placed the parchment back into the pouch and tied it securely. It had taken a second raid for Ian Blackstone to respond to her, his message gracious despite what she had done. If she were to act as Kolyn, she would accept his offer, but as the MacGregor she could not. She walked across the hall to the boy who stood waiting for her reply just inside the front doors.

"Tell Lord Blackstone that . . ." She paused, uncertain for a moment what to say, then shoved the pouch at him, making him grab it before it fell to the floor. "I don't want his offers of peace. I shall take what I want and when I want. He owes it to me."

"I dinna ken your meanin'," muttered the messenger in obvious confusion.

Kolyn felt sorry for the boy, his nervousness apparent. But she couldn't allow him to see her own confusion, her own weakness. "You don't need to understand. Just tell him he owes it to me. No more, no less."

He nodded, and all but ran from the castle.

Kolyn whirled around, stopping short when she saw Dwight watching her. She wanted to make excuses for the look on his face, the glow that lit his eyes, but she could no longer deny what she saw. Too much had changed. Nothing was the same.

"Is there something you needed?" she asked.

"No," he answered, giving no hint of what was going on in his mind. "I merely wondered what the rider was wanting."

"It is nothing. I have taken care of it."

"Aye. I believe you have at that."

Suspicion rose inside her. "Have you been drinking again, Uncle?"

"Aye, that I have."

"Why are you doing this?"

"What, lass?"

His tone was infuriating, but she held on to her temper. "Are you planning to drink your life away?"

He considered her question, then nodded. "Aye, I'm thinking it be a good way t' die. It takes away what I feel."

"Not to feel, that's what you want?"

"All these questions . . . what is it you want from me, Kolyn?"

"The truth, Dwight. I want the truth." Kolyn studied him, but found no answers to any of her questions.

"Sometimes," he said softly, his voice husky and strained, "'tis best that we not tell what truly lies within our hearts."

His words hurt Kolyn. "I am your family."

"No," he said, a pain of his own moving his stony features into a sad expression. "You're no longer just family, Kolyn MacGregor. You're a woman. And I'm a man."

It was slow, the meaning of what he said taking shape in her mind. At first shock kept her silent; then a numbing despair claimed her. "Oh, Heavenly Father."

When she looked up, Dwight was gone.

Chapter Five

"The woman is mad."

The wiry little man nodded in agreement with what Ian said. He held his hat in hand, the frayed brim crunched in his fists as he nervously waited for Ian to continue.

Ian paced back and forth in front of the fireplace, careful to keep his face a stone mask. He tried to keep from displaying what he was feeling, to hide the irritation that ate at him, but it was a difficult task to accomplish. The fact was he was not only irritated, but angry.

Ian stopped and leaned against the heavy oak mantle. The witch was pushing him too far. She had rejected his offer of peace and in the last month had persistently raided his tenants, taking whatever she pleased, whenever

Fela Dawson Scott

she pleased. Yet what was he to do? Make war with a woman? Never! There must be some way to appease her, to make her forget this feud her father had started.

"Lordy, it's been over five years. Don't they ever let go?"

"A Scotsman can't."

Ian turned to see his mother enter the room. He welcomed her advice. His mother was always calm and rational when he was not. "She hit Murray's farm last night," he said.

Ainsley Blackstone nodded. "Yes, I heard." She smiled warmly at the older man who stood waiting to be dismissed. "My son appreciates you taking the time to come and see him concerning this matter, Murray. I hope this unpleasantness hasn't disturbed you or your family. Please give my love to Patricia."

The graying head bobbed and he wasted no time in starting for the door, his discomfort apparent by the relief lighting his eyes.

"Don't concern yourself over this, Murray. I'll take care of Kolyn MacGregor." Ian's voice was hard, his tone saying even more than his words.

Again the shaggy mop of hair moved, and Murray disappeared out the door. Ian frowned for a moment, and then turned back to his mother. "Why are you smiling?"

She shrugged her petite shoulders and continued to smile. "I was just wondering how you plan to take care of Kolyn MacGregor."

A sort of snort was Ian's first answer. Then he elaborated. "I don't know. I seem to be at a loss as to how to handle an angry woman. No, let me clarify that—an angry Scotswoman who thinks she has a score to settle."

"Doesn't she?"

He had not expected his mother to say such a thing, and it brought forth instant anger, anger that was already smoldering inside him. "And what does that mean? I've only done what I had to. The MacGregor's sons each challenged me, not the other way around."

"I know that, Ian. You needn't be angry with me. I'm just telling you that Kolyn MacGregor has lost her brothers and father to your sword. Were they your brothers and father, what would you think? What would you do?"

"I don't know," he confessed, confusion taking the edge from his fury. "What am I to do? Let the woman take whatever she feels like taking? She's raided three of my farms. Do I let that go?"

"You could. She is doing no one harm."

"So far, she has done no one harm. What about the next time? And when will she stop?"

Ainsley looked thoughtful, and then said, "When she feels she has collected all the debts you owe."

Flashes of each fight, each man succumbing to his sword raced through Ian's mind. He lived with his actions; he had no choice. But he couldn't fight a woman, he couldn't kill a woman, and he had no doubt that was what it would come to if she continued such reckless acts.

Ian sighed, thinking that was exactly what she wanted. "And what if she decides to collect the highest payment of all—my life? Would you still be so approving?"

"Of course not," Ainsley declared. Then she looked worried. "You do not think the woman would be so foolish?"

Ian was thoughtful. "I don't know. Perhaps." Then he smiled widely. "I have learned never to underestimate a Scotsman—or a Scotswoman either!"

A twinkle came to his mother's eyes, and he marveled at how beautiful she was. He could understand why his father had left England behind to be with Ainsley and live in Scotland.

"Ian, my son, your Scottish blood is overriding the English in you." Then her playfulness was gone, and in its place came a serious thought. "Be patient. The girl has a lot of grief to get past. You've had your own share and it has been difficult to get free of it."

This touched a nerve in Ian, one that was not pleasant to feel. Would he ever be rid of the guilt, the pain? He despaired ever having a normal life again. "It's the MacGregors who persist. They are the ones to end this, not me."

"Well, let's pray that Kolyn MacGregor will come to her senses."

"You do that, Mother." Like a breeze blowing, Ian felt the anger ease from him, and in its stead settled a great sadness. "While you're saying your prayers, say one for me. Pray I find an answer before someone does get hurt or killed."

The sun inched behind the mountains and the air was touched with coolness. Kolyn knew they should go in, but was unwilling to give up the enjoyment of watching her son ride his pony. Horses, manure, hay, and dust all fused into a strong, musty odor, a smell she always associated with the stables. She didn't mind the smell; she rather liked it. It was earthy and natural.

"That's very good, Drew."

Kolyn ran alongside the pony, holding the bridle as Andrew sat tall and proud making his rounds in the stable yard. His laughter was echoed by hers, his high and shrill, while Kolyn's was sultry, a warm counterpoint.

"Let go! Let go!"

Andrew tugged at her grip, trying to free her hand from the bridle. Kolyn was afraid to let go, but knew he wanted to ride without her help. She took a deep breath and released the pony.

Taking charge with authority, Andrew stayed astride as the animal trotted along. His cries of victory brought tears to Kolyn's eyes. She clapped and cheered in response to his newfound expertise and bravery.

"Look at you," she called, turning in a circle as her son rode about. "You're such a big boy."

"Look, Uncle Dwight." Andrew let go with one hand and waved, but quickly grabbed hold once again as he became insecure. "I'm riding all by myself."

"Aye, you are at that, lad."

Kolyn felt a sense of uncertainty as Dwight walked over to stand beside her. He said nothing. They just watched Andrew as he continued to ride, his small body bouncing up and down in rhythm to the pony's slow, choppy gait.

"He's a fine lad, Kolyn. You've done a good job raising him."

"I've done my best."

A tense silence descended once again. Kolyn wondered about her uncle's thoughts, but was afraid to ask. At times, she even convinced herself she had imagined it all, that what he had said was spoken in drunkenness and was not what was in his heart. He was her uncle, her family. Surely she had been wrong. Shame filled her, leaving her shaken and trembling.

"Is there something wrong, lass?"

Kolyn turned to Dwight, her gaze meeting his straight on. He didn't remember. She was certain of it now. "Nothing's wrong."

It was a lie, but Kolyn dared not let him think she was afraid of his feelings for her. It haunted her like an echo in a cavern of rock, bouncing back again and again. It was true. She was afraid of his loving her, not in the way a family loves, but the way a man and a woman love.

This revelation touched her with its power, making her anxious and twisting her stomach into a painful knot. It was impossible! Kolyn tried to argue with her own thoughts and emotions as they ran rampant.

"Drew," Kolyn called out, unable to take any more. "We'd best let the pony rest. We'll ride again tomorrow."

Andrew trotted over and reined the animal to a precarious stop. Pride seemed to explode from him, his golden eyes alive with accomplishment. "Can't I ride some more?"

"No, it's getting dark. You need to get ready for bed, lad."

His lower lip pouted, but he did as Kolyn said and slid off into her waiting arms.

"You used t' do the same, lass. You'd have slept on your pony if you could."

Nostalgia touched her lightly, easing some of her apprehension. Dwight had been the one to teach her to ride. "I still miss that pony. What was her name?"

"You called her Flower."

"Flower." Andrew giggled at the name. "That's silly."

"Just as silly as Blackie." Kolyn tickled his tummy and Andrew's giggles turned into laughter. "Let's get you ready for bed, Drew. It's getting late."

"Good night, Kolyn."

Kolyn turned to Dwight and smiled, the awkwardness she felt hidden. "Good night, Uncle. Is everything prepared for tomorrow night?"

Dwight nodded but said nothing. Kolyn was aware he thought it too soon to strike again, but that was the very reason she wanted to— to remain unpredictable.

The sound of laughter, conversation, scraping benches, and crackling fire was like an old friend to Ian, The Raven like a second home. It wasn't so much the strong ale they served that he found appealing, but the company he kept there. Ian liked to spend time with his men, and always welcomed Geoffrey's companionship. He knew they were more at home at the tavern. Stonehaven's stiffness was too formal for their rowdiness. And they all, Ian included, respected and loved Ainsley too much to subject her to their drinking, so they kept to the tavern for such occasions. Ian looked forward to the quiet evenings he spent with his mother, and she did not mind his nights spent away with his men. She had grown used to his comings and goings, and never complained about the many nights he stayed at the inn, understanding his dark moods better than he did himself.

"Tell me, Geoff. What would you do?"

Ian watched his friend closely, the good humor and teasing Geoffrey had engaged in coming to a halt as he thought upon Ian's question.

"'Tis a bit of a problem, Ian. If it was a man, you could handle it as you have in the past. But since the MacGregor is now a woman, I've no clue what to do about it."

"Mother thinks I should just leave her be, let her work this tantrum out."

"Do you think 'tis but a tantrum?"

"I don't know. Time will tell us the answer, I'm sure."

Someone entered the tavern, distracting Ian and Geoffrey from their conversation. The man's excitement stirred everyone up.

"Looks to be a fire! 'Tis the grain!"

Both Ian and Geoffrey stood in unison, the wooden benches nearly toppling as they bolted for the door. Within minutes they were on their horses and headed toward the fire, its glow guiding them in the darkness, the smoke disappearing into the night sky.

When they arrived, the fire had already been put out. A woman stood in the midst of the smoke and ashes, beating the last of the flames out with her plaid. She was covered in soot from head to toe, and there was not an inch of flesh left unmarred with black. Her hair hung in tangles, heavy with ash and dirt, sheaves of wheat clinging to it.

Kolyn looked up to see two men on horseback watching her. She stopped and coughed to clear her lungs of the smoke she'd inhaled.

When the fire broke out she had ordered Dwight and her men away. Now she wished she hadn't. But she would not run. She stayed her ground, facing them in all her unkempt glory.

"What are you doin', lass?"

"What does it look like I'm doing?" They were close enough for Kolyn to read the looks on their faces. They obviously hadn't expected her to be so cocky. A warning went off inside her head, telling her it was best not to be that way, but she ignored it.

"Are you puttin' it out or are you startin' it?"

Kolyn watched them closely. The taller, dark-haired man remained silent. He was the one she kept her eyes on. "I'd be asking your own men who started the fire. Dropping a torch in the middle of a granary is not a smart thing to do."

"So you were puttin' it out."

"Actually, I was stealing it."

This they definitely did not expect. But neither did Kolyn expect the dark man's reaction. He began to laugh, not a quick laugh, but a long, heartfelt one. She thought he might fall off his horse he was laughing so hard.

Kolyn ran over to him and grabbed a big, booted foot and shoved with all her might. The giant man toppled from his steed, landing with a thud on the ground.

"I don't take kindly to those clods burning my grain. I expect payment in full. You tell

Blackstone, payment in full."

Standing, he brushed off the dirt and cast a quick glance to his companion, stilling his chuckles. He casually walked up to Kolyn. He was over a full foot taller than her, his shoulders broader than any she had seen. The humor still lingered in his eyes, but a seriousness had smoothed out the laugh lines. His eyes were a vivid gold, surrounded by features so prominent they looked to be carved from stone, each line strong and sharply defined. His black hair was pulled straight back and neatly tied at the base of his neck, the hair as dark and rich as the night sky. Boldly, she examined the full curve of his mouth, and she found herself wanting to touch it.

"I suppose it is time we met. I am Ian Blackstone."

Kolyn's voice was gone, as was her intense scrutiny.

"I would assume I have the pleasure of meeting Kolyn MacGregor. Am I right?"

"I assure you, Blackstone, there is no pleasure."

Mirth returned to his eyes, and Kolyn saw them twinkle. Anger began to seethe and guilt twisted in her as she realized she had thought him handsome.

"I thought so," he said.

"What exactly is it you're thinking? Are you wondering what to do with me? Are you angry with me, Blackstone?"

"Yes, I am angry with you. You've been causing me a lot of trouble lately."

"And I'll cause you more before it's over."

"Damn you, woman. What do you want from me?"

It was a fair question, and Kolyn wanted to answer it. But she wasn't sure she could. "I want . . ."

"What, woman? What?"

"I want you to pay for what you have done to me."

Ian looked at her for a long moment. "Nothing I have can ever replace your family."

"No, nothing can do that."

"Then what is it you want? What will get you out of my life?"

Kolyn moved closer, standing toe to toe with him. She craned her neck to look into his disturbing eyes. "I want your life, Ian Blackstone. I want you dead."

At first, she thought she read anger in the eyes she studied up close. Then she saw the twinkle return.

"You're a bonnie lass, I'll give you that." Then he started to laugh again.

This time, she struck him hard across the face. His laughter ceased. The look he gave her would have frightened most men, but Kolyn did not take heed. She plunged on.

Stepping back, she pulled her sword. "Perhaps I'll kill you now and be done with it."

The briefest flash of a thought ran across

her mind, but it came and went so fast it didn't remain long enough to create caution. She had said herself she couldn't fight the Black Wolf and win, but at that moment she didn't care. Never had she been so angry. Emotions churned inside her. She waited, but Blackstone made no move to draw his own weapon.

"I will not fight a woman."

His words were soft, unlike the fire that sparked in his eyes. Kolyn replied in the same gentle voice. "Draw your sword, or I'll cut you down where you stand."

Still, he made no move. Kolyn didn't stop to consider what she was implying. It no longer mattered. If she must, she would murder him.

Ian just stood there, stunned. From the look on the woman's face, she meant it. She meant to fight him. Admiration gentled his anger. "Be sensible, Kolyn."

"I am the MacGregor, and I challenge you. Does the Black Wolf accept or not?"

She was pressing him, pushing him against a wall with no way out. To deny the challenge would be cowardly. To accept and fight a woman would make him unworthy of his own code of honor. "I will not fight you."

"Coward," she hissed.

It rankled Ian, but he would not take the bait. He turned to leave. Kolyn attacked, her cry as unnerving as that of any Highlander he had encountered. He twisted and pulled his sword, intending only to disarm her. Their blades came together, clashing with the force of each swinging arm. In one quick jerk, Kolyn's weapon was dislodged from her hand. It landed with a thud somewhere in the soot and ash that surrounded them.

Yet Kolyn was not to be stopped. When Ian glanced away to see what Geoffrey was about, she lunged at him. His instincts took control, and he brought his hand up, piercing Kolyn's shoulder with the tip of his sword. This stilled her attack.

"Damn it, woman. I could have killed you. Don't you understand that? This isn't a game, and it's time you stopped this tantrum of yours."

As if on cue, lightning lit the black sky, quickly followed by thunder. Rain splattered down. The storm echoed the emotions that warred within Kolyn's heart.

"I hate you Blackstone. I will see you dead."

Had he heard her threat? She couldn't be sure. He merely walked over to his horse and mounted. The other man leaned closer to hear what he was saying, then rode off, leaving Blackstone behind.

He looked back where she stood and hollered above the rain beating down on them, "You're mad, and I'll not fight you, Kolyn MacGregor."

"I'm not mad!" Kolyn screamed at him as he rode away. "I'm not mad, you son of a . . ." Her curses trailed off when she realized he could not hear her. Wasting no time, she found her mount and followed.

It was difficult to keep him in sight, his steed carrying him with great speed. Storm clouds covered the moon, blocking the light it had given her earlier, making the ride dangerous. She would not give in to the elements. The anger inside her churned into a mighty force she could not deny, pushing her faster and harder.

He thought she was mad!

A dull ache finally reached her mind, an insistent throbbing reminding her she was wounded. Still, she did not let up. It wasn't until they were well into the forest that Kolyn realized the terrain had changed. Her horse slowed its pace, and she hung on with all the strength she had left. Cold numbed her, keeping her from feeling the limbs tearing at her from the never-ending wall of trees that surrounded her.

It was several moments before she realized she no longer knew where Blackstone was. It was too dark to find her way, let alone find him. Regretfully, Kolyn pulled her horse to a stop and wearily slid from his back. When her legs touched the earth they refused to hold her, and she fell.

She trembled, as much from the cold as from the loss of blood. Every part of her body hurt, but her shoulder was on fire. Unable to stand, Kolyn crawled to find a spot that might provide protection from the rain. She rolled beneath some heavy ferns and curled up into a ball for warmth.

Weariness overtook her, but she did not close her eyes. Something kept her alert. Finally, she saw the animal. His golden eyes glowed in the darkness, shining like small suns against a black sky. She recognized the black wolf. Stories flashed through her thoughts, tales of the Black Wolf her father and brothers had frightened her with. She recalled her first encounter with the wolf and quickly discounted the legend. Why didn't she believe her father and brothers? Had they used the wild tales merely to perpetuate the feud, to support the hatred they clung to so righteously?

Her eyelids fluttered closed but she forced them open, trying to stay alert against their stronger will. They drooped, defying her intention.

"I hope that I am right, that you are my friend and not my foe. You protected my son, now I must trust you as I sleep. I pray it is God's wisdom that has given me this thought."

Chapter Six

Ian moved through the darkened forest with ease, the trail he followed familiar. Anger surged inside him, firing his blood. He couldn't believe the nerve of the woman. She actually had expected him to fight her. She must be crazed. Mad!

Yes, he decided. *She was mad.*

The terrain became steeper and his mount carefully picked its way along the rocky path, which twisted and turned. They climbed continuously, finally arriving at a stone cottage nestled in the trees on the mountainside. Smoke drifted up and curled before disappearing into the dark sky. Geoffrey had already arrived. Ian eased from the saddle. He led his horse to the lean-to attached to the house.

"I thought you would come up here, to work the anger out."

Ian finished pouring the bucket of oats into the feeder before he turned to face his friend. "She must be mad, Geoff. I don't know what to do with the woman."

"Aye, she does pose a problem."

Geoffrey and Ian walked into the cottage in silence. Ian stood by the fire and watched the flames take hold of the dry wood. Geoffrey sat upon a bench at the trestle table.

"You were right not to fight her. You cannot fight a woman, even if she is the clan chief."

"I've never seen such anger in a woman's eyes."

"Her father and brothers have passed on a legacy of hate, a feud of honor they couldn't finish. This is a heavy burden for a woman to carry in her heart."

"Aye," Ian mumbled, his mind recalling the MacGregor as she stood facing him, defiant and angry. The remaining anger eased from him, and he laughed. "She looked quite ugly. She looked manly in those pants."

Geoffrey laughed too. "There wasn't an inch of the lass that wasn't covered in soot. It will take her many washin's to scrub the filth from her."

"I don't think it will help much." Ian grinned, still amused by his vision of the MacGregor. "She's a homely maiden in need of a man to put her mind right and to give her other things to think about than killing me."

This brought a frown to Geoffrey's face. "Do you think she really wants t' kill you, Ian?"

"I've no doubt, my friend. No doubt at all."

Kolyn opened her eyes and saw a woman sitting beside her. Confusion played havoc with her muddled mind. She looked about, trying to determine where she was. It was all unfamiliar. A large, stone fireplace dominated a single wall of the small room, a table and benches placed in the center. A rocker sat near the fire and a worn sideboard braced one wall. The outside door was next to a large old chest.

The woman was young, yet a hard life had left its marks upon her face. She was getting close to childbirth, her extended belly obvious as she reached to wipe Kolyn's brow. Her touch was gentle, soothing. Kolyn liked the kindness in her dark brown eyes, the look on her small, round face. She trusted her.

"Where am I?" Kolyn whispered, her voice hoarse and dry.

The woman pulled back in surprise. "Thank the Lord," she whispered, tears shining in her eyes.

Kolyn smiled. "I think I owe thanks more to you than the Lord."

The woman looked horrified at first, then smiled. "It wouldn't hurt to thank the Lord too. You've been terribly ill."

"I feel as if I'm dead."

"You came close, lass."

Kolyn closed her eyes, weary beyond description. "I am grateful for . . ." were the last words she spoke as she drifted into sleep once more.

"Perhaps she has realized the futility of the feud, Ian. It's been over two weeks since the granary fire."

Ian looked up from the rose he carefully trimmed of thorns and shrugged at his mother's statement. The flower's scent was sweet, but today it brought him no pleasure. The garden, usually a source of comfort and peace, could not help him. Over and over he continued to relive the ugly scene at the fire. "Perhaps. But somehow, I think not. I saw the look in her eyes plainly."

Ainsley took the rose and added it to her basket, already overflowing with beautiful buds. "It could be that Kolyn MacGregor is much like this rose. Once the thorns are removed, she is harmless. Your encounter has removed her thorns."

"I harmed a woman with my sword," Ian said with disgust. He worked on the bush, trimming away dry, faded blooms.

"You . . ." His mother laid her hand upon his, stopping him. Ian turned to look into her eyes.

"You had no intention of harming her. Surely you do not blame yourself for what happened."

"I do. I should have more control of my temper."

"And what of her temper?" Ainsley asked. "You cannot be responsible for her anger and her actions. It was her own doing that caused her injury. Besides, you said it was but a scratch."

Ian said nothing.

"The roses are beautiful this year. If only your father could see them." Ainsley caressed the velvety petals with reverence. "He did love his roses."

"I remember him best right here in his garden." Ian's voice had taken on a soft, longing tone.

"Yes." She smiled, remembering too her husband's love of flowers. "When we married he vowed he could leave England behind as long as he could have me and his roses."

"My men find it amusing that I tend his garden."

"Does that trouble you, Ian?"

This time he smiled. "'Tis no trouble. We all must have some sort of amusement. I'm glad to be theirs."

They walked up the path that wound from the castle into the gardens Blackstone had created. They paused before going inside. Ainsley looked up at her son, towering above her petite form.

"What sort of amusement do you allow yourself, Ian?"

A shadow descended over his face, his eyes

becoming hard and unreadable. "I've plenty
to amuse myself. You needn't worry yourself,
Mother."

She understood his way of keeping his heart
closed to her. Someday he would allow her in
so she might share his pain. "That's good, Ian.
That's good," she said. Someday.

Kolyn walked to the small shed where the
cow and horse were kept, the scent of hay and
animals drifting to her. It was pleasant. She
saw Daniel, the son of the couple who had
taken her in and had tended her. The little
boy brushed his horse, his strokes loving and
gentle. Kolyn guessed him to be eight, maybe
nine. He looked up when Kolyn approached,
her steps slow and shaky.

"'Tis good t' see you up and about, miss."

"I have you to thank for that, young man. If
you hadn't found me, I would have died."

He smiled, blushing at her praise. "I dinna
ken how I found you. You were curled beneath
some ferns, hidden from view."

"I am very glad you did."

They were silent for a moment, each at ease
with the other. Kolyn spoke first. "Could I ask
another favor?"

"Anythin', miss."

"I need to get a message to someone. To
Father McCloud in the village at Gregor Castle.
Can you do this?"

"Aye, I can go tomorrow, miss."

"My name is Lynn." Kolyn felt a twinge of guilt at not being totally honest with the boy, but she was uncertain where this family's loyalties lay.

Again he smiled. "'Tis a pleasure, Lynn, miss."

This made Kolyn laugh. "Mine too, Daniel, sir."

"There you are," his mother, Jean, called out, walking toward them, drying her hands on her apron.

"I needed some fresh air," Kolyn offered, seeing the look of worry upon Jean's brow.

She nodded. "Aye. The cottage can get cramped and gloomy. My husband has filled our tub. I thought you might enjoy a bath."

Kolyn pulled at her filthy hair and grinned. "Do you think I can possibly get the grime washed away?"

"Aye, but it will take the two of us, I'm afraid. Daniel, your father is waiting to go huntin'. Find us a plump bird for the pot."

Kolyn and Jean watched Daniel scurry off in search of his father, his face bright with exuberance. Kolyn could see a mother's pride on Jean's face, her hand folded and resting upon her belly. She was dressed in a simple wool dress, her feet bare, her brown hair neatly pulled back into a braid that fell down her back. It was the gentleness of her eyes that made Kolyn feel welcome and at home. Ronald and Jean were strangers, perhaps even her enemies, but Kolyn felt no fear. She trusted the couple, and so far they had asked no questions of her.

"I have a dress you can wear if you'd like. As you can see, I am unable to wear it."

"You've been most kind."

Jean shook her head, then took Kolyn's arm to walk back to the cottage, making certain to give her support should she need it. "I find it a pleasure havin' another woman's company."

"Isn't it dangerous, living so far from the villages?"

"No one bothers with us." Jean stepped inside the cottage, her hand sweeping about to make her point. "We've little enough for thieves to take."

"It is peaceful here."

"Aye. Ronald and I have chosen to live away from the feudin'. The troubles of others are no business of ours."

Kolyn smiled, understanding her meaning. "You are both good people. I shall always remember your kindness."

Jean moved to the fireplace and removed the large kettle, then poured the bubbling water into the small, wooden tub that sat in the center of the floor. "That should make it plenty hot for you, lass." She set the kettle aside and moved to stand beside Kolyn. "Here, let's get them filthy clothes off you."

Kolyn allowed Jean to help her undress, her strength failing her after the short foray to the shed. The tenderness of her hurt shoulder seemed to keep her an invalid. So for the moment, she gave in to Jean's mothering.

The water was heaven, the warmth seeping into Kolyn's sore muscles. It felt wonderful to let Jean wash the soot and dirt from her stringy hair. The steam drifted about her, her mind relaxing, her eyes closing. Then they were there. Golden eyes watched her, studied her.

Kolyn jerked, swinging at the air with her fist.

"What is it, Lynn?"

Jean's question penetrated Kolyn's sudden anger, and she took a deep breath. "Nothing," she lied, quickly covering up her distress.

"Here, wrap up in this before you catch your death." Jean bundled Kolyn up when she stood, then sat her before the fire.

Kolyn started to brush the tangles from her hair, but found it difficult with her sore arm.

Gently, Jean took the brush from her. "Let me, before you tear it out by the roots."

Putting her mind on other things, Kolyn made idle chatter. Anything to put the golden eyes of the Black Wolf from her. "How far along are you, Jean?"

"Nearin' my eighth month. Won't be long now."

Kolyn couldn't hold her head up. She found it difficult to concentrate. "Do you want a girl or another boy?"

"You need to get back to bed, lass. You're

Fela Dawson Scott

tired out." Jean helped Kolyn to stand. "A little girl would be nice, but I'll be happy if God blesses me with a healthy child." She tucked Kolyn into the bed.

Kolyn fell to sleep immediately.

104

Chapter Seven

Only a soft spray of light touched the sky, the early morning hour cloaking Kolyn and Ronald in darkness. A hard November frost cloaked the trees and road, casting the world in a chilling white blanket. The wagon lurched and bumped over the rough road, and they did not try to speak above the noise. Kolyn welcomed the sense of solitude.

Her mind dwelled on the day to come. When Ronald mentioned the night before he would be going to the village the next morning to deliver the tables and benches he had made for the innkeeper, she had asked to go along. Jean had fretted, saying she was not well enough for the long trip. Kolyn was not to be swayed, a strange determination claiming her. What did she hope to accomplish by going? The village lay at the base of Blackstone's castle . . . enemy territory. Yet something made her want to go, and she followed that feeling.

Slowly the day dawned, as did her doubts. With the light of day came apprehension about what she was doing. Still, she was determined. She must learn about the Black Wolf; then she could kill him. Kolyn made her plan.

Ronald maneuvered the wagon past the vendors and stalls that lined the busy streets. It took most of the morning to get to the village, and he wasted no time pulling up to The Raven. Kolyn knew Ronald wanted to turn around and start home as soon as he could, his worry about leaving Jean alone too long apparent. He was a quiet man, a man of few words. But the love the couple shared was obvious to Kolyn. It was a love she envied, a love she longed for.

Kolyn brought her thoughts to a halt, surprised at the path her mind wandered on. She climbed down from the wagon, her legs numb from the long miles they had traveled without stopping. She followed Ronald inside.

The tavern was busy, most of the tables full of patrons. Kolyn scanned the room, then turned away when she found herself the center of attention. The owner was easy to find, a burley man with an apron tied about his rounded belly. He seemed glad to see Ronald, and quickly disappeared to the back room.

"You'd best have a seat while I help Mr. McNeil unload."

She looked up at Ronald and smiled. "I think I've sat long enough. I'll stand while I have the opportunity."

"Damned women," cursed the innkeeper, returning. "Me wife's gone t' the market and who know's what that girl Leslie's about."

"Probably still abed, she is," said a man who stood nearby. "'Tis always abed, that lass."

The innkeeper's face puckered as everyone laughed. Kolyn was embarrassingly aware of their joke.

"Can you wait till me wife returns, Ronald? I'll be able t' help you with the tables then."

"Aye," Ronald said, nodding at the same time.

Kolyn knew he had wanted to start back as quickly as possible. "I'll see to your customers, Mr. McNeil," she said.

Two more men walked in just as she made her offer. "Have you ever done this kind of work before, lass?" the innkeeper asked, his look doubtful.

"No," Kolyn replied honestly. "But I did have three brothers to wait upon. And it's only for a minute or two while you unload the wagon."

Mr. McNeil handed a full pitcher of ale to her. "See t' the men who just came in, then refill any who need it."

She took the pitcher in her right hand, grabbing a couple of mugs with her left. She felt a small twinge of pain in her shoulder, but she paid it no mind. Carefully, she moved through the crowded room. Talking hushed as she passed each table. She reached the table by the fire and placed the mugs before the two men. Then she began pouring their drinks.

Kolyn avoided meeting their gazes, and purposely ignored the comments that she heard.

"Thank you, lass."

The voice was soft, familiar, and she brought her eyes up to look at the man who spoke. Then she froze, spilling the ale upon the table as the mug filled. Horrified, she pulled back.

"'Tis nothing," Ian assured the girl, the look on her face telling him of her discomfort. "Bring a rag, and we'll wipe it up. No harm done."

She just stood, staring.

"You've frightened her," Geoffrey said with a laugh. She shifted her gaze to look at him. "See, she's gone all white in the face."

"Surely not." Ian smiled. "What's your name?"

She said nothing.

Geoffrey was enjoying this. "Good God, Ian. You've struck her dumb too."

"Lynn," she finally replied.

"I've not seen you before, Lynn. Where are you from?" Ian watched the young woman place the pitcher down on the table, the look in her eyes now thoughtful. She seemed to be considering what to say.

"She came with me," Ronald said, stepping into the inn, holding the end of a table. "Lynn's stayin' with Jean an' me for a while."

Ian's intense gaze moved back to Kolyn. She was certain there was no recognition in his eyes. He had no idea he had seen her before, no idea who she was. This made her feel powerful, with danger no longer an immediate concern. She smiled. She saw a definite reaction, a reaction that surprised her. Suddenly, her brother's words came to her, haunting her with their meaning. "... *you, dear sister, are too beautiful for any man to resist.*"

Kolyn had never thought herself beautiful, feeling only the harshness of her life reflected in herself. Yet when she looked around, it was obvious, so obvious even she could not deny the effect she had upon these men, and upon one man in particular.

"McNeil," Ian called out to the innkeeper, who had followed Ronald into the room, his breathing strained from exertion as he carried his end of the heavy table.

"Aye, Lord Blackstone," he replied, wiping the sweat from his face with his hand, which he wiped on his apron.

"You should have Lynn help you out here in the tavern. You're always bellyaching about your help. Or lack of it." Ian laughed, then tossed her a coin. "She'd be a welcome change."

Many agreed, their own encouragement added to Ian Blackstone's.

"Perhaps she does not want t' work. I've little enough t' pay much more than room an' board."

Ian looked directly at Kolyn, and her heart stopped.

"I'd wager she'll make a good wage with tips," he said.

This prompted her to look at the coin she had caught. It was much more than she deserved. She walked over to where Ronald stood.

"You are welcome t' stay as long as you need with us, Lynn. Jean has enjoyed your company well enough."

"I know I am welcome in your house, but with another child coming soon, you don't need the extra burden, Ronald." Kolyn gave him a quick hug and slipped the coin into his hand. "For the dress Jean lent me."

The plan formed so fast, she had little time to contemplate the danger. Her mind buzzed from the excitement, and fear danced inside her. She thought of Andrew, how much she had missed him these past few weeks as she recovered from her wound. How could she bear to stay away longer? Kolyn focused on one thing—she would be near the Black Wolf. She could end the feud and give her son a life free of hatred and killing.

"I would like to work here, Mr. McNeil, if you will have me."

Mr. McNeil didn't look like he had the

courage to deny her, so he just nodded. "Get on with your work then, lass. These men are dyin' of thirst."

Ian leaned back against the stone wall, feeling rather pleased with himself. He watched Lynn closely as she filled the tankards, carefully avoiding the wayward hands and pinching fingers. She was beautiful, with snapping green eyes and flaming red hair. But there was something else, something he couldn't quite figure out, that made him curious, more curious than he ought to be and more curious than he had been about a woman in a very long time.

"I was beginnin' to fear that Blair had killed the man in you, my friend."

Geoffrey's words brought Ian's attention back.

Geoffrey was not put off as Ian's eyes darkened dangerously. "If I'd known a redhead would bring you back to life, I'd have found you one long ago."

This made Ian chuckle. "'Tis not the red hair, though it is the prettiest I've ever seen. 'Tis the look in her eyes, Geoff. I'd almost think it was anger."

"Aye, but you'd best be prepared, Ian. 'Tis a look that says no. She's been here only a few minutes and I can see she'll not be warmin' your bed."

"'Tis not my bed needs warming," Ian said softly. "'Tis my heart."

*   *   *

When the innkeeper's wife returned, she took Kolyn to the attic where she would sleep. Mrs. McNeil merely pointed up the ladder, not wishing to climb it. Kolyn thought that was best, considering her portly girth.

"Thank you, Mrs. McNeil. I'll be fine."

"Call me Molly, girl. Come on down t' help serve supper. Then you and Leslie can tend t' the tavern."

Kolyn nodded. The main stairwell led to the rooms on the upper floor where travelers stayed, and the small ladder she climbed was the only way up into the attic. She looked about her. It was dark and drafty, two straw mattresses upon the floor and a single, shuttered window at the end looking out over the stables. Two small trunks, a wash stand, and a single chair were the only other furnishings.

A low moan sounded from one of the mattresses, the crumpled blanket upon it moving. Slowly, a woman sat up, her eyes finally settling on Kolyn.

"Who are you?"

"I am Lynn. You must be Leslie." Kolyn remembered the comments made earlier in the tavern.

"Why are you here, Lynn?"

Her words were short and rude, but that did not annoy Kolyn. She had had much practice with Emmett's continuous sarcasm. "I will be helping you out in the inn."

112

Leslie considered this before she spoke. Narrowed and wary, her pale blue eyes appraised Kolyn. "I didn't know I be needin' your help."

Kolyn cleared her throat and then plunged on. "I understand you work very late. I'll be helping Molly out more during the day."

"You'll be gettin' up t' help with breakfast?" This seemed to appeal to Leslie.

"Yes. That way you can sleep." Kolyn was aware of what Leslie did with her night hours, but it didn't matter much to her. She wanted only to get along with the girl so she could concentrate on her other plans. She didn't want trouble from Leslie.

Leslie pulled herself up off the mattress and ran her fingers through her blond hair, somewhat combing it before pulling it back and braiding it. "Well, I cannot fault you for wantin' t' work, Lynn. But if I find you are takin' me night work too, I'll bust that pretty little nose of yours."

Kolyn took in the information impassively. "The night work is all yours. I promise."

Leslie looked Kolyn square in the eyes. "I can see you've never been hungry. Believe me, my pretty, when hunger's gnawin' at the back of your belly, your morals no longer carry any meanin'. You could make a lot of money with your looks."

"You are right, Leslie. I've never been hungry. But there are offenses worse than what you do." Kolyn thought about her oath to kill

113

Blackstone. "Believe me, my sins are greater than yours."

Leslie smiled, then offered her hand in friendship. "Then we understand each other."

Kolyn shook Leslie's hand. "Completely."

"Leslie, are you sharin' all your secrets with Lynn?"

Kolyn couldn't help but smile as Leslie approached the man who spoke, a definite swagger to her hips as she planted her hands on them and looked quite confident of herself.

"There are some secrets a girl's got t' be keepin' t' herself. I'll teach her how to wait on you slobs, but I'll not be teachin' her how t' bed you slobs. 'Tis me secret alone, and no other's."

Kolyn no longer blushed at the conversation. She laughed along with everyone else. As brash and bold as Leslie was, Kolyn liked her. She was a survivor.

By the time Kolyn had cleared all the tables and scrubbed the tankards, she was nearly exhausted. Her shoulder ached and she felt exertion throughout her body. Morning would come too soon, so she wasted no time in climbing to the attic and her bed.

She welcomed the tiredness for it helped her sleep without dwelling on the loneliness that consumed her. She missed Andrew terribly, and hoped the second message she had sent by way of a traveling peddler would reach

Father McCloud. Certain he would explain her absence to Drew, Kolyn made her plans. Intentionally, she did not send word to Dwight or Emmett. If her plans failed there would be no need of explanation. Reprisals for her failure could be much worse than their anger at her disappearance.

It was near dawn before Leslie made it to her own mattress. Kolyn merely turned over and went back to sleep. It wasn't long before Molly called her and Kolyn made her way downstairs to start another day.

Chapter Eight

Kolyn dipped the brush into the bucket and sloshed more soapy water onto the floor, then started to scrub once again. The floor seemed endless, but her mind wasn't on it. She dwelled instead on Ian Blackstone. Not once in the last week had she seen him alone. His men were always nearby. Each night he came to the tavern, each night he watched her, each night he left with Geoffrey at his side. She longed to go home to Andrew, but was determined to see this out to an end. Kolyn sat up and rubbed the ache in her back.

"What a pretty picture you make."

Startled, Kolyn twisted about to see who spoke and found herself staring straight into dark eyes, as gold as any she had ever seen. A shiver touched her despite the heat of her labor. She pushed back the stray strands of hair that clung to her face and started to stand.

"Please." Ian stepped forward and offered his hand. "Allow me."

She hesitated before accepting his help. Not realizing how long she had knelt on the floor, she stumbled, her legs numb. Ian steadied her, his strength keeping her from falling. "Thank you," she mumbled, unnerved by his touch.

When she tried to pull her hand away from his, he didn't let go. Instead he reached for the other.

"Your hands are raw from work," Ian said softly, turning them over to examine her palms.

Kolyn managed to free herself from his grip. "It's nothing to trouble yourself with, Lord Blackstone."

"Oh, but I do."

These simple words made Kolyn's heart race, and she found it difficult to breathe. She admitted he frightened her, but the feeling he was causing at that moment was not fear or anger. How could such a giant of a man sound so gentle? He had killed her brothers and father, yet he showed concern that her hands were chapped and split. Was this how the devil worked? To charm and disarm?

"Come here, Lynn."

Again, he startled her, having moved to the doorway without her hearing. She whispered a short prayer before following him into the kitchen. Ian looked about, then searched the cupboard before turning his attention back to her.

"Come over here," he repeated. When she didn't move, he laughed, though with a touch of sadness. "I won't hurt you. I promise."

Did it disappoint him that she was afraid of him? Or was she more afraid of herself, of the feelings he seemed to arouse at will? Mystified by the man, she moved to stand beside him. He took her hand into his, then carefully rubbed some lard into the sores. It soothed the dryness and softened the skin. He did the same for the other hand. Then he wiped away the excess grease with a rag. Kolyn knew she should move away, but she couldn't.

Ian watched the play of emotions across Lynn's lovely face and wondered what went on inside her pretty little head. He knew she was afraid of him. Why shouldn't she be? He was well aware of the legend, the curse he supposedly carried. He had even encouraged the fierce reputation that men feared. Now, as he looked down at Lynn, he regretted it. He didn't want to see fear in her forest-green eyes, he wanted to see . . .

What exactly did he want to see? He didn't know this wisp of a lass. He didn't even know where she came from or her family name. Ian knew nothing except that she made him feel alive, something he hadn't felt inside himself in a very long time. A warmth touched him, melting the ice inside him. Lynn aroused his desire. What man wouldn't desire her? But more, she made him feel emotions he thought dead.

He leaned down, wanting to feel her lips against his. He paused, wondering at the madness that seemed to claim him, looking deep into her eyes. Her mouth was parted, her breathing shallow. The moment went on forever.

Lynn turned away and mumbled, "Thank you for your kindness, sir."

"Lynn," Ian called to her, frustration so fierce inside him he could not hide it. "Don't run away from me."

Kolyn stopped and looked back. The look on his face struck her hard, causing her to wonder at the power he had over her. "I have work to do." She left him standing in the kitchen.

"He's not had a woman in years."

Kolyn looked up from the chicken she plucked and stared at Leslie. "Who hasn't?"

Leslie's eyes rounded in exasperation. "You know who—Lord Blackstone."

"How do you know that, Leslie?" She didn't know if she really wanted to learn so much about the man, but found herself asking anyway.

"Ever since his wife died, he's taken no woman t' his bed." She lifted her brows in a knowing way. "He found her with another man an' they say he's never trusted a woman since. I never heard of a man bein' so . . . so . . ."

"Chaste?" Kolyn found the word for her.

"Yeah." Leslie grinned wide. "'Ceptin' a holy man or such."

Kolyn looked down, hiding her face and smile from Leslie. "Is that so?"

Leslie punched her on the shoulder playfully. "Come now, I know you're curious. He's been watchin' you with that look in his eyes. I was beginnin' t' think he was a bit odd." Again she lifted her eyebrows and rounded her eyes. "If you know what I am talkin' about."

Embarrassment warmed Kolyn's face. "He has not been watching me, and I think we should talk about something else."

Molly appeared from the kitchen, her face showing she had been listening to their chatter. Nothing was more enjoyable to the woman than a good round of gossip. "Leslie's right, Lass. I'd say Lord Blackstone has designs on you."

Leslie's and Molly's laughter was friendly, and Kolyn couldn't help but laugh in turn. "I don't care, I tell you!"

"Go on," Leslie chided. "He's the handsomest man I ever saw, and you're pretendin' t' not care? You can't fool me, Lynn."

The warmth on Kolyn's face increased. "He's very handsome. I'll give you that."

"Then what's stoppin' you, girl?"

Leslie's question made Kolyn wonder what

was holding her back. Her plan was to get him to bed, yet she ran away each time he made an advance in that direction. Kolyn realized Molly and Leslie were waiting for her answer, their faces animated with anticipation. "I don't know if it's what I want."

It was the truth either way, an answer to their question as well as her own.

Leslie squealed, her eyes round with wonder. "Lord, Molly, she's a virgin!"

Kolyn felt the warmth increase, creeping up her neck and over her face.

"Oh, dear me," Molly muttered, her own amazement clear. "'Tis a wonder, lass, that with your looks no man has taken you t' his bed."

Again Leslie's laughter filled the room. "Where have you been, Lynn? A nunnery?"

The laughter was contagious and Kolyn couldn't help but giggle, thinking their conversation unlike any she had ever had before.

"'Tis nothing to laugh about, Leslie." Kolyn tried to look serious but failed. Leslie just laughed harder.

A deep sigh came from Molly, her gaze turned wistful. "Oh, t' be so young and beautiful." She brushed a pudgy finger over Kolyn's hot cheek. "Oh, t' have Lord Blackstone as my first lover."

Leslie sobered as well. "Aye." Then she shook it off with a giggle. "We'd best be teachin' this lass a thing or two, Molly. We wouldn't want

122

the man t' be disappointed in our girl."

Kolyn looked from one woman to the other. They were quite serious and she knew it would do no good to argue with them.

"Lordy," was all she managed to say.

The vendors barked their wares, drawing attention to each stall or cart. Ian walked beside his mother patiently, giving her the pleasure of moving at her leisure. Every once in a while she stopped and examined a small item or two.

"You seem to spend a lot of your time of late at The Raven. Is there any particular reason, or have you developed a taste for drink, Ian?"

Ian grinned, trying to waylay her serious look. "I've always had a taste for drink, Mother. Not any more now than before."

She didn't seem satisfied. "Could there be a lass then?"

Ian knew she had already spoken with Geoffrey, and between the two of them they knew more about what was happening with him than he did himself. At least they liked to think so. "And if there is?"

Ainsley tried to look surprised, but she wasn't very good at it. "So, there is a woman? A tavern girl?"

"Would it bother you if she were a tavern girl?"

"I . . ." Ainsley was taken off guard by his

question. "I don't believe so. I merely want what makes you happy."

They were silent for a moment, then Ian spoke. "I don't know what will make me happy. Perhaps it is something I will never know. But this woman sparks interest in me. More so than any other woman has in many years. For now, that is enough."

"Then it shall be enough for me also." Ainsley smiled and patted her son on the arm.

A flash of red caught Ian's eye. "Please excuse me for a moment. I won't be long."

Kolyn had stopped to look at the poultry, picking out some chickens that looked fresh and plump. She added them to her basket.

"Good morning, Lynn."

The last thing Kolyn had expected was to see Ian Blackstone. He had not struck her as a man who spent his time at the market. "Good morning, Lord Blackstone."

He made no move to leave. He merely stood in her way. Kolyn tried to walk around him. "I have much to do, if you'll excuse me."

"May I walk with you?"

"I . . ." She didn't know what to say. "Don't you have better things to do?"

She didn't mean to sound rude, and regretted that she had.

Ian removed the basket from her hand, then took her elbow to guide her through the crowd of people. She stopped when they passed a cart.

"Molly needs some fresh vegetables." She pointed to them.

Carefully, Ian picked out the best the man had, holding up first one vegetable, then another for her approval before placing them in the basket he still held. Once she got over her amazement, she felt amusement. Never before had she seen such a thing—a fierce warrior walking about with a basket on his arm, picking out produce in the market. It was hilarious.

"I like seeing you laugh, Lynn. But I get the impression you are laughing at me."

"I am, sir."

Ian spread his hands out wide and smiled. "Please, call me Ian."

Dimples creased his cheeks, his resemblance to Andrew striking Kolyn. At first, a warm and tender emotion tickled her. Then, just as suddenly, a sick feeling descended, leaving her weak and shaken. These past years Kolyn had loved Andrew like her own son, at times even forgetting he wasn't. Ian Blackstone was Andrew's father. She would never let him take her son from her.

"Are you all right?"

He was speaking, and Kolyn tried to concentrate on his words, to take her thoughts from the cruel reality encroaching upon her mind. She failed. She must kill this man. She must do as Emmett said and keep Andrew safe. She must.

"Are you all right?" Ian repeated, concerned

by the sudden paleness of her skin.

"Leave me be," she whispered, grabbing her basket. He reached for her, and she stepped back. She was frightened of him and herself. "No."

Ian watched Lynn turn and run from him. "Damn, what did I do?" She was always running away. This disappointed him, much more than he wanted to admit.

"Ian," his mother called out. She approached him and hooked her arm through his. "I would like some wine. Shall we stop at the inn before we return home?"

"Yes." Ian smiled. "Let's share some wine."

Kolyn placed the basket she carried upon the kitchen table and sat. She grasped her hands, twisting them together to still the shaking. Confusion assaulted her. Why was she confused? It was simple. She must honor her promise to her father. Simple.

No, it wasn't simple.

Molly poked her head into the kitchen. "Lynn, dear. Could you bring a tray of wine out?"

"Yes, Molly. I'll be right out."

Kolyn took a deep breath and calmed herself. She prepared a tray and entered the tavern.

Ainsley watched the young woman bring the wine over, and knew she carefully masked her discomfort as she served them. She was truly a beautiful woman. She could understand her son's attraction.

"You have the most beautiful hair," Ainsley commented, drawing the sharp green eyes to her.

"Thank you, Lady . . ." She could not finish.

"Lady Blackstone. This is my son, Ian."

Kolyn curtsied and dared only a glance toward Ian. He was grinning. "It's a pleasure to meet you, Lady Blackstone. I hope the wine is to your satisfaction."

"Yes, it is fine. And your name?"

"'Tis Lynn."

"Lynn, would you share a glass of wine with us?"

"I . . ." Kolyn felt shocked, unable to respond with any intelligence. "I . . . I couldn't. I have work to do. Please excuse me, Lady Blackstone."

Kolyn fled back to the safety of the kitchen. *He had a mother! He was a nice, likable man with a mother!*

"God help me," she muttered, then began to laugh. *I like the very man I'm supposed to kill. How ironic!*

Ian sat upon his mount and watched the full moon's path as it climbed high into the night sky. Too many years of grief were embedded in his soul, and he could not shake the black mood that had descended on him. Even the pleasure of seeing Lynn could not overtake the cycle of emotion each full moon brought.

Intentionally, he headed into the dark forest. The night and the wolf would be his only companions. When the blackness turned pink by morning's light, then he would return to the inn for a bath and bed. Just as he had for too many years.

That night Ian wasn't at the inn. Kolyn tried to pretend it didn't make a difference, that she was glad. But she lied to herself. All afternoon her mind had stayed on the man, giving her no respite from the torture it conjured. The harder she tried not to think of him, the more she did just that. She thought she might go mad.

She poured Geoffrey another pint, careful to avoid his eyes.

"He'll be back when the sun comes up."

Kolyn tried to look unconcerned. "Who will be back?"

Geoffrey's lips pulled into a wide grin. He was obviously enjoying his game. "There's an evil moon tonight."

Kolyn felt her own eyes widen, and she wished she could control her reactions more skillfully, for Geoffrey seemed to watch her every move.

"Ian will show up when the sun comes up. You might prepare his room and a bath for him, Lynn. He'll expect it."

"I'll see to it, sir." She wondered what Ian was really doing this night.

Geoffrey took her hand when she turned to leave and stopped her. His smile never faltered and the twinkle in his eyes never dimmed. "Will you see to my friend's needs, Lynn? Will you take care of Ian?"

"I'll see to his room." She understood his meaning and pulled her hand away. "Nothing more."

"Don't be so stubborn, lass." His voice teased her. "He's quite taken with you."

"Why?"

Geoffrey looked surprised. "Have you never looked in a mirror? Can't you see your own beauty?"

"There are a lot of beautiful women. Let him find another."

"Bring Ian to life, lass. Let him know what it is to love and be loved in turn."

Tears stung Kolyn's eyes. She didn't want to hear this. "No, I cannot. Leave me alone." She backed away. "Please, leave me alone."

Kolyn made it to her room before she started to sob. How could Geoffrey tease her about loving and being loved? His words brought forth a yearning she had always denied—a need she kept hidden, a need for a love she would never know. It rushed in on her with such insistence that she was left helpless to its destruction.

Finally, she fell into an exhausted sleep, tears still upon her face. When she woke, her candle had sputtered out, leaving her in total darkness.

"I'll light a candle."

"Leslie?" Kolyn's mind was muddled with sleep.

"Aye, who else did you expect?" She struck a flint to the wick. "Maybe Lord Blackstone?"

"No, of course not."

"You cannot lie to me, Lynn. I'm not blind. He's had nothin' but eyes for you since you came. He'd take you as his lover if you'd just let him."

Leslie was trying to tease, but a hint of hurt underlined her words. Kolyn wanted this conversation to end. "I've got to go downstairs."

"Yes, he'll be comin' in soon. He likes his water hot."

Kolyn hesitated before descending the ladder. "What does he do on the nights of the full moon?"

Leslie considered her question a long time before answering. "He struggles with the demons inside him."

A chill ran over Kolyn, and for the first time she wondered what demons Ian Blackstone might have. Did Blair's ghost haunt him? Perhaps her brothers, or father. Did he regret all the killing?

Without further comment, she went downstairs to start a fire and prepare Ian Blackstone's bathwater. One thought after another ran across her mind, tumbling into each other, creating chaos. She couldn't think. Nothing made sense.

One by one, she hauled the buckets up the stairs and to Ian's room, filling the large wooden tub that sat before the fire. She put one last kettle to boil over his fire just after the sun came up. She prepared to leave.

"Would you not stay and help me undress?"

Once again he had come upon her, entering his room so silently she had not known it. It unsettled her already strained nerves. "That and nothing more."

Quietly she assisted him, taking his sword and dagger. As she placed them upon the dressing table near the bed, her fingers lingered upon the hilt of the dirk. It was heavy and quite long. She returned to help him remove his leather tunic. She could smell the dampness of the earth and the stronger scent of his war-horse. Kolyn laid the tunic across the chair. She heard him splash into the tub and turned to him.

"Is there anything else, my lord?"

"Wash my back, lass."

"Must I?" she asked weakly, uncertain why she feared doing so. It was not an uncommon thing to assist a man in his bath. She had done so many times for her father's guests.

"Is it so much to ask, Lynn? I'll behave myself. You've my word on it."

Hesitant, she moved closer. She took the sponge he offered her and began to wash his back. When she was done, she handed the sponge back to him.

131

It seemed warm in the room, too warm.

"Rinse me."

Whether it was a statement or a question, she didn't know. "That you can do yourself." Then she added begrudgingly, "My lord."

He only smiled at her. "Would you be so kind as to bring me a towel then?"

Ian stood and Kolyn quickly turned away. She grabbed a towel, then stopped. The dagger lay before her. Shaking fingers touched it, wrapping about the cold steel.

"Have you forgotten my towel?"

She pulled her hand away. "Not at all," she whispered, shaken by his sudden closeness.

Kolyn could feel the wetness that clung to him soak into her dress, chilling her heated skin. A lightness invaded her head, and she thought she might embarrass herself by fainting.

Ian placed his hands upon her shoulders, then slid them down the full length of her arms, finally entwining his fingers in hers. She was truly on fire.

"Lynn, stay with me."

His voice was so hushed she almost wondered if it were her own thoughts conjuring the words. She wanted him to continue to hold her close. She wanted . . . to kill him.

Conflicting thoughts crashed into each other, startling her from her reverie. Shame washed through her like a flash flood, leaving her stripped of the warmth that claimed her. A cold hardness claimed control, and she pulled away from him.

"Leave me be, Ian Blackstone."

Ian did not go after her. A deep ache touched his heart, one he thought he could never feel again. He shouldn't allow this woman to unnerve him. He knew the danger, yet he could not let this redheaded wench be. That he understood.

Chapter Nine

The goose was only a foot away, wagging his tail feathers angrily at her. Kolyn inched forward, careful not to move too fast. Just as she touched the tip of a feather, he moved off at a fast waddle, honking loudly, perhaps even laughing at her.

She pretended to ignore him, then lunged at his plump, white carcass. He still escaped in a flurry of feathers and down. Kolyn chased him about, hunched over, grasping at air time and time again. From the feathers that clung to her dress and hair, she thought he should already be plucked, saving her the effort later should she ever catch him. Still, he evaded her.

Frustrated and tired, Kolyn gave one last

jump, landing unceremoniously on her backside, the goose watching her with what she was certain was a gleam in his black eyes. She moaned and covered her eyes with her hands, not wanting to look at him anymore.

The goose pecked at her hands, then nibbled on a curl that hung loose about her face. Kolyn peeked between her fingers, afraid to move lest he run away. He continued his appraisal of her, and when she moved her hand down, he did not flee. Instead he honked and nibbled some more. She laid her hand upon his back, then grasped him firmly in her arms.

"I got you my fine, feathery friend."

He seemed not to care, intent on investigating the long length of hair that hung over her shoulders in a very loose braid. He quietly honked, a subtle, almost friendly sort of noise.

Suddenly, tears filled Kolyn's eyes, and she looked deeply into the animal's round beady eyes. He was cute, in a fowlish sort of way. He rubbed his head under her chin. The tears spilled over, and she knew she had lost.

She began to sob outright. Whether it was solely for the goose or for herself, Kolyn really didn't know. She just cried. She let the goose go, shooed him away.

The goose came back and nestled upon her as she sat on the ground.

Ian remained quiet, leaning against the kitchen wall. Lynn's back was to him and he wanted to say something, but he couldn't find the right words. He had never known anyone so gentle of heart. Her attempt to catch the goose had been funny, yet sad. He knew Molly's plans for the goose. She had tempted her customers with the mouth-watering delight for months as she fattened it for the pot. Suddenly, he had no appetite for a goose dinner.

"Looks like you've made a friend."

Kolyn recognized Ian's voice, and could not bring herself to look up, her cheeks warming as she recalled the intimacy of the night before. She felt the fool, sitting in the chicken yard with a goose in her lap. "I don't think Molly will be so happy to learn that instead of killing and plucking her goose I've made friends with him."

"You've a kind heart."

She lifted her gaze and dared to look at him. He was sincere. This made her feel guilty. *How was she supposed to kill this man when she couldn't even kill a silly goose?* "Oh, God," she moaned and closed her eyes.

Ian knelt beside her. "I'll see to it that Molly has a goose. Two, just to be sure."

She felt even guiltier and moaned again.

"All right, no goose. I'll send a pig over."

This made her laugh. She was worried about having to kill this man, and he was worried that she didn't want to eat a goose. "No." She finally looked at him. "I can't ask you to do that."

"You didn't ask." Ian stood and offered a hand to help her up.

She accepted, but regretted it the instant his hand touched hers. He was warm, his touch gentle. She wanted to hate him and was finding that difficult.

"I will pay you for them." She reached down into the pocket of her dress and removed the coins she had received in tips.

A strange expression filtered across Ian's face, one she didn't know how to interpret.

"I wouldn't dream of your paying, Lynn. I just don't want to see you cry again."

This confused her even further. "I . . ." She didn't know what to say.

Ian picked a feather from her hair. Curious, he lifted a long curl and twisted it about his finger. It was as soft as he thought it would be. He wanted to see if it smelled of heather, as Lynn did, but he refrained. He could see that his first small gesture had stiffened her back and turned her face away. Pink tinted her cheeks. He longed to taste of the rosy lips she puckered in dismay.

"You are very beautiful, Lynn."

"Thank you, my lord."

"Could you call me Ian? I would prefer it."

She finally turned back to him, her eyes wide and troubled. He wondered at the sadness he read in them.

"I think it best I do not," Kolyn whispered.

Disappointed, Ian asked, "And why do you think this?"

Kolyn wasn't prepared for such a question. "I . . . I don't expect to know you well enough, my lord."

"But"—Ian grinned—"I thought we might get to know each other better. Much better."

"And why did you think this?"

"Because I am very attracted to you."

She nibbled her lower lip, not liking the direction of this conversation. "I have been told"—Kolyn chose her words carefully—"that there has been no woman in your life since your wife died."

"That is true," Ian replied.

She watched him from beneath lowered lashes. "Why me, my lord?"

Ian's eyebrow raised as if he truly couldn't understand why she would not know his reasons. "Have you had no men desire you, Lynn?"

"No," she answered quietly, honestly. The only men in her life had been her family, her son, and Father McCloud. No one had ever come to court her. Her father had been preoccupied with his anger and hate, and the fact that Kolyn might long for the love of a husband had been beyond his realm of feuds and challenges. She herself had thought little of it, grief claiming most of the past years. And she had Andrew. Kolyn had needed little else these past years.

"I find that hard to believe." Ian lifted her chin to gaze into her wonderful green eyes, so clear and sharp in color they left him breathless. "Women as lovely as you are women to die for."

Kolyn felt her heart tighten painfully. Once again she thought of the irony of it all—Ian could very well die for her love.

Ian leaned down, his lips brushing hers, ever so softly. Ever so sweetly. He stepped back and bowed low, exaggeratedly gallant. "I shall look forward to seeing you tomorrow night. Please give me the smallest hope you will save a dance for me?"

Kolyn couldn't help but smile at his foolishness. "Perhaps, my lord, perhaps."

"Your smile is my reward," Ian muttered, then turned and left.

A short time later she heard Molly's cackle as he strode through the kitchen and out of the tavern. Molly's large form filled the doorway.

"What's this, lass? Has Lord Blackstone gone mad? He's tradin' two hogs for that goose. Says I'm not t' cook it."

"Aye." Kolyn felt the culprit pecking at her feet, his soft honks melodious. "I couldn't kill the goose."

The village was filled with people, the harvest celebration a time all enjoyed. The night air was chilly, but everyone stayed warm with dance and laughter. A bonfire blazed in front of the

tavern, and people milled in and out with
tankards of ale and mugs of wine. Everyone
brought food and ate their fill, Ian's two hogs
turning into four. He had even taken Kolyn
to Stonehaven to help him fill a wagon from
his own storeroom for the event. She had
worked since early that morning, and now
felt weariness drag at her, but the jubilation
around her was undeniable.

Ainsley Blackstone stood only a few feet
away, and Kolyn studied her. She was a
graceful woman age had forgotten to dull. Her
hair was as black as a raven's wing and her skin
the color of cream. She was beautiful. Her eyes
were the softest brown, a touch of gold glistening in them. Kolyn could see where Ian had
gotten the intense color of his eyes—there was
a hint of it in his mother's. All her movements,
her manners, her smile were gentle and caring.
Kolyn knew she could have liked the woman.

"That's very pretty," Ainsley said, stepping
over to Kolyn and touching the small flowers
entwined in her hair.

"Thank you." Kolyn returned her smile.
"Leslie did it for me. I've never been very
good with my hair."

"You are very different from Leslie."

Whether it was a statement or a question
Kolyn wasn't certain. She sensed Ainsley was
not waiting for an answer.

"Yet you are her friend. Many would not be,"
Ainsley said.

"We all have our sins, Lady Blackstone."

"Aye." Ainsley's look grew sad. "The Lord forgives us our sins . . . if only we can forgive ourselves."

"Sometimes, it's not so easy."

"I believe you promised me a dance."

Kolyn glanced nervously between Ian and his mother. Ainsley's look was one of amusement now, the sadness all gone.

"I did no such thing," Kolyn said.

"I see your friend has not left your side." Ian pointed to the goose that rested at Kolyn's feet. "He is my witness you did indeed promise me a dance."

Kolyn felt the heat rise in her face, his persistence annoying, yet thrilling at the same time. "If I say no, will you leave me alone?"

"Of course not."

"Then let's dance, my lord." She turned to his mother. "Please excuse me, Lady Blackstone, while I appease your son."

Kolyn offered her arm to Ian and allowed him to lead her out into the crowd of dancers. The goose followed, his honking blending with the music and laughter. He was underfoot and in danger of being stepped upon. Kolyn tried to shoo him away, but he remained close by. Laughing, Ian picked the goose up, and they finished the dance with the animal tucked securely under his arm.

The music ended. Out of breath, Kolyn took her goose and nodded politely. "Thank you, my lord." She walked back to where she stood before.

Ian followed.

"Thank you, my lord," Ian mimicked, irritated by her coolness. He grabbed her free hand and pulled her behind him until they were alone and out of sight. He stopped and whirled about so suddenly she ran right into him.

"Excuse me," Kolyn muttered, confused by his sudden anger.

Even though she tried to pull free of his grip, he did not let go of her hand. He held her firmly.

"Please let me go."

He ignored her.

Suddenly, Kolyn was nervous. He seemed so dark, so sinister. He no longer smiled and teased her. "I'd best get back."

He said nothing.

"What do you want from me?" she asked weakly.

"A kiss," he whispered, his voice deep and husky. "All I want is a kiss."

She considered this and wondered if he was lying to her. If she kissed him, then what? Would he expect more? Was she willing to give more? Kolyn looked away, embarrassed by her own thoughts. Kolyn set the goose down and turned back to Ian.

"One kiss, that is all?"

"One kiss."

She stood on her tiptoes and found she was

still too short to reach him. He didn't make a move to lean down. Kolyn glanced about, and spotting a tree stump, took his arm and pulled him over to it. She climbed up on it and found herself staring into Ian's golden eyes, their softness drawing her in. She gathered her courage.

Kolyn had never kissed a man. Not a man who openly desired her. She felt her stomach tighten and jump. She licked her lips to moisten them. It was hot, too hot. Even the coolness of the night could not chill the fire inside her.

Every strong line of his jaw, even the slightest shading of his beard, was before her gaze. She saw the contour of his lips, the subtle indentation where his dimples showed at rare times. She wanted to touch them, found herself doing so. Ian remained still under her scrutiny; only the slightest reflex in his jaw showed he was even aware of her. Blackest lashes framed his eyes, eyes of melted gold.

A kiss. That was all he asked. Kolyn prepared herself. She cocked her head to the side and kissed him. When she pulled back, his arms went about her, pulling her closer, enclosing her in a circle of muscled arms. She could not escape.

His tongue pried open her lips. The tip played with her own, sending tremors through her. The fire exploded within and consumed her body and mind. She was lost.

Ian drank long of her kiss, like a man dying of thirst. Her body fit so neatly against his, her softness molding to his hardness. Longings rose in him like a giant roused after a long sleep. At first, slow and drowsy, then fierce and demanding. He pulled away, afraid of his own yearnings.

"Thank you, my lady." Ian's voice broke from the intensity of his reaction to her. "I must go now, or I shall need more than a kiss."

With that, he disappeared, leaving Kolyn standing upon the stump. Bewildered and confused.

"Does the lady need assistance down?"

Startled, Kolyn looked about to put a face to the voice. Geoffrey stepped forward from the night shadows.

"No." Embarrassed, she stepped down. "Do you always lurk in the shadows?"

Geoffrey's laughter filtered to her. "As long as there are men who would kill Ian."

"Are there many?" Kolyn asked.

Geoffrey shook his head. "No. Most of Ian's enemies are dead."

Thankfully, Geoffrey could not see Kolyn's reaction in the dark. "Then why do you still protect him?"

"They are not *all* dead." He laughed again. "It is what I do, lass. I know no other life."

Curiosity got the best of her. "You would kill for Ian?"

He looked amazed, as if it were a silly question. "Of course, Lynn. I'd kill for him, and I'd die for him."

"That's extremely loyal, Geoff. How is it Lord Blackstone has such a friend?"

"You ask a lot of questions," he said, looking uncomfortable.

Kolyn had never seen Geoffrey serious, a mischievous grin always on his lips, laughter always there. This made her hope he would continue.

"Ian saved my life when I was young. He gave my life back to me. Then he provided a life for me. To watch over Ian seems little enough for all he has given me these past years."

"And what's that?"

"His friendship."

Kolyn was quiet a moment, then threw another question his way. "Do you think I would harm Ian?"

This change of subject obviously confused Geoffrey. "What?"

"You were watching over Lord Blackstone when he was with me. Do you think I will try and kill him?"

It was a dangerous question. Kolyn knew this. But she couldn't stop herself from asking anyway.

"Aye." He smiled. "All women are suspect. Women can kill a man without a weapon. I suspect you will break Ian's heart, Lynn."

Anger touched Kolyn. "You make fun of me,

Geoff." She turned to go back to the tavern.

"No, lass," Geoffrey called after her. "I'm deadly serious."

Kolyn felt tired. It was time to slip away up to her attic room for some much needed sleep. It had been a long day. She went inside the tavern, the room filled with people still eating, still drinking. Perhaps sleep wouldn't be coming anytime soon. She moved through the crowd to the stairs.

"Hey, lass."

Someone grabbed her arm and stopped her. She turned to see who had spoken to her. It was a man she had seen only a few times in the inn, usually quite drunk. Tonight was no exception. He was dirty. Kolyn tried to pull her arm from his hand, but he persistently held tight, hurting her.

"Please let go of me," she said much more politely than she felt.

"I seen you go off in the dark with Blackstone. How 'bout sharin' some of what you are givin' t' him."

His breath was foul, and Kolyn thought she might be sick just thinking about kissing someone like him. "I'm tired. Let me go."

"Now, lass," he whined, but he stopped when a giant shadow fell upon him.

"What do you want of the lady?"

Ian's voice was as hard as his look.

The man cowered before his fierceness.

"Nothin', my lord. Was not wantin' anythin' of the lady."

"Then go have another drink and leave her be."

His words brooked no argument, and the man didn't give any. He slunk away into the crowd around them. Ian turned to Kolyn.

"He's harmless, Lynn. Just a man who drinks too much."

"I suppose." She wasn't convinced.

His dark brows wrinkled together. "Did he frighten you?"

"No." She wouldn't admit it if he had. "He's just a harmless drunk."

"Are you retiring for the night?"

Kolyn eyed him suspiciously. "Yes. I'm very tired."

"I'll see you upstairs then," he said matter-of-factly.

She didn't argue. She was very tired and didn't even want to talk anymore. Kolyn stopped at the foot of her attic ladder and turned to Ian.

"Good night, Lord Blackstone."

Ian looked down at her, his eyes expressing everything. But he said only, "You'd best take the ladder up, so no one will accidentally disturb you."

Whether it was to keep the drunks out, or Ian himself, Kolyn really couldn't decide. "What of Leslie?"

"Leslie won't be around for a long time after

a celebration like this. Take the ladder up."

Deciding it was best, she climbed the ladder and he helped lift it up behind her. She peered down at him, his head not too far from the attic's entrance. She wasn't sure what to say.

"Good night, Lynn."

He turned and walked away. Kolyn moved over to her straw mattress, wishing she were at home in her own large, comfortable bed with Andrew curled up beside her. She had been away from home five weeks, much too long. She missed Andrew terribly. It was time for her to see this to its end and go home. Having decided this, Kolyn slept.

Ian's soft mouth found hers, his lips moist and wet. His kiss was like fire, its heat sweeping through her wildly. She thought she would die with longing. Suddenly, his face contorted with pain. She looked down at her hand and found she held his dagger, blood dripping from its tip. When her gaze moved back, Ian was deep down in a grave, the earth sliding in to cover him. She began screaming, clawing at the dirt that threatened to swallow him. His eyes opened, the golden light accusing.

Kolyn jerked awake, clamping her hand over her mouth to still her screams. Sweat trickled down between her breasts and she struggled for breath, the air seeming thin. Hot tears assaulted her and sobs shook her.

"Dear God," she moaned, sickened by her

own dream. What was she to do? She must kill the very man she desired—the very man she was growing to love. Her heart ached with longing and pain at the same time her mind condemned her for disloyalty, betraying her family and clan.

Chapter Ten

Kolyn stared in disbelief at Ian as he sat upon his horse looking down at her. He seemed so serious.

"I have work to do, Lord Blackstone. I cannot go riding with you."

She hoped this would put an end to his idea. Then again, he didn't look like a man who discouraged easily.

"I've spoken with Molly. She said you worked very hard yesterday preparing for the festival. She's given you the afternoon off."

"I cannot."

"And why not?" he asked, sliding off his mount to stand beside her.

She shielded her eyes against the sun and looked up at him. He was smiling. His dimples were irresistible. "I . . ." She couldn't think of another excuse.

"Then it's settled." He took her hand, guided her to the saddle, then lifted her up.

"I should get my shawl." Kolyn pointed inside.

"I'll keep you warm, Lynn."

She already was regretting this, especially when he mounted and settled into the saddle with her wrapped securely in his arms. He was much too close, but she couldn't get away. She was certain that was his ploy.

"Where are we going?"

Ian nudged his horse into a gentle gallop. "I thought I'd show you some of the country."

"Show off your land is what you mean." She laughed, already feeling lighter in spirit to take a break from her work.

"Aye." He grinned, his dimples popping. "To show off."

It was true. Ian wanted to show Lynn his home, his work. To let her know what was important to him, to have her meet the people who were a part of his life.

Kolyn had to admit Ian acted the gentleman, never once taking advantage of their closeness. This allowed her to relax and fully enjoy the beautiful countryside. Blackstone land covered a vast expanse, the terrain varying from thick woodland and mountain forests to lonely moors and enchanting sea cliffs. MacGregor land was inland, not so far from the sea.

Still, Kolyn had never seen the sea. Every moment, every new experience was a delight. She couldn't remember the last time she had enjoyed herself so much. For the time, she let everything slip from her, all her anxieties gone in the rays of the sunshine.

Ian left his special place for last, higher up on the mountain that overlooked Blackstone lands. When they reached the spot, Ian jumped down from his horse, then helped Lynn to the ground. Without a word, Ian took Lynn's hand and led her to the very spot where he had spent many hours himself, the spectacular view taking his breath away each and every time. He watched her closely for her own reaction, and was not disappointed.

"It's beautiful, Lord Blackstone."

She felt him tense, and knew it was an irritant to him that she wouldn't concede and call him Ian.

"My father was a loyal Englishman, but he said there was nothing to compare to the Scottish Highlands. They are truly magnificent."

"Do you ever wish to live in England?"

He shook his head. "I went to school in England; 'tis all I want to see of it."

A sudden sadness attacked Kolyn as she looked down over the farmland, neat patchworks of fields readied for winter's snow, a slow, winding river running through them. She saw areas of mountain meadows nestled among the thick woodlands, meadows where she was certain a wealth of cattle and sheep would roam in the summertime. Stonehaven castle sat at the edge of the village, its protection and comfort like a beacon of light in a fog, marking the presence of its lord and master. Even at the best of times, MacGregor land had never been so lush and fertile.

"Everything is so well taken care of. You do a fine job with your lands."

"It does not pay to let things go to ruin. My father worked hard to make these lands prosper. I'd be a fool to let that slip away because of ignorance or inattention."

"I thought you must not do much." She tried to smile. "You are at the inn so much."

This made him smile. "Aye, of late I've been a bit preoccupied with a certain lass. She has made my work suffer."

"You shouldn't. It's not worth your time at the inn."

Ian looked at Lynn and wondered why she tried so hard to discourage him. He knew she desired him—once in a great while she would let it show. "Why do you fight me so hard? Why can't you just let—"

Kolyn put her fingers on his lips to stop him, her face showing her pain. "Do not talk so, my lord."

He grasped her hand and kissed the palm. "You are the strangest lass I've ever known."

"You don't know me," she whispered. "You don't know who I am or where I come from.

You know nothing about me."

"That is what I want—to know who you are and where you come from."

She pulled her hand from his and turned away. "Why can't you just leave me be?"

Frustration exploded inside Ian. He wanted to make her look at him. To kiss her doubts away. But he didn't. "You make me feel something I thought I could never feel again. Is that so bad, Lynn? Is it so terrible to want you to feel something for me?"

"I cannot feel anything for you." Tears blurred her vision. She couldn't feel desire for him. She couldn't love him!

This time, he did make her turn to look at him. "I don't believe what your beautiful lips are saying. You do feel something. I can see it."

"No . . ." She tried to say it to his face. "I . . ."

She couldn't. She felt great shame. She had failed her father, her clan, Andrew, herself. She could not hold back her tears.

Ian pulled her into his arms and comforted her.

"Don't cry, lass. I didn't mean to make you cry."

He seemed so lost, so at a loss, when she cried. It was something she wouldn't have expected from such a fierce-looking man. His tenderness shook her even further.

"Please take me home."

It was the last thing Ian wanted to do, but he agreed.

They rode in silence.

"Where is everyone tonight?" Kolyn asked, looking about her at the empty tables as she swept the floor.

Leslie motioned with her head. "At the stables. The dog fighter came t' the village today and they be tryin' their luck. I hear Samuel is fightin' his dog."

Kolyn stopped cold. "The dog fighter?"

"Aye, they'll be in as soon as there's a winner."

" 'Tis a cruel thing," Kolyn mumbled, thinking it awful that people would bet on such a thing.

"I went t' one." Leslie paused, apparently recalling her experience. "Was enough for me. Bloody awful it was."

Kolyn went to the door and opened it. She heard the yelling, then heard the dogs. Suddenly, one let out a low howl. It sounded as if it were dying. Reacting rather than thinking, Kolyn headed toward the noise, her broom grasped firmly in hand.

The stables were dim, a lantern swinging from the rafter. The smell of smoke, ale, and too many humans assaulted her, but she drove through the wall of backs. Surprised to see her, many let her pass, stepping aside as she brandished her broom at them. She worked her way into the center of the ring of men.

It was a horrible sight. The larger dog had the other by the neck, his yelps going unheeded by the crowd of onlookers. Blood was everywhere. Kolyn stepped forward.

"Get him off," she yelled toward Samuel, but he was caught up in the thrill of winning.

"I said," she screamed at him, finally drawing his gaze, "get him off."

"Now, Lynn. Why would I be doing that?" Samuel looked at her as if she was crazed.

"Get him off now, or I'll give him a knot on his head he'll never forget." She raised her broom ready to strike.

"But he's winning, lass," he whined. She didn't retreat.

When he made no move to stop the dogs, Kolyn stepped forward, her broom aimed. She whacked the larger dog on the head, getting his full attention. He growled at her.

"Get him off, Samuel!"

Samuel finally moved forward and grabbed his dog. He pulled the dog away, shaking his head. "I could have won a pile o' coin."

Kolyn reached into her pocket and retrieved her tip money. "Here. Take it."

She was furious. She knew it showed, in her voice, her movements, her look. When he hesitated, she stomped over to him. "Here's your bloody money, Samuel." She shoved it into his hand, ignoring the growls of his dog. "Now go on home before you spend it all on ale."

The dog snipped at her, and she turned back and swung her broom with accuracy. The wispy straw struck the dog a second time. "You be quiet." She rounded on the gathered men. "You ought to be ashamed. All of you!"

The dog clamped his jaw shut and sat down. The men began to scatter.

A man stepped forward. "Jus' who the bloody hell are you?"

Kolyn was not swayed by his anger. She pointed at the smaller dog. "You must be the man who brought this poor animal here to fight?"

"Aye," he sneered. "He's me dog all right."

"Not anymore," she said so matter-of-factly it took him back.

"What's tha' you said?"

"You heard me." Kolyn was beyond irritation. She had no patience with this man. She knelt beside the dog. "He's near dead, and I'm taking him."

"Like hell you will," he yelled, grabbing her by the arm.

He whirled her about, but she brought the broomstick up under his chin, knocking what little teeth he had together. "Don't try and stop me. I will have this dog."

Her threat seemed to slide off him like water from a duck's back. "You are a feisty lass, I'll give you tha'. But you'll no' be taking me hound."

"If the lady says she wants the dog, then she can have him."

The man's attention was diverted to Ian, who stood only a few feet away, Geoffrey by his side. "A dead dog will get you nothing. Let her have him."

The man seemed to think the situation over and stepped back. "He's near dead anyway," he said, then walked away.

"I didn't need your help," Kolyn said to Ian.

He looked at Kolyn and wondered at her sanity. To do what she did was totally without sense. Then she had the audacity to stand there and say she didn't need his help. "Have you lost all your senses, Lynn?"

"No, and I'd appreciate it if you'd just stay out of my affairs. I was doing just fine without you."

She bent down and tried to lift the dog, but he was too big. Still, she wouldn't ask Ian's help.

Ian had to fight back the laughter that tickled him. He walked over and gently pushed her aside. "I'll carry him over to that pile of hay." He pointed to the exact spot in the barn. "Go get some hot water and bandages from Molly."

This time, Kolyn didn't argue. She ran to do as he said. Ian carried the animal over to the corner and laid him upon the soft straw. He knelt down to examine the dog's wounds. The dog was bleeding badly.

Kolyn came back with the water and cloth

and sat upon the dirt floor beside him. Carefully, she cleaned away the dirt and blood. The dog lifted his head to look at her, and she talked to him softly.

"It's going to be all right boy. I'll take care of you."

The animal seemed to understand her words, his look one of trust. She continued with her work.

Ian watched Lynn closely, helping when asked. Neither spoke except when necessary. When she had done all she could, Lynn sat with her back against a stall post, the dog's head in her lap, her hand stroking him with love.

The night was nearly gone, but Kolyn continued her vigil—she didn't want to leave the poor animal alone. Her hand could feel his uneven breathing, each rattled breath a struggle. He lifted his head.

"Ssshhh, be still, boy. You'll hurt yourself."

The dog looked up at her, his eyes dull and pained. Kolyn felt angry at how his master had abused him. Gently, he licked her hand.

"It looks like you've made another friend, Lynn." Ian sat across from her. "You're getting quite a menagerie of animals. The tavern will never be the same."

Kolyn brushed away the tears that filled her eyes. It seemed all she did was cry lately. "You don't need to worry about that," she said sadly. "The dog is dead."

"I'm sorry, lass. You did your best to save him."

She lifted her head and looked at Ian, his eyes sympathetic. "I'd like to bury him. Perhaps by the creek among the trees."

Ian said nothing more. He stood and walked to where some tools were hung. He grabbed the shovel and left.

Kolyn continued to hold the dog, her hand still stroking his head.

When Ian returned, he lifted the dog from her arms. She followed him outside. The sun was coming up, a spray of pink softening the black sky. The spot Ian had chosen was beautiful, and Kolyn was touched by his consideration. Whether it was for her or the animal she neither knew nor cared. It only mattered that the dog would rest in peace along the bank, tall birch trees to watch over him.

Gently, Ian placed the animal in the grave he had dug, then shoveled the dirt over him. Lynn pulled her shawl tighter about her, the chill of the late fall morning touching her. Ian finished and moved to stand beside her.

She turned to him. "Thank you, Ian."

Ian watched her go back to the tavern, pleased she had called him Ian. He knew it meant more to him than it should. Still, he could not help but wonder if it was to be short-lived, if the next time he saw her she would call him *my lord* again. He strolled back to the stable.

"You look quite pleased for a man who has sat up all night with a mongrel dog."

Ian stepped past Geoffrey, who leaned casually against the barn door, and placed the shovel back on its peg.

"Aye." Ian smiled. "I think the woman has taken away all my sense."

Geoffrey chuckled. "Aye, that she has."

Ian slapped his friend upon the back. " 'Tis time to ride home, my friend."

Geoffrey stared at Ian, amazement rounding his eyes while laughter pulled his lips into a broad smile. "You *have* lost all your senses, Ian."

"Aye." Ian's deeper, long laugh mixed with Geoffrey's shorter one, filling the tavern's stable with their blend of sound.

Ian sobered, but the twinkle remained in his eyes. "This slip of a woman has me thinking and doing strange things. I seem helpless to stop myself, even if it means risking your ridicule, my friend."

" 'Tis good to see you smilin'. I'll do my best to refrain from laughin' at you." Geoffrey failed almost immediately, unable to keep his chuckle down. Just the sight of Ian holding that mongrel dog was too humorous to keep from laughing. "Do you think it will work?"

Ian set the dog on the dirt floor, the mutt's dark brown eyes never leaving Ian, looking anxious to please. "Limp," Ian commanded and the animal immediately obeyed, limping forlornly across to the door. He looked back, waiting for Ian.

"You're a sneaky man, Ian Blackstone. 'Tis something I dinna ken about you."

"I just want to see Lynn smile again." Ian thought back on the few times Lynn had smiled with genuine happiness. "I am a fool, but I don't seem to care much these days."

"Just remember that, my friend, when she breaks your heart." Geoffrey laughed again and slung his arm about Ian's shoulder. " 'Tis amazing how short our memories get when we become a fool over a woman. God help us if we ever stop lovin' the fair maidens—God help us when they stop lovin' us."

Geoffrey's warning struck the small, hidden memories Ian fought so hard to forget, but they couldn't rise above the good feelings inside him. "Stay here with the dog while I get Lynn."

"You're determined to mix me up in your schemes." Geoffrey cast a mock look of being disgusted. "Aye, go get the lass. This I've got to see."

Ian left the dimness of the stable, the scent of hay and horses still strong in his nostrils. The sky, overcast and cloudy, emitted streams of sunshine sporadically through the floating blackness, as if it couldn't make up its mind whether to clear or not. Ian strolled into the inn, his purpose in mind. He still couldn't believe he would go so far for a simple smile.

Instantly, his eyes found Lynn, drawn to her by feeling more than sight. It amazed him how beautiful she was, dressed simply in a wool skirt and blouse, no frills to take away from her loveliness.

Kolyn heard the door open, the cool blast of air in the staleness telling her someone had entered, the strange thrill that tickled her insides telling her it was Ian. She delivered the mugs she carried, trying to calm herself before acknowledging his appearance. He didn't give her much time to accomplish such a difficult task.

"Lynn."

His voice was soft, stirring. But it paled in comparison to what his golden gaze did to her when she turned to face him. "Good morning, Lord Blackstone."

She saw his eye twitch slightly with disappointment, but he gave her a big smile nonetheless, his dimples showing.

"Good morning, Lynn." He stepped closer. "I've a favor to ask."

Ian's look had turned so serious she could not deny him. "What is it you need?"

He took her hand and guided her toward the door. "I found a dog as I took my morning ride. He seems to be hurt."

Tears sprang immediately to her eyes, an old heartache blended with a new one. It had been a week, but she still couldn't keep from crying when she thought of the cruelty the mongrel she had tried to save had endured. "The poor thing," Kolyn whispered, brushing an escaped tear away before Ian could see it. "Where is it?"

"In the stable. Could you look at him?"

"Of course." Kolyn untied her apron and laid it on a nearby table. She turned back to look for Molly, finding her standing in the kitchen doorway waving her to go on. Ian took Kolyn's arm and walked with her to the stable, his touch unnecessary but pleasant.

It took a moment for her eyes to adjust to the darkness. Then she saw the dog, lying on the straw-littered ground. He lifted his head as she approached, his eyes large and warm as his curled tail thumped a happy rhythm stirring the dust. Tan, wiry wisps of hair stuck out in every direction, giving him a homely look. Kolyn immediately fell in love with him.

"What's the matter with him?" she asked, turning her gaze back to Ian's. For the first time, she noticed Geoffrey standing just behind him, a strange grin plastered across his face. Suspicion nudged her.

"He's limping pretty badly."

Kolyn moved a few steps away. "Come on, boy," she cooed, coaxing him to stand and walk.

"Limp," Ian stressed, then finished when Lynn looked at him curiously. "See." He pointed. "He's limping."

165

Fela Dawson Scott

The dog struggled over to Lynn, one leg lifted as he hopped along on his three others. She kneeled down and pulled him into her arms. Gently, she examined the animal.

"His leg doesn't seem to be tender to the touch."

"Somethin' must be wrong. He's limpin' quite badly," Geoffrey observed. Ian felt he was enjoying himself much too much and cast him a warning look.

"Well." Lynn stood, bewilderment clear on her face. "I don't know what it could be."

"Perhaps he just needs some love," Ian said.

Kolyn felt stifled by his look, the heat in it flowing to her. "I couldn't . . ."

She stopped when she saw the disappointment on Ian's face. "I already have the goose to take care of. How could I possibly take care of a dog too?"

Ian stepped closer, too close for Kolyn's comfort. She tried to step back but found herself surrounded, Geoffrey having closed in behind her.

Ian took her hand into his. "He needs your help, Lynn."

She was trapped with no way out, but it was a pleasant dilemma. Ian looked too serious, and Geoffrey . . . looked too amused. Kolyn smiled. "You two are up to no good. I can feel it in my bones."

Ian's lips quivered as he tried not to smile, and Kolyn knew she had been right. She

166

glanced back at the dog, who still sat where she had left him, then called to him. "Come here, boy." Before Ian could say anything she put her finger to his lips to stop him. They all watched the dog scatter over to her, his limp suddenly gone. He jumped into the air and barked, twisting about in a healthy, rambunctious manner.

"Look," Ian declared, his tone overly anxious. "He's better already."

Kolyn tried to keep from laughing, wanting Ian to suffer a little for his teasing. She failed as the little dog did his best to get her attention, and laughed wholeheartedly. He was more than adorable. She gathered him into her arms happily.

"You two are terrible." Her scolding came off with little success.

"I told you she'd not be fooled." Geoffrey slapped Ian on the head, just as they had since they were boys. Not wanting to take any blame for Ian's fool-hearted behavior, Geoffrey protested, "I had nothin' to do with this, Lynn. Blame *that* culprit, if you will."

"What a friend you are," Lynn teased back. "Do you always run at the faintest sign of trouble?"

Geoffrey liked this side of Lynn, and he too wished they could see more of it. "Of course. What are friends for?"

"Thanks, Geoff," Ian mumbled under his breath. His look played into a scowl, but it didn't reach the twinkle in his eyes. "I'll remember this."

"Well, I've got to go." Geoffrey winked at Lynn, then quickly made his exit.

"Are you angry?" Ian watched the top of Lynn's head as she played with the dog, her manner loving, caring. When she lifted her eyes to meet his, he had his answer. It pleased him.

"No," Kolyn whispered, knowing it wasn't worth the effort to try to pretend otherwise. "Where did you find him?"

"I bought him from some traveling players. He is trained to do all sorts of tricks."

"Including limping?"

"Aye." Ian smiled, looking much like a child caught in a lie. "Including limping."

Kolyn liked the easy feeling that had descended upon them. Determinedly, she did not allow anything to sneak in and destroy it. "And you were very convincing." She hugged the dog to her, his wiry hair tickling her cheek.

"Will you keep him?"

"You went to a lot of trouble, Lord Blackstone. I don't know if I understand why."

"Isn't it obvious?"

Ian's voice sounded gentle, drawing Kolyn further into a warm sense of comfort and pleasure. She should go back to work, but couldn't bring herself to do so. She wanted to know all his reasons, even if she chose later to deny or disbelieve them. "No, I don't seem to understand, even if it is obvious."

" 'Tis simple enough," Ian conceded. "I wanted to see you smile, my lady."

Ian watched Lynn turn her face away from him, her cheeks flushed pink with embarrassment. He knelt down and turned her face to him. "My efforts have been rewarded. You are even more beautiful when you smile, Lynn."

Kolyn couldn't help the nervous giggle that escaped. "You only wanted me to smile?"

"Aye."

Amazement, embarrassment, pleasure . . . it all danced inside her and she did just that. She smiled. The dog's wet nose rooted beneath her hand, wanting her to continue her petting, impatient she had stopped.

"He's very demanding." Kolyn scratched his head and when he rolled over, scratched his belly.

Ian reached out and picked him up, his look serious once again. "Now, let's get something straight, you mangy-looking rat."

The dog's tail never missed a wag as Ian lectured him kindly. "I didn't bring you here to occupy the lady's time and attention."

He turned his gaze back to Kolyn, his look now intense. "There are others who long for her affections as well."

Kolyn wanted to kiss Ian. Slowly, she leaned closer. Her mouth was slightly open, inviting him to her. Her body had claimed control over her mind. The warnings it could have

Fela Dawson Scott

given, the sense it could have offered, she never considered. She wanted to kiss Ian.

Her lips touched his, their softness molding to hers. He tasted good. He smelled good. Kolyn moved her hand to his neck and pulled him closer. Ian felt good.

Kolyn's kiss started sweetly, curiously, but deepened with passion with each strong beat of his heart. Ian pulled away and held her at arm's length, holding the dog between them. Her smooth forehead wrinkled together in dismay.

"You didn't like it?" Kolyn's voice sounded hurt, the slight quiver to her lower lip adding to Ian's turmoil.

"No." Ian tried to gather more air into his lungs, her one kiss having stirred him greatly. But his pause caused more dismay to Kolyn. He rushed on. "No, Lynn. I more than liked it."

Her face did not show any understanding.

"I liked it too much, lass."

Slowly, her lips turned up into a small, shy smile, her eyes pleased. Kolyn stepped closer, but Ian stepped back.

"Have mercy," he muttered, his own voice sounding strange, strained. "One sweet kiss and I'm tempted to take more, and more."

Kolyn felt confused. He had always made it clear he wanted more from her. She asked the obvious question. "What is stopping you?"

His sigh touched her. It was sad, apologetic.

"Because I want more than a quick dalliance in the stable, Lynn."

She still didn't understand what he was saying.

"When I make love to you," he explained, "I want to do so with leisure. I want to enjoy each moment and every inch of you. I don't want to push your skirt up and take you in the hay."

Ian leaned closer, his words now whispered into her ear. "I want to smell the sweet heather that scents your soft skin, the firelight dancing off its milky complexion in temptation. I want to lose myself in the tangles of your hair filling my senses with its aroma. I want to taste the salty sweat on your belly as our passion heats our bodies."

Kolyn struggled for air, feeling as if she had run miles when she hadn't taken a single step. Ian handed the dog to her and walked to the stable doors. He turned back to say, "His name is Dax."

Then he was gone. Trembling, Kolyn hugged Dax to her.

"Oh, my," she said softly. She buried her heated face into his wiry fur. "Oh, my."

Chapter Eleven

"How much coin would it take t' warm me bed, lass?"

Kolyn twisted free of the grabbing hands, and despite her irritation, she smiled and filled the men's drinks. "No amount of money you have could get me to your bed. Now keep your hands on your mugs and off me."

The same man spoke again, his two mates eager with pinching fingers and leering grins. "Now, lass. No need t' be that way. Me friends an' I just want t' have some fun."

Leslie stepped between Kolyn and their wandering hands. "How about me, lads? I'll see t' your needs right enough."

A large hand pushed Leslie aside. "I be in the mood for a redheaded wench." He looked up at

Leslie. "Not a blonde, lass."

Kolyn tried to ignore his comment and went about her work. She was grateful to Leslie for trying to distract them. She quickly glanced to the table where Ian and Geoffrey always sat, but instantly regretted it. The scowl on Ian's face was ominous. Never had she seen him so fierce. His eyes bore holes in the three men, who seemed unaware of Ian's anger. Obviously they were strangers, or they would have been more cautious.

As awful as they were, she began to fear for them. The last thing she needed was trouble from Ian. Deliberately, she avoided their table, leaving it for Leslie to serve. The three men continued to drink heavily, their ribald comments and stares growing with each mug of ale they finished.

"'Tis her job, Ian. Perhaps you'd best leave if you cannot sit here and keep hold of your temper."

Ian turned away from the source of his anger and looked at Geoffrey, a great heat rising inside of him. "I'll keep my temper in check. But they best not touch her again."

"Look," Geoffrey pointed out. "Leslie's serving them now. She'll keep them away from Lynn."

Ian wasn't convinced. Something inside him remained suspicious of these men. Silently, he watched them.

Molly stopped Kolyn and whispered in her

ear. "Perhaps you should leave for a bit, lass. Till they have had their fill of drink."

Kolyn nodded and set down the pitcher she carried. She slipped into the kitchen and out the back door. Her goose was immediately under foot, his honking a comfort in the dark. She walked for a bit, enjoying the crisp night air. The tavern was crowded tonight, the air tight and stale. But mostly, she enjoyed getting away from Ian's watchful eye.

She wandered to the small creek where they had buried the dog, her heart still aching from his pain-filled death. Kolyn paused a moment at the small mound of earth, but moved on to the creek's edge. She heard the bubble of water. Soft moonlight reflected off its shimmering surface. It was a pleasant sound, the air fresh as a breeze cleared the smoky haze of village fires from it.

Kneeling down, Kolyn cupped some water in her hands and drank, the near-winter chill parching her thirst. She splashed the rest over her face, cleansing her skin of the sweat from her work. She shouldn't stay gone too long. Leslie might need her help.

"You're a bonnie sight, lass."

The man from the tavern stood before her, blocking her way, his two companions just behind to his right and left.

Kolyn tried to remain calm. "I told you, I'm not interested in your offer."

He just smiled. "Well, I'm not a man who

Fela Dawson Scott

much cares what you have t' say, lass."

His threat registered in her mind, and she was afraid. She felt helpless, vulnerable, and this made her angry. "Don't threaten me, you bastard."

He stepped forward. "'Tis no threat, 'tis fact. I'll be takin' what you will not share."

A big-fisted hand grabbed for her, but she slipped from his grasp. When she turned to flee, she tripped over the goose that huddled at her feet and fell to her knees. The goose flapped his wings in fright, and a large foot kicked at him, sending him running toward the tavern, his cries loud in the still night.

The man was on top of her before she could right herself, slamming her to the damp ground with his weight. All her breath left her lungs, and she found it difficult to fill them again with his large body on top of hers. His face loomed above her, ugly and coarse, his breath foul.

"I'll show you what a man can do for you, lass."

She felt his hand beneath her dress, slowly sliding up the length of her leg to her hip. He squeezed it painfully as he thrust his groin against her hips. Kolyn felt sick. She struggled against him. She opened her mouth to scream, but his hairy hand clamped over it to still her cries.

He pulled his trousers open. Kolyn kicked and struck out, but her blows seemed to be of little effect on his meaty body. Pulled above

her waist, her skirt no longer offered protection
against him. She screamed into his hand, the
muffled sound heard only in her own head.
Tears blurred her vision of him as he raised
above her, his partners pulling her legs apart
for his ease. Never had she been so shamed.

The growl that reached her ears was animal-
like, causing the hair on her neck to rise. The
ugly man was lifted from her like he was a mere
boy, not a large, burly adult. He was flung into
the air to land in a heap upon the hard earth.

Ian faced the other two men, slowly pulling
his sword from its scabbard. They dropped
their hold upon Lynn and pulled their own
weapons to meet Ian's challenge. They seemed
confident with the odds and pushed their
advantage. Ian met them with a smile.

Within seconds, Ian had disarmed one and
wounded the other. But he was distracted by
the man he had pulled from atop Lynn. He
turned his attention to him, as if pleased to
kill him first.

Kolyn pushed herself up onto her shaking
legs. She looked about and spotted Geoffrey,
his posture at ease as he watched Ian fight the
three men. Confusion clouded her mind. Why
was he not helping Ian?

It soon became apparent that Ian needed
no help. He seemed to play with the man,
drawing out the obvious end to its fullest.
Kolyn was horrified. Ian's look, his manner,
spoke of danger. Indeed at that moment he

was the wolf, the predator hunting its prey. His sword sliced through the man, shredding his flesh like a velvet ribbon. Again and again his blows fell, leaving no room for the man to strike back. He was almost defenseless against Ian's power and skill.

"Stop!" Kolyn cried out.

Ian did not.

"No, Ian!" She ran to interfere. He stopped only when she stepped into the path of his sword.

"Get away, Lynn. The man deserves to die."

"Please stop," she pleaded.

He looked confused, but his sword remained ready. "I'll not stop. He cannot live for what he has done!"

Kolyn moved closer to Ian so he alone could hear her words. "Can't you see? I cannot live with his death upon my conscience."

Darkened gold eyes studied her, a brief flicker of disappointment crossing them. "After what he tried to do to you, you would plead for his life? I swear, Lynn, I do not understand you."

"I do not expect you to understand, only to do as I ask."

"And why should I?"

"Because he offended me, not you, my lord. I am the one who must live with the shame, not you. 'Tis my choice if he lives or dies, and I ask that you let him live."

"Bloody . . ." Ian dropped his sword to his

side. "You ask much, lass."

Kolyn turned to the man, who had fallen to one knee. "If I ever set eyes upon you again, I swear, I shall kill you myself." With that, she turned and fled to the tavern. Ian was right behind her.

He caught her and whirled her about. "You're the damnedest woman I've ever known."

"Leave me be," Kolyn cried, her emotions spent.

Angry eyes accused her, and she cringed from him.

"You're trouble," he said, "and yet I cannot keep from you."

Her own anger began to warm her dull mind. "Trouble? I did not ask you to interfere."

"Interfere?" he asked with amazement.

"Yes," she screamed, losing control. "Every time I turn around, you're there . . . interfering in my life."

Gold eyes narrowed. "I would think you'd be grateful for my help."

"Grateful? Is that your game, my lord? Do you think if I'm *grateful* for your help that I might *thank you* by letting you share my bed?"

Kolyn knew it wasn't true, but she couldn't be beholden to this man. She needed to hate him, to despise his very existence.

"Is that what you think?"

His words had softened, and his expression showed his hurt. Kolyn thought she would die from shame. The shame of letting her promise to her father guide her mingled with the shame of letting this man know how unworthy she could be. She thought of Andrew and how much she loved him. The lies came easier when she shored up her determination with a fierceness to protect her son from all the ugliness that had entered her life. The fact was Ian could not give her enough reasons to ignore her promise, and the clan, her father, and Emmett had given her many reasons to keep it. She must remember this.

"Yes, it is what I think. But you're right, I should be grateful." She reached out and took his hand, blood staining his flesh. She did not pull away. Instead, she raised it to her lips, a strangeness taking her in its grip.

"I shall thank you properly, my lord. Let's go to your room." She kissed his hand. "Come, let me thank you."

Kolyn pulled on his hand, but Ian did not budge. She had never seen such a look in his eyes. She failed to heed the warning they gave.

"I'll make you feel good, my lord." She stepped closer to him and placed her hand upon his chest. Kolyn looked up into his scowling face.

"Kiss me, Ian," she whispered. "Take me to your room."

Ian pulled away. "Why do you change so quickly from one moment to the next? What goes on in that pretty little head of yours?"

"Do you not desire me?"

"Aye," he answered, his voice gruff. "But I'll not be taking you up on your sweet offer, Lynn."

Confusion wound full circle and ran head on into her angry determination. "I'll not offer again, Ian Blackstone. Remember that."

She turned and walked away, fury in her steps.

Ian did not go after her this time. Never would he understand her. One moment she was throwing his advances in his face; the next she wanted him to take her to his room. He felt sick. He wanted her to come to him of her own free will, because she desired him. Not because she was grateful. He wondered how the hell she had come up with that?

"How do I manage to act so foolish?" Kolyn muttered to herself in anger. Feelings cascaded through her, one after another, leaving her totally and completely confused. Every time she was around him she seemed to get more absurd—more irrational.

Kolyn came around the corner to the kitchen door and nearly ran head on into Geoffrey. He blocked her way.

"He's right, you are trouble."

Geoffrey's words were hurtful, but Kolyn's anger refused to let her feel it. "Let me pass, Geoff."

He didn't move. "I thought you'd be good for Ian, help him feel again. But I was wrong, and I don't like bein' wrong."

"What do you want from me?" They all wanted something of her—something she did not understand.

He considered this. "I want you to leave Ian be."

Frustrated, she threw up her hands. "Make up your mind, for God's sake. First, you ask me to take him to my bed, then you want me to leave him be. 'Tis no wonder I'm confused."

He grabbed her by the shoulders and shook her. "Well, you've managed to confuse the hell out of him. I just wanted you to make him see there can be other women. What I don't want is for Ian to be hurt again."

Hurt? Kolyn's mind reeled back to Blair's death, the woman dying in the streets like a beggar. She had feared this man's wrath to the point of fearing for her son. Kolyn had witnessed Ian's anger that day, pushing him to the point of killing. This same man crippled Emmett, and killed Malcolm, Gilles, and her father. She almost laughed at Geoffrey's compassion.

"Your devotion is admirable, but the man is quite capable of taking care of his own affairs. I'll not speak of this again."

Kolyn twisted free of his hold and stepped past him. She wanted to be left alone and went directly to her attic room. It was just a few minutes later that Leslie poked her head above the floor.

"Are you all right, Lynn?"

"Aye, I'll be fine."

Leslie started to go back down the ladder, but came back up. "I've been tryin' t' get Ian t' me bed for near five years now. You've been here a few weeks and he's willin' t' kill for you. Do you not see how lucky you are?"

Kolyn thought it sad Leslie would think this. "Don't you ever think of love and marriage, Leslie?"

The girl folded her arms and laid her chin on them. "Sure I do. All women dream of such things. But 'tis not for the likes of me, especially t' a man like Ian Blackstone."

"And not for the likes of me?" Kolyn asked.

Leslie shrugged. "You are not like me, Lynn. Even I can see that. But men like Ian marry ladies. 'Tis not enough t' be pretty."

Kolyn snuggled down in her bed. "I don't want to marry Ian Blackstone."

"You are a fool, Lynn." Leslie moved back down the ladder. "A plain and simple fool."

Kolyn felt the fool and buried her head into her pillow. She was falling in love with a man she was supposed to hate, a man she was expected to kill. Father McCloud's advice drifted through the haze of pain . . . *look into your heart for the answers.*

This frightened her above all else. If she followed her heart, she would betray all for the love of her enemy. Shame forced her to lock her feelings away, to hide them from herself and all she might be disloyal to. There could be no considering her heart's desire.

She must leave this place soon.

The wind was icy, winter's promise just around the corner. Kolyn was cold, but she did not go back. The chapel bells rang out, announcing Sunday services. She watched the people file into the small church, looking much like ants from her perch upon the hill. She envied their simple lives.

"If I didn't know you better, I'd think you were about to jump."

Kolyn didn't turn to Ian, his sudden appearance not so surprising anymore. "What makes you so sure I wouldn't jump?"

He looked past her and down the steep cliff at the treacherous descent. "You've too much fight in you. To jump would be too easy."

"I don't want to fight you, my lord."

He laughed, though his tone held a note of irony. "You've done nothing but fight me, Lynn."

She finally looked at him. "I don't mean to. When you are around, I don't seem to know what I am doing . . . what I am saying. Please forgive my foolishness."

Ian stepped closer. "I have been rather single-minded in my pursuit of you, and I apologize. I guess . . ." He paused, then went on. "I had forgotten how pleasurable it was to be attracted to a woman. You're very intriguing. I've lost control with you, Lynn, and I didn't stop to think of your feelings. I am sorry."

Kolyn's breath was taken away, her heart nearly stopping at his sincerity. Somehow, she knew he was not the kind of man who apologized frequently. She was moved beyond reason, and could not speak for the lump that formed in her throat.

"I've taken a room at the tavern for the next week." Ian saw her question and answered it without her asking. "I don't trust those men not to come back. I want to be certain you are safe."

"That's very kind, but you needn't—"

He raised his hand and stopped her. "I couldn't sleep in my bed at Stonehaven wondering if you were in danger."

For the first time he saw fear in her eyes.

"You think they would come back?" Her question came out meek, frightened.

Visions came back to assault Ian, bringing with them the anger that had exploded inside him when he had come upon Lynn about to be raped by the three men. Never had he felt greater rage. Even over Blair's betrayal. He could easily have killed them. Such men deserved to die. It still confused him that Lynn had asked for mercy.

"I don't think so," he offered in comfort. "And

if they are so foolish, it shall be the last thing they do."

Kolyn felt a tremor pass through her, the steel in his voice enough to convince her, let alone the fierceness she knew existed barely hidden beneath the surface. Was this what her brothers had faced? A man who prompted fear by his very existence?

"Is it hard to kill a man?"

It was obvious her question caught him off guard.

"Is it hard?" she repeated. "Is it something all men do easily, or can it be learned?"

This time his laugh was nervous. "To kill is never easy."

"Have you ever regretted killing someone?" What pushed these questions into her head and out her mouth, she didn't know.

The look that passed over Ian's features was unmistakable. "Yes, there is one death I regret."

"I must go back," Kolyn declared, growing uneasy with her own curiosity. She moved past Ian.

"Lynn," he called after her, and she paused. "Sometimes I see fear in your eyes. Don't you know I would never harm you?"

"You've a fierce reputation, and I cannot help but fear it."

"Aye, my strength and temper have caused me much grief in the past. But God as my witness, I'll never harm you, Lynn. I've enough ghosts to haunt me."

Kolyn squeezed her eyes shut to keep the tears from them. How could she believe him? How could she trust him—he had abandoned Andrew, his own son, to die while still inside his mother's womb. Kolyn could never chance his knowing about Andrew. Never.

She all but ran back to the inn.

Ian watched Lynn as she disappeared over the knoll. He wanted to chase after her, to make her understand how he felt, but he didn't. He would be patient, something he wasn't good at, but something he was learning.

Chapter Twelve

Ainsley watched her son closely as he packed a few things he would need during his stay at The Raven. She felt pleased with the light that shone in his eyes. "Are you sure it's only for her protection that you are going to stay at the tavern?"

"It's true I can't seem to see enough of her," Ian confessed, boyish dimples showing as he broke into a smile. "I'm totally and completely infatuated with the woman."

"I can see that." Ainsley returned his smile, her heart filled with love for him. She walked over to the side of his bed and hugged Ian. "It is good to see you happy, son, but I worry."

Fela Dawson Scott

Ian's brow wrinkled as he looked down at her. "Whatever for?"

"You've your father's passionate heart. I fear you may be to enamored too quickly. You know nothing of this girl. Not even her full name."

"I know all I need to know."

Ainsley took his hand and placed it against her cheek. "I only want what is best for you."

"I know that, Mother." He cupped her face with his large hand. "She's a pretty lass that has captured my eye. It will pass."

"'Tis not a bad meal you've eaten, Ian. The woman has captured more than your eye—she has your heart. Do you think when you've bed her you will no longer be so taken with her?"

He turned away. "'Tis no way for a mother to speak."

She turned Ian back to her. "That is what you are thinking, isn't it? Do not think that because I am your mother that I do not know the ways of men. Be careful. You'll not rid your mind nor your heart of Lynn once you've made love to her, Ian. Most likely you'll embed her in your soul."

"You're making too much of this." Ian felt uncomfortable with her talk. He made to leave, but stopped when he saw her look, that of a mother unhappy with her child.

"Is she worth the risk?" Ainsley asked.

"What risk is that?"

Ainsley looked down at her hands, remembrance bringing her own pain. "The risk of

190

being betrayed . . . of the pain and heartbreak?"

"Aye," Ian said softly, his voice deepening with emotion. "She's awakened a need in me I cannot deny. I must see this to the end, whatever it may be."

Ian walked from his room. It was true, he couldn't walk away from Lynn. It had been a long time since he had allowed himself to feel anything for a woman, and now it was beyond his control. Sometime during their strange and rocky relationship, his desire had developed into something else—something stronger, something irresistible. Maybe it was love, he didn't know. Whatever it was, he couldn't stop it, anymore than he could stop the seasons from passing or the sun from rising.

He would see this to the end.

Kolyn pulled the ring from around her neck and placed it under her pillow, careful to tuck the old string she had hung it on underneath as well. She had felt it best that no one see it, even Ronald and Jean. Picking up a candle, she made her way down the ladder and to the kitchen on the lower floor. It was Sunday night and everyone had retired, leaving Kolyn a few private hours. Molly had said she could bathe in the kitchen, that no one would bother her. Like a child at Christmas she anticipated the quiet time, longed for the heat of the water to soothe her aching bones.

Within minutes she was soaking in the

hot water, tiredness easing from her. Visions floated across her mind torturing her heart with emotion. Ian's golden eyes haunted her. Had she thought that killing a man would be easy?

She should hate him. Hate him with every fiber of her being. He had killed her father, her brothers, even wounded *her*. Yet she was having a difficult time remembering all those things. Especially when he touched her. One touch and she was lost.

A sick feeling twisted her stomach. She should hate him. How could she desire him?

Unable to deal with the shame any longer, Kolyn slid beneath the water to dampen her hair, then proceeded to scrub it with a vengeance. She would kill him. She must.

Ian heard soft footsteps on the stairwell and stepped outside his room. When Lynn reached the top of the stairs, she stopped.

"Good evening, Lynn."

Lynn stood very still. "Good evening, Lord Blackstone."

"I thought we had decided you would call me Ian." Ian stepped closer, noticing her wet hair and the blanket she huddled beneath. "If I had known you were bathing below, I might have taken advantage of the situation."

Kolyn knew he was teasing, but her emotional state was too tense to take it as such. "I must go."

She started to turn, but Ian reached out to stop her, his hand touching her cheek. His thumb ran over the fullness of her lips, bringing a frown to his face.

"You're trembling," he whispered.

"I'm cold," Kolyn replied honestly, her legs shaking beneath her.

"You need to warm by a fire." Ian took her hand and started to guide her to his room. She pulled back. "No, I'll go to my room, thank you."

"Is there a fire in your room?"

She thought he must know they had no heat up in the attic, and frustration undermined her already fragile emotions. "I have no need of a fire."

He seemed not to take her comments to heart. Instead he forcibly moved her to his room, then pushed her down in the chair that sat in front of the fire. Without further comment he grabbed one bare foot and began to rub the chill from it. She just stared at his bent head, clutching the blanket about her.

"Give me your dress, Lynn."

"What?"

Ian pried her finger from the wet dress she held, then laid it near the fire. "It should be dry by morning."

He returned to rub her other foot, his hands gently massaging up her calves. The chills finally left Kolyn and in their place came drowsiness. She fought to stay awake,

193

to keep her senses alert. The Devil charms, then disarms. She must stay awake.

Kolyn came awake with a start, the room dark and quiet. Too quiet. It took a minute for her eyes to adjust to the dimness, the faint light the embers provided allowing her to see shadows of the furnishings. Slowly she inched across to the bed, Ian's even breathing telling her he slept. She started to leave, then stopped, her gaze resting on the dagger that lay upon his nightstand. They were alone, and the knife was within her grasp. Taking a deep breath, she reached out.

Ian's hand seized Kolyn's, sending her heart to her throat. Her gaze met his. She understood what he wanted. What he needed. Suddenly, she had no fear. She understood what she had to do.

Without words, she let the blanket drop away. His gaze was hot upon her, sliding over every inch of her. She allowed Ian to look at her nakedness before she climbed into the bed. Kolyn felt the long, muscled length of his body as she pressed against him, his flesh heating hers. A strange warmth stirred deep in the pit of her belly teasing her with its power.

Hesitant, yet determined, Kolyn ran her hand along the taut ridge of muscles in his arm, her touch causing them to bunch in reflex. Shyly, she explored the broad width of his chest with the sensitive tips of her fingers, the fine hair causing them to tingle. She was pale compared to his tanned skin, smooth against his scarred flesh. Gently, she kissed the old wounds, wanting only the feel of Ian beneath her lips. Her tongue tasted his flesh, her nose smelled his scent, musky and male. Her mind filled with Ian, his short, heavy breathing a melody. Nature guided Kolyn and she wanted to get closer, to claim his lips with her own.

Ian pulled her face up and kissed her, long and deep. No longer was there any denial, any hesitancy. Lynn returned his kiss, her tongue stroking, twisting with his. He wondered if he was dreaming, but knew it was too good to be fantasy. She was alive and in his arms, giving of herself.

He moved his lips to feel her cheek, soft and velvety. The scent of heather mingled in her freshly washed hair, as it did on the gentle curve of her neck. He studied the contour with his lips, moving along the length of her arm and on to the tips of her fingers. Her hands pulled his face back to hers, her lips searching for his. He responded willingly. Longingly.

The heat broke into fire, and he thought he might have died, gone to heaven. Lynn's body moved beneath him, innocent, yet seductive. Her hands clutched his back, pulling him closer, her hips arching to him, telling him of her need, of her desire.

His attention moved downward, captured by a tender nipple, taut and erect. His tongue glided over it. Ian claimed it with his lips, causing Lynn to moan. He kissed a line down to her belly, the pink flesh quivering with each wet touch. She smelled sweet, delicate.

Kolyn trembled from the delightful torture his lips inflicted on her. He moved to the sensitive skin of her thighs, then on to the ticklish backs of her knees. Ian discovered her toes, nibbling and licking till she could take no more. She wrapped her legs about his, pulling him closer, the full length of him touching her body, his hardness promising pleasure. She moaned and arched to meet him, to take his fullness inside her. Newly awakened sensations gathered inside her, and she feared she might explode from wanting.

His golden eyes met hers, the gentleness in them touching her, stilling the beating of her heart. He pulled back, a sudden question in their depths. She smiled and drew him back to her, guiding him within her. His eyes closed, and she felt him tremble as he drove past her maidenhead. The flash of pain only added to her need, and she accepted him fully, clinging to him. Again and again he lunged, bringing her beyond and above the realm of reality, satisfying her aching need. Never had she expected such pleasure as he gave to her. Never had she expected the Black Wolf to be such a gentle lover.

Kolyn lay curled within the warmth of his strong arms, a satisfied, lazy feeling permeating her. He lay for a long time holding her, neither of them talking, neither moving. She waited for him to sleep, but sleep found her instead.

For the second time that night, Kolyn awoke with a start. Holding her breath, she listened, then breathed with relief when she found him asleep. Carefully, slowly, she left the bed.

Her legs felt rubbery. Whether it was the aftermath of their lovemaking or her fear that robbed her of her strength, she wasn't certain. Kolyn licked her lips, the flesh sensitive from his kisses. Shame moved in, taking away the pleasure she had known only a short time before. How could she have enjoyed his touch so much? She felt a pain in her chest as her heart broke with each memory her mind conjured. Each touch, each kiss was forever branded in her mind.

With shaking hands she covered her eyes, tears hot on her flushed face. Angry, she wiped them away and gritted her teeth. She must stop acting like a woman and act like the MacGregor. Kolyn reached for the knife. The metal was cold in her hand as she pulled it from its sheath. She breathed deeply to still her trembling hands.

She watched Ian, his sleep sound and undisturbed. Kolyn raised the knife above her head. Dark hair framed his face, a boyish innocence softening his features. He was devilishly hand-some, his dark looks and golden eyes enough to melt any woman's heart.

"But not me," she whispered hoarsely, grip-ping the knife harder. "Not me."

Still, Kolyn could not strike. She stood for the longest time, prepared. Yet she could not move. He lay before her, his heart bared, unprotected. She closed her eyes and clenched her jaw. He had killed her father!

Guilt collided with hesitancy. Confusion clouded her mind, flashes eating away at her. *I promise to see the Black Wolf dead . . . Black Wolf dead . . .*

Tears blinded her. Slowly she lowered the knife, her heart constricting from the shame of her failure, the pain of what that failure might mean to her, to Andrew, to her clan. Never had she expected Ian Blackstone to touch her as he had. Never.

Kolyn set the knife back on the table and moved to where he had put her clothes to dry. She pulled them on, feeling numb. She intentionally willed her mind blank. To think was painful. Without looking back, she left Ian's room. It was time to go home to Andrew, to salvage what she could.

Ian rolled over and reached for Lynn, but found the bed empty. A small alarm went off inside his head, but he ignored it and pulled himself up. Her dress was gone. He grabbed a towel and wrapped it about him as he walked down the hall to the attic entrance. Quietly he climbed the ladder.

"Lynn," he called out.

No answer came.

He looked about the small attic room and found it empty. Again the alarm sounded. This time he paid heed. Ian wasted no time in going downstairs and searching for Lynn. He realized she was nowhere to be found. By the time dawn came, Ian's anger was beyond control.

"We've searched the entire village, Ian. She's gone."

He didn't want Geoffrey to tell him that. He wanted Lynn found. Something inside him snapped, and he grabbed his friend's arm. "Search again. She's got to be here."

Geoffrey pulled free of Ian's grip and shook his head. "I dinna ken your anger, my friend. She's just a pretty lass. What has possessed you?"

Ian sat down on the wood bench, pushing back his hair in frustration. He didn't know what possessed him—only that he couldn't face Lynn being gone. "Why would she leave, Geoff? Without even a word."

Geoffrey laughed, trying to lighten the mood. "Who's to say why a woman does what she does?"

Ian agreed, his attempt to laugh with his friend failing. He sighed instead.

Geoffrey felt concerned about Ian's intense reaction to the girl's disappearance. This was exactly what he'd feared would happen. How could Ian become attached to the girl in so short a time? "You barely knew the lass, Ian. Why are you so upset?"

Darkened eyes looked up at Geoffrey, the look haunted. "I can't explain it, my friend. I thought it was just an infatuation with a pretty girl that made my blood run hot. All I could think of was having her in my arms and in my bed. But when I found her gone . . . I thought I'd never feel that kind of pain again."

"Just shows you Blair didn't leave you dead inside. 'Tis time to go on with your life again." Geoffrey slapped Ian upon the back, trying to get a smile from him. "Come, let's take a ride."

The two men walked to the tavern door, but stopped when Molly called out to them.

"Just what am I t' do with these two?" She pointed to the goose and dog. "They've been carryin' on for that lass all day. Can I cook the goose now, my lord?"

"Aye." Ian waved his hand through the air as if to clear it of the memories of Lynn. Again he started to leave, but thought better of what he had said. Without saying another word he walked over to where Molly stood, Lynn's goose at her feet. He picked up the goose and tucked it under his arm, then handed the dog to Geoff.

"I'll see to them, Molly."

"Are you goin' t' cook him?" she asked, her eyes round with surprise.

"No. He's not to be a meal upon our table."

Geoffrey laughed, drawing Ian's menacing glare. "Now I've seen everything!"

Geoffrey left before Ian could say anything in return, the wiggling dog firmly in hand.

Leslie turned and went back up the ladder to her room. She had heard Geoffrey return and couldn't help eavesdropping. She had liked Lynn, but jealousy hit her hard, twisting inside her, creating anger and hurt. Why had Ian taken to Lynn and not her? She had given him every opportunity to have her. She had made it very clear she desired him. Yet he'd always remained politely distant.

She kicked out, striking the mattress Lynn had used. Then, with a carefully placed foot, she hurled her pillow across the room. Something fell onto the floor at her feet, and Leslie bent to pick it up. Her eyes grew big with surprise as she held the ring up to examine it.

"Blessed be," she murmured in awe. It looked expensive, and this made Leslie smile. She placed the cord around her neck. "Thanks, Lynn, or whoever you are." Leslie dropped the ring down her blouse between her breasts. She yawned and sprawled out on her bed. Maybe she could get a coin or two for it.

Chapter Thirteen

"Where have you been, Kolyn?"

Dwight moved to stand directly in front of Kolyn where she sat curled up in front of the fire. Dwight's question was not unexpected. In fact, Kolyn had marveled at his restraint all that day until they were alone and Andrew was tucked in his bed. As if to make up for lost time, she had spent every minute with Andrew. He looked to her as if he had grown during the six weeks she was gone.

Kolyn took a sip of the wine from the goblet she held, trying to find the right words. All day long memories had stifled her, tearing at her heart and soul like demons from hell. Surely it was what she deserved. She had lain with him, like a common whore, giving of herself and loving him. Shame assaulted the reasons she had so steadfastly held onto—the feud, Emmett's threats. Even now, under Dwight's angry glare, she remembered the pleasure of Ian's touch, the desire he so easily aroused in her. How could she explain that she found him attractive, that he was gentle and loving? How was she to live with the fact she couldn't kill him, even to save Andrew from her brother's threats? How was she to live with the fact that she had even tried?

"I'm waiting." As if to stress his point, Dwight sat across from her, the fire crackling loudly in the silence that followed.

She drew a deep breath, wishing she could draw courage from the air to still the harried beating of her heart and keep her hands from shaking. "I'm sorry you've been so worried, Dwight. I had hoped you would not be."

"Would not be worried? You disappeared that night of the fire. Your horse showed up the next day. You did not. What happened?"

His look was fierce. Kolyn had to give him some sort of explanation. "I stayed to put the fire out and two men rode there from the village. One was Ian Blackstone."

"The Black Wolf," Dwight muttered, his look incredulous.

"Yes," Kolyn said, "the Black Wolf himself. We argued, and I foolishly challenged him. He laughed at me, and it angered me. I struck out, and he reacted in self-defense, wounding me in the shoulder. He rode off, and I followed. I don't think he even knew I did—it was raining hard and stormy. I got lost, Dwight."

Her story came out stilted, without emotion. She could not let him hear the truth, not even in her voice.

"You lost your way?"

"I lost a lot of blood. It was dark and I found myself in forests I'd never been in before. Blackstone's land. I decided to wait till light to find my way out, but by dawn I was fevered and unconscious. The boy I sent to Father McCloud found me, and his mother nursed me back to health."

Her uncle was silent for a long moment, as if taking in her story. He watched her, his eyes doubting. Was her own guilt showing? Could he see that she had betrayed her father and the clan?

"What else happened, lass?"

"Nothing else, Uncle. You know I wouldn't stay away from Andrew any longer than I had to." The lie was difficult, but to tell the truth was impossible. What she had hoped would bring this horrible nightmare to an end only complicated it. What would she do now?

Dwight didn't believe her. There was something . . . something different about Kolyn. He couldn't place words to it, couldn't define it or explain it. He just knew. "Aye, Kolyn. Andrew's missed you fiercely."

He stood and crossed to Kolyn, and knelt in front of her. "I too missed you fiercely." He took her hand and brought it to his lips. He felt her tremble and looked into her eyes, feeling lost in the green pools. "I have nearly gone mad with fear for you. Certainly you can see the foolishness of these raids. 'Tis time you came t' your senses, lass."

"Foolishness?" Anger tingled deep inside Kolyn. She pulled her hand from her uncle's, uncomfortable with his touch. "He thinks that because I am a woman he cannot fight me. So we shall continue our foolishness and see how long it takes for him to change his mind."

But as soon as she said the words, she knew they came from only one part of herself. She felt split, torn apart inside. She'd never wanted any part of the feud. She'd been coerced by her father, her brother, a sense of shame, of obligation. Then she'd met Ian, and had grown to know the man. Had grown to love him. Where in all this was the right path for her to take, to protect Andrew, to pull herself together, to find some sanity and peace?

Dwight stood, his body stiff and unyielding. "I'll challenge him in your name, Kolyn. Do not be so stubborn."

Confusion reigned free, tearing at Kolyn and her thoughts. As the MacGregor, the Black Wolf had ridiculed her, laughed at her. As Lynn, he had made love to her. Which was it to be? She wasn't *Lynn*. It had been a deception. A means to get close to him. Close enough to kill him. But she had failed. She'd had the chance to put a knife through his heart and she hadn't. She was weak. She had allowed herself to feel something for a man she had sworn to kill. A man who despised her. What a fool she had been to allow his charming ways to disarm her. *Never again!* This she swore to herself.

"We shall ride out tomorrow night, Dwight. Have the men ready. I'll not hear your arguments again."

Dwight gave no further argument. He started to leave, but paused and asked, "Why do you not wear the ring of the MacGregor, Kolyn?"

Kolyn felt for the ring about her neck, and for the first time realized that it was gone. She had left it under her pillow at the inn. "Oh, my," she whispered in despair.

"What is it, lass?"

She couldn't meet Dwight's look of concern. "I must have lost it in the forest." Quickly, she tried to cover up her fear. She couldn't risk returning for it. It would be too dangerous.

"I'll have another made for you," Dwight said. "A smaller ring, so it will fit you better and not slip off."

"No," she said as calmly as she could. "'Tis my own carelessness at fault. I can do without it."

Dwight frowned. "'Tis a symbol of who you are."

"It would cost too much and we've more

important things to worry about at this time, Dwight."

When she said no more, Dwight left.

She prayed no one would find it.

Ian wanted to go crazy with the anger built up inside him, but he held it down, chilling its heat with indifference. He looked at the couple sitting across the rough-hewn table, their faces showing little as he continued to question them. Ian had known Ronald and Jean a long time, helping them when he could, but mostly leaving them be as they wished it. They were proud people and he admired their fortitude.

"Ronald, I would like to find Lynn. I need to see her again." Ian looked from Ronald to Jean, neither seeming to understand fully the situation. The past day had been pure hell.

"If she had wanted you t' know where she's gone, she would have told you, Lord Blackstone. We cannot help you."

Ronald's comment caused the muscle in Ian's jaw to twitch, his patience to run quite thin. "I mean her no harm, surely you know that."

"Aye," Jean said softly. "We do not fear for her. We just don't know more about her. She came into our lives a stranger and left the same. We knew her only as Lynn."

Ian felt confused by these people who kept to themselves. "You never asked her where she came from?"

"Did you?" Ronald asked quietly.

"No," he mumbled. "I didn't even know her full name."

"Perhaps she will come back." Jean touched Ian's hand in a kind, sympathetic way.

"Perhaps." Ian stood. "Thank you for your time. If you see her again, will you tell her I am looking for her?"

"Yes." Jean smiled. "I will tell her."

Ian left the small cottage and walked to where Geoffrey stood with the horses.

"Do you think she'll come back here?" Geoffrey asked.

Ian shrugged. "I just don't know, Geoff. Nothing about the woman seems predictable."

Kolyn looked at the door before her, preparing herself for the confrontation she knew lay ahead. She had put her brother off for a full day and knew she could not do so any longer. Pulling her shoulders back, she opened the door and stepped inside.

"So, you've decided to pay a visit to your dear brother after all. I thought maybe you might have forgotten me."

As usual, Emmett was in a foul mood. Kolyn shut the door behind her. At least Jacob wasn't about. "Of course I wouldn't forget you, Emmett." She crossed to him and kissed him on the cheek he had turned away from her, much like a child in a tantrum.

"I think it's dreadful I must learn of your

return from the servants. You disappear without a trace, then reappear just as mysteriously. What have you to say for yourself?"

"Nothing, actually." Kolyn had no patience for this. "I'm back, and that is what counts."

His eyes narrowed dangerously. "I agree with Dwight. You aren't telling us everything."

"Make of it what you will, Emmett. Surely between you and Dwight you can make up a wild tale." What an intolerable person he had become. She punched the pillow she held, then placed it behind him.

This made Emmett laugh. "My, you seem to be spirited, dear sister. I will be curious to find out exactly what did transpire during your absence." He grabbed her arm, his grip painful. "I will find out, Kolyn. Remember, I know all your secrets."

She wrestled her arm free, then stepped away from the bed.

"How can you be so hateful?"

"How?" Emmett screamed. "How, you ask? You know damn well how, you bitch! You'd best be taking care of that promise you made me, or I'll see you never forget how hateful I am. Get out!"

When she didn't move, he picked up a book from his nightstand and hurled it at her. She easily ducked it, and it slammed against the wall.

"Get out," he yelled, his eyes wild, his face screwed up with hate.

Kolyn left.

*   *   *

Only the smallest sliver of a moon hung from the dark sky, but Kolyn studied it for the longest time before moving to the rocking chair in front of her fire. It had been a long, emotionally tiring day, yet sleep did not come easily. She sighed and closed her eyes. Visions immediately disturbed her.

"Mommy."

Andrew's soft voice broke through, and she opened her eyes to find her son standing by her. "Why aren't you in bed, young man? It's very late."

"Can I stay with you?"

She reached out and pulled him into her lap. "Of course you can." She kissed his forehead, and he cuddled against her, his head resting upon her shoulder. In moments, he slept, his soft breathing comforting to her ears. Once again, a fierceness struggled forth, claiming control of her emotions. Whatever she must do to protect her child, she would do. That was the one thing she knew for certain.

Ian stared at the ceiling of his room, wondering where Lynn was that night. Did she have family to go home to? Did she think of him?

Frustration and anger surged through him again, causing him to stand and resume his pacing. The fire had burned low, but he didn't stop to replenish it. He only stopped every now and then to drink from the flagon of wine he carried. Maybe if he drank enough he could sleep. Maybe he could wipe the visions from his mind: the sparkle of sea-green eyes, the velvet of her skin soft beneath his touch. Rose-tipped lips beckoned to him. Mere thoughts aroused him. He took another drink.

Ainsley stood outside the door to her son's chambers and listened to him pace. She knocked.

"Enter."

She opened the heavy door and met his golden gaze, the sadness in them disturbing to her. "Ian. What has upset you so? You've said little since coming home tonight."

"'Tis nothing. Go back to sleep, Mother."

Disappointment tempted her to ask again, but she did not. "I'll not pry. When you are ready to speak to me, I shall be ready to listen." Ainsley turned to leave.

"It's a great comfort to know you'll be there."

"I love you. When something troubles you, it troubles me. 'Tis the way of mothers. Good night, Ian."

Ian watched the door close. It wasn't that he was keeping secrets from her. What could he tell her? That she was right? He had succeeded in seducing Lynn? Even worse, that he had seduced a virgin and when he'd awakened she was nowhere to be found? Had Lynn been so horrified at what she had done that she'd fled? Was his mother right about her touching his soul? Why else did he want to find her so badly? And if he did, then what?

Ian had no answers to these questions. It would be a long night. A long night indeed.

Chapter Fourteen

The clash of metal on metal rang out, accented by the groans of each man as he strained beneath the other's attack. A long, slow grin crossed Geoffrey's face as he pressed Ian with his assault.

"You are gettin' as slow as an old woman, my friend."

Ian's answer was more like a grunt than a word, but he expressed his response better with the swing of his claymore, the blow stilling Geoffrey's smile. Again he brought the sword around. Again Geoffrey met his blow, the sound echoing about the courtyard. The two men worked hard, one gaining the edge, then the other.

"Old woman," Ian ground out. "You seem a

mite tired yourself, Geoff."

The smile came back. "Not at all. Not at all."

Both men were bare-chested despite the cold, sweat bringing a shine to their skin. Muscles strained, their arms tiring beneath the weight of steel.

"Have you had enough?" Ian asked.

"Not nearly," Geoffrey said, meeting Ian's great blow with the last of his strength. He sank onto a knee, but held strong.

Out of the corner of his eye, Ian saw Ainsley, her step quick as she moved toward them.

"Well, *I've* had enough for today," Ian declared, helping Geoffrey to his feet. "You're as strong as a bull, old friend."

Geoffrey slapped him across the back and laughed heartily. "You are a liar, Ian, but that's what I like about you."

They walked to where Ainsley now stood waiting, and Ian greeted his mother. "Good morning. What brings you out here, Mother?"

"Good mornin', Lady Blackstone," Geoffrey said with a nod.

Ainsley smiled, but her smile looked forced. "It seems, son, that Kolyn MacGregor decided to help herself to a few of your pigs last night."

A tremor went through Ian. Whether it was anger or dread, he didn't know. He had hoped she was done with this nonsense. "How many is a few?"

"A dozen or so."

Ian remained silent for a long moment, uncertain what to do about this woman who had made such a nuisance of herself. There had been a long break with no raids, then suddenly, twice in one week. "I think I will go hunting. Do you want to join me, Geoff?"

Ainsley couldn't hide her surprise. "Hunting?"

"Yes. We could use some venison in our cellar. You said so just the other day." Ian took her hand and kissed it gently. "I'll be gone a week or so. Can you manage?"

"Of course," Ainsley said softly. Then she smiled. "I am proud of you, Ian."

"Whatever for?"

"For not allowing this woman to anger you."

"It's just a few pigs. I gladly give them to her." He turned to his friend. "We leave within the hour, Geoff."

Andrew's high-pitched squeal made Kolyn laugh. Andrew ran after one puppy, then another. His excitement reached the mother dog, and she started barking, adding to the chorus of her offsprings' yapping, the mixture of noises echoing about the great chamber. Andrew picked up a cuddly puppy and returned him to the giant basket where his mother lay, then retrieved another. As fast as he brought them back, they scurried out, finally tiring

Andrew out. He sat near the basket, and the bitch licked his flushed cheeks as he hugged a tiny fur ball to him.

Kolyn thought of Dax and hoped he was being taken care of. She hated leaving him and the goose behind, but she'd had no choice. It was best this way, just as it was best she had left that part of her life behind. If only the feelings were so easy to be rid of.

" 'Tis good t' see you smiling again."

Kolyn glanced up to where Dwight stood by her chair, but she couldn't bring herself to look into his eyes. She looked back to where Andrew sat among the litter of puppies, his attention on them. She didn't say anything.

Dwight remained standing. "I thought I would go mad with worry for you, Kolyn. But 'tis naught compared t' the madness you create with your silence."

She bowed her head and studied her hands as they twisted together. "I've had little to say."

"Why do you not trust me, lass?"

This brought her gaze up to meet his. "I trust you, Dwight. You are my family."

" 'Tis my weakness that disturbs you."

A rush of emotion robbed her mind of its control. "I must confess that your drinking does disturb me. It will bring only destruction to you, Uncle. You must stop."

"You lie and that hurts me," he cried out, his tortured eyes haunted, pained. "Is my love for you so unbearable?"

Kolyn wanted to run away, to pretend he had not said the words she dreaded to hear. "Uncle, you know it cannot be. You must never speak of it again."

Dwight grabbed her by the arms and jerked Kolyn from her chair, his face reflecting his fury. "Do you think I have not tried t' put it from me? That I have not prayed t' God t' save me wicked soul? This passion consumes me, Kolyn. I cannot deny it any more than I can deny I love you."

His words struck deep and painful, the horror of what he said clear in each tormented word. She tried to pull away, to free herself of his hurting touch. "Dwight, do not say more, I cannot bear it!"

He paused, as if he were understanding the suffering he caused. Then he pulled her closer, his arms like steel about her. "I cannot stop loving you. I cannot."

His lips came down on hers, demanding and cruel. Kolyn twisted to free herself, but to no avail, his strength so much greater than hers. Panic seized her and quelled all tenderness to his agony. She struck out, her nails raking across his face. "No," she mumbled, and bit down on his lip.

Yelling, Dwight pulled back, his look murderous.

"Mommy!" Andrew ran to where they stood.

Kolyn lifted him in her arms. "I'm all right, Drew. It's time to go to bed."

Timidly, Andrew reached out and laid a chubby hand on his uncle's cheek, obviously confused by their argument. "Good night, Uncle Dwight."

The big man stepped back, guilt washing across his features. Unable to look at Kolyn, he muttered, "Good night, my boy."

Andrew in her arms, Kolyn ran from the room.

Dwight watched Kolyn leave, then turned away, sickened by his own actions. He slumped into the chair, still warm from her body. His heart ached and his mind revolted. He could not trust himself to go upstairs, to go near where she slept.

Tears came to his eyes as the shame played out its destruction in him. "God help me!" he cried out to the empty room. He dropped his head into his hands. "God help me."

Kolyn set the candle aside and knelt by the old trunk. The attic was damp and cold, but she was not ready to go back to her room and the sleepless night that lay before her.

The hinges objected as Kolyn opened the old trunk. Its musty smell reminded her of the years it had been shut away. Memories came with each item she removed, taking her back to a happier, gentler time. She cradled the small hand-carved doll in her arms, the doll's dress lovingly made by her mother. She discovered the old wooden blocks, their paint chipped, the figures on each side worn smooth. A book covered in faded fabric lay on the bottom, nearly hidden by old baby clothes. Kolyn dug it out.

At first, Kolyn didn't recognize it. When she opened it, she recalled the long hours Emmett had spent writing in it. His words were youthful, vibrant, romantic—all of which were no longer a part of the man she knew today.

It seemed so long ago. Kolyn closed the book and laid it aside. She continued to examine each item, piling the baby clothes and toys to the side. What she didn't need, she placed back inside the trunk. She closed the lid, along with her memories, taking the small pile of things for Jean's baby. And the book filled with Emmett's poetry.

Ian stood among the trees, his presence obscured by the evergreens, his scent drifting away from the buck he watched. He remained still and quiet, the only sounds the natural noises of the forest. Slowly, he raised his bow.

The red deer stag darted off, its long legs bringing it to a full run in seconds. Ian and Geoffrey raced after it, crossing a small meadow to follow it into the dense forest. The animal forded a small ravine, and they continued pursuit, never slowing their pace as they pounded downhill, then scrambled up again, their feet barely touching the moss-covered ground. They closed in, their prey within sight.

At a full run, Ian brought his bow up and fired. His aim was true. The buck fell. Ian and Geoffrey came to a halt beside the dead animal, its rack large and proud. Ian leaned upon his bow and caught his breath.

"Thank you, Lord, for providing us such a worthy and noble opponent. This mighty animal shall provide food for many."

"Aye," Geoffrey agreed, his eyes still bright from the challenge. "It has been a good trip, Ian. 'Tis time to go home."

"We'll start in the morning, Geoffrey. I think I'll take this one to Jean and Ronald. We'll still have plenty to take back to Stonehaven."

Geoffrey smiled. "Do you think she's come back to their place?"

Ian didn't like being reminded that he still could not put the lass from his mind. "I always take some venison to them. It has nothing to do with Lynn."

"Of course not," Geoffrey quipped, agreeing but certainly not believing. "I'll take the rest of the meat back to Stonehaven."

"You shouldn't have brought so many things, Lynn."

Kolyn hugged Jean warmly. "They are of no use to me and I thought the baby could use them."

Jean glanced at the pile of baby clothes and other things Kolyn brought. "We cannot thank you enough."

"You saved my life, remember." Kolyn squeezed her hand once more before walking to her horse. "That is something I can never repay with just a few old things I found in the attic."

She mounted with Ronald's help. "Should anyone ask about me, I'd prefer you didn't say I was here."

Ronald and Jean exchanged glances. Kolyn felt terrible placing them in such a position. "I wouldn't ask if it wasn't very important."

"I know, Lynn," Jean said. "We'll not mention your visit should Lord Blackstone ask."

"Thank you," Kolyn said in relief. She trusted them at their word. "I'll be back when I can. Take care of yourselves."

Kolyn rode off, wondering when that would be.

Ian rode from the cottage with a strange feeling plaguing him. He knew Jean and Ronald had lied to him. He had seen the look on their faces when he arrived. What were they keeping from him? And why?

Sensing their discomfort, he had stayed only long enough to leave the meat and question them about Lynn. He knew nothing more now than after his last visit. This frustrated him.

Not wishing to go back to the castle yet, Ian rode deeper into the forest. He remembered a beautiful loch not too far away, and decided it would be a quiet place to spend the afternoon. Perhaps give him time to sort out his feelings.

Kolyn leaned down and drank from the loch, the chilled water soothing her thirst. She leaned back against a boulder and pulled her knees up to rest her chin on them, her wool shawl wrapped snugly about her to ward off the cold. Snow covered the earth, blanketing the world in its frozen whiteness. Soon, she wouldn't be able to get to this place. As December passed it would bring more storms, limiting travel . . . limiting her raiding.

She dreaded being bound within the manor. How would she continue to deal with Dwight? And what of Emmett and his madness? A chill touched her. Not one of cold from the briskness of the air, but one of fear. Kolyn prayed she find a solution.

Suddenly she felt his presence even before she saw him, sitting on his great war-horse across the water. She did not move for fear he would see her. Emotions played havoc with her attempt to remain calm. He looked larger than life, sitting tall in the saddle, dark and ominous. It was difficult for her to believe this was the same man who had made love to her so tenderly. So passionately.

Unable to deal with the sight of him, Kolyn squeezed her eyes shut, praying for him to go away.

Get Four Books Totally FREE— A $19.96 Value!

▼ Tear Here and Mail Your FREE Book Card Today! ▼

PLEASE RUSH
MY FOUR FREE
BOOKS TO ME
RIGHT AWAY!

Leisure Romance Book Club
65 Commerce Road
Stamford CT 06902-4563

AFFIX
STAMP
HERE

* * *

Ian's heart nearly stopped inside his chest, and he even feared to breathe. Lynn sat upon the opposite bank. Were his eyes deceiving him? Slowly, silently, he moved.

She did not disappear, even as he rode near her.

"Are you real, Lynn? Or just my imagination playing cruel tricks on me?"

Her heart jumped into her throat, keeping her from speaking. She wanted to run, but her legs also failed her.

"Have you nothing to say?"

Kolyn pushed herself up onto her trembling legs. "Leave me be. You must leave me be."

Ian wasn't sure he had heard her right, the words she spoke barely above a whisper. "How can I? You've cast a spell on me, lass. How can I fight such witchery?"

" 'Tis no witchery," Kolyn cried out, her eyes widening in horror. "You must not say such things."

Confused by the fear he saw on her face, Ian slid from his mount. When he turned back, she was gone.

"Lynn," he yelled out, but no answer came.

Kolyn heard him call to her, and ran deeper into the trees. Uncontrolled fear pulsated through her with each hurtful beat of her heart. She feared him, she feared herself, she feared the turmoil seeing him brought her.

Kolyn heard him crash into the brush in pursuit. She felt much like an animal in flight from a hunter. He closed in fast, and Kolyn had no choice but to seek cover. Quickly, she scurried beneath an outcropping of rock. Huddled there on her hands and knees, Kolyn watched him pass. The pent-up breath in her lungs burned until she felt safe enough to let it out. Another silent prayer crossed her lips.

She crawled out, her skirt making it difficult. She untwisted the woolen from about her legs and started to stand. She stilled.

Before her crouched the black wolf. The same one she had seen twice before, black-coated, with gold eyes that pierced her soul with intent.

He inched forward.

"Remember me?" she whispered.

The wolf stopped.

She swallowed hard and sat back on her heels. "Are you Ian's wolf?"

The wolf yelped in an almost puppy-like way.

Kolyn closed her eyes in disbelief. When she opened them the animal was gone.

"Can it be?" she whispered. In answer an eerie howl surrounded her, touching her with its chill. It came and went in one long, haunting breath. Lengthening shadows told her the lateness of the day, that darkness would fall on the loch quickly. Fearful the wolf would return with Ian, Kolyn fled to find her horse.

* * *

"Damn it, man." Ian tried to bring his irritation under control, not wanting to offend Ronald. "I know she was here. You don't need to protect her any longer."

"We aren't protectin' Lynn, Lord Blackstone. She asked that we not mention her visit t' you."

Ian smoothed back his hair, trying to find the right words. Frustration ran free inside him. He had searched everywhere at the loch. Somehow she had gotten away. She'd even gotten past the wolf. "Please, I must speak with her. That's all I ask."

"I don't know where she lives. I don't know anythin' about her. She brought Jean an' the baby some things."

"You know nothing?"

Ronald shook his head, regret showing on his face.

"I delivered a message for Miss Lynn," said a small voice.

Ian turned to Daniel, but it was his father who questioned him. "You did not mention this before, son."

He shrugged his shoulders. "Miss asked me t' do this. I didn't think it was important you know."

"Where did you take this message, Daniel?"

Daniel looked to his father, and replied only when he saw him nod. "T' the church in the village at Gregor Castle. She asked I give it t' Father McCloud."

"Do you know what the note said?"

Again the boy shrugged. "I cannot read, Lord Blackstone."

Ian shook Ronald's hand and tossed the boy a coin. "Thank you for taking care of Lynn, Daniel."

"Was my pleasure, sir."

It was the middle of the night, but Ian couldn't wait until morning. He pounded on the small church door until he roused the good father.

Father McCloud's gray head peeked out, his hair mussed from sleep. His eyes widened when he saw Ian and Geoffrey standing before him. "What on earth . . ."

"Father McCloud?"

"Aye. I'm Father McCloud. What is so urgent that you would wake me from my sleep?"

"I must speak with you."

Wary eyes watched Ian. Then slowly, the door widened to allow them in. He shuffled over to a pew and sat, motioning for them to do the same.

"I'm sorry, I know the hour is late. I am Ian Blackstone."

Father McCloud only nodded, not surprised.

"I am looking for a woman named Lynn."

Nothing registered on Father McCloud's face. "I don't know such a woman, Lord Blackstone."

Ian thought he would go mad. "I was told a young boy named Daniel delivered a message here from her. It's been over two months ago, near three."

"Could you describe her?" Father McCloud asked.

"She has beautiful red hair and startling green eyes."

"You say her name is Lynn? Do you know her Christian name?"

"No." Ian felt quite foolish. "I do not."

"Might I ask," Father McCloud ventured, "why you wish to find this woman?"

Ian's voice came out strained, tired. "I want to speak with her, nothing more."

The priest considered this. "It seems, if she wished to speak with you, you would know where to find her."

"Aye," Ian confessed. "Please, Father. It's terribly important I find her."

Father McCloud did not seem convinced.

Ian stood. "I will find her. Even if I have to return with my men tomorrow and search every cottage in this village."

"This is MacGregor land, Lord Blackstone. I don't think that would be wise. People could get hurt."

"Aye, it wouldn't be wise, Father. I'm sure we both know if the MacGregors fight, they will not win."

His point was made and Father McCloud conceded. "I will see if I can find the lass for you. But mark my words, if harm comes to her I'll fight you myself."

Ian held his hands up. "I've no wish to harm Lynn. You've my word on it."

"Come back tomorrow night, Lord Blackstone. Late. It would not do for you to be seen here."

Chapter Fifteen

Kolyn heard the horses ride up and knew that Ian and Geoffrey had arrived. She sat alone in the chapel, having convinced Father McCloud that she must meet Ian alone. He had retired to his room, assuring her she only had to call out if she needed him. She tried to calm herself. The door opened, then closed. His footsteps were soft, almost unheard, amazing Kolyn as she thought of what an imposing figure Ian made with his great height and broad shoulders.

She didn't look up when he stopped beside her, fear keeping her gaze glued to the floor. Her hands clenched her wool skirt into a knot as she tried to think of something to say.

Ian knelt down and gently pried the fabric

from her fingers. "Lynn."

Kolyn still couldn't look at him. She knew she would be lost to his golden gaze if she did. She must be strong. Pulling away from his gentle touch, she stood, her back to him.

"Why couldn't you just leave me alone?"

Ian was silent a moment. "How . . ." His voice broke and he cleared his throat before starting again. "How could I stay away?"

Finally, she faced him. "Surely you must understand by now that you and I can't be together?"

"Because you live here? Among the clan MacGregor?"

"Aye." Kolyn didn't elaborate, uncertain where her lies would take her. It was impossible for him to know the truth.

"Why didn't you tell me?"

Kolyn laughed.

Ian thought a moment, then said, "She sent you. Didn't she?"

"What are you talking about?" Kolyn was confused by his sudden change in tone.

"That witch, MacGregor," he accused. "She sent you to spy on me, didn't she?"

This wasn't going well—the tone in his voice was not to her liking. Kolyn swallowed, trying to keep her own anger from surfacing. "No, the MacGregor knows nothing about us, and she mustn't. Not ever."

"Come back with me, Lynn." Ian took her hand into his. "Tonight."

This took Kolyn by surprise. She wasn't certain what she should say. "That's impossible." She pulled her hand free. It was too difficult to think when he touched her.

"Why is it impossible? Leave here."

"You ask too much, Ian. Would you leave your family to be with me? Would you betray your clan?"

Ian threw up his hands in dismay. "No, I wouldn't. But for you it's different."

The pink on Lynn's cheeks darkened to a bright red, and Ian saw the anger spark in her eyes.

"Why is it different for me? To betray my clan and leave behind the love of my family would not matter, perhaps hurt less? And for what? To be your lover?"

He hadn't thought beyond convincing Lynn to come back with him. "Would that be so bad? Surely I can give you a better life than you have here."

"You assume too much."

Ian was frustrated and he felt his patience slipping. "Why are you so loyal to the MacGregor? She's a fool to persist in this feud. She can't win."

"Perhaps it's not a matter of winning."

"Then she should give it up."

Kolyn sighed. "What of honor and loyalty to her people? What of her father and brothers you have laid in their graves? Should she forget all this? Would you?"

"For me it would be different. She's a woman, Lynn."

"No." Kolyn closed her eyes in vexation. "She is the MacGregor. She is bound by honor. An honor that knows not whether she is a woman, or a man. An honor she must live up to or die. And I am loyal to the MacGregor and will not betray her."

"Then you are as foolish as she."

"Aye. I'll not go with you, Ian." Kolyn felt near tears. "Promise me you'll not come here again."

Ian said nothing.

"Please," she whispered. "I beg you."

"Did our one night of love mean so little to you, Lynn? Will you make me stay away?"

"You must stay away."

Ian took a step towards her, then turned and walked away.

"I must have your promise," she said.

He stopped. "I cannot give it."

Kolyn watched Ian leave, her heart breaking, the tears no longer held back.

Kolyn stared at her accounting of their winter stores, a deep sense of despair pulling at her. How could her father have let things go so much? Winter had set in with its certainty. Christmas was only a few days away. How was she to provide her clan with holiday celebrations when there was so little left?

"How am I to get them through the winter?" she cried out to the empty cellar. At that moment, she despised her father, angry he let his hatred obsess him to the point of neglecting all else. Even his family. She couldn't remember the last happy time they had had as a family.

She laughed, the word family such a loose term when used in reference to what they were. Her father's sons had been merely a means to an end . . . the death of the Black Wolf. Douglas MacGregor had sacrificed them to his own hatred, this feud. The shame inflicted on the MacGregor by Ian Blackstone's actions had killed his last two sons, and driven him to his own death. Kolyn tried to understand this, but could not.

The death of the MacGregor had not put an end to the hatred, the promise Kolyn had given him lodging it upon her own shoulders. She felt confusion tear at her mind, shame rip apart her heart. She had betrayed everyone, but mostly, she had betrayed her own son. Had she not sworn to protect him, to keep him safe from the man who did not want him? Ian had sent Blair away knowing she carried his child. He had not cared enough to save the child from the same fate as his mother. She hated him for this.

Why hadn't she been able to kill him when she had the chance? Did she truly love Ian? Is that what had stopped her hand? He thought

Fela Dawson Scott

her a fool—and she was. A fool to allow her heart to guide her, to keep her from her duty.

Perhaps that wasn't what made her weak. Had it been her own conflict about the feud? Some deeper feeling? Regardless, she knew what she must do. She must not fail her clan again.

Kolyn stood and carefully folded away her lists. This was her most pressing need at present. She must find a way to feed her people.

"Come here, Drew."

Kolyn picked Andrew up and carried him, his small legs tiring in the fresh snow. His cheeks were red from the chill, but his eyes shone brightly from excitement.

"I'll take him, lass."

Dwight reached out to carry the boy, but Kolyn pulled away. "No," she said, then caught herself. "I'm fine, Dwight. Thank you."

His eyes were bloodshot, his face lined with age. Drink would put him in an early grave. She could not help but pity him, even love him. He was her family. And right now, the only family she had in addition to Andrew was a drunkard and a madman. Kolyn cuddled Andrew to her fiercely. He was the only sanity she had in this world. She clung to that.

The small church was filled with villagers, the gathering of the MacGregor clan for the Christmas service. Kolyn had emptied her cellars so they could celebrate as they always had, but she feared the New Year would not dawn so bright. She had such a short time to find a solution. Until then, she would rejoice with them and pray for a miracle.

"My child," Father McCloud said, interrupting her thoughts.

"Yes, Father." Kolyn smiled up at him.

"You look so sad. 'Tis a time for celebration." He sat down in the pew beside her.

She never could keep her feelings from the good father. "I'm afraid I am not such a worthy clan leader. I am the MacGregor, and I can do nothing to help my people."

"Your father has left you with a terrible burden, child. Pray and God will provide."

She wanted to pray, to believe what he was telling her. But she couldn't. "I fear even God cannot help me now."

His brows came together in concern. "Do not forsake him now, Kolyn. He is your strength."

"It is me he has forsaken, Father McCloud."

"Perhaps it only seems that way. In time, you will know his meaning. Be patient." Father McCloud patted her hand, then stood. "Be patient."

Kolyn stared toward the window, patterned panels of colored glass allowing a rainbow of light to cascade upon the floor in front of her. Snow fell again outside. Andrew struggled from her lap and ran to play with the other children, their laughter mingling with the lower pitched voices of the adults.

She looked up to the altar, studying the crucifix that had graced the church for over a hundred years. Jesus looked down at her, his face serene, his eyes gentle. She wondered what he would say to her if he were here, sitting beside her.

"Forgive me, Lord. I know not what else to do."

"I thought you might like some company."

Kolyn knew she was insane to seek the company of her brother, but it was Christmas and she thought . . .

Emmett watched her as she crossed the room to his bed. "So, you've brought me some Christmas cheer, have you?"

She held her breath, fearing he would be in one of his foul moods. Instead he smiled. It had been a long time since she had seen him really smile.

"Merry Christmas, Emmett." She leaned over and kissed him on the cheek. She handed him a small gift, wrapped in a colorful bit of cloth.

He took it and looked away. "I have nothing for you, Kolyn. I am stuck abed."

Again she held her breath. "It isn't much, brother. We've so little these days."

"Aye," he agreed. "I understand our stores are depleted. Quite a legacy our father has left us, wouldn't you say?"

It was the first time he had ever referred to them as a family. "Open it," she prompted.

"'Tis a book," he deduced, though it was not hard to discover that much by the shape and hardness of it.

"I found it in the attic, among some of our possessions when we were children." Kolyn saw his fingers tremble. "I thought I might find some things for Andrew. Instead I found this book. Do you remember it?"

"Aye," Emmett mumbled, his voice cracking from emotion.

"You used to read it to me, Emmett."

He let the small book drop from his hand, and Kolyn picked it up. "You wrote beautiful poetry. You made me promise never to tell Father that you wrote poems. You thought he might think it silly."

She knew she was rattling on. Emmett remained silent.

"We were happy as children, Emmett. What went wrong?"

He finally turned his gaze back to her. "I fell into a living hell and wanted everyone's company. I'm only happy when I know everyone else is miserable as well."

Tears came to her eyes. "Then you should be extremely happy, dear brother."

"Aye," he agreed. "Only one thing can make me happier."

She knew to what he referred. "I'll not speak of it on this day. 'Tis a time for celebration." Isn't that what Father McCloud had said to her?

239

For once he gave in to her. "Then pour me some of that wine, and we shall toast this day."

Andrew was fast asleep in her arms. She gently laid him in his bed. Lovingly, she tucked his covers around him. It had been a long and exciting day for the lad, and he couldn't hold his eyes open. He fell asleep again at once.

"Good night, my sweet boy." She kissed his forehead, then blew out the candle by his bed.

"You've avoided me all day, lass. I just wanted t' say good night."

She could see Dwight's large outline against the doorway, but she could not see his face. She couldn't tell if he had been drinking heavily or not. His voice seemed quite clear.

"Good night, Uncle." She didn't move from Andrew's bedside. She wanted her uncle to leave first.

He stood for the longest time, as if waiting, as if wanting her to come out of the room. Finally, he moved on down the hall to his own rooms.

Kolyn hated this, dreading her own uncle's company. Yet he made her uncomfortable. More than that, he frightened her. It was best she avoid any confrontations with him if she could.

Returning to her rooms, she crossed to her windows and spread the curtains aside. The snow still fell. She sat upon the sill and studied the cloud-ridden sky, masking all stars that might have brightened the blackness. Sudden longings assaulted her, robbing her of her will. She thought of strong arms curled around her, warming her, comforting her.

Guilt followed and collided with her tender feelings. It twisted into a ball of heartache and despair. Emmett would be delighted. She *was* miserable.

A knock sounded at her door.

"I need t' speak with you, lass."

Kolyn's heart sank. "'Tis late, Dwight. Can we speak in the morning?"

There was a long pause, then he conceded, "Aye, it will wait."

She breathed a sigh of relief.

"Merry Christmas, Kolyn."

"Merry Christmas, Dwight."

"As God is my witness, the man and the wolf are one."

Kolyn wanted to grab the man who sat across the table, to scream it couldn't be. But she didn't. She had known John McNee her whole life, the village smithy being a favorite place for children to gather. He wasn't a man to lie. He believed what he said.

"You have seen this?" she asked, much more calmly than she felt.

"Aye, lass. I have. I shall never forget the sight."

Drawing in a calming breath, Kolyn smiled, then said, "Please, John, tell me your story."

John pushed back his stool and stood. He stepped closer to the fire and placed another log onto the flames. He leaned against the stone mantel of his one-room cottage and studied the orange blaze. Kolyn remained patient, allowing him to gather his thoughts.

"I was hunting, some four years back it was. I suppose I had traveled a bit farther than I should, somehow wandering onto Blackstone's land. I shot a deer and carried it upon my back for a good distance before I stopped to rest. It was a good-sized buck and I despaired of getting it down the mountain. Quite sudden-like, he was there, standing before me. He is a giant of a man. I feared my life had come to an end."

"Yet he did not kill you, John. Obviously," Kolyn added in the silent interim.

John nodded. "He made no threat. Instead, he lifted the deer upon his back and carried it down to level ground. I was out of breath just keeping pace with him, yet he barely broke a sweat. He never spoke a word. It was dark by then, and he gazed up at the full moon rising above us. I too watched it. When I looked back, the man was gone and in his place stood a black wolf."

Kolyn couldn't believe John. "Perhaps he stepped into the forest as you watched the moon." She recalled the many times he had appeared without any noise to warn her of his presence.

"I would have heard something. Not a leaf or a branch stirred. I took a step forward, to search for the man, but the wolf stopped me, his bared teeth giving me warning to stay. Then he ran into the darkness of the trees."

Now Kolyn was convinced the wolf was friend to Ian. "John, surely, you cannot—"

John held up his hand. "I didn't look away but a second, and I am not a man subject to imagining such things. I'm a God-fearing man with a family, and believe me, I've had my own misgivings on what I saw."

"Forgive me, John. I didn't mean . . ." She did not finish.

"I cannot deny what I saw. Ian Blackstone is the Black Wolf. What sort of evil this is, or if it is evil at all, I cannot say. I know only a man to be feared showed me a kindness, yet the same man became a wolf."

John looked back into the flames again. "This man has slain your brothers in combat. Even your father died from the fierceness of his sword and the inhuman strength of his arm. Yet he showed generosity to a stranger trespassing on his land and carried the poached deer upon his own shoulders."

Visions teased Kolyn's mind. "A gentle giant." She spoke softly. She looked up at John and stood. "Thank you for telling your story to me, John."

* * *

Golden eyes pierced her mind . . .

Kolyn sat up in bed, her sleep disturbed by the dream, the same one she had experienced over and over in the last month. Ian Blackstone's golden eyes haunted her even as she lay awake.

She hated him. No, she loved him.

Tears came to her eyes, and she made no effort to stop them. She allowed her sobs to comfort her troubled mind and aching heart. She was lost to this living nightmare. Alone with nowhere to run.

Kolyn stepped into Emmett's room, curious that he had sent for her. He never did that. "What is it you need, Emmett?"

"I've something for you," he said, smiling.

Something inside her quivered. She didn't like the look in his eyes, belying the smile on his face. Cautious now, she took his offering.

"Sit," he cooed.

She knew something was wrong.

"It's a poem, a sort of present for the New Year. I wrote it for you, dear sister. Like I used to."

Unable to do anything else, she unrolled the parchment and began to read.

There once was a girl named Lynn . . .

Her gaze met Emmett's. He knew.

"Yes," he drawled lazily, enjoying each moment like a child eating candy. "I found out your dirty little secret, Kolyn. I told you, I always do."

Her heart began to pound fiercely within her chest, making it hard to keep her breathing even. She didn't want him to know the effect he had on her. She continued to read the limerick.

Who took a job at the inn.
She caught the lord's eye,
so she plotted and plied,
to revenge family and clan honor.

Kolyn felt herself sway, but willed herself to be still, to stand before his cruel eyes and read.

There once was a girl named Lynn
the lord took to his bed on a whim.
After, the lord wasn't dead,
or so it is said.
She had failed. 'Tis said she regretted.

Kolyn swallowed hard to relieve the dryness of her mouth.

There once was a girl named Lynn,
who ran home to her family in sin.
The lord planted his seed
in her belly indeed.

Emmett poked at her arm, drawing her tear-filled eyes to look at him. "I wonder what the New Year will bring us?" he chirped, then burst out laughing.

"Stop it," she cried, wadding the poem up in her hand. "You are such a cruel bastard!" Kolyn threw the ball of parchment at him, striking him in the face harmlessly. He laughed even harder. She ran from the room, all but bowling Dwight over as he entered.

"What's the matter with Kolyn?" Dwight asked, his eyes following her down the hall.

Pretending indifference, Emmett shrugged his shoulders. "I guess she took offense to my poem. Who can figure women out?" He couldn't help but be pleased with himself. And Jacob. The man had always been an invaluable source of information, but his servant had out-done himself this time by discovering where Kolyn had been during her absence. Much of his limerick had been a guess, but now Emmett was certain his hunches were correct. He laughed again. Perhaps even his prediction that she would swell with Blackstone's bastard child would come true. That could prove useful in the future.

Dwight moved to stand beside Emmett's bed, and picked up the parchment she had thrown at him. He read it, and as he did, a dark cloud descended over his face. Emmett watched Dwight as he nearly exploded with fury.

"She betrayed you, Dwight. And me. The bitch spread her legs for the bastard and didn't kill him. She didn't even try."

Dwight took Emmett's words as truth, his anger wanting him to believe it.

Emmett went on. "You've more reason than ever to kill that son of a bitch. He's taken what was rightfully yours."

Doubt crept in, making Dwight step back, both mentally and physically. "Kolyn would no' do such a thing."

"Wouldn't she?"

"She's a good lass."

"Is she?"

Emmett's words were maddening. "She'd not waste her virtue on the Devil. Her faith's too strong."

"Ask her, Uncle." Emmett continued to smile, an all-knowing smile that said everything.

Dwight shook his head. "'Tis not my place."

"You are to be her husband. 'Tis your right to know if she is a virgin or not. 'Tis your right to know if that bastard's seed grows within her belly. Ask her!"

Kolyn waited in her room, expecting Dwight to appear. But when he finally did, she was frightened at the anger on his face. That too was expected, but never had she envisioned what she witnessed at that moment.

"Tell me 'tis a lie."

"Tell you what is a lie?" She wouldn't make it easy on him.

His fists clenched at his side, and Kolyn wondered if she should find a weapon. Carefully, she looked about for one, spotting the log just behind her near the fire.

"Did you lay with the Black Wolf?"

It was a direct question. She wouldn't lie. Lies, she had learned, could only make a dreadful situation even worse. "Yes."

If he had expected more of an explanation, she didn't give it. He waited. She didn't offer more.

"Why?" he finally asked, his voice quivering with emotion.

"Why?" she repeated. "Do you not know why?"

He got frustrated, impatient with her. "No, lass. I do not."

"If I must explain it to you, Dwight, then you will not understand."

He blinked a few times, as if he could not see her properly. "Explain it," he ground out menacingly.

"I'll not explain my actions to you, Uncle. Get out."

He did not move.

"Believe what you will and get out." Kolyn used her most authoritative voice. Still, he did not move.

He seemed not to know what to do, what to think. But the anger still existed. She was terribly aware of it. He stepped toward her, his look hurt.

Suddenly, he struck her full across the face. Kolyn stumbled back, then fell. She scrambled to her feet, grasping the log firmly in her hand. She faced him again, club raised.

Dwight came for her. She raised her weapon higher and yelled, "Do not."

He stopped.

"Strike me again, Uncle, and I'll kill you." Her voice sounded strange to her ears, almost distant.

Did he believe her? She waited, her breath held till he turned and left. She didn't lower her club until he was out of sight.

Chapter Sixteen

A strange sort of existence had descended on Gregor Castle in the last two months. Kolyn avoided her uncle whenever possible. Dwight remained surly, yet made no mention of their fight again. Now she had no choice but to seek him out, the urgency of an empty cellar pressing her to action. She found Dwight in the great chamber, drinking. When she told him her plan, he just stood and stared at her. Kolyn wondered if he would reply at all.

"Will you see that everyone is ready tonight?"

"I have feared that madness had consumed you. Now I'm certain of it."

Kolyn refused to let him anger her. "Aye, I am mad, Dwight. See to it."

"How do you plan t' raid Blackstone's stores?

It will take us into the belly of his castle. 'Tis too risky, Lass."

"His storeroom is full. Ours is empty."

Dwight turned away, his anger apparent. "We shall fill it another way."

"No." Kolyn's voice had hardened. "No, we shall fill it tonight. With the supplies of Stonehaven Castle."

He stood like a rock, unmoving.

"Mark my words, Dwight. I'll ride with or without you. 'Tis your choice."

With that, Kolyn left the room. For a brief moment, she wondered if she was indeed mad. What drove her to think she could steal from the Black Wolf and not suffer reprisals? What if he discovered who she really was?

"Kolyn," Dwight called to her.

She turned back.

"We'll be ready, lass."

Kolyn nodded and walked away. Mad or sane, she would continue on the path she had chosen. It was the only thing she could do now.

Kolyn watched the last wagon roll away, its bed heavy with barrels. She quickly went back to the storeroom and motioned for her men to ride out. She waited until the room was empty, then followed.

"What is it you're doin', lass?"

She stopped, her path blocked by a burly man a good foot taller and a few feet wider than she.

"You'd best go on," yelled Dwight, bringing the man's attention to his back. "I'll be there shortly."

When the man turned to face Dwight, Kolyn grabbed a torch and struck him on the head. He slid to the floor unconscious. "Get the men out of here, Dwight."

He hesitated.

"Now," she said, this time more firmly. He did as she asked. Kolyn looked about one last time, then made her way along the narrow hall and up the steep stairs. She heard the horses riding away as she closed the last doorway behind her. It was a dark, moonless night. It took a second for her eyes to adjust.

"If I were to guess, I'd say I'm in the presence of the MacGregor herself."

Geoffrey's voice was familiar. She didn't need to see his face to know him. She saw no need to deny who she was, and assumed he could not see her face any better than she his. "Your guess is correct," she answered, disguising her voice with a heavy country accent.

The dark shadow leaned against the stone wall. "Are you totally without your senses?"

She feigned ignorance. "I don't know what you're meanin'."

"Of course, you do!" He laughed. "'Tis time you learned who you are dealing with, MacGregor."

He reached out and grabbed her arm and pushed her in front of him. Kolyn made no move to resist. She walked with him.

"Are you scared, lass?"

"No." Kolyn wasn't afraid.

"You should be." Geoffrey chuckled.

Kolyn stopped, causing him to bump into her. She didn't turn around. "Should I?"

Geoffrey stood directly behind her, his head high above hers, his body pressed against her own intimately. "Yes, you should," he whispered hoarsely.

She sensed his sudden confusion. "Blackstone has taken everything from me. I have nothing more to fear from him."

Something strange forced its way into Geoffrey's mind—even more so, into his heart. Sympathy rarely touched him, and he wasn't used to it. It made him feel odd, uncomfortable. Suddenly, he could smell heather, and he couldn't resist pulling off the plaid that covered her hair. It spilled over her shoulders and down her back. He recalled the only other time he had seen her, covered from head to toe in soot and mud. This time, he wasn't laughing. He could feel the arch of her back, gently curving to form her backside. Somehow, even though he had not, could not now see her face, he no longer thought her an ugly woman.

He reached out and gathered a handful of hair, the softness curling about his fingers, the scent strong in his nostrils. He leaned down to smell, and wished he could tell the color of it in the dark.

Kolyn twisted and brought her knee up, hard and deadly accurate. Geoffrey doubled over with the pain her well-placed knee caused his groin. She couldn't help but smile as she thought her brothers would have been proud that their lessons had not been wasted. She jerked free from his hand, pulling a hank of hair from her head.

Geoffrey dropped to his knees, his moan loud in the silent night. This brought a guard's attention to him. As the guard made his way toward Geoffrey, Kolyn armed herself with a lid from a barrel. His eyes were on Geoffrey, and she attacked, knocking him out with one swift blow to his face.

She made her way to the castle wall and silently slipped out before a call went up to stop her. Her horse was tied where she left it. She mounted.

"What has taken you so long, Kolyn?"

Dwight's voice startled her. Before she could answer they heard horses riding out of Stone-haven. They wasted no more time in leaving.

Geoffrey pulled his horse to a halt, the animal fighting to go on. He watched the two riders disappear into the dense woods. He knew who they were and where they were going. There was no need to follow, but something disturbed him. She'd seemed familiar. Why did he feel he knew her from somewhere else?

Whatever the answer, right now he had to

face Ian. To tell him what this woman had done under his very nose.

Dwight slid from his mount even before it had come to a halt, turning to Kolyn as she rode into the courtyard behind him. In two long strides, he was beside her horse, pulling her from the saddle.

"You've set your mind on killing yourself. I'll not be a part of it."

He hauled her like a child into the great hall, anger pushing him further into his world of pain.

"Put me down, Dwight."

Kolyn squirmed in his arms, struggled to free herself from him. He held on tighter. "If you persist in this game, I'll surely go mad."

She stilled. "Put me down."

"I'll kill you myself before I'll watch another strike you down."

Anger burst inside Kolyn. She struck out, landing a blow to Dwight's chin, then catching him with her left hand on his lip, splitting it.

"You sorry bastard!"

She hit him again. "Put me down!" she yelled.

He dropped her, and she landed on her backside. His look remained murderous.

"You want to kill me," she goaded him as she quickly stood up. "Then do it!"

She faced him, standing close, taunting him. "Do it, Dwight." She grasped his hand and wrapped it about her throat. "End your torture now."

Dark eyes watched her.

His grip tightened as the pain on his face increased.

"End it all, Dwight. Put us both out of our misery."

Why she was doing this, she didn't know. Did she really want to die? Did she really believe Dwight would kill her? His hand cut off her air, and the hall began to whirl about her. Blackness threatened her. He let go.

"I cannot," Dwight cried out, his voice full of anguish. "You sorely tempt me, but I cannot!"

Fury took her blindly on. "You cannot! You will not!" She hit him hard across the face with her doubled fist. "You coward!"

He caught her hand before she could strike him again. She tried to get free.

"Forgive me, Kolyn."

"I'll not. You've gone too far, Dwight. I'll not forgive you this time." She reeled out of control, but she didn't care. He pulled her into his arms, stilling her struggles.

"I hate you," she screamed against his chest. Darkness drifted over her. "I hate you."

Kolyn fainted.

Ian sat very still, wondering if he had heard wrong. Surely he had. The fire crackled loud in the great chamber where Geoffrey had found

Ian and Ainsley, a game of chess having kept them up to this late hour.

"I dinna ken how she did it. Stealin' the stores from under our very noses."

Geoffrey's statement made it clear Ian had heard him correctly. But his harried pacing told him even more. "Yes," Ian drawled, keeping a tight rein on his emotions. "How did she do it?"

"Too easily," Geoffrey conceded.

Ian turned to his mother, whose expression showed her worry.

"If they are truly in need of our food, I for one would gladly let them have it," she said.

"I agree," Ian replied softly, his mother's reaction again a surprising one. "But," he added, "I'd prefer she ask rather than take."

"She doesn't seem to be a woman who will ever seek your help, Ian."

"She's gone too far this time. I can't have her coming and going as she pleases in my own home."

"What do you intend to do?" his mother asked.

"I think it's time to put this whole feud behind us. Once and for all."

Geoffrey watched Ian leave the room. Whatever Ian had in mind, Geoffrey would be interested in the ending to this tale. Something told him there were still a few surprises in store.

Chapter Seventeen

Kolyn opened her eyes to a dark room. Her first thoughts were confused, distress underlining them. Slowly, she realized she was in her own room. She tossed back the bedcover and crossed to her window. Light streamed in when she pulled the drapes aside, the angle of the sun telling her it was early morning.

She recalled the fight she'd had with Dwight, and felt ashamed at her loss of control. Kolyn let the velvet drop back over the panes of glass, casting her back into darkness. She wished she could block out her thoughts and feeling as easily as she did the sunlight.

Nellie's soft knock sounded, and Kolyn called for her to enter. The cook ambled in, her large frame filling the doorway, her arms filled with a tray loaded with food.

"Lass, what are you doin' out of bed?" She bustled across to set the tray on the table. "You are t' do as I say."

"I'm fine, Nellie. Really I am."

Kolyn's objections went unheard as the woman bundled her up and tucked her back into bed. "You need your rest, child. You've been pale an' your appetite is sufferin'. 'Tis time you let your Nellie take care of you."

Before she could object, Nellie had the tray set in her lap. Hot scones with gooseberry jam, porridge, and tea tempted her, but her stomach rejected the thought. Suddenly, she felt light-headed and her stomach lurched.

"I'm not hungry, Nellie. Please take it away."

Nellie's brow furrowed, and her lips pursed, but she removed the tray from Kolyn's lap and placed it on the bedside table.

Kolyn laid her head back on her pillow, closing her eyes to still the whirling of the room.

"I'll just lie here a while," she said to Nellie.

Noises drifted to Kolyn's ears, the sound of many horses riding into the courtyard below causing her to open her eyes.

"Nellie." Kolyn looked at her servant. "Please see what is going on."

Nellie did as asked, but quickly pulled back from the window. The fear on her face prompted Kolyn to stand again, despite her stomach's objections.

"Oh, lass, you must stay abed," Nellie moaned, her hands twisting her apron into knots.

"Go back to your kitchen, Nellie. I'll see to this." Kolyn threw back the curtain and peered out. She too felt fear prickle the back of her neck. She ran from her room to her father's for a better view.

"I wish to see the MacGregor!"

Ian's words were clear, demanding. Kolyn stepped back, the back of her hand held to her mouth. She swallowed her fear.

"What is it you want?"

Ian recognized Dwight MacDougal as the man stepped through the manor doorway and faced him and his men. He looked bedraggled, not at all like the strong-hearted man Ian remembered.

"I want to see Lady Kolyn." Ian was not a man who liked repeating himself, but today was a day of many unpalatable things.

"She does not want t' see you, Blackstone. 'Tis best if you leave now, afore we come t' blows."

Ian continued to sit on his mount, looking down at the man. "I've come to make peace with the woman, Dwight MacDougal. I'll not leave till she sees me."

"Then you'll die," Dwight growled.

"Then someone will die."

"What do you want, Blackstone?" a voice called out.

Quickly, Ian studied the many windows, determining from which the woman had spoken. "I've come to speak with you, Lady Kolyn."

"As I said." Kolyn's voice remained hard, revealing nothing to him. "What do you want?"

"I want peace." Ian still could not see her but a familiarity swarmed over him.

"I've nothing to say to you. Go, while you can."

"Will you not show yourself?" Ian shouted up to the blackened windows, aggravation running strong inside him.

She did not answer.

Ian's horse moved impatiently beneath him. "What is it you want from me, MacGregor? You've helped yourself to my cattle, my sheep, my pigs. You even dared to take from my storeroom."

Still no comment.

An idea teased Ian's mind, forming a thought he did not want to recognize. "I'm glad to give it all to you. You are welcome to whatever you need. I'll not let your people suffer for your father's neglect."

"It's not enough," Kolyn screamed, shame pushing her anger forth.

"What more do you want?"

Ian's question made Kolyn question herself again. *What did she want?* She had sworn to kill him. And she had failed. She had failed her father and her people. She had failed to protect Andrew. She had failed everyone.

"I want you dead, Blackstone! I want you dead."

Slowly, Ian rode forward, closing the distance between where she stood at the upper window and him.

"Then kill me, Lady Kolyn." Ian raised his empty hands in the air, showing her he held no weapon. A nagging sense of recognition lay just beyond his grasp. "Kill me now and be done with it."

As if in a dream, Kolyn grasped the bow from her father's mantel. Her gaze locked onto the image of her father, the damage she had inflicted upon the painting like scars upon his soul. Guilt, shame, fear—it all bore down upon her. His eyes stared at her, filled with anger at her failings. Kolyn returned to the window. Stiff, trembling fingers placed the quill of the arrow against the string. She pushed all thought from her mind. She raised the bow, took aim, then fired.

Ian saw the flash of the arrow tip, but did not move. The arrow embedded itself in his chain mail, only the tip piercing flesh. Ian glanced up and saw Kolyn MacGregor look out, the sun setting fire to her hair. Then she was gone.

Recognition pounded across his mind, so brief yet so powerful. He looked to Geoffrey, wondering if he had seen her. He had not.

Ian pulled the arrow out and flung it to the ground. His war-horse raised up high on its hind legs, pawing the air fiercely. Ian twisted around as the horse came back to the ground, his words carrying the cold, icy anger he could no longer control.

"Tell your mistress she had her chance. I'll not stand for any more of her tantrums. If she wants something, she has only to ask. But if she wishes to continue on with these childish raids, I'll have no choice but to put an end to them."

Dwight's face twisted into a mask of rage. "You just try and stop us."

Ian pointed his finger at Dwight. "I'll start with you, Dwight MacDougal. You'd best talk some sense into her. She's a damned pest."

"I'll fight you here and now!" Dwight yelled, stepping forward, his hand upon his sword.

"No. It will be on *my* terms when I kill you." Ian whirled his mount around. "Not till then."

Kolyn watched Ian ride out of the castle's courtyard. The bow she held slipped from her fingers and clattered to the floor.

"What have I done?" she whispered.

Guilt overwhelmed her, bringing tears to her eyes. She should feel disappointment, not relief. She had failed to kill the Black Wolf, and she was sickened—not by her failure, but by her attempt.

She stared at her hands, wondering what they were capable of. As she had watched the arrow arc across the courtyard the consequence of her actions had hit her. The fierce pounding of her heart had stopped for one brief second, until she saw the arrow had caused no harm. Her hands still shook from the realization that had come during that moment—to kill Ian would kill a part of her he now controlled. Two distinct sides were at war inside Kolyn. On one side, she held the promise to her father, the threats of her brother, and the desire to protect Andrew from all the evilness that surrounded her. Was Ian part of this evil? In the eyes of her clan he was, but in her heart she believed he was not.

That was what lay on the other side. Sensitive, confused feelings for a man she barely knew. Yet a man she had made love to. Not in horror or distaste, but with pleasure and immense desire. A desire that still remained. A desire that haunted her every moment. And a love that she could no longer deny or hide away.

"Should we ride out an' attack the bastard?"

Dwight filled the doorway with his bulk, drawing Kolyn's tearful gaze to him.

She shook her head. "No, he came in peace. Let him go in peace."

"You cannot mean—"

"I can and I do!"

She could see how much he wanted to go after Ian. It was plainly written on his face, and it frightened her.

Dwight left her standing there, alone and confused.

* * *

Ian rode hard all the way back to Stonehaven, his temper pounded out with each slash of his horse's hooves. Ian slowed only when he entered the stable yards.

How could he have not known? Once again he felt the fool. Lynn . . . no, Kolyn must be having a good laugh at his expense. The cold fury settled in his heart, its strength pushing aside the newer, tender emotions he had allowed to revive.

"I should strangle the witch!" He jumped from his saddle and handed the reins to the stable boy.

Geoffrey's laughter echoed off the stone walls, somehow saying *I told you so*, bringing a warmth to Ian's face.

"Tell me, Geoff." Ian smiled, lazy and slow. "How is it that this woman was able to walk in to Stonehaven without meeting any resistance? Except, of course, the two men she knocked cold."

"Obviously"—Geoffrey shuffled his feet uncomfortably—"she knew her way about."

This prompted a serious nod from Ian. "Aye. I thought that strange." A MacGregor had never set foot inside Stonehaven, but Lynn had. She knew exactly where he kept his winter stores because he had shown her himself before the harvest festival.

Once again, Geoffrey felt a strange feeling of knowing Kolyn MacGregor. "Do you ever get the feelin' we ken the MacGregor?"

"That we know her?" Ian asked innocently. He wasn't ready to face acknowledging Lynn's true identity.

"Aye." Geoffrey rubbed his chin thoughtfully. "Sometimes it feels as if we should ken the woman."

"We ran into her when the grain caught on fire. Remember . . . the woman was covered in soot from head to toe. It was hard to take her seriously. Couldn't weigh a hundred pounds, soaking wet."

"She's a spirited lass, though," Geoffrey reminded him with a big smile.

"Yes, she has proven to be a pain in the ass. Even more so than her father. At least when I faced the MacGregor men, I knew where I stood. With a woman, I'm at a loss. I can't fight her, yet I can't let her go on with this feud of hers."

"You have no way of winnin', my friend."

"Aye," Ian conceded. How ironic—he loved the very woman he hated. "Seems I've had no luck with my women, Geoff."

Geoffrey agreed with a small laugh. "You can't get one woman out of your life and the other won't be a part of it. No luck at all, my friend."

"Perhaps they're in league together, to make my life hell."

A thought flashed across Geoffrey's mind so unthinkable it left him breathless.

"Geoff."

Ian's voice broke into his jumbled thoughts.

"You look quite troubled. Are you all right?"

Geoffrey nodded. "Yes, I'm fine. Just had a strange thought, 'tis all."

"Anything you wish to share?"

"No." Geoffrey stepped away. "I've got to tend to some business, Ian. I'll be seein' you later."

Ian wondered at what disturbed Geoffrey, since his friend's mood was generally jovial, but Ian had his own problem to tend to. Kolyn MacGregor.

Chapter Eighteen

Kolyn knocked on her brother's door and waited for him to answer. She had missed taking Emmett's breakfast up and felt she needed to check on him. No answer came. Quietly, she opened the door.

"What the bloody hell . . ."

Emmett looked up, meeting Kolyn's shocked gaze. She stepped inside and closed the door behind her. Kolyn recognized the woman. Her name was Juanita. Many believed her to be a witch-woman, and feared her magic powers. Kolyn felt only anger.

"What is she doing here, Emmett?"

A smirk crossed his lips as Juanita gathered up her potions and powders. "I would think that it was obvious, sister."

Kolyn turned to Juanita. "Get out."

"You've no need to be angry," Emmett said.

She looked back to her brother in disgust, then walked over to the table by his bed and grabbed a bottle that lay on it. "She's here to practice her witchcraft and you think I shouldn't be angry."

"It will help me walk," Emmett mumbled through gritted teeth.

The look in his eyes was murderous. Kolyn knew she had hit on the truth. She threw the bottle across the room, smashing it against the wall. "You will never walk, Emmett. You know that."

"I don't know that!" he screamed. "Juanita can help me, and you'd best stop interfering!"

"What is he paying you?" Kolyn nearly choked on her anger. They were nearly destitute, and Emmett was wasting money on this witchery. She crossed to stand before Juanita. "What is he paying you?"

Juanita merely sneered at her.

Kolyn reached out and twisted Juanita's arm behind her back, bringing a yell of pain and surprise. Indignant fury gave Kolyn the strength to push the larger woman out the door and down the long flights of stairs. Once outside, she gave the witch-woman a hard shove. "Get out and don't come back. There'll be no more money for your worthless cures."

Juanita smoothed her skirt and straightened her blouse. "You would be wise not to anger

270

me, Kolyn MacGregor. I have the power to reveal the secrets within your heart." Casually, she strolled up to Kolyn, putting her face only inches from hers.

"I can reveal the secret that lies within your womb."

Juanita laid her hand on Kolyn's belly, and suddenly Kolyn was afraid.

Juanita smiled. "I may be the only friend you have when it comes time to rid yourself of this curse."

"Leave me be," Kolyn muttered, her anger gone, weak and shaking.

Juanita's laughter made her wince, the sound trailing behind the woman as she walked away, the evil sound remaining even after she disappeared. Kolyn ran inside to escape it.

She heard Emmett screaming her name, and knew she had to face him. Slowly, she climbed the stairs and returned to his room.

"What lies have you told that woman, Emmett?"

It was obvious he was beyond anger, his face hideously twisted with emotion. "I tell no lies. It is you who keeps the truth from me."

"Me!" Kolyn was amazed at how his mind worked. "You spend what little money we have on that woman's witchcraft, wishing your life away on her spells and potions. She cannot make you walk. Nothing will make you walk."

His laughter was vicious, cruel. "I'm no fool. I know what the future holds for me. But I fear if I stop trying, I'll die. I'll die a pathetic cripple."

"I . . ." Kolyn didn't know what to say to his intimate confession.

"I would prefer your anger to your pity, Kolyn. Do not pity me!"

Kolyn felt tears sting her eyes, but fought to keep them from falling. "Sometimes I hate you."

This made him smile. "Yes, that's better."

"This woman frightens me," Kolyn confessed, instantly regretting it.

"You'd be wise to fear her. She's quite wicked."

"I cannot let her come back here."

"Did she threaten to tell about the child you carry?"

Shock bolted through Kolyn. First, that it was her brother who had implanted this idea into Juanita's head. Second, that it had not been just a madman's rhyme. The sickness in the mornings. The swell of her stomach. She was going to have a baby. Ian Blackstone's baby.

"Did you not know this, Kolyn?"

She hadn't realized. No, it couldn't be. "How did you know? No, how did *Jacob* know?"

Emmett snickered in his usual annoying way. "You can be so innocent. Nellie's been quite concerned about your lack of appetite, your sickness in the mornings. It doesn't take a genius to put two and two together. Even with my New Year's prediction, you were caught unaware?"

Again she didn't answer, yet he seemed to read her mind anyway.

"You are such a child, dear sister? Should I demand *he* make an honest woman of you?"

"You needn't concern yourself, dear brother." She cleared her throat nervously. "I shall take care of my own problems."

"The way you're taking care of the Black Wolf?" His words were full of contempt. "You missed him on purpose this morning when the bastard came to make his peace with you. Didn't you?"

"That's not true."

"Isn't it? How many other times have you tried and failed? You slept with him to kill him, yet you failed? Why?"

She remained still, fearing even to breathe lest he see the truth.

"Why did you not kill him, Kolyn? Do you want the Black Wolf, the father of the bastard child you carry, dead?"

Kolyn wanted to turn and run. To get as far from Emmett as she could. But to run would admit her guilt. She stood her ground.

"Tell me, was it so good for you that you can forget your promises? Did he make you squirm and scream with desire? Did you cry out for more?"

"You bastard," Kolyn screamed. She stepped

273

to the side of the bed and raised her hand to slap her brother across the face, but his hand was quicker. His grip was cruel. But not near as hurting as his words.

"You little whore. You slept with him, and you liked it."

"No!" she denied.

"Yes!"

His mouth was close to Kolyn's ear as he whispered to her, his breath hot on her neck. "Did he touch your breasts?"

Kolyn cringed, tried to twist free. His hand remained clamped about her arm, keeping her next to him.

"Did he kiss the softness of your neck?"

Kolyn began to sob openly.

"Did you spread your legs for him willingly, or did he take you by force?"

Kolyn screamed, "No."

Emmett threw Kolyn from him. "You'd best learn to be nice to your dear, crippled brother. Or I'll have that witch-woman rid you of that bastard inside you."

"You wouldn't," Kolyn whispered.

"You forget who you're dealing with, Kolyn. Cross me and I'll see to it that not only does the bastard child die, but Andrew as well. I'd get much pleasure in sending both carcasses to the Black Wolf. Maybe even yours."

Kolyn couldn't hold back the bile that rose in her throat. She emptied her stomach upon his floor.

"Get out, before you make me sick!" he screamed.

She ran from his room.

Kolyn nearly ran over Nellie as she made her way to her room.

"Slow down, lass. You'll hurt yourself running blind like that."

Just hearing Nellie's voice calmed Kolyn. "Would you see to packing some of Andrew's things? I'm taking him to Father McCloud's for a while."

"'Tis almost dark. Couldn't you wait till mornin' child?"

"No," she said, trying to keep her voice even. "I promised the father I'd be there tonight. I didn't keep track of the time. The church isn't so far away."

"I'll see to it, lass." Nellie scurried off, then stopped. "I near forgot. This was delivered for you."

Kolyn took the note, no seal giving her any idea of who the sender might be. She went to her room before she opened it.

It read, *I know that Lynn, the tavern maid, and Kolyn MacGregor are one and the same. Meet me tonight where the grain was set on fire. Geoff*

Slowly, Kolyn gathered her shattered nerves and tried to think. First she would take Andrew to Father McCloud's. He would protect Andrew. Then she would meet Geoffrey. Perhaps he would kill her and end this nightmare.

Fela Dawson Scott

* * *

"Is there something amiss, child?"

Father McCloud's face showed his concern, even in the dimly lit chapel where they stood.

"I must settle my life, Father. I would worry less if Drew were with you. I know you will keep him safe."

"Should I worry for your safety, Kolyn?"

"Take care of Drew." She handed the sleeping child over to the priest and turned to leave. "Tell him that I love him. More than life itself."

"God will watch over you, Kolyn MacGregor."

"Aye, Father."

Kolyn watched the moon as it made its path into the sky, the pale yellow sliver giving little light to the darkness about her.

"I dinna ken if you'd come."

Geoffrey's voice was deep and soft, holding no threat. Kolyn hoped this was a good sign. "I didn't have much choice but to come."

"It took me some time to figure out that you and Lynn were the same woman. I was not happy to learn it."

"I must confess I am not so happy either."

A sigh drifted to her ears.

"What is it we should do about this, Kolyn MacGregor?"

Kolyn was surprised by his question. "Why should we do anything?"

"You tried to kill Ian, didn't you? That night

276

when you were together?"

"No," she lied, but it came out a croak as her throat swelled up.

"It was your intent," Geoffrey persisted.

"I don't know."

Suddenly Geoffrey grabbed her, his hand wrapped about her throat, shutting off the air she breathed.

"You are lyin' to me. You tried to kill Ian, just as you tried this mornin'. I should kill you now and be done with it."

Silently, she prayed he would.

"Oh, God," he whispered, then released his hold, pulling her into his arms to cradle her. Kolyn began to cry. "What are you cryin' for? I'll not harm you."

Kolyn pulled back and wiped at her tears, shamed by her weakness. "I'm crying because I wanted you to kill me."

Geoffrey's sharp intake of breath and awkward silence made his surprise obvious. "I'd not kill a woman, no matter what you did."

"Even to protect Ian Blackstone?"

Again he was quiet.

"I am bound by honor to kill Ian," she said.

"You've tried three times and failed," he reminded her.

"I cannot fail again."

"What am I to do, Kolyn?"

Kolyn felt his agony. "Nothing."

"I must tell him the truth."

"Why?" she asked. "Why tell him the woman

he made love to is his enemy? The very woman he hates. Would his best friend tell him such a thing?"

"I don't know."

"It seems we both have difficult choices to make."

Kolyn walked away, leaving Geoffrey to make his.

Chapter Nineteen

Kolyn walked quietly up the darkened stairwell, the skeletal staff of servants having long since gone to their beds. She stopped when she heard Dwight's voice. She glanced across the landing and saw the door to his room stood ajar. His giant shadow moved back and forth, waving in the flickering candlelight. From the mumbling and cursing that reached her ears, she knew he was drunk. She moved on to her own rooms and entered silently. She bolted the door.

A great tiredness made her shoulders sag, but she knew sleep would be hard to find. Kolyn crossed to the washstand and poured some water into the bowl. She cupped it into her hands and splashed it over her face. The coolness felt good.

"Let me in, Kolyn. I wish t' speak with you."

Dwight's loud voice startled Kolyn, and she instinctively took a step back. He tried to enter, but found the door locked. He pounded on the door and called to her again. Still, she did not move.

"Go away, Dwight. It's late, and I'll not see you as you are."

He was silent, but only for a moment. "And how do you ken how I am? You do not ken what I feel or what I think."

"You're drunk. That's all I need to know."

"Aye," he hollered, his speech slurred. "I drink t' get you out of my mind. Yet I can smell the heather you wear when you come up the stairs."

"Go away." She tried to sound firm.

"Where have you been, lass?"

Frustration churned inside Kolyn. "'Tis no concern of yours."

"No concern of mine?" he asked, his voice rising in anger. "You sneak off and you mock me for asking."

She did not reply.

"Open this door, Kolyn, or I'll be bustin' it down."

The threat was real, but she would not open it willingly.

When the ax struck the door, Kolyn nearly jumped from her skin, the sound was so loud in the quiet of night.

"Stop it, Dwight. I'll not stand for your insolence."

He merely laughed and continued hacking at her chamber door.

Dwight rammed the door with his shoulder, and it gave way, the wood splitting and splintering beneath his strength. Kolyn faced him with her anger. "How dare you."

His laughter stopped. "Tell me, lass. Where were you tonight?"

Kolyn pointed to the door. She wished her finger did not shake so much. "Get out, Dwight. I'll not ask again."

"Did you go t' your lover?"

"Lover?"

"Aye, your lover. The man who planted his seed in your belly."

Dwight dropped the ax he still held and stepped forward, his eyes full of anger and hate. "Did you go t' him, Kolyn? Did you beg him t' take you t' him? T' give you more of what you like?"

"I have no lover, Dwight. You are drunk, and you are scaring me." Kolyn knew he was out of control, and for the second time that day she knew terror.

His hand reached out and grabbed her before she even had time to react, his vise-like grip on her wrist unbreakable. He pulled her to him, his eyes glazed with madness.

"I love you, Kolyn. It should be my child inside you."

"Dwight, you're hurting me. Please let me go."

"No!"

Kolyn closed her eyes to block the vision of agony reflected in his face. She wanted to scream, to allow madness to take her mind from the reality she was forced to live.

"My bonnie sweet Katey."

"I am not Katherine, Dwight. Katey was my mother."

"Aye, Katey gave you to me when I could not have her."

"No." Kolyn struggled to make Dwight understand. "She did not give me to you."

His hand reached out and stroked her hair, loosening it from its plait. "Her hair was afire like yours. But you've more fire in your blood than Katey."

"No one *gave* me to you, Dwight. Listen to me—"

"Your brother promised you t' me. You're mine, Kolyn."

He pulled her into his arms, his mouth seeking hers. Kolyn twisted away, his lips hot on her cheek. Easily he picked her up, carried her to the bed, and threw her upon it. She tried to scurry away, but he hauled her back.

"I want what you gave t' your lover, lass. I want what should have been mine."

"No," she screamed, but he dropped his weight upon her.

"We'll rid your belly of the bastard, and you'll

be mine, Kolyn. I cannot stop loving you, even when you've betrayed me this way."

He ripped at her dress, his large hands shredding it easily. Kolyn struck out, bringing her knee up into his groin. This gave her the moment she needed, and she scrambled off the bed and retrieved the ax he had dropped near the door.

"Get up, Dwight."

Dwight rolled over, then slowly stood when he saw her standing before him, ax in hand.

She pulled on the servants' cord to waken them from their sleep, the frequency and intensity telling them to come quickly. She watched the many emotions travel across Dwight's features, but the one she feared was the hatred. Only a few minutes passed before Nellie bustled in. Instantly she was at her side, pulling a plaid about Kolyn's tattered dress.

"Oh, my dear," Nellie moaned, wringing her hands with worry.

"I'm all right, Nellie. He didn't hurt me."

Four guards entered on Nellie's heels.

"Escort Dwight MacDougal from MacGregor land." She faced her uncle. "Never shall you be welcomed here again, Uncle. If you should ever return, you shall pronounce your own death sentence."

"You've no right to banish me, Kolyn Mac-Gregor."

"I have every right." She stepped closer, looked him straight in the eye. "I shall never forgive you this shame you have cast upon me."

"I'll see you dead before another can have you."

Kolyn turned to the guards and ordered, "Take him away."

She went to the window. Silently, she watched Dwight as the group of men rode out of the courtyard. Would she ever see him again? She prayed she would not.

Her hand slid down to feel her belly, the roundness quite apparent now. How could she not have known she was with child? She felt the fool. Everyone else seemed to know, even Dwight. Obviously, it was something she needn't try and hide.

A sad sigh escaped her lips, and she wondered what she would do now. At least Dwight would no longer be a threat. But she still had to deal with her mad brother. She had never felt so alone in all her life. Alone and frightened.

Kolyn walked along the garden path, Andrew's tiny hand cradled in her own. The last two weeks had passed in a numbed haze, her only delight her daily visit with Andrew. Yet each visit ended with agony as she had to leave him behind in Father McCloud's care. When they neared the door to the church, she lifted him into her arms.

"Can I go home with you, Mommy?"

Her heart broke as she looked into his dark

eyes filled with hope. Hope she knew she must dash. "Not yet, lad. You will have to stay a while longer with Father McCloud."

"How much longer?"

A child's innocence made him question her, but it was an adult dread that filled her heart. "I don't know, Andrew. You know it won't be longer than necessary. I miss you."

"I miss you too."

Andrew kissed her, then hugged her tight. Tears blurred her vision. "I love you, son. I'll be back as soon as I can to see you."

"Aye," he mumbled, tears filling his eyes.

"Be brave for Mommy." Kolyn couldn't bear to see him cry, and he did his best for her. "Go on in. Father McCloud is waiting for you."

Kolyn watched her son run inside, and had to force herself from calling him back. Her life was stalled, nothing happening, nothing resolved. For the last three weeks she had merely existed, feeling nothing. It was as if she were awaiting something. What, she didn't know.

Only one thing seemed certain—she knew she needed to keep Andrew safe with Father McCloud. She wanted him with her, to ease the loneliness she felt. But it wasn't the time.

She turned away and started for home. Absently, Kolyn made her way through the narrow streets, her mind dwelling on her sadness, not her surroundings. It wasn't until her instincts pushed their way forward that she became aware of the feeling that someone followed her. It was strong and undeniable. She glanced around, trying not to panic, trying not to let on she suspected. She saw no one. She heard nothing.

Feeling silly, Kolyn ignored the sensation inside her and walked on. Yet it persisted, even when she shut the door behind her, safe within the manor. She decided it was just her imagination and went about her day's work, but the feeling never went away.

"What is going on here?" Kolyn ask Jacob as he exited her father's chambers.

"Your brother has moved from the tower, my lady."

"Is Emmett inside then?"

"Yes, my lady."

She entered her father's room.

"You have ignored me of late, dear sister."

"Have I?" Kolyn feigned ignorance, but the truth was she had not been able to face him since their last encounter.

He seemed to have forgotten the ugliness of it. "Yes, and I'm quite hurt by it. But I'll forgive you if you come sit with me a while."

She moved to the side of his bed . . . her father's bed. "Are you comfortable in Father's rooms?"

"Yes, quite. You don't mind do you?" He seemed to want something from her.

"Not at all." It all seemed so polite, so civilized. She wanted to scream. She wanted to slap him across his smiling face.

Emmett watched her closely, but Kolyn allowed nothing to show on her face.

"After the accident Father hid me away in the tower room. He was ashamed of me."

"No, he wasn't, Emmett."

"Yes." His voice was raised. "He was. You see, I became a cripple. An invalid. He couldn't bear that. It would have been better if I had died honorably. Like a man. Like my other brothers did. He was so proud of them. But me . . ."

Kolyn felt her patience waning. "You were a stubborn, willful boy who couldn't control his temper. But that doesn't mean he was ashamed of you."

Emmett only laughed. "You are so innocent. Always willing to believe the best. Good, sweet little Kolyn. Everyone loves Kolyn."

Kolyn wanted to change the subject. His mood was dangerous. "Do you want me to read to you, Emmett?"

"No," he snapped. "You never told me why you banished our dear uncle. What did he do to deserve that?"

She looked at her feet, unwilling, unable to look at Emmett's smiling face. "You knew how he felt, didn't you?"

"Whatever are you talking about?"

"You promised me to him. For what? What did he promise to do for you in turn for me?"

"Kill the Black Wolf."

Kolyn looked up and met his gaze. "It wasn't his right to kill the Black Wolf. You shouldn't have asked him."

"Why? Because the right to vengeance is yours? As the MacGregor, the honor of the clan rests in your hands? Is that what you think? And what of me? What right do I have as the eldest son and heir, the rightful chief of the clan?"

"I would give anything for Father to have acknowledged you as the MacGregor, but he didn't."

"Aye," he sneered, bitterness strong in his voice. "He didn't."

She turned away, sickened by the sight of his hate.

"I've not finished with you."

She stepped toward the door. She was finished with him.

"What do you intend to do about your promise to Father? From what I've determined, you've done nothing but sleep with your enemy. Now you are with child by the very man you're supposed to kill. That wasn't exactly what I had in mind when I suggested you spread your legs for him, sister."

"I don't suppose it was exactly what I intended either, brother."

He chuckled, obviously enjoying her misery. "Was there a touch of self-pity in that comment?" he asked. "I know how you hate self-pity."

Kolyn turned back to Emmett. "What is it you want from me?"

"What I want hasn't changed. I *want* you to kill the bastard."

"I don't know how," she whispered.

"Find a way." His voice was steel, ungiving, much like his expression. "Find a way, or I'll have to kill his son. Then, if that's not enough to make me feel good, I'll kill the bastard you're carrying inside you."

Tears came to her eyes. Her heart pounded strongly in her ears. "You're my brother . . . how can you speak of such things?"

His laughter resounded against the walls, mocking her, taunting her. "Ian Blackstone killed your brother! What you see here is but a shell. Only hatred keeps me living."

Kolyn looked at Emmett. He was right. Her brother was dead. In his stead lay a madman whose cruelty she feared.

She said nothing more.

Her silence made him laugh again. Wicked and sinister, it struck the very soul of her being.

His laughter waned. "Kill the Black Wolf, or you will suffer."

The truth of what he said washed over her in waves of emotion. Sickened, she ran, his shouts trailing after her to her own rooms. Even when she slammed her heavy door shut, she heard him, her mind echoing his threats over and over.

She covered her ears, yet the sound of his voice persisted. "No," she screamed. "No."

Dwight rolled over, the stones that cut into his back making him grumble. It had been a long while since he had slept upon the ground, and he longed for the comfort of his own bed. When sleep did come, dreams plagued him, causing Dwight to rouse and stare at the night sky that peeked through the canopy of trees. Visions of Kolyn haunted him even when awake, and restful sleep was not easy to come by.

"I'll have you yet, my Kolyn. I'll not be denied what I've been promised."

That said, he once again closed his eyes, though sleep never did take his thoughts from the MacGregor. Anger warmed him when the cold, forest earth should have chilled him. Like a criminal, he crept into the village, hiding his face from any who might recognize him. He no longer wore the MacGregor plaid with pride—no colors graced him at all. He was a man without a clan, without a family. Without Kolyn.

"I'll not be denied."

Dwight knew if he was patient he would find an opportunity. Then he would have Kolyn. Until then, he would continue to follow her, to watch her. Then he would seize her. She would learn that Dwight MacDougal was not a man to be scorned.

* * *

"Well, so far we haven't heard a peep out of our MacGregor. Do you think she actually took to heart what I said?"

Geoffrey looked up from the pint of ale he studied. He shrugged. "Could be, Ian. She'd be smart if she did." Silently, he prayed she had. He felt guilty. He had discovered who Kolyn MacGregor really was and had not told Ian. Many times he thought of their meeting—of her soft voice, her heather scent, her flaming red hair. He couldn't blame Ian for having fallen for her when she was here. No man could be immune to such beauty.

Kolyn's tears had haunted him, tearing at his tough warrior heart, softening him to the point of weakness. Was she really disappointed he had not killed her? What made her so sad?

"You certainly have been a moody sort lately, Geoff. What's been on your mind?"

Geoffrey pulled his thoughts back from the dangerous ground they were on. "Moody? Me?" Geoffrey feigned hurt, trying to change the subject. "And what about you, my friend? Sulking about like a wounded puppy, you are. It's time you forgot the woman."

This brought a frown to Ian's face, where only moments before a smile had lurked. "I can't, Geoff."

"Why not?"

Ian ran his hand over the night stubble of his chin. "I don't know."

Geoffrey asked the one question he had avoided. "Do you love her?"

Dark eyes looked at him, filled with emotion Geoffrey rarely saw, causing his own guilt to magnify.

"I think I do love her."

"You lads are much too serious-lookin'," Leslie said, interrupting their conversation. "You need another drink."

She turned to Ian and slid onto his lap. "Perhaps you need Leslie t' put a smile on your face?"

Ian pushed her from him with gentle persistence. "Not tonight, Leslie."

Leslie's lower lip pouted, and she leaned forward, slowly unbuttoning her blouse to allow Ian a better view of her breasts.

"I know Leslie can make you feel good, Ian," she whispered huskily.

Something caught Ian's eye and he reached out to touch it. He noted Leslie's smile as his long fingers plied between her breast, but her smile disappeared when she saw he was looking at the ring she wore on a string about her neck.

"What's this, Leslie?"

She shrugged and tugged on the string to get the ring back from Ian. "Just somethin' I found."

"You found this?"

He had not intended his words to sound doubtful. Leslie's look turned nervous. "Aye, I found it. Do you want t' buy it?"

Ian nodded and produced enough coin to prompt Leslie to take it off. He turned toward the fire for better light. He recognized the ring of the MacGregor. Leslie giggled and put her money away. Satisfied, she turned to leave.

"Where did you get this, Leslie?"

"I told you. I found it." She sounded defensive.

"Where," Ian repeated, trying to be patient, "did you find it?"

"It's mine. I had a right t' sell it."

Leslie backed off a step or two, and Ian gentled his look as well as his tone. "It was yours. Now it's mine, and you get to keep the money, Leslie. I just want to know where you *found* it."

"What's the matter, Ian?" Geoffrey too felt Ian's change of mood. A dangerous mood. He reached out for the ring, and Ian placed it in his hand.

Leslie spoke up. "That girl . . . Lynn. She left it behind. Hid under her bedding. I figured it was mine since she never came back for it."

"Lynn," Ian said.

Geoffrey stared down at the ring of the chief of the Clan MacGregor. *Bloody hell.*

Ian didn't say anything else. He just stood and left. Geoffrey followed right behind.

"What are you goin' to do?"

Ian stopped, his hand resting on the pommel of his saddle. "I suspected it was she when the storeroom was robbed, but I've *known* for certain since the day we rode to Gregor Castle. Yet I still don't know what to do."

"You knew?" Geoffrey's shock was apparent. Then he laughed.

"What's so funny?" Ian frowned, but Geoffrey's laughter did not stop.

"You bloody well could have told me. I've been feeling damn guilty about not telling you."

"Then why the hell didn't you tell me?" Ian tried to be angry with his friend but couldn't. Then he too laughed. Long and hard. "That woman has turned us both into fools."

Geoffrey agreed, but a seriousness claimed his good nature. "She did what she thought she had to do."

This brought Ian around to face Geoffrey straight on, his gold eyes questioning. "What do you mean?"

Geoffrey swallowed hard, not liking the feelings inside him. It was strange for him to take her side against Ian's. But he would not back down. "Damn it, man. She did no less than you or I would do in the same situation. This feud has been laid upon her. Look at her lands— they're in sad condition. The lass knows nothin' but hate. What do you expect from her?"

"I would expect her not to sleep with me to kill me."

"You look unharmed to me."

"She tried three times to kill me, and you

think that's all right?" Ian looked fierce.

"She's a persistent lass, I'll say that."

The fierceness vanished, and Ian laughed. "Bloody persistent!"

"Aye." Geoffrey laughed with him. "And mighty comely too."

Ian turned serious again. "I can't get her from my mind, Geoff. She lives with me day and night, every blessed minute."

"Go see her, Ian."

"And say what? She's made a fool of me. She's made a slave of me! I no longer have control of my will. I'll be damned before I go see her."

Geoffrey did not reply, but let Ian think of his own foolishness.

"I'm already damned," Ian said finally.

Chapter Twenty

The fire had burned low, and the room lay cast in shadows and darkness. Kolyn did not move to stoke the fire. She sat huddled in her chair. Waiting.

It was clear to her now what she had to do. She couldn't stay. Emmett was mad. Where she would go, what she would do, she didn't know. Only that she must go.

Tears started fresh, her thoughts moving to Andrew. She couldn't risk taking Andrew with her. It would be difficult enough without him and to take him would place him in danger. He would be safer with Father McCloud.

Determination swept through Kolyn, and she brushed her tears away. She had cried too much lately. It was time to take her life into her own hands, to stop Emmett.

Kolyn stood and picked up the small tapestry bag she had packed earlier. Second thoughts, even now, and fear caused her tenacity to lag, but she drew a deep, cleansing breath and crossed to the door. She opened it. The hall was dark and quiet. She stepped out. Instantly, her heart began to pound against her chest, making it difficult to breathe.

Each step seemed to take forever, the long hallway going on and on. The stairwell loomed before her, the single torch on the wall sconce casting shadows over the stone steps. Her legs were shaking and threatened to buckle as she stepped down, but she worked her way along using the cold wall as support. She reached the bottom, the huge double doors of the back entrance only a few feet away.

Slipping through the entrance, she carefully made her way through the castle grounds to the village, each noise, each shifting shadow, each imagined danger stretching her nerves to the edge. Kolyn slipped past the cottages, her heart stopping when dogs barked in alarm. She thought she would never make it through the village, the manor, and small cluster of stone homes.

One last glance over her shoulder and she bid all she had known in her life farewell, then ran across the open meadows and disappeared into the safety of the forest. Taking a moment, she crouched down to gather her thoughts and catch her breath. She pulled her plaid tighter about her shoulders, the chill that shook her from the fear in her heart, not the night's cold. Kolyn closed her eyes to think. To decide what her next move should be.

"You should not be wandering out alone, lass. 'Tis dangerous."

Kolyn started at Dwight's voice, his presence the very thing she feared. She tried to gather her courage and wits. "It seems my home has turned into a prison. I thought it best to leave, Dwight. Do not stand in my way."

He laughed, the sound sending a chill over her. She looked for an escape.

"There'll be no one t' rescue you this time, Kolyn."

Suddenly, anger saved her from the fear. "I need no one to rescue me, Dwight."

"I've risked much, lass." His voice was soft, almost apologetic. "I'll not leave without you."

"You will," she said in her most defiant voice. "Now."

"I cannot."

A thousand thoughts rushed across her mind. He was no longer reasonable. She didn't know what to do. She studied his face, obscured by darkness. Yet she saw enough to see the emotion etched upon it.

"Do not do this," she said softly.

Pain filled his eyes. "I'll not hurt you, lass. I love you."

"Dwight," she choked out, "you are hurting

me more than you can ever imagine."

"I'll be good t' you and you can learn t' love me."

It was a statement, yet Kolyn heard the question in it. He wanted her to say she could love him. "Never," she whispered.

Dwight stepped closer and grabbed her by the arms. "Do not say that."

"Never," she said louder. "Never!"

His grip tightened. "You *can* love me, Kolyn. You will."

Dwight leaned down, his lips seeking hers. Kolyn turned away, but his hand caught her chin and forced her to look back at him. His eyes were angry.

"Do not turn away from me again."

"Or what?" she challenged, refusing to give in to her fear.

He forced his kiss on her, but she clenched her teeth against his searching tongue. When he finally intruded into her mouth, she bit down. Dwight yelled and pulled away.

Kolyn shoved him with all her strength. He stumbled back. She tasted his blood. She ran.

It was too dark to see, the cloud-covered moon giving little to no light to guide her. Instinct placed her steps, taking her away from Dwight. Suddenly, arms reached out and pulled her off her feet. A hand clamped over her mouth to keep her cries silent, a strong arm held her securely.

Dwight ran by, then stopped, standing so

close she could hear his heavy breathing. He looked about, staring right into the darkness that hid Kolyn from him. She struggled against the man who held her, but to no avail. After a moment, Dwight went on.

The man lifted Kolyn and carried her away. They came to a horse and he whirled Kolyn around. Before she could mutter a sound, he stuffed a filthy rag into her mouth, then tied her hands. He lifted her into the saddle, then climbed on behind her.

As they rode back through the village Kolyn tried to get a look at her captor. She twisted around, but his face was cloaked in darkness by the hat he wore, the brim pulled low over his brow. He forced her back around.

When they arrived in the MacGregor court-yard Kolyn became confused. Then afraid.

She was hoisted upon his shoulder like a sack of potatoes. She kicked and screamed, but to no avail. The man took her inside and up the stairs. He put her down and untied her.

As soon as her hands were free she swung at the man, his hat flying off as he ducked her fist. She stilled when she saw his face.

"Did no' think you'd be seein' me, Lady MacGregor?"

Kolyn snapped her mouth shut and tried to gather her composure. "No. I guess I hadn't."

"He's been quite informative, dear sister."

She turned to her brother. It shouldn't surprise her so that he was the culprit behind this whole matter. She chose to say nothing to him. He just smiled at her silence.

"How fortunate for me that Donald came to our village, and even more, that he saw *you*. He was very helpful so I asked him to stay. He's already proved quite useful, wouldn't you say?"

Again, she did not reply.

"You interfered in me business an' took me dog."

"Yes," Emmett drawled. "Donald wasn't very happy about that, Kolyn. Perhaps next time, you'll think twice before you interrupt a man doing business."

"It's not a business!" Kolyn felt her anger return as she thought of the poor dog and the abuse this man gave him. "It's a cruelty, and he should be whipped for his treatment of animals."

"Bloody bitch," Donald sneered, stepping closer to her.

Kolyn moved away, but found herself trapped between her brother and his new conspirator. She turned to Emmett.

"Tell him to get out," she demanded.

He did not. He patted the bed for her to sit beside him. She sat. Emmett took her hand into his, his touch surprisingly gentle.

"You ran away. I told you not to."

The hair on the back of Kolyn's neck rose. She tried to pull her hand back, but he held her tight, though he made no attempt to hurt her. She did not trust he wouldn't.

"You give me so little choice, Emmett. I fear your madness."

"Madness?" he said, his voice soft, belying the hard anger that filled his eyes.

"Aye," she whispered, wishing she had not said it.

Emmett looked at Donald, who stood close by. Too close for Kolyn's comfort. "She thinks me mad."

His and Donald's laughter echoed about the room, mocking her, robbing her of what little composure she had. She stared down at her lap, unable to face the madness that consumed her brother.

"What should I do with you, Kolyn?" He reached out and cupped her chin, forced her gaze to meet his. "You know I must teach you a lesson."

She swallowed hard, trying to think, but couldn't. She blinked back tears, refusing to allow herself to cry. "You needn't worry, brother. I can see now it was hopeless to try and run. I'll not do it again."

This made him grin, but his head shook back and forth anyway. "I know you won't try it again, but that's not enough. You must pay for your actions."

A loud ringing in her ears deafened her, and she fought the terror that rose inside her. "What . . ." Her voice faded. "What will you do?"

"What do you suggest, Donald?"

Kolyn too looked at the man, waiting for his answer. He was a coarse, ugly fellow, something she hadn't noticed upon their first encounter. She had been too engrossed in saving the dog to pay much attention to the man's appearance. But now she did. His slow smile made her cringe.

"I could beat her," he offered, his hand clenching into a fist as he thought of it. He licked his lips as if the mere thought brought him pleasure and delight.

The grip on Kolyn's hand tightened. Slowly, Emmett pulled her closer. His breath was hot on her face and she thought she would be sick.

"Should I let him beat you?"

She knew he really didn't expect an answer, so she gave none. Kolyn concentrated on keeping her fear under control.

Emmett whispered in her ear. "I think I will."

Kolyn struggled to pull away, but he jerked her head back with a handful of hair. "You may beat her, Donald. And I want you to make sure she loses the bastard she carries inside her."

His cold eyes looked to Donald. "Make certain she loses the brat," he said again. "I want her to know better than to cross me."

"No," Kolyn cried out, tears choking her. "You can't, Emmett!"

He looked down at her, his face so hard and

unfeeling Kolyn knew she could never reach him. All compassion was gone. All feelings of kinship and love were destroyed by hatred. Emmett placed his hand on her growing belly.

"Do you want to feel the bastard child Lord Blackstone has put in my sister?"

She squirmed to get away from his hands. Even more so from Donald's. They laughed as they touched the roundness.

"Kill it, Donald." Emmett all but threw her from him.

Kolyn landed in a heap on the floor at Donald's feet. He kicked her.

"Do not," Emmett interrupted him, "mark her face. My sister still has a promise to keep. Don't you, dearest Kolyn?"

She crawled over to the side of his bed. "Please, Emmett. For God's sake, you cannot kill my baby."

"And why not?"

He'd asked the question so casually, as if he honestly couldn't see any reason why not. She was horrified by what she saw. "Please, you cannot."

Emmett seemed to like her begging. "You should have thought of this before you went against my will."

"I promise, I'll never cross you again."

"Never?"

She shook her head to stress her promise. "Never again."

A gleam of satisfaction came to his face.

Fela Dawson Scott

"Why do you beg for the life of this bastard child, Kolyn? I would think you'd like to be rid of it."

Tears spilled onto her cheeks, blurring the vision of her brother's twisted soul. "'Tis but an innocent child within me, Emmett. He knows nothing of this hatred. Why must the child pay for my sin? I cannot let you harm my baby."

"How noble," Emmett snickered. Then he pushed her away. "Beat her, Donald."

Kolyn screamed as Donald dragged her across the floor.

"Do not harm the brat," Emmett called out. "As long as the bastard and his brother live, she will do as I say."

Kolyn remained huddled in the corner of her room for hours. Her tears had long dried up, the pain eased into a dull throb. Donald had done as Emmett had said. He hadn't marked her face. Her body had suffered his abuse, yet she thanked God her baby had not been harmed. She had been a fool risking Andrew's safety and that of her unborn child.

Gently, she rubbed the swell of her stomach. She wondered for the first time if she would have a boy or a girl. A small flutter of joy stirred her heart. She had been a mother for five years, yet this would be her first child to come from within her. She recalled Blair giving birth to Andrew. Kolyn had cut the cord and cleaned the blood from him. She had loved him with all her heart from that first moment of his life.

She thought of the strangeness of life. She had been the one to take Andrew as her son, only to give life to his half brother. If God worked in mysterious ways, she wondered at his purpose.

With a pained slowness, Kolyn stood, her legs numb from sitting on the floor. She found the comfort of her bed, but experienced a sudden loneliness as she hugged a pillow to her. She longed for something, but that something remained unclear. She didn't have time to give it much thought as sleep overtook her.

Andrew played happily with the other children. His laughter drifted to Kolyn as she stood at the chapel window and watched him. Her heart ached with missing him.

"You look a little pale, lass," Father McCloud said, concern etching his face. He took Kolyn's hand into his own and patted it, fatherly love shining in his eyes.

Kolyn smiled, though she knew her attempt wasn't as convincing as she would have liked it to be. "I'm fine, Father."

"Drew misses you. He's been here near three weeks. Can't you take him home with you now?"

"No," she said a little too quickly, causing the father's gray brows to raise in alarm. "Not yet."

"What is it you fear, Kolyn?" He led her to a

pew and they sat, his hand still holding hers in comfort.

"Time will work things out, Father. We must be patient. Then I can take Drew home with me. Believe me, I'll not stay away from him a moment longer than needed."

He patted her hand again. "I know that. Just promise me you'll come to me if you're in trouble."

She knew his kindness and generosity were unlimited, but even Father McCloud could not help her. To involve him would only place him in danger as well. She needed him more to care for Andrew. The father was the only one she could trust with her son.

"You have my promise. Don't worry so. I'll be fine. I'm just tired is all."

Andrew ran into the chapel and crawled into Kolyn's lap. She winced slightly, but hugged him to her. A slight desperation grabbed her heart, and she thought she might cry. She loved him so much. She could not imagine life without him. She kissed his head and brushed back the thick hank of hair that hung down into his face. His cheeks were red from playing and his eyes sparkled.

Could she ever provide him a normal life?

This question haunted her.

"I'll pray for you, Kolyn."

"Thank you, Father McCloud. I need all the help I can get."

Andrew looked up at her, his eyes full of love.

"I'll say a prayer for you too, Mommy."

Her throat tightened with pride. "I love you, Drew."

"I love you too," he whispered, his dimples appearing.

Kolyn would not let anything hurt her son. She would do anything to protect him.

"I promise you," she said softly, determination stiffening her words, "that nothing will ever separate us. Nothing."

He reached up and touched his mother's cheek. "I will never leave you."

"I know, Drew. And I'll never leave you."

"I'll take good care of him, Kolyn," said the cleric.

"I know you will."

"Remember, my child," Father McCloud said with tears in his eyes, "let your heart guide you through your troubles. It will never fail you."

"Sometimes my heart is filled with an ugliness I cannot understand. How can I follow such grief?"

"I do not believe this of you, Kolyn Mac-Gregor. Your heart is good. You should never doubt that."

"I'll try to remember what you've said, Father."

"Trust your heart and you'll not go wrong."

Chapter Twenty-one

Kolyn closed the door to her bedroom chambers and locked it. The room was dark, the fire having burned low. She crossed to the stone fireplace and stirred the coals into flames, then added wood to it. A cool breeze from her window made her pull her plaid tighter about her, the woolen nightgown she wore thin from wear. She wondered who had opened her window, the drapes moving with the stiff March breeze. She closed the leaded panes and pulled the coverings tight across it.

When she turned about, Ian Blackstone stood before her, the surprise nearly causing her to faint. She swayed, and his strong arms reached out to support her. Kolyn could smell the musky scent as he pulled her close. Nothing she had dreamed of could have prepared her for the reality of him. The need within her immediately roused from its deep sleep, the sensation so powerful she could think of nothing else. She should hate him. But she didn't. She should kill him. But she wouldn't.

His lips came close, the flesh so delicate in contrast to his lean, clean-shaven jaw. She wanted to touch him, to taste of the lips she saw.

"What have you to say for yourself, *Kolyn?*"

She swallowed, uncertain what he meant. Her mind was not following any coherent trail. Suddenly, she understood. Shock struck her like lightning across a dark sky, causing her to pull back and twist free of his grip.

"You risk much coming here," she said.

This seemed to amuse Ian. "Aye. But I couldn't stay away any longer. I wanted to see for myself if what I learned was the truth. I can no longer deny it."

"You've seen the truth. Now go."

The tone of her words told Ian she was getting angry. This made the fire in him return. "I'll go when I damned well please."

"Your coming here will only make matters worse."

"Worse?" Ian said. "How can they get worse?"

Kolyn laughed, though her laughter seemed sad, even fearful. "Believe me, Ian Blackstone. You would not want to know."

"Are you going to tell me more of your lies, Kolyn?"

"No," she said softly. "I've no need to lie anymore."

Ian felt some sense of victory. "Why did you make love to me? Why did you come to me so soft and sweet? Was it to stick a knife in my heart while I slept?"

She was quiet a moment, uncertainty crossing her features. He watched her, wanting to know, yet holding his breath in fear.

"Yes. I made love to you to kill you," she replied softly.

No lies to soothe his ego, no lies to ease the pain in his heart. The hurt he felt caught him off guard, leaving him vulnerable to her. At that moment he hated himself more than he hated her.

The fact that her words had caused him pain was plain enough to see, and it took Kolyn's breath away. She stepped closer, her hand reaching out to caress his face, to erase the hurt from it.

He grabbed her hand, as if her touch would be unbearable. His fingers crushed hers, but she ignored it. Dark golden eyes searched her soul, sapping her strength and purpose. Only the need remained. She put her arm about his neck and stood on her toes. His breath was hot on her face, his body hard against hers.

Ian twisted his hand into her hair and pulled her head back. "Bitch," he sneered.

"Yes," she whispered, sliding her leg up his before curling it around him.

He moaned and kissed the expanse of neck before him, his hand now cradling her head gently. Ian worked his way up until his lips claimed hers, freeing her captured hand to pull her closer to him. She felt his need hard against her own softness causing the heat within her body to rise.

"Kill me now and be done with it," Ian moaned in desperation.

"Later." Kolyn pulled his lips back to hers, then pulled her nightgown up. Ian lifted her against the wall and took her, fierce and wanting. Angry and hurt. Never had she needed anything more, her own desire unbridled and demanding.

When Ian's heavy breathing quieted, Kolyn continued to hold him. She kissed the place on his temple where his pulse beat strong, but he stiffened, then moved away. Without Ian holding her, she felt chilled. She stepped back to the fire.

Finally, Ian spoke. "You've cast a wicked spell on me, Kolyn MacGregor, and I've no way to fight it."

His choice of words made Kolyn nervous. "I've done nothing to you, Ian."

This only seemed to bring back the anger to his eyes. "Done nothing to me! You've been a royal pain in the ass, stealing and raiding my property. Not to mention the *three* times you've tried to kill me. That certainly isn't nothing."

"You owed me all that."

"Owed you?"

It came down to the very thing she wanted to avoid. "Yes, for the grief and pain you've caused my family."

"And what of my grief and pain?"

This question didn't hold the power and tone of the previous one. It was an honest, forthright question. But Kolyn didn't know how to answer it. She knew only her situation. Before her stood the man she had sworn to kill. The father of the child she carried in her womb.

She considered all this, but one thing stood dominant in the chaos of her mind. This was the man who had banished his pregnant wife to die in the streets. What could she expect from him if he were to discover she was with child? Her fear was too great to overcome.

"Did you feel grief when Blair died?" This came from nowhere. Even Kolyn wondered at the words she heard coming from her mouth. Instantly, she regretted it.

"What do you know of Blair?"

Ian's voice was quiet, belying the emotions that twisted his gut into a million knots. A cold chill claimed his heart, putting a deadly edge to the anger that lay barely beneath the surface of control.

"I know you banished her to die in the streets like a dog. Did you think of the pain you caused her? What of the child she was carrying? Did you grieve at all for your son?"

Shock waves surged in every direction. Never before had anyone said she had had a boy. A son—a dead son. Many years of guilt bewildered him, shattered his heart. He couldn't move. He couldn't breathe. He couldn't speak.

Kolyn waited for an answer, but none came. Was he so indifferent? Disappointment crashed in, causing anger to rescue her from the moment of weakness.

"You bastard," she mumbled, tears scorching her eyes. "You unfeeling bastard!"

She turned to wipe at the tears that spilled down her cheeks. When she looked back, Ian was moving toward her, a strange look on his face. She shrank back from him, fear taking her into its grip.

"Don't touch me."

He stopped, but then reached out and grabbed her wrist. "Come here, Kolyn."

His voice was hard, unfeeling. She shook her head no.

Ian forced her to him. "Come here," he repeated.

He gave her no choice, and she submitted.

Without saying anything, he whirled her about, her back against him. Slowly, his hands slid over her belly. Back and forth, feeling the roundness of it. Suddenly, she understood what he wanted.

She turned to face him. His expression terrified her.

He let her go, then left without another word.

Kolyn stared at the window in horror. Ian knew she was going to have his baby. Then she felt the hurt. *He didn't care.*

Ian scaled the wall even faster than when he had entered Kolyn's bedroom. Never had he been so close to losing total control as he had the moment he discovered Kolyn to be pregnant. Yet he didn't know if he was happy, sad, angry, or devastated. Too many conflicting emotions, too many memories cascaded one upon another, leaving no room for clear thinking. He had no choice but to leave. He had to get away from the very thing that caused him to struggle with each breath he took.

Once he was clear of the manor, he stopped. What could he do? The woman he was infatuated with wanted to kill him. He was to be a father, but the mother couldn't be trusted the moment his back was turned. Ian saw it in her eyes . . . she feared him. But it wasn't the challenges he had fought with her brothers and father that caused it. She thought he'd killed Blair and their child with his callousness. That was what she was afraid of.

"I'll not let you touch my bonny Kolyn again."

Ian whirled about, tense at the sudden danger.

Dwight MacDougal stepped from the dark

shadows. "'Tis time for you t' die. I'll not let your evil touch her."

He lunged at Ian, but Ian was prepared and swiftly pulled his own claymore in defense. The sound of metal hitting metal was loud in the silent night, rousing the dogs of the village to their fight. Soon lights appeared and shouts went up.

Dwight paused in his assault, then backed down. "Another time, Black Wolf."

He disappeared as fast as he had appeared. Ian even wondered if he had imagined the man, but the sweat on his brow told him he'd been real enough. He had heard Dwight MacDougal was banished from MacGregor land, and this confirmed it to be fact. At least the man knew when to leave.

Someone shouted not far away, and Ian determined it was time for him to leave as well. It wouldn't do to be caught on MacGregor land himself.

Kolyn stood before the fire watching the flames dance about the wood, licking and devouring the pulp with its orange tongue. The heat warmed her skin, but her heart remained cold. No thoughts or feelings seemed to touch her mind. She was lost to the numbness that took her.

Without giving thought to what she was doing, Kolyn walked from her room and made her way down the long corridor to where

Emmett slept. She went inside. It was dark, but she knew where the large bed was and crossed to stand by it. She just stood and stared down at her brother.

"Are you going to smother me in my sleep?"

She didn't start at his sudden question. His eyes came open, and he grinned at her, the ever-present sarcasm apparent even in the darkness.

"Should I?"

"Perhaps," Emmett replied, shrugging his shoulders indifferently. "Perhaps you would be doing me a great favor, little sister."

"Aye," she murmured, still unable to shake the numbness, the near-paralysis that held her. "Perhaps it would be best for us all, Emmett."

Emmett watched her, uncertainty showing in his eyes. "You couldn't kill your enemy while he slept. What makes you think you could kill your very own dear brother?"

"Perhaps I like my enemy more than I like you."

His eyes squinted, warning Kolyn of the perilous mood he'd descended into. "Do you love your enemy, Kolyn?"

She considered this. Yes, she did. Yet she also feared him. How could one love and fear at the same time? "I fear him," was all she offered.

"As well you should," Emmett sneered. Then he grabbed her arms and pulled her closer, his face nearly touching hers. "Do you love him?"

"I . . ." Kolyn's mouth went dry, and suddenly, her dullness disappeared. "I don't think that matters—whether I do or don't. I must kill him, mustn't I?"

"Yes." Emmett pushed her away in disgust. "You must."

This time, Kolyn laughed, and Emmett's eyes got thinner with anger. "I think I could kill *you*, sweet brother. After all, it is what you want, isn't it? To die?"

Whatever possessed Kolyn, she didn't know. She only knew that the men in her life were pushing her toward lunacy.

"God help me, Emmett. God help me."

When Kolyn walked away, Emmett shouted after her. "God won't help you, Kolyn. We're on our own, you and I. God's forsaken this house."

Kolyn paused, her hand upon the handle of the door. "Then I shall do what I must do without his guidance."

"You do that, sister."

She opened the door.

"Next time you go to see Drew at Father McCloud's . . ." He paused to give her time to comprehend what he was implying. "Give him my love."

She tried to ease the sudden dryness in her throat. "I . . ." Her voice cracked. "I will."

Once again, Emmett had won their battle of wits, had assured her that the threat to her Andrew was real. Kolyn returned to her rooms.

Chapter Twenty-two

Ian reclined in the chair, stretching his long legs out in front of him. He studied the fire intensely, yet his eyes did not see the orange and red flames. Instead, his mind's eye saw the flame of her hair, the flash of her green eyes, the blush upon her cheeks.

"I see you've been out. Is everything all right, son?"

He turned to his mother as she entered the great chamber. "I thought I'd better take care of some unfinished business," he said. "I couldn't find excuses any longer."

She took a chair next to him. "Would this unfinished business be Kolyn MacGregor?"

"Aye," Ian confirmed. "I went to see her tonight."

"And . . ." Ainsley prompted.

Ian felt a renewed pain as he recalled their encounter. "It was a disaster." He dropped his head into his hands, his misery complete.

"Do you love her, Ian?"

His mother's question was simple, yet the situation wasn't. Ian tried to explain that. "At the moment, that seems to be irrelevant. Too many things complicate this relationship."

This word struck him as funny, and he laughed. "Relationship. It's not even that much."

"What is it that is so difficult for you? Is it that she is the MacGregor?"

"That's one of the problems," he admitted. "She hates me and she wants me dead. That's another *difficulty*."

Ainsley seemed to think on this. "I think if Kolyn MacGregor wanted you dead, you would be dead."

Ian's brows tugged together. "What makes you think that?"

"If she wanted you dead, son, she would have killed you the night you two were together."

Ian brushed his hair back and looked directly at his mother. "You always had a way of knowing what went on in my life, perhaps better than I do myself."

"It's part of being a mother."

Her soft words made him wonder what Kolyn thought about the baby she carried. His baby.

"Do you think Kolyn MacGregor is happy to be the mother of my child?"

Ainsley was truly surprised. She gasped. But she quickly recovered and leaned over to cup her son's face in her hands. "You are going to be a father?"

"Aye," Ian said, feeling the delight for the first time. "I am going to be a father."

"Then you must marry the lass." She said it so matter-of-factly, so simply.

"Marry her?" Ian was in shock. With so much trouble in their way, he hadn't given marriage thought.

"Of course, Ian. You must marry her and soon. I want to know my grandchild. You will want your child with you."

"She'll not marry me, Mother. It's the last thing she'll want to do."

Ainsley frowned. "Do you know this?"

"No," he admitted, but he couldn't see it any other way. He recalled too easily the look on her face. The fear in her eyes. Kolyn wouldn't want to marry him. "She hadn't even intended for me to know about the baby."

"The poor child," his mother muttered sadly.

Ian shook his head in amazement. "You always seem to feel sorry for the lass."

"Think of it," she said, her eyes wide with worry. "She's your sworn enemy, Ian. Her clan would not understand her carrying your child. She must be extremely frightened."

Guilt assaulted Ian. "I hadn't thought how

Fela Dawson Scott

Kolyn must be feeling. I've been too immersed in my own misery."

"You've allowed Blair's death to fill your life for over five years. It's time you stop feeling sorry for yourself and do something good for yourself. Marry the lass and bring your baby home."

"What if she does not want to marry me?"

His mother got a determined look in her eyes. "See that she has no choice. It's up to you, Ian, to see that the right decision is made for the child's sake. Do not take no for an answer."

"Are you saying I should force her to marry me?" Ian knew his surprise was apparent.

"Yes," she said calmly. "Carry her away by force if you must."

"Mother," Ian said with as much seriousness as he could muster. "You really are devious."

She smiled and squeezed his hand. "I'm going to be a grandmother, and I intend to see that you two stubborn children don't destroy that."

"I'll do my best, but I can't speak for Kolyn. She may not be as easy to convince."

"That too will come with time."

Ian squeezed her hand in turn. "I hope so, Mother. I truly hope so."

He watched his mother stand and walk to the door. She turned back to him. "You bring home the bride and I'll take care of everything else."

"Perhaps I should let you bring home the bride." His smile returned. "And I'll take care of everything else."

324

"Bring her home, Ian." Again she started to leave the room, again she stopped. "She's very smart, Ian. And brave."

"Why do you say that?"

"To do what she did was quite clever," she replied in amazement. "It's not easy to get you alone, without Geoffrey watching you."

"Yes," Ian mused. "I suppose it was."

He watched his mother leave. Ian wondered how difficult the task at hand would be. Kolyn MacGregor would not fall into his arms grateful that he wanted to marry her. Most likely, she would not be happy about it at all.

This made him laugh out loud. *That* was an understatement. She would be mad as hell. But he wouldn't let his own temper interfere with what he had to do. This time, he would keep it under control. This time, he wouldn't lose his baby.

The old pain ripped him open, but a new joy fluttered forward to mend it. He was going to have a child, perhaps a son. He would never forgive himself for what he did to Blair. He'd killed his child without even knowing he had done so. This time, he knew about the child and he wouldn't let the woman go. He couldn't.

His mother's question came back to him. Did he love her? He didn't know if what he felt for her was love, but he did love the child she carried. They had had so little time together, and most of that time was filled with deception and hate. Could they overcome all the obstacles ahead of them? One thing was certain. Ian wanted to be a good father to his child. Tomorrow, he would bring home his bride . . . with or without her consent.

"You're insane," Geoffrey cried as they reined their mounts to a halt.

Ian looked out on the village, the Mac-Gregor castle just beyond it. He smiled at his friend's comment. "Aye, I've gone mad for the woman."

"Do you think there will be trouble, Ian?" Geoffrey looked about him nervously.

"Don't look so worried, my friend."

"You have gone mad," Geoffrey exclaimed. "We're ridin' into MacGregor territory in broad daylight to ask your sworn enemy to marry you. What has possessed you, Ian?"

He twisted back to glance at his friend as he urged his mount into a trot. "She's with child, and I'm going to be a father."

Geoffrey just sat for a moment, taking in what Ian had said. Then with a holler, he caught up to him. "She's goin' to have a baby?"

"Aye." Ian grinned widely. "And I'm taking my bride home, where we'll be married this afternoon. I'd be honored if you'd stand up with me, my friend."

"My honor, Ian. But what if the lass says no?"

Ian slowed his mount down as they reached

the edge of the village. "I'll not be denied my child, Geoff. Keep your sword ready. We shall take her by force if necessary."

Geoffrey nodded, his look serious once again as his hand rested upon the hilt of his claymore. Side by side they rode through the village streets, drawing curious stares or sending people into their homes in panic.

Ian rode up to the manor door, all of the MacGregor men having let him pass without trouble. He could see the fear in their eyes. None had the courage to challenge his passage. He dismounted and walked up the steps. Geoffrey remained on his horse, alert and ready. Ian pounded on the heavy wooden door.

"Tell the Lady Kolyn that Ian Blackstone is here to see her." Ian's voice rang clear across the courtyard. He knocked on the door again.

The door opened, and Ian walked in. Geoffrey moved to the doorway and remained only a few feet away.

A servant cowered nearby, and Ian turned his attention to him. "Tell the lady I am here."

"I am well aware that you are here."

Ian looked up to see Kolyn standing at the head of the stairs. Slowly, she walked down. He was surprised to see her dressed so simply, but as he looked around he understood. The castle was in grave disrepair, like the lands. For the first time he understood her motive, her need to feed her people. He was shamed he had stood in her way at all.

"What do you want, Lord Blackstone?"

Her voice was low, confusion and hurt apparent in her tone. Ian felt his heart go out to her. "I've come to take you home, lass."

"My home is here. You've wasted your time."

She turned to leave, but his words stopped her. "I intend to be a father to the bastard child you carry. I'll not be denied what is mine."

Kolyn stood, for the longest time, with her back turned to Ian. Then she turned, slowly. His gaze met green fire.

"*You* will not be denied. How dare you come into my home and declare such a thing?"

"'Tis my right," Ian said calmly.

"What makes you think that?"

"It's my child," he explained, "'Tis my right."

Kolyn walked down the rest of the way and stood before him, her eyes angry and proud. "It isn't your baby, my lord. So go home."

He wanted to grab her, to make her tell the truth. But he didn't. "You've no need to lie, Kolyn. I know it's my seed inside you."

"How could you know that?" Kolyn felt the anger seething inside her, his foolish demands an insult to her tender emotions.

Ian lowered his voice so she was the only one to hear his words. "You came to me a virgin. I'll not forget that."

She felt renewed shame at what she had done, all in the name of revenge. Now her worst nightmare was coming true. Ian wanted to take his child from her. Kolyn could not bear that.

"But there have been other men since that night I stayed with you, Lord Blackstone. I couldn't say who the father is."

Ian merely laughed, the sound soft, saying as much as his words. "I don't believe you, lass."

His gaze met hers, taking her breath away, stilling her heart.

"I will not let you take my child." She ran up the stairs and Ian followed her.

Before she reached the top, he caught her. "I've come to marry you, Kolyn MacGregor, and I'll not leave without you."

"Let me go." She tried to twist free of his grip. "I'd never marry you."

"You've no choice, lass."

His persistent smile irritated her beyond description. She wanted to scratch it from his handsome face—to erase the dimples that reminded her so much of Andrew. She was afraid. Afraid of herself as much as of him.

"Do you think you can just carry me off and marry me against my will?"

"Aye," Ian said seriously. "I plan to do just that."

Her eyes narrowed. "You wouldn't dare?"

"Of course I would."

She looked around for help but no one seemed to be about.

"There'll be no one to rescue you, Kolyn. They all seem to be afraid of me." He smiled broadly, then swept her into his arms.

"No," she screamed. "I'll not marry you!"

"Of course you will."

Ian carried her, kicking and screaming, down the stairs. His smile never faded. He handed her to Geoffrey, mounted his horse, then took her back into his arms.

When she persisted with her struggles, he whispered in her ear, "You'll hurt the baby, Kolyn."

Kolyn stilled despite her need to strike out at him.

"Do not worry. I'll be a good husband and father."

Stubbornness tilted her chin up in defiance. "You've no right to do this, Ian Blackstone. I'll never forgive you."

He looked down at her, his smile gone. "That's a decision I can live with."

Kolyn allowed herself to be ushered into Stonehaven and into a sitting room. Much like a child, Ian sat her down in a chair.

"My mother will help you dress for the wedding. I have some things to attend to, so I will see you in the chapel."

She said nothing, merely turned away from him. If he expected cooperation, he expected too much.

"I will see to everything, Ian." Lady Blackstone had entered the room, and moved to stand by Kolyn. Ian left them alone.

"Are you feeling well, Kolyn?"

It was hard to be rude to her. "I am feeling fine, despite everything."

"I'm sorry for the inconvenience and haste. But you do understand the need for that haste." She took Kolyn's hand and urged her to stand. She walked with her into her private bedchamber.

"Your son seems not to care what I think on this matter," Kolyn's words came out sounding petulant. She had not wanted them to. "It's all so sudden and confusing."

"Even when you've had plenty of time to prepare for marriage, it is still sudden and confusing, my dear. You will adjust."

Kolyn looked at her. "Will I?"

"I promise," she said, and gave her hand a reassuring squeeze. "You've brought me much joy, Kolyn. I want only happiness for you and my son."

She didn't want to like this woman, her future mother-in-law, but somehow Kolyn understood she would fail at this. "In what way have I brought you such joy, Lady Blackstone?"

"Ainsley," she corrected with a smile. "You have given life back to Ian, and you have a new life inside you. I thought I'd never become a grandmother. It suits me completely."

Tears rushed forward. Kolyn fought to keep them at bay. She didn't want to show so much emotion to a stranger, yet she couldn't help her reaction to the woman's heartfelt words. "I . . ." her voice failed. "I am grateful for your kindness."

"I had hoped you wouldn't mind wearing my wedding gown. On such short notice it was all I could think of." Ainsley motioned to the bed, where her gown lay, the shimmering white satin like fresh-fallen snow across the tapestry bed covering.

It took Kolyn's breath away. Not only the beauty of the gown, but the sentiment of Ainsley's gesture.

"I thought it would fit you perfectly." Ainsley picked it up and held it to Kolyn. "I was your size when I married."

"I think you are the same now, Lady . . ." Kolyn stopped and smiled shyly. "Ainsley. It's the prettiest dress I've ever seen."

Ainsley blushed with pride, her eyes aglow with pleasure. "Let's see what you look like." She started to help Kolyn. "Then I will fix your hair. What a lovely bride you will be."

Kolyn turned away so Ainsley wouldn't see the pain on her face, the tears that finally slipped down her cheeks. It was all wrong. She had never really spent much time dreaming of marriage and weddings . . . but it wasn't to be like this. To be forced into marriage because of the child she carried had not been part of her dream. And never had she dared to foresee she would marry her enemy.

Yet she was unusually touched by Ainsley's

apparent joy. She put the gown on and experienced a thrill of pleasure. When Ainsley had finished with her hair, she looked in the mirror. Again she felt a thrill. Never had she been so elegant. So beautiful.

A soft knock sounded. Ainsley went to the door and opened it. "We are ready."

Ainsley returned for Kolyn. Intense green eyes stared at the older woman, fear deep in their depths. She put her arms about Kolyn's shoulders and tried to comfort her.

"You'll be fine, lass. 'Tis natural to be nervous."

"Nervous?" Kolyn laughed and turned away, the sound of her laugh reflecting the very thing she talked of. "I'm near frightened to death."

Turning Kolyn about to face her, Ainsley looked straight into her eyes and said softly, "So much sorrow has befallen you. I cannot think of a more courageous lass to marry my son. He is very fortunate indeed."

It wasn't what Kolyn had expected. She found it very difficult to know what to do, what to say. So she said nothing, and followed Ainsley from the room to the chapel.

Ian was already there, Geoffrey standing by his side. It seemed fitting even to Kolyn that Geoffrey be there. Ainsley took Ian's hand and looked up at her son, pride showing in every move, every look, every word she spoke.

"Ian, you will need a ring for Kolyn. I would like you to give her my wedding ring." She pulled it from her finger, never having taken it off since her husband's death. Ainsley placed it in her son's hand.

Kolyn objected. "Ainsley, you can't give up your own ring. I do not need one."

"Of course you do, dear."

"No—"

Ainsley interrupted her before she could go on. Her eyes returned to her son. "This was your grandmother's ring, then mine. Now it will be Kolyn's. Someday, when your own daughter marries, it will be hers. I am honored to have Kolyn wear it."

A brief thought prompted Kolyn's curiosity. Why hadn't Blair been given the ring? But Kolyn had known Blair well enough to understand why. Yet she wondered that Ainsley was so willing to accept her, a total stranger and a clan enemy. This woman had a remarkable sensibility, something that Kolyn was drawn to strongly.

"Are you ready, Kolyn?"

Ian's deep, soft voice struck a thousand chords in her. She wanted to scream that she wasn't ready. Not now, not ever. But she held her tongue, not wanting to destroy the look on Ainsley's face. She granted this fierce-looking man one thing. He had an amazing mother.

A sudden and intense wave of distress overtook her, taking away all other feelings. Thoughts of Emmett and his wicked threats reminded her of the danger, both from the

Black Wolf and from Emmett himself. What would Emmett's reaction be to her wedding the man he wanted dead more than anything else in this world? Would he blame Kolyn?

She was certain of it. Silently, she said a prayer.

Chapter Twenty-three

Ian waited for his mother to say good night to Kolyn as he stood outside the doors to his own room. He wondered what Kolyn was thinking, her face having shown little expression throughout the ceremony. Only once had she hesitated, and Ian had thought she might say she wouldn't take him as her husband. Instead, she had looked at him with hurt eyes and said yes. He still felt the guilt of forcing her to marry him, yet he knew it was for the best. He would not chance losing this baby, no matter what he must do.

His mother stepped into the hallway and joined him. "She hasn't spoken two words to me since I brought her home," he said.

Ainsley put her arm about his waist. He

Fela Dawson Scott

casually put his arm over her shoulder, and
they walked down the hallway together. "She
will adjust. Give her time, Ian. She's frightened
and angry. She doesn't know us very well. It
must be quite disheartening to be in a strange
place with strange people."

"Aye," he agreed.

His mother looked up at him and smiled.
"She's a very brave lass, but you must be
patient."

Ian smiled too, admiring his mother's percep-
tive ways. "You've always seen her side with an
amazing clarity. How is that, Mother?"

"You only need to remember that there are
always two sides to everything."

He laughed. "But generally a right and wrong
side."

"This is true, but a person can be wrong and
fervently believe she is in the right. That is what
you must consider."

Ian thought on what his mother said. "Kolyn
MacGregor may be wrong in what she has
done, but in her mind she thinks she is doing
the right thing."

"Exactly," Ainsley said. "We must sympathize
with her situation. She knows nothing about
you except what her father and brothers have
conveyed, and I'm quite certain their hatred has
been her only inheritance."

Something strange occurred to Ian, and for
the first time he thought he might understand
Kolyn a little better. "It's sad to think what it

338

has been like for her. Now she is to have my baby. The child of the very man she considers her enemy."

Ainsley stopped and placed her hand upon his chest, her eyes filled with tears. "The very man that has killed her brothers and father. How can she understand such a thing?"

"I believe . . ." Ian stopped to consider what he wanted to say. "I believe she has feelings for me, that there is more than desire inside her. But she is afraid to let it show. Something keeps her from saying what is in her heart."

"She is afraid. But what has her so frightened? Is it you, Ian? That wild tale they whisper about you turning into a wolf?"

They started to walk again, her arm upon his. "I don't know. I would think she knows there is no such nonsense."

"What of Emmett?"

Every muscle in Ian's body tightened with tension. "He still lives."

"He is a cripple, a man that must hate you more than life itself. I wonder what kind of relationship she must have with her brother, the only family she has left."

"I have heard he is quite mad. Vengeful."

"Perhaps he is behind her attempts to kill you."

"You may be right, Mother." Ian had a new thought. "Do you think I have placed her in danger by this marriage?"

Ainsley looked quite distraught. "That is

something I had not thought of."

They stopped at the doors of her sitting room. Ian kissed her on the cheek. "I shall watch over her, do not worry." He turned to leave, but paused. "I love her, Mother. I thought I'd never be able to love another woman. How strange that it would be a MacGregor."

"Be patient, Ian, and she will love you in turn." She watched him walk away, then called after him. "Ian."

He stopped and waited.

"Perhaps you should not expect her to be wife to you right away."

Ian understood and grinned. "I've had another room prepared for me. I'll only say good night to my bride, though she is quite lovely and a great temptation."

Ainsley was overwhelmed with pride and love. In her heart, she knew that in time they would be happy. She went inside.

Ian did not go into his rooms right away. He stood outside the door, his mind abuzz with what he and his mother had discussed. How was he to act? What could he do to take the fear from her eyes?

He knocked. A slight, almost non-existent sound told him to enter. Kolyn sat in a chair near the fire, still dressed in Ainsley's wedding gown. She stared at her hands, and did not look up when he crossed to stand beside her.

"Is there anything you need, Kolyn?"

She shook her head.

"Mother laid out a nightgown." He pointed to the bed where it lay, but she did not look. "Shall I help you with the buttons?"

Kolyn stood, like a wooden doll, stiff and unemotional. Ian carefully plied the silk loops off each pearl button. He could smell heather and wanted to hold her close. Instead, he stepped away when he was done.

"There, I think I managed them all."

"Thank you."

"Kolyn." Ian wanted to say something to make her feel better, but he didn't know what words would accomplish the task. "If you need anything, I'll be next door."

He saw the surprise in her eyes before she masked it just as quickly as it had come. Ian reached out and ran his finger over the contour of her chin. Her flesh was soft, supple. He closed his eyes a moment to gather his purpose and deny his yearnings.

"I'll see you in the morning, lass."

"Thank you, Ian," she whispered, almost so softly he didn't hear.

It took every bit of willpower not to take her into his arms and kiss away her sadness. "Would you like me to take you home tomorrow? I didn't give you time to speak with your family about our marriage or to gather your personal things."

Kolyn turned away, unable to deal with the surge of pure fear that shook her. "I . . ." Her voice failed her. She tried again. "I think it best if you do not go with me. If you trust me to go without you."

"Then I will have Geoff take you. You should not go alone. It wouldn't be safe."

On this point she agreed, but she didn't know how to say it. So she said nothing.

Ian broke the silence. "Do you have much you would like to bring from home? I shall send someone with a cart to bring it back if needed."

"No," Kolyn said. "There is very little I need." Yet her heart cried out, *except for my son.* But the persistent fear kept her silent.

"I shall speak with Geoff first thing in the morning."

Kolyn watched Ian leave, pulling the door shut behind him. She almost expected him to lock it, but he didn't. This puzzled her immensely. Why would he trust her not to run away? Then again, why would she? As horrible a situation as this seemed, it was no better at home. Home. It seemed an unsuitable word for what her life had become.

For the first time, she looked around at her surroundings. She could not help but be impressed at the plushness of Stonehaven. Since she arrived, she had seen very little of it, only a few rooms. Yet each one had a warmth and friendliness that her own home lacked. It was obvious Blackstone was wealthy. It showed in every room she had seen so far.

She guessed it would be so in every room of the large estate.

She walked about, looking at and touching the fine things. This was Ian's room. It was obvious from the masculine touches. Yet it too had a quiet comfort to it. Her gaze was drawn to the huge canopied bed that occupied one wall. Tapestry hangings draped the bed, huge carved hardwood posts supporting the dark, green velvet-covered mattress. The silken gown Ainsley had left looked small and delicate on the bed, out of place in the room of dark hues and rich textures.

Kolyn slipped the wedding gown from her shoulders and stepped from it, careful to lay it neatly aside to return to Ainsley in the morning. She dressed for bed. She felt quite strange, quite alone in the enormous room, and even more so when she crawled into bed. She could see Ian would need a bed to fit his great height, but she felt small as she curled up in it alone.

Shyly, she laid her hand upon the empty pillow next to her and wondered if they could ever truly be man and wife. Her heart longed for such a thing, yet her mind told her the futility of such a hope. A dark anger seeped into her mind and took away all her dreams. To trust a man, any man, would be foolish. Men had only brought fear into her life. Her father's hatred, Emmett's madness, and her uncle's obsession had taught her the cruelty of men.

Was Ian any different? Kolyn couldn't forget Blair's fear of him. He had cast her aside, knowing she was with child. How could he be so heartless? Blair had betrayed him, and part of Kolyn understood his anger and hurt. But the child was an innocent. She thought of her sweet Andrew, and hated Ian for rejecting him. How could he love the child she carried unconditionally and not his firstborn son?

These thoughts collided with a newfound tenderness creating havoc inside her. She was confused, and frightened. How could she risk Ian not wanting her son . . . his son? She couldn't. What was she to do? She was now legally his wife. To be apart from Andrew was torture. What could she do to be with him again?

And what of Emmett?

This frightened her the most. She understood what Emmett was capable of. How was she to protect Andrew from his madness? It all came down to the same agonizing solution. She must kill Ian.

She felt sick, and her heart tightened painfully as it told her quite plainly the impossibility of it.

"Good mornin', my lady."

Kolyn blushed at Geoffrey's courtesy. "You weren't nearly so formal when you thought me a tavern maid."

"But now you are Ian's wife, not a tavern maid."

He looked away, and Kolyn knew he was uncomfortable with that. "Do you not approve?" she asked.

"'Tis not important whether I approve or disapprove of what Ian does. He asked that I take you home. We should go."

Geoffrey helped her up onto her horse. For some reason, she did not want him to disapprove, and this confused her. "You still watch over him, don't you, Geoff?"

He mounted, and this time he didn't turn away. She saw the anger in his eyes. "Aye. You place me in an awkward position, lass."

"And Ian has not placed me in an even more unpleasant one?"

This took him aback. "In what way?"

"I shall be lucky if my clan does not banish me for my disloyalty to them. You do recall that I am a sworn enemy to the Black Wolf?"

"'Tis hard to forget." His face was grim, so unlike his normal mood of laughter and smiles. "But you have a new home and will lack for nothing. It seems you are better off than you were."

"In what way?" she asked. "I have no family left, to speak of. They have been taken from me by Ian's sword. Everything I've known has been destroyed by the feud. In what way do you think I am better off?"

"I see little of worth on MacGregor land. You

will be wealthy as Lady Blackstone. You lived with a family of fools, Kolyn MacGregor. Your father was foolish and allowed his hatred to risk his sons to Ian's sword. It was not Ian who took them from you. And this same foolishness caused his own death, not Ian. Emmett is forever doomed to be a helpless cripple and it was his own foolishness that caused it. He cannot blame Ian for it."

She did not like his tone, and even more, she did not like what he said. It was too close to the truth. "And what of Ian? He is totally blameless?"

Geoffrey did look away for a moment, then turned back to Kolyn. "Ian's only fault was to love a woman who did not deserve to be loved. Blair knew nothing of being a faithful wife and loving mother. She was selfish and shameless."

"Aye," Kolyn admitted. "She was . . . Blair."

"Ian would not hear the truth about her. He was infatuated and unable to see what she was."

Kolyn moved her mount forward so she could lean close to Geoffrey. "And she paid for her mistakes. Just as my father and brothers paid for theirs. What of Ian? Am I to forgive and forget so easily?"

"You are to have his child," Geoffrey said flatly. "I think it would be best if you did."

"I cannot." She pulled her horse around and urged the mare forward.

Geoffrey watched her ride away, her back stiff with pride and anger. A mixture of emotions ran through him. He wanted to throttle her; he wanted to hold her close and take her pain away. He admired her, he disliked her. His loyalty to Ian made him feel guilty for the sympathy he held in his heart for her situation. He stood between two people, both hurting and in need of healing. His heart told him Kolyn needed a friend, but he could not be that. He could not be friend to her and betray Ian. His loyalty to Ian was stronger than his desire to befriend this woman who claimed to be the MacGregor, now wife to the Black Wolf.

Kolyn slowed her horse's pace, thinking better of allowing her anger to make her careless and risk harming the baby. Geoffrey caught up with her easily, his war-horse's stride much greater than her mare's. They did not speak, and Kolyn was grateful for the silence. She was too confused, and feared she would make an even bigger fool of herself if they continued speaking.

As they neared MacGregor land, she felt the apprehension of facing Emmett overwhelm her. She wanted to turn and flee. To ride back to Stonehaven and never see her brother again. But she understood this was not to be, and tried to find the strength she would need to face him. She must know that Andrew was not in danger from his insane anger.

Riding through the village was difficult. The

people she had grown up with showed no
kindness to her. They turned away, their eyes
not meeting hers. Those who did look showed
the anger and hate she had feared they would
have. It was no surprise, yet it hurt just the
same. These were the people she had loved
and cared for. She had stolen and risked her
life to see to their needs. Now they merely
walked away, rejecting her in her own time
of need and sorrow.

Refusing to let Geoffrey see her pain, she
rode with her head up, pride in her every
move. She did not hesitate when she rode into
the castle yard. Geoffrey helped her down.

"You had better wait here with the horses. I
won't be long."

"Are you certain you do not need my help?"
Geoffrey looked at the front door as if it were
the danger. "To help you carry your things," he
added when he turned back to meet her eyes.

Kolyn understood the hidden meaning in his
words, his need to protect her as Ian's wife.
Did he suspect Emmett might harm her? This
thought made her uneasy, and she wanted to
take him with her. But that was impossible.
She could not bear anyone to witness Emmett's
total madness, her shame. It was something she
must do alone.

"As you said before, I have little of worth I
need to bring with me. I merely wish to see
my brother and say good-bye. I had no time
yesterday."

Geoffrey nodded. "Aye, my lady. I will wait here."

Her knees were shaking, and she thought she might stumble when she walked up the stone steps. She drew the last of her strength and entered her home. It felt strange, as if she no longer belonged.

"Don't be ridiculous," she mumbled to herself, unwilling to give in to this simple thought that seemed to betray her family and clan. She went straight up to Emmett's rooms and knocked.

She did not wait for his leave to enter.

"So," Emmett drawled, his voice lazy and snide. "My dear sister has returned. Is the honeymoon over already?"

Kolyn flinched. "He didn't give me much choice in the matter, Emmett."

"Yes, I understand he carried you off." He turned away from her stare. "Ian Blackstone seems to be good at carrying women off and marrying them."

This almost made Kolyn laugh. She hadn't thought about the coincidence. "What am I to do?"

This brought his angry eyes back to her, and she wished he would turn away again. Still, she stood her ground.

"What do you want to do?" he asked.

She swallowed and tried to put the right words together. It was so difficult discussing anything with Emmett—any word could be the wrong one. "If I come back here, he will only take me back to Stonehaven. I don't think I have much choice."

"You could kill him, Kolyn. As you promised me. As you promised Father."

"That is simpler said than done."

"Why?" he screamed, his voice hysterical. "Why would that be so hard a thing to do? You are now his wife. It seems to me it would be quite easy."

"I cannot—"

"I'll have no more of your excuses. I've grown weary of you and this whole matter. Kill him. Now!"

What could she say? "I will try."

Emmett pushed himself up with his arms and leaned closer. "You had better do more than try, or you will suffer greatly for it." He motioned toward the window. "Look outside, Kolyn."

Dread claimed her mind, his eyes telling her there was something to fear out in the courtyard. She looked out, but saw nothing. She turned back to Emmett, her look questioning him.

"Look near the stables."

This time she saw them—Donald holding Andrew. Her heart exploded inside her chest, the pain nearly rendering her helpless.

"If you do not do as I say, Drew will die. Then I shall take great pleasure in ridding you of that brat you carry. And . . ."

His pause caused Kolyn to look at him. He smiled, his eyes gleaming with sinister delight. She wanted to close her own, to block the ugly sight before her, but she was frozen in place.

"And if you are of no use to me, Kolyn, I shall have to kill you too. I really would hate to kill my own, dear sister. But if I must, I will."

"Do not harm my son," she whispered, trying to keep her world aright as it whirled precariously about her.

"You may see Drew on Saturday morning. Donald will take him to Father McCloud's church, and you will have an hour. Call it a reminder. You will have this one time with him. If you haven't accomplished what I ask by the next Saturday, it will have been your last time with the lad. Donald has instructions to slit his throat."

She felt the blood drain from her face. This was madness. What made her think she could reason with him? He was beyond that. "You disgust me."

This made him laugh. "Of course I do. I disgust myself."

"May God forgive you, Emmett." Kolyn walked to the door.

"God abandoned me to this living hell long ago. I do not need his forgiveness, nor yours. Remember, I'll not be patient any longer. Kill him for me, Kolyn. I'll be forever grateful."

Tears came to her eyes as she walked from her home. She could never return, she knew that now. She was no longer a MacGregor. She was a Blackstone.

Geoffrey helped her up onto her horse, his brows knitting together. "Are you all right, Kolyn? You're as pale as a ghost."

"I'm fine, Geoff." Her reply came out weak, her voice shaky, but he did not question her further.

"Whore!"

Kolyn whirled around just as the dirt clod struck her in the face, splitting her lip. The villagers had gathered into a group and tossed whatever they could grab at her, their curses hurting her more than the objects that hit her.

"The bitch has bred with the Black Wolf! Traitor!"

"You've betrayed your clan and broken your oath, be gone with you!"

Geoffrey shielded Kolyn from most of the abuse, but he could not keep their words from her. He grabbed her horse's reins and rode through the crowd, his large war-horse guaranteeing passage. They galloped from the village.

Once they were safely away, Geoffrey stopped and handed Kolyn back her reins. "Did they hurt you?"

"Aye." She tried to smile bravely, but failed as tears threatened her. "But only my pride."

"You're bleedin', Kolyn." Geoffrey nudged his horse closer and wiped at the blood from her split lip.

Kolyn looked away in shame. "'Tis nothing."

"Why are they so angry? 'Tis more than your marryin' Ian."

"They think I have married the Devil, Geoff, that I have betrayed my clan and family."

"They must know Ian gave you no choice. No, there is more to this than mere superstition. And what of this oath they spoke of?"

She could not look at Geoffrey. She hated to lie, but she had no choice. "There is no oath. Please, let us go."

"Ian will be angry. He had not expected this."

"Please," she put her hand upon his arm. "Please, Geoff. Do not mention this to Ian."

His brows furrowed together in confusion. "I must."

Her eyes pleaded with him. "'Tis my shame, Geoff. Ian need not know."

Geoffrey saw the tears in her eyes, the shame written upon her face. His heart went out to her, leaving him helpless to her whim. He nodded begrudgingly. "If that is the way you want it, my lady."

"Aye, that is the way I want it."

They rode home in silence.

Chapter Twenty-four

When Kolyn and Geoffrey arrived at Stonehaven, Ian met them before they had even dismounted. He helped Kolyn from the saddle, setting her gently on the ground.

"Did everything go all right, Kolyn?"

"Aye," she lied, turning away from his concerned look.

She knew he wanted to know more, but refrained from asking. She was thankful for that. His look moved to Geoffrey, perhaps hoping to discover more from his friend. Geoffrey took the horses to the stable.

Ian turned back to her. "I thought I could show you around. If you're not too tired?"

Anything was better than being left alone

with her confused thoughts. "That would be nice."

"Are you sure?" he asked again. "You look tired."

Irritation touched her, but Kolyn kept it hidden from Ian. "I'm fine, really I am. Show me your home."

He took her hand and placed it in the crook of his arm, escorting her across the immense courtyard. Everywhere she looked, it was neat and tidy, not a single thing out of place. Ian greeted each person they came across with a smile, calling them by their first names, sometimes even pausing to ask about their families or if they were feeling better. Kolyn was introduced to each one, their responses filled with warmth and kindness, their respect for Ian carrying over to her. None seemed to care that she was a MacGregor. They showed only their genuine happiness Ian had married again.

Perhaps it would have been easier had everyone hated her. As they toured his home her defenses came down, and she found herself actually enjoying Ian's company. The morning's ugly events became a distant shadow, sneaking up every now and then to pull her away from the sunshine. What she would do, she didn't want to think about. Yet at times, it all flooded back to take her pleasure away.

Ian was acutely aware that something was bothering Kolyn, something deep and troubling. Just when he would capture a smile from her, a deep sadness would take it away. He had to remind himself many times not to intrude, that she would tell him if she wanted to. His pride was hurt by her silence, but he understood the distrust in her eyes. His mother had cautioned him to be patient, and he would do his best to be so.

When they entered the glassed terrace, he smiled at her reaction. Plants filled the room, creating a kaleidoscope of color and smells.

"It's beautiful, Ian!"

"My father had this terrace built so he could close in his roses for the winter. The harsh Scottish weather was too much for the delicate bushes."

Kolyn walked about, touching and smelling the blooms, so out of place that time of year.

"In the spring, I will remove the glass panes and open it up to the sunshine."

Kolyn had never seen anything like it before. "Did your father bring these from England?"

"Aye," Ian said, pride touching his voice. "He did love his flowers."

"Who cares for them now?"

"Ian does."

Ainsley entered the greenhouse and walked over to stand by her son. "Ian dotes over them as much as his father did."

Ian's dimples showed as he smiled down at his mother, his arm draped casually about her tiny shoulders. Kolyn felt a twinge of envy over the relationship they had. She had never known a mother and son to be so comfortable and loving with each other. Her own brothers would have been chastised for such behavior by their overbearing father. Douglas MacGregor had not been outwardly affectionate, even to his wife, and certainly would not have abided his sons showing such emotions in public.

This made Kolyn wonder what kind of man Ian's father had been. A man who had given up his life in England to be with the woman he loved in Scotland.

"I'm having refreshments served," Ainsley said. "I thought you might need to sit and rest a while after your long ride."

"Yes," Kolyn replied, trying to smile despite her tender lip. She was careful not to start it bleeding again and draw Ian's attention. "That would be nice."

As they walked to the sitting room, Ainsley continued with polite conversation, Kolyn responding when necessary. Finally, they were seated, and Kolyn was provided with a hot cup of spiced wine. Ainsley sat across from her. Ian remained standing, a glass of wine in hand. She felt their eyes upon her.

Finally Ainsley spoke up. "What will the MacGregor clan do now that you are here, Kolyn? Is Emmett able to act as the clan chief? Will your lands fall to ruin?"

Kolyn had not thought on this matter before, and was quite surprised Ainsley had. And that Ainsley would approach her on such a delicate

subject. Then again, Ainsley was a straight-
forward, honest woman and would deal with
Kolyn in this same manner.

"I don't know." Then she added as an after-
thought, "My lands seem already to be in
ruin."

"If there is anything we can do to help,
please ask."

Sincerity rang in Ainsley's statement, and
Kolyn accepted it as it was meant—as kindness,
not insult. "Thank you for your offer, Ainsley.
To be honest, I haven't given any of this a lot
of thought."

"Yes," Ainsley mused, setting her cup aside.
"It all has been rather sudden, hasn't it?"

Kolyn merely nodded agreement. It was still
so confusing, so distressing. Once again, Emmett's threats rolled through her mind, sending tremors through her. She relived the moment she saw Andrew, no longer in Father Mc-
Cloud's safe care, but instead with Donald. This
prompted visions of every horror imaginable.

"Dear," Ainsley said, interrupting her torture.

"Yes?"

"You looked quite shaken. I'm so sorry if we
haven't been sympathetic to your feelings about
this situation. I must admit my prejudice about
your baby, my grandchild, and my son."

Kolyn had not meant to alarm Ainsley. She
had been nothing but generous and kind. "I
did not mean to imply . . ." What could she
say? Embarrassed at her lack of composure,

359

Kolyn stood. "Please excuse me. I am feeling rather tired and would like to lie down."

She all but ran from the room, tears already running down her face. How could she explain that her own brother, her own blood, was the cause of her unhappiness? He had her backed into a corner and was forcing her to kill someone she was finding to be a gentle and loving man. She almost wished Ian could be as fierce as his appearance portrayed. It would be easier. And what was now more confusing was the knowledge he had turned away from Blair when she was carrying his child. It did not make sense, not if he were being true to her, his love and devotion to her own unborn child real.

Too many thoughts collided inside her mind, leaving her spent and worn. It was as if a storm raged, leaving in its wake total devastation. When she reached her rooms she entered and fell upon the bed sobbing.

Ian entered quietly, not wanting to startle Kolyn. Her crying tore at his heart and tormented his mind. He stood for a long while, just listening, wanting to comfort, but knowing it would not be accepted.

"Kolyn," he said softly, drawing her swollen eyes to him. They were empty and dull, the vibrancy he knew so well gone. He wanted to say the right thing, but what it was, he didn't know. "I'm sorry."

Her delicate brows wrinkled together as she

continued to stare at him, confusion deep in her green eyes. "Why?"

It was his turn to be confused. "Why? Have I not done enough to you to be sorry for?"

Still she stared at him. She sat up, pushing the strands of hair that clung to her wet face away. "Are you sorry I am with child and you had to marry me?"

"I didn't have to do any such thing, Kolyn. I wanted to."

"You—" Kolyn paused, not believing what he was saying. "You wanted to marry me?"

Ian walked over to sit on the bed beside her. "I nearly went crazy when I woke up at the inn and found you were gone. It takes me a while sometimes to figure out what it is I want. But I wanted to marry you."

"That," she said, a sliver of a smile touching her lips, "is madness. You don't even know me—what I like, what I don't like."

"I'll learn all those things. What I do know is that you have made me very happy. I have longed for a son and now you shall give me one."

"What if it's a girl?"

"Either way." He grinned, his dimples showing. "I will be the happiest man alive."

She didn't know whether to believe him or not. "You're making light of me, aren't you?"

"I've never been more serious in all my life."

This wasn't at all what she expected of him. "What of your first son? Did you hate Blair so much that you couldn't love your child? Why did you want him dead too?"

The shock that tore through Ian was cruel and ugly. He took a deep breath and held it. Slowly, he released it, along with the anger that claimed his mind. "Is that what you think?"

"Aye," she whispered, frightened by the look in his eyes. Like a cloud his face had changed from light and airy to dark and stormy. "You killed an innocent child because of what Blair did to you, and now you want me to trust you with mine. How can I do that? How can I take the chance that you won't banish me into the streets to die like an animal?"

He stood and looked down on her—all his tenderness gone. "I guess you can't trust that I won't. Especially if you are a lying, betraying bitch like Blair was. Are you, Kolyn?"

"I'm not Blair, but you don't know what lies in my heart or my reasons for what I do."

"Then we are in agreement on one thing. We can't trust each other."

"It seems that way," she said, wanting to take back all the cruel things she had said that took his dimples away. But she didn't. She couldn't, and she knew it. It would be better if he hated her.

Ian started to leave, but stopped. "Oh, I meant to give this back to you earlier but forgot."

He tossed the MacGregor's ring to her. It landed on the bed in front of her. Surprised, she picked it up.

"How did you get this?"

"Leslie sold it to me." He gave no more explanation and she didn't need more.

"We've much more to overcome than just you being a MacGregor and me a Blackstone, don't we?"

Kolyn raised her eyes up to meet his. "Yes. It seems so."

A sudden look of hurt crossed his features. "Why couldn't we just be two people trying to love one another?"

"That is an impossibility, Ian. We cannot deny who we are any more than we can deny what we feel. And they do not go together."

"I had hoped they could," he whispered hoarsely, his dark gaze intense.

Whatever she hoped, she could not say it. "You had hoped wrong."

When Ian closed the door it felt like her heart was being torn from her chest. She would have cried, but there were no more tears. Kolyn understood what she must do— kill Ian Blackstone, her husband and the father of her child. But she also understood what her heart had been telling her all along—she loved Ian Blackstone.

Ian berated himself for losing control of his temper. It galled him she thought so little of him. Kolyn had actually accused him of killing Blair's child. He hadn't known she was pregnant. If he had . . .

The same tormenting thoughts plagued him, just as they had for the last five years. Would it never end? Would he never come to peace with himself over her death and the death of his firstborn? He feared the answer was no.

What a fool he was! To think Kolyn would change into a loving wife and mother merely because he had married her. His mother was right. She had too many reasons to hate him and at that very moment he hated himself. Perhaps he should have told her he had not known of the child, but something told him she would not have believed him. There was no reason for her to. Maybe in time she would learn the truth.

Ian looked out and saw the full moon hanging in the night sky. For the first time in over five years he had not even noticed, until now. Finding the strange room closed in and unbearable, he left, seeking the comfort of the dark forest.

Unable to sleep, Kolyn watched the night sky and its full, rounded moon. She saw Ian leave Stonehaven and go toward the stables. She pondered about this strange man, so fierce, yet gentle. Curiosity overcoming her, she quickly pulled her shawl about her and left for the stables.

Ian rode off on his black war-horse, and Kolyn was careful to conceal herself in the shadows. Soon, she was on her own mount and following him into the distant forest. She wondered about the legend and what he did when he went off at night—and why.

Kolyn hoped to discover something about Ian that would clear some of the confusion that cluttered her mind. It was difficult to keep up with his larger horse, but she gently urged her mare to do so. She would not let him slip away into the darkness.

Ian stopped his angry ride through the forest, an unusual feeling bringing him to a complete halt. Quietly, he dismounted and listened to the clamor of the night, intent on the sound he had heard. It too had stopped, yet he remained alert.

A low growl sounded, and he knew his faithful wolf was nearby, warning him of what he had sensed. Someone or something was out there. With the stealth of an animal, Ian slipped into the cover of the trees, hiding himself from whatever or whoever watched him. He waited.

The growl reached Kolyn's ears, sending a shiver down her spine and making her mare shift nervously. It came from where Ian stood by his horse, and she almost believed he had made the sound himself. She closed her eyes for a second, to calm her fear. When she opened them again, he was gone. She searched the trees that surrounded her, the shadows hiding many things from her. Something moved, snapping a twig. She settled her gaze on that spot, intent on seeing what crept up on her. It was like a ghostly apparition, melting into nature's outline.

The first thing she saw was his eyes, the golden spheres surrounded by black. Then, slowly, she saw his head, then his chest and front paws. The wolf watched her, just as she watched him, neither moving. Then he moved off into the blackness, making no sound, no threat.

It was a full minute before she looked away from the place he had been. She slid from her horse to the ground, thinking to follow the animal. The howl began as a low, mournful sound, climbed to reach a startling pitch, then receded and diminished, a long echo following.

The silence that descended upon Kolyn was more nerve-wracking than the wolf's eerie howl. It was too quiet.

"You're a foolish woman," Ian said, coming up behind her.

Kolyn jumped, his sudden appearance catching her off guard. She had to take a deep breath to calm her racing heart before she could speak. "You frightened me."

"What are you doing out here? You could have hurt yourself." His voice scolded and his eyes told her his anger. "You could have harmed the baby, Kolyn."

He was right. She did feel ridiculous. "I'm sorry, I didn't think."

"Aye, you didn't think." Ian was not ready

to forgive her such foolishness. "I asked what you were doing out here in the middle of the night."

She tried to think of a lie, but couldn't. "I followed you." Now she felt even more stupid than before. What had she been thinking?

"Why?"

Frustrated, she pushed him away from her, unable to think standing so close to him. "I wanted to know what you do when you ride off in the night."

"What do you think I do?"

His questions were starting to irritate her beyond all else. "I don't know. That's why I followed you!"

Ian closed the distance between them in one long stride, his face towering above her, watching, waiting. She feared to look up. "'Tis dangerous out here."

"You seem quite at home," she countered, still unable to look at him.

Finally, he pulled her chin up to look at him. "Why are you so curious about what I do?"

"I don't know," she whispered, wondering that herself. His stare bewildered her, sending her composure fleeing.

"You seem to know very little tonight."

Kolyn cleared her throat and licked her dry lips nervously. "Perhaps I'd best go back."

Ian could feel her shivering and pulled her into his arms. "You're cold."

She started to pull away, but his warmth sent

the chill away, so she snuggled closer. "Aye. I am cold."

"I'll take you home." Ian lifted her and carried her back to his horse. "Next time you want to know what I am doing, just ask, Kolyn. I'll not have you riding all over the country by yourself."

He put Kolyn in front of his saddle, then mounted. "Are you comfortable?"

She nodded and settled back against him.

Ian rode to where her mare stood and picked up the reins. Slowly, they rode through the forest, his senses guiding their way in the darkness.

"Kolyn," Ian said softly, bringing her eyes open.

She looked about her in confusion, having fallen asleep on the way back to Stonehaven. Realizing how close Ian held her, she pulled away, embarrassed.

Ian swung his leg over his saddle and landed gracefully on the ground. He reached up and lifted her into his arms, but he didn't put her down. Instead he carried her to the manor.

"I can walk."

"'Tis a pleasure, my lady."

His voice was soft and husky, making it difficult to think clearly as sleep clouded her mind. Her body reacted to his closeness, leaving no room for her weakened will to respond. She wanted to despise his touch. Instead she longed for more. Just being near him awakened the desire inside her. She loathed such weakness, but she could not keep the need from stirring within her.

When they arrived at the door to her bedroom, Ian set her down, his arms still wrapped about her. Kolyn made the mistake of looking up. All her resolve was lost to his golden gaze.

Ian pulled her closer and kissed her, the instant passion between them deepening the kiss. The tiny warmth in the pit of her stomach ignited into an intense heat, the hot blood that ran through her veins scorching her flesh, searing her mind. Gone were the thoughts of distrust and hatred. Only his kiss mattered.

When he pulled away, Kolyn couldn't hide the disappointment.

"For a woman who thinks so little of me," Ian muttered, his own feelings reeling out of control, "you seem quite amiable. Tell me, Kolyn, what am I to do? It is hard to resist such temptation."

"Aye," she agreed with him, pulling back from his caress.

"Good night, Kolyn."

"Good night, Ian." Kolyn went inside, leaving Ian to stand alone in the empty hallway.

Chapter Twenty-five

Ainsley watched Kolyn for a few moments before she entered the terrace where she sat. Kolyn looked up, and Ainsley thought she looked troubled, her eyes sad. Dark smudges marked them, telling Ainsley of Kolyn's sleepless night.

"Good morning, Kolyn."

"Good morning," she replied, her voice as listless as her look. This worried Ainsley.

"Would you like to walk into the village this morning, dear? You look a little pale. Perhaps some fresh air will bring some color to your cheeks."

"That would be nice. I'll get my wrap."

"I'll walk with you," Ainsley said, hooking her arm through Kolyn's. "Spring will be here soon.

371

Winters always seem so long and dreary, don't you think?"

Kolyn nodded, glad to have the company but not in a very talkative mood. She allowed Ainsley to carry the conversation, and her new mother-in-law didn't seem to mind that she did. Kolyn politely answered when necessary, allowing her mind to be diverted from her troubles.

As they walked into the courtyard, Kolyn felt something brush against her, the feel familiar, especially when he let out a raspy honk. She knelt down to stroke her goose.

"What is he doing here?"

Ainsley smiled, then laughed, the sound soft and gentle. "Ian brought him home from the tavern. A dog too. Molly threatened to cook the goose, and for some strange reason Ian didn't want the animal touched. When I asked, he just growled and said he liked the damn thing."

Kolyn's throat tightened and, again, amazement touched her. Ian's actions were a puzzlement—never had she known a man quite like him. A deep heartache began anew. She tried to ignore its pain. What kind of man Ian was didn't matter.

They began to walk, and the goose followed Kolyn, his quiet noise like a shadow behind her. Ainsley stopped and tried to shoo him back, but he couldn't be swayed.

"He is fine, Ainsley. I don't mind his company."

A bright twinkle lit Ainsley's eyes, and Kolyn thought she might be suspicious of whose goose this had been all along. But she said nothing.

It took some time for them to walk through the village, everyone stopping to speak a kind word or two to Ainsley. She introduced Kolyn as Ian's wife, making her feel uneasy, yet warm congratulations finally calmed her hidden fears. Her own people had rejected her, but Ian's took her into their hearts. Hurt swarmed over her, but the genuine devotion Ian's people willingly gave helped ease the pain.

"Would you like some wine?"

They had stopped in front of The Raven, and a sudden uneasiness descended on Kolyn. She couldn't hide it from Ainsley. "I don't think so," she said softly, hoping Ainsley would understand.

"I'm sure Molly would like to see you again. Even Leslie seemed quite fond of you, Kolyn."

"I lied to them about who I was."

"That's the past, dear. They'll think nothing of it, I'm sure." Ainsley linked her arm in Kolyn's and led her inside.

Molly was there instantly, her face smiling, her arms extended. "You found her, I see."

Before Kolyn could say anything, she was engulfed in a tremendous, smothering hug, the woman's girth swallowing her.

"Bless me, lass," Molly wheezed. "What made you run off without even a good-bye?"

Kolyn felt the warmth creep up her face, and knew she had just reddened to a brilliant shade. Ainsley came to her defense.

"Now Molly." Her voice took on a soft chastising tone that said more than her words. "I promised Kolyn we'd not pester her with our questions. All that matters is that Ian did find her."

"And married her, I hear," Molly said, her eyes rolling widely. She grabbed Kolyn and gave her another hug. "I cannot believe it. 'Tis a miracle."

"Aye," Ainsley agreed, her eyes misting with emotion.

Before Kolyn could catch her breath, she was comfortably seated before the fire. Leslie brought their wine, a small smile greeting her.

"'Tis hard t' believe you've married Lord Blackstone, my lady." She set the wine down. "I wish you much happiness."

"'Tis Kolyn, Leslie. There's no reason for you to be so formal with me."

Leslie laughed, then shared the thought that prompted it. "For a fine lady, you certainly served the ale up fine."

"You worked hard," Molly added coming up behind Leslie. "I've had no luck replacin' you."

"I figured you were different." Leslie's smile faded and she turned serious. "That you were a lady."

Leslie drew a deep breath and went on. "But you never acted as if you were better than us.

I be admirin' of that an' proud t' call you my friend. If," she added, "you still call me friend."

Kolyn stood and faced the blond girl whose downcast eyes studied her bared feet. Kolyn pulled Leslie's chin up to look into her eyes. "I still call you my friend."

Tears swam in the blue pools, and Leslie shyly hugged Kolyn. "I've work t' do."

"Aye." Molly tried to sound stern, but failed as her voice broke with emotion. "We've both work t' do."

They bustled off, Molly kicking out at the goose as she went, her laughter telling Kolyn she was merely being playful. The goose ignored it altogether as he wandered about at his leisure. Finally, he settled at Kolyn's feet.

Kolyn began to feel comfortable. She and Ainsley sipped their wine, neither feeling the need for conversation, the quiet moment enjoyable. When they prepared to leave, Molly returned, a gleam in her eye.

"'Tis a celebration we be needin', Lady Blackstone." Her gaze moved from one Lady Blackstone to the other. "A great celebration for this miracle."

Ainsley readily agreed. "I think that would be splendid, Molly."

"We can have it right here, where Ian met this lass." Molly reached out and squeezed Kolyn's hand.

"I'll have my cooks bring down the food,

Molly. And put the ale on our bill. If there is anything else you need, just ask."

Molly bustled off in a flurry of apron. "I have it all under control, my lady. It will be a great celebration."

Ainsley led Kolyn out the door.

"What does she mean by a miracle?" Kolyn asked.

"Only love can conquer hate, Kolyn. With you and Ian married, the clan feuding is over. Everyone feels it's a blessing, or a miracle."

"Oh," was all she could think of to say, the reminder dragging her mood down again. For just a few moments, she had forgotten what ugliness she must be about.

Ainsley looked concerned. "I'm sorry, dear. Did I upset you?"

"No. You've been more than kind."

Ainsley did not seem convinced. "You looked so . . ."

She couldn't seem to find the right word, but Kolyn understood. "I am fine. It's all happening so fast, I just need time to understand everything that's running around inside my head."

"You will, Kolyn. You will."

Ainsley pushed a stray curl from Kolyn's face, much like a mother would do. It stirred a strange longing in Kolyn, who still grieved for her mother, so long dead, yet so strong in memory. Kolyn liked Ainsley, and this made her turmoil even worse.

All the worry and strife that had plagued her

during the long night returned in a rush. It stole her simple pleasure away, leaving only disturbing thoughts. She felt sick and wanted to be left alone with her misery.

"I think I need to take you home to rest," Ainsley said.

"Yes," Kolyn agreed. "I could use some rest."

As the two women left the inn, a sudden intensity touched Kolyn, as if warning her of something. It increased as they walked through the village, the feeling distracting Kolyn from Ainsley's conversation.

"Are you looking for something, dear?"

Kolyn turned back to Ainsley, her question bringing her mind back from the danger she felt. "No, not at all."

She tried to relax, to tell herself nothing was amiss. Still it dogged her every step back to Stonehaven. Ainsley stopped for a moment to speak to an elderly man, hunched in front of his tiny cottage. Just as Kolyn came to the decision it had been merely her imagination, she saw him. Dwight stood only a few feet away, his stare sending a tremor through her.

She plainly saw the anger, the hate, glow in the dark depths of his eyes, and she now understood the danger her instincts had been warning her about. Kolyn stepped closer to Ainsley, hoping her presence would deter Dwight from doing anything rash. They were close to Stonehaven, close enough so that he would be foolish to try to take her. She turned away, unable to stand the look on his face any longer.

When Kolyn dared to glance back, he was gone. This discovery sent another wave of shivers down her spine. It was almost better to know exactly where he was than to imagine it. Her nerves strung as tight as they could go, Kolyn wished Ainsley would hurry.

"Ainsley," Kolyn said, interrupting her conversation. "I think I'll walk on ahead if you don't mind?"

"Of course, Kolyn. I'll catch up to you. I'll not be long."

Kolyn set her sight on the gate into the courtyard and walked as fast as she could without actually running. Dwight stepped out in front of her, and she collided with him, his arms keeping her from falling.

"Do not touch me," she hissed beneath her breath, trying not to draw anyone's attention as she twisted away. "You are a fool, Dwight."

"Aye," he agreed. His voice was flat, but his eyes told her what to expect next. "I'm a fool for you, lass."

He reached for her again, but she put her hand up to stop him. "Touch me and I'll scream. Every man in Stonehaven will come, perhaps even Ian. You'd best leave while I am feeling generous enough to let you go unharmed."

"Generous," he sneered, his lips twisting into

a frown, creating an ugly look of hatred. "You are so innocent. I'll not let you go, Kolyn. Marriage or not. You are mine, now and forever."

Angry words came to her lips, but he left before she could utter them. Ainsley came up behind her.

"There." Ainsley smiled. "I wasn't so long, was I?"

"No. You arrived in time."

Ainsley's look turned curious, but she didn't ask Kolyn to explain. They walked the rest of the way home in silence.

Before Kolyn had time to dwell on what had happened, she was home and lying in bed. Ainsley quietly closed her door, leaving her to nap. At first, Kolyn thought it silly to rest during the day. But it was only a moment before her eyes drooped and sleep overtook her, despite her mind's activity.

"Kolyn."

She opened her eyes, the dream so real she found it difficult to bring her mind back from it.

"Drew," she whispered hoarsely.

"'Tis Ian." Ian sat on the bed and pushed her tangled hair out of her face. "You've been dreaming, Kolyn."

Finally she realized where she was and who she was speaking to. She sat up. "What are you doing in here?"

Her question had come out accusing, sharp.

She had not meant it to. She turned away from him, embarrassed that he found her so disoriented.

"Who is Drew?"

A tremor went through Kolyn, a tremor of dread and horror. "No one."

"You were sobbing and crying his name. That is what made me come in."

She said nothing.

"You don't cry out no one's name."

Kolyn remained silent. What could she say?

Ian grasped her by the shoulders and shook her, his frustration showing in his fierce look. "How can we truly be man and wife if you keep things from me?"

"We can never be man and wife," she screamed, stopping him. "Don't you see that?"

"No," he ground out between clenched teeth.

"Don't be a fool, Ian. It can never be."

He stared at her, unbelieving. Kolyn would not give in to his look. Ian's hand slid from her shoulders and down the length of her arms, his hands warm on her flesh. He didn't stop. His hands moved back up to her neck. His fingers massaged her muscles, relieving the tension along the ridges. She began to relax, his persistence making her feel languid. His hand pulled her close, his lips nearing hers.

Kolyn could smell his musky scent, his breath sweet like wine. His teeth were white against the dark tan of his face, a faint line of bristle starting to show on his cheeks. She had never seen him shave, and had the urge to shave him herself. To feel the strong curve of his jaw in her hands as the razor slid over each inch, scraping the remnants of his beard away.

She wanted to feel his lips on hers, but he held back, teasing, tempting. Licking the dryness from her own, she leaned forward, their lips nearly touching.

"Do you love Drew, Kolyn?" His voice was soft, seductive.

"Yes, very much."

Kolyn didn't even realize what she had said, not even what he had asked, her mind preoccupied with his touch. Ian pulled away.

"You love this man called Drew?"

Confusion shook her, bringing her back to what he said. "What?"

"You said you loved Drew. Supposedly a no one."

"Y . . . you . . . tricked me," Kolyn stuttered, unable to comprehend what she had said as anger took away all other thoughts but one. He had tricked her. But worse, she had fallen right into his arms.

"Who is this man?"

She pushed Ian away and scrambled from the bed. "Get out!"

Ian stood and walked over to her. "Who is this man?"

"Get out!" She felt as if she would explode with anger, and began to push at him. "Get out of my room."

"Your room," he yelled back. "I do believe it is *my* room."

He was right, but it didn't matter. "It's my room now, and I've asked you to get out."

"Ask all you like, my lady. I'll leave when I damn well feel like it."

She gave him another shove, but he did not move an inch, his great height towering above her. Kolyn began to pound on his chest in earnest. "You better damn well feel like it now."

Ian crossed his arms over his chest, her attempts to evict him useless. She struck out, slapping him across the face, the sound loud. Kolyn could feel the blood drain from her face, and she stepped back. Caution finally made its way into her mind, bringing with it the sense she needed.

His eyes darkened dangerously. She took another step back instinctively, to protect her from his anger. She turned to flee, but his arm snaked out and grabbed her about the waist, pulling her back to him.

"Leave me be," she whimpered, anger no longer forging her courage.

He lifted her into his arms and carried her back to the bed. He tossed her on it, and she sank down into the soft mattress. Like a sinking swimmer, she struggled to gain her balance and get up.

Before she could do so, Ian was there, his muscled length lying beside her. His long legs captured her, bringing her struggles to a halt.

He laughed, soft and low, his eyes alight with mischief. His slender fingers played with her blouse, pulling it free of its ties, the fabric sliding down, revealing her shoulder to his gaze.

His lips were hot on her flesh, moving up to the curve of her neck. Kolyn felt her own heat renewed, fast and unrelenting. She tried to ignore it, to will it away, but failed miserably. It controlled her, consumed her. It started in the pit of her belly, causing a tightness between her legs. She closed her eyes against the look in his eyes, the look that told her he had control and he knew it.

She hated him. No, she loved him.

"Do you want me to leave, Kolyn?"

Kolyn opened her eyes. Victory lightened his golden ones. "You are cruel, Ian."

"Aye." He smiled wickedly. "Tell me you want me to stay."

She wanted to throw his words in his face but couldn't. Kolyn was beyond going back. "Don't go."

Her words came out so softly Ian almost wondered if his own longing had created them. But when he reached out to stroke a soft cheek, flushed with desire, he saw it in her eyes. She wanted him to stay. He lowered his head to kiss the silken lips he'd dreamed of so often. Kolyn opened her mouth to let his tongue explore, to taste the sweetness inside. He pulled her closer, anxious to feel her against him, flesh against flesh.

His kiss moved down to her slender neck, to one breast, then another. They seemed fuller, firmer, motherhood filling out her body for his child. Never had he felt so fulfilled, so aroused. Quickly, he pulled her clothes off, revealing to his gaze the rounding of her stomach, so slight, yet apparent to his keen eyes. Gently, his hands felt the swell, the marvel in every touch.

Ian kissed her belly, her flesh quivering beneath his moist lips. Kolyn thought she might go mad with his persistent examination, each tender touch leaving her breathless with wanting. Finally, she pulled him up to her, her fingers tearing at his breeches to remove them. He helped her, and in seconds he lay naked beside her. Her lips sought his, demanding their attention. He gave it.

At that moment, nothing else mattered. Promises, threats, vows—it all melted away in the light of something stronger, more demanding. She wanted only one thing, one man.

Ian quietly slipped from the bed and pulled his clothes on. He looked down at Kolyn as she slept and felt a pang of guilt assault him. They always seemed to be at odds, yet their passions could surpass their fighting and bring them together. But when it was past, the truce was over. This he regretted with every part of his being.

He stood for the longest time just watching

Kolyn sleep, her slumber deep and undisturbed. His thoughts returned to what had brought him to her room to begin with, her cries alarming him as he had walked by. The dark circles that lined her eyes told him her sleep was fitful, and he wondered what haunted her. Was it this Drew she had called out for?

Jealousy slithered into his brain and took control of his emotions. She had confessed to loving Drew, and this made Ian's heart tighten painfully. Who was this man? And why had she lied about him when Ian asked?

Questions rolled about, twisting into a horrible knot in the pit of his stomach. Unable to bear it any longer, he walked away.

Chapter Twenty-six

The dream came upon her again, awakening Kolyn from her deep sleep. It was so real, so frightening, she couldn't discard the emotions it triggered. Awake now, alone in her dark room, she continued to see Andrew, fear in his eyes, his arms outstretched to her. He called for her to help him, but she was unable to.

Something deep and stirring gripped Kolyn, a fierceness so great it startled her. This same feeling guided her, pulling her from the bed. She put a robe on, but still didn't know what prompted her. Giving in to its power, she allowed it to guide her, to take her from the room and out into the hall. Slowly, she moved to the next doorway. Ian's room.

She opened the door and silently maneuvered in the darkness. When she stood beside his bed, she hesitated, not fully understanding what she would do. Her eyes had adjusted to the room's light, and she looked about, instantly spotting his dagger on the night table. It was where he always kept it, easy to reach should he ever need it. Kolyn studied it, the long handle glistening in the dark.

Kolyn stretched her hand out, touching the intricate markings. It felt cool, while she felt a strange heat moving inside her. She felt vicious, ugly. Her hand slowly wrapped about the dirk, her grip strong and unwavering. Power surged through her as she thought of Andrew.

If Ian had not cast his son aside with his hatred of Blair, Andrew would not be in danger now. Even the fact she would never have been a mother to him would be more acceptable than what she was being forced to do now. She must kill to save her son's life. She knew she would do anything to protect Andrew, even take a life. Wouldn't she?

This thought surprised Kolyn, drawing the air from her, sucking the smallest bit of doubt from her with it. She despised herself, yet it made no difference. Motherhood dominated all else. It was stronger and more firmly rooted in her than this new and confused feeling of love.

She closed her eyes and lifted her arm to strike. Visions of Andrew calling to her haunted her—creating a will that moved her. Ian stirred. She hid the knife behind her back.

"Kolyn?"

Her mind snapped, and emotions flooded in. She ran the gamut—fear, hate, love, anger, confusion. They all mixed and ran headlong into one another. She could not speak, she could not run, she was frozen, body and soul.

Reaching up, Ian touched her cheek. It was like a shock, moving her back a step.

"What's wrong, Kolyn?"

She felt the table at her back and laid the dagger down. Kolyn shook her head. "Nothing," she finally whispered.

An alarm sounded in Ian's head, as it did when he was facing danger. Yet he pushed it aside, not wanting to acknowledge Kolyn could be the cause. "Why are you in my room? Something brought you here. What is it?"

"Nothing," she repeated woodenly.

Ian ran his hand down her arm. She felt cold. "You'd best get back to bed. You're freezing."

"Aye." Kolyn turned away and left the room.

He watched her leave, then sat up in bed. The alarm still sounded in his head, and he quickly searched the room. His gaze settled on the night table and his dagger. Ian's heart sunk. Kolyn had moved it. Disappointment was quickly replaced with anger. What was she about?

Then he felt sheepish, foolish. What had he expected? Did he really think she would give up trying to kill him just because he had married her? And what of the baby? Did he think that would change her thinking?

It was true, he was the biggest of fools. He had been gullible enough to trust Blair in his youth, and it seemed he had not changed all that much since. Time and the feud had only hardened him, not really changing his true nature.

The anger toward Kolyn turned inward, and he could not forgive himself for his childishness. He would have to be more careful. Obviously, she could not be trusted. Why couldn't he love a simple-minded woman who wanted only to please him in every way?

Ian lay back down to sleep, then thought better of it. He stood and went to the door. He wanted to rest without worrying about Kolyn sneaking in and stabbing him in the night. He threw the bolt and returned to his bed.

"Damn woman," he muttered, jerking the covers over his shoulders before settling down.

Kolyn stood for the longest time, staring out her window into the darkness, her mind seeing only her nightmares. She had no feelings, her tormenting thoughts killing them.

Time inched by, and soon the sun began to rise, the mist that lay across the moors swirling in the graying light, finally disappearing as the sun's warmth touched it. Tonight would be the celebration Molly planned, the village turning out to congratulate Lord Blackstone on his marriage.

This thought prompted a wry smile. If only the people knew the truth . . . what would they think? A soft knock interrupted her turbulent thoughts. Kolyn did not answer, she merely stared at the door. Slowly, it opened.

Ian looked in, then walked to where she stood by the window.

"I couldn't sleep," he said.

Kolyn still said nothing, her mind clinging to the image of Andrew in danger—dwelling on her helplessness, her despair, her desperation.

"Please tell me what you are thinking."

Ian tried to pull her chin up to look in her eyes, but she turned away.

"If I didn't know better . . ." Ian paused, looking down on her head, her back stiff and unyielding. "I'd think you wanted to kill me."

This brought her gaze back to his, her look murderous. Ian realized it wasn't just indignant anger that caused it, but a real desire to see him dead. Now he regretted his words. "The first time I saw you, I asked what you wanted from me. You declared that you wanted me dead."

Kolyn remained silent and frustration pushed him on. "Let's not play at games, Kolyn. Why don't you just tell me the truth? You still want me dead."

"And if I do confess such thoughts, what do you plan to do? Be the gentleman and kill yourself for me?"

He couldn't help but laugh, despite the strangeness of their conversation. "I never said I was a gentleman."

"No." She did agree with him on that point. "You never did."

Ian leaned down and whispered close to Kolyn's ear, his warm breath sending tingles to her toes. "What must I do to convince you I am worthy of your forgiveness?"

Kolyn closed her eyes to gather her will. How could one man do so much damage to her reserve? "'Tis not a matter of forgiveness, Ian. I forgave you long ago."

It was true. She had continued to speak the words, to claim to all he must pay for the death of her brothers and father. But deep in her heart, she had forgiven him. She bore him no malice for his part in their deaths. How ironic she would discover this now.

"You have a strange way of showing it, Kolyn."

"Aye," she said sadly. "I only hope there is forgiveness in your heart as well."

"What is it I am to forgive?"

"My weaknesses." She spoke softly, more to herself than to Ian. She had said too much already and knew she must be more careful. He was suspicious, and that made things more difficult.

Ian didn't understand what she meant, but he let it be. It was enough she no longer thought him totally responsible for the feud. He had never truly felt guilt for meeting the men of her family in challenge—it was a matter of honor, the way of men. But to have her feel he was the reason for what had happened in her life had caused him grief. He felt good to be rid of it.

Ian didn't speak again as they watched the sun climb higher into the early morning sky. He recalled their lovemaking—tender and beautiful. He relived their arguments—ugly and hateful. Their relationship remained so confused, they didn't know whether they loved or hated.

"I will be back tonight to take you to the village. Mother said she would bring you something to wear."

Kolyn's voice was soft, tormented. "It doesn't seem right."

Ian didn't know to what she referred. "What doesn't?"

She looked up, her eyes filled with doubt. "It doesn't seem right to celebrate our marriage. It seems a lie."

"Is it a lie, Kolyn?"

Kolyn felt her throat tighten and tears were close by. "Aye. Marriage should be about love, not just a child created by accident."

"In time—"

She put her hand up and stopped Ian. She couldn't bear to hear him say it. "No." She knew better. "Please go, Ian. I wish to rest for a while."

Kolyn watched Ian leave. She did not rest. Instead she paced the room, her mind running through a cycle of continual torment. When Ainsley's knock sounded, it startled her, the passing of time having no meaning in her mind.

When Kolyn didn't answer straightaway, Ainsley opened the door and called to her. "May I come in, Kolyn?"

"Aye." She had managed an answer, but her mind still whirled away from collected thoughts.

"I thought you might like a hot bath, and I've brought you something to wear. I hope you don't mind."

She struggled to maintain her composure. "Not at all. It was very thoughtful of you, Ainsley."

Ainsley smiled. "I'll return, if you like, and do your hair. You mentioned once that you were not good at fixing it."

Kolyn nodded. "Yes, I did. If it's not an inconvenience, that too would be nice."

"I'll be back soon. If you need anything, just ask one of the servants to bring it to you. You are part of the family now, Kolyn. Don't hesitate to ask should you need something."

"Thank you," Kolyn mumbled, her mind darting from one disheartening thought to another.

The door closed, and she continued her pacing until another knock interrupted her.

She assumed it was the servants to set up her bath. "Enter."

As they did so, she stared out the window, not really aware of who entered and left. Kolyn turned her attention to the girl only when she touched her on the shoulder.

"'Tis ready, my lady."

Again she muttered a weak thank you.

"Would you like me t' stay and help you?"

"No, I can manage," Kolyn could not stop the deep sigh. "I'm sure you have plenty of other matters needing your attention more than I do."

The girl's eyes widened. "Oh, no, my lady. It would be my pleasure t' help." She took Kolyn's hand and guided her to the bath. "I could wash your hair. 'Tis so thick an' pretty."

The servant girl couldn't be much younger than she, and Kolyn liked her congenial manner. So she allowed the girl to assist her, and when Kolyn stepped into the steaming tub, it felt wonderful. For a short time, Kolyn was able to empty her mind and enjoy the simple diversion.

"What's your name?"

The girl smiled shyly, "'Tis Mary."

Mary began to lather Kolyn's hair, the gentle massage relaxing Kolyn so totally, she drifted off to sleep for a moment. Mary wrapped her hair in a soft towel, and Kolyn couldn't suppress a wide yawn as she settled back again in the copper tub. Her eyes closed, and she fell asleep for the second time.

"Shall I wash my lady's back?"

Kolyn's eyes flew open, and she found herself staring into Ian's dark, gold eyes. "Where's Mary?"

"I sent her away." He smiled, kneeling beside the tub. "I told her I would assist you with your bath."

It amused Ian that Kolyn blushed.

He lifted a brow. "Do not look so mortified, Kolyn. After all, I am your husband." Ian picked up the heather-scented soap and smelled it. His smile widened. "Shall I wash your back?"

"No." Kolyn stiffened, her voice as tense as her back.

He turned his smile into a frown. "Even if I promise to behave?"

"No."

Ian's sigh was long and sad. It did not change her mood. "You do know how to take the fun out of being married, lass."

Instead of making Kolyn angry, his words hurt her deeply." "'Tis not what I imagined it should be either."

"When you were a little girl, what did you dream of?"

Kolyn closed her eyes to keep the tears back, not wanting Ian to see her cry. "It was so long ago, I can't remember."

Ian's finger brushed her cheek, opening her eyes to his. "Was not so long ago, lass. You've barely passed twenty."

She pushed his hand away. "I feel much older, and I no longer dream childish dreams. My nights are haunted with nightmares that I cannot chase away. This marriage holds no future for me."

Ian said nothing. He stood and left the room. A few minutes later, Ainsley returned and helped her dress as promised.

Chapter Twenty-seven

Kolyn had never seen so many people gathered together at one time. People came in from all over. It amazed her that the word could have spread so fast. Everyone came to meet Kolyn and wish the Lord of Stonehaven the best. She felt as if she were deceiving them all, not just Ian and Ainsley.

"Ian has gained the respect of his people," Kolyn said quietly to Ainsley in a short spell with no interruptions. "I admire that. My people mostly feared my father. He was known for his temper and harshness."

"Each man deals with people in his own way. Your father's way was just different from Ian's. My own father was much like yours, and until I met Ian's father, I had never known a truly gentle man. Seems almost unfitting for a Scotsman. My son, luckily, is a good combination of both. He has a temper." Ainsley looked to Kolyn as she finished. "But you know that, don't you? When he was younger and less likely to listen to advice, he acted rashly."

"You did not want him to marry Blair, did you?"

A pained look crossed Ainsley's pretty features, then disappeared with obvious control. "No. I knew she would hurt Ian. But . . . he would not listen to reason where she was concerned."

Kolyn suddenly found herself wanting to ask a question she knew she shouldn't, but could not keep from it. "You would do just about anything to keep Ian happy, wouldn't you, Ainsley?"

She looked surprised but answered honestly. "Aye, I would. 'Tis the way of mothers. This is something you will learn about soon."

No—it was something Kolyn knew about now. "How far would you go for your son?"

"I don't know if I understand what you mean."

"How far would you go to protect Ian? Would you kill to keep him from harm?"

The questions seemed stark, absolute, when spoken out loud. Kolyn held her breath, wanting, no, needing to know what Ainsley would do for her child.

"Yes, if need be, I'd kill to protect him."

Kolyn turned away from Ainsley, unable to look her in the eye any longer. Her breathing became strained, she couldn't get enough air into her lungs. Guilt assaulted her—she couldn't kill Ian to protect her son. What kind of mother was she? "If you should ever look back on this time and wonder about what I have done and why, remember that I loved with the same determination and strength as you do Ian. Then, perhaps, you will not hate me so much."

Ainsley pulled Kolyn's face back to hers, her eyes filled with concern. "I should never hate you. Tell me what it is that keeps you so far from us, Kolyn. You frighten me."

"I cannot," Kolyn whispered. Then she pulled away and lost herself in the crowded room. The hours dragged by as she waited for the night to pass, anxious for the next day, Saturday, to arrive. She needed air, and headed for the door.

The cool night brought immediate relief to her heated skin, and she breathed in great gulps of its freshness. She wanted to disappear into the dark shadows that lined the forest's edge just beyond, but thought better of it. Kolyn stayed close to the inn and sought solace in being alone, away from the clamor of the people inside.

Still, a feeling disturbed her, stealing away the peacefulness she sought. Kolyn looked out into the darkness, studying the shadows intently. Dwight stood among the trees.

Kolyn whirled about to go inside, and ran straight into Geoffrey.

"I didn't mean to startle you."

"Y . . . You didn't." She glanced back to see Dwight was gone. "I was just going back inside."

"If you wish to stay, I'll not disturb you."

"That's all right, Geoff." She tried to still the fear that threatened to engulf her. "I don't need you to watch over me. I'll not wander off."

"I don't mind keepin' you company, my lady."

This made Kolyn angry, rescuing her from the fear. "I'm not a child and I don't want your company."

Her anger embarrassed Geoffrey and he looked away.

"I'm sorry, Geoff. I know you are only doing as you are told. 'Tis Ian I should be angry with, not you."

"Ian's only concerned for you and the child. I think it would kill him if this child . . ."

He didn't finish, but Kolyn understood. "He should have thought of the consequences before he sent Blair away. He knew she couldn't survive, not with a babe on the way."

Geoffrey looked confused. "Ian didn't know Blair was with child. He would never have banished her if he had."

"You lie," she accused him bluntly. Blair had

told her Ian knew. Even Emmett had known about the baby.

"I have no reason to lie to you, Kolyn. Ian did not learn that Blair was going to have his baby until he heard of her death and that a child had died with her. He has lived with a guilt all these years he does not deserve. I had hoped that the child you carry would ease the grief that still burdens him."

"How can that be?" Kolyn whispered, the walls of her world crowding in on her. She couldn't breathe.

Geoffrey's strong arms supported her, or she would have fallen to the ground. He was speaking to her. She saw his lips moving, but she could not hear the words. A great roaring filled her head, and she feared she would be sick.

Kolyn bolted from Geoffrey and returned to the celebration. It all mocked her—the laughter, the smiles. Everyone . . . everything. Each face became grotesque to her, and she fought to get past them. She needed to get away.

Ian saw Kolyn leave again, and knew something was wrong. She was pale, her face drawn. He spotted Geoffrey as he entered the inn, and moved through the throng of people to find out the problem.

"What's wrong, Geoff?"

"I don't know. She looked ill."

"Aye," Ian said, already heading for the door. Once he was outside, it took a moment to locate

Kolyn. She was going inside the stables. "Is she going home?"

"She wouldn't be so foolish," Geoffrey exclaimed.

"I think she would."

Kolyn had a horse pulled from the stall before Ian stopped her. "Do you never listen, woman?"

Her green eyes looked at him so filled with pain it took the harsh words he had been about to say from his mouth. She pushed past him, her grip still on the mare's reins.

"Kolyn . . ."

She ignored him, but the wild look in her eyes told him something was terribly wrong. "I'll take you home."

"Please . . ." she cried out, her tone as strange as her look. "Don't interfere, Ian. You cannot help me. Don't you see that?"

He grabbed the reins from her. "I cannot let you go out alone. Just let me take you home."

"Send me away, Ian."

Ian did not understand what was wrong. "We'll go home and talk this out. Everything will be all right. I promise you."

"How can you promise such a thing?" She began to laugh. "You don't even know what is going on."

Ian stilled, then took her by the shoulders. "What is going on, Kolyn? I want to understand."

"I don't want to hurt you," she mumbled,

touching his face tenderly. Then her look became confused, doubtful. "But I must."

"Why must you?" he questioned, still baffled by her bizarre manner. "Why must you hurt me? Do you hate me so much?"

"No, I've never hated you. I love you."

Her confession was as strange as her actions, taking Ian by surprise.

"I love you, Ian. But I love another more. One of you must die, and I could not bear to lose him. He has been a part of me too long. My heart would break, and I could not live. He is just an innocent in all this ugliness."

Ian tried to be patient. "You are not making any sense. Let's go home. Then we will talk."

Kolyn began to sob, and Ian drew her into his arms, holding her close, uncertain how to comfort her.

"No," she cried, and pulled away. She grabbed at his knife and jerked it from its sheath. Kolyn lunged, the blade slashing in a frenzy, much like her manner, her mood.

The dagger bit into his arm, drawing blood, but Ian caught her wrist before she could make another swing. He pried it from her hand, and it dropped to the ground. Tears streaked her face, and she struggled to free herself. Ian lifted her and carried her to his horse. Geoffrey stood, waiting, the horse saddled and ready.

Kolyn suddenly stilled.

"She's fainted," Ian offered, seeing the unasked question in Geoffrey's eyes. "Tell

Mother I've taken Kolyn home." Ian mounted and rode off.

Ian watched Kolyn as she slept, her face as white as the sheets she lay upon. He heard his mother's soft knock and went to the door.

"How is she?"

"She's still sleeping." Ian ran his hand through his hair, worry scorching his mind, her odd behavior still clear in his memory. "She's not awakened since she collapsed at the inn."

His mother took his hand into hers, tears in her eyes. "She carries a great trouble that we cannot imagine."

Her eyes fell to the blood on his arm.

"'Tis nothing," Ian assured her. "She was saying things I can't understand. What am I to do?"

"When she awakens, we will speak with her. She must trust us with whatever it is that has her so frightened."

"Yes, when she awakens."

Ian closed the door and returned to his chair, to his vigil. He would be there when she woke up.

Kolyn heard his heavy breathing even before she was fully awake. She lifted her swollen lids and peered in the direction of the sound. His head had dropped down onto his chest as he slept in the chair he had pulled up next to her bed. The sun's light hurt her eyes, and she realized how late it was.

Slowly, she reached out and grasped the vase that sat on the night table, then hid it beneath the covers. She closed her eyes again and let out a soft moan. It was all it took to bring Ian awake. He leaned over and brushed the hair from her face.

"Kolyn," he whispered.

She turned over and slowly opened her eyes. His eyes were filled with concern, tenderness. Kolyn placed her hand upon his cheek and whispered, "Forgive me, Ian."

He looked confused. Kolyn brought the vase up and smashed him firmly on the back of his head, knocking him unconscious. He slumped down upon her.

Kolyn wiggled out from beneath him and rolled him over into the bed. She felt his head and found a lump, but no blood. Her eyes fell to his dagger. Kolyn reached out and stroked the long handle, then grasped it firmly in her palm. Determination rushed through her, and she pulled it free of the sheath.

Ian did not move as she crawled from the bed and stood over him. Again, she laid her hand to his cheek, the roughness of his unshaven beard scratching her tender flesh.

"I love you, Ian."

Kolyn left the room, careful not to be seen. By the time Ian awakened, she would be gone. She must go to Andrew.

* * *

Ian moaned and rolled over, nearly falling off the bed. He held his head in his hands as he swung his long legs over the edge.

"She's gone," Geoffrey said, standing in the doorway.

Ian looked up and nodded. His splitting headache told him that. He didn't need Geoffrey to tell him.

"Where has she gone?"

"I don't know, Ian. Your mother was out riding and saw her. The groom says she is following her and will return as soon as she can."

Ian stood, his head spinning as he did so. He stumbled when he started to walk across to Geoffrey. His friend held out a hand to support him.

"Damn woman," Ian mumbled.

"What should we do?"

"Wait until we know where to find her."

Geoffrey looked unhappy.

"Do you have a better plan?" Ian asked testily.

"No," Geoffrey looked sheepish. "I didn't mean to—"

"I know. It's damn frustrating, isn't it?"

"Yes." Geoffrey noticed Ian's dagger was missing, and this confused him more. "If she wants you dead, Ian, why didn't she use your dagger while you were unconscious?"

His hand moved to his empty sheath, and

he wondered that himself. There was nothing about Kolyn he understood. But today he would find out what was behind her misery. That he promised himself.

"I need a drink," Ian declared.

Geoffrey agreed, even though the hour was early.

Chapter Twenty-eight

Kolyn wrapped her shawl around her head, not wanting to risk recognition as she rode into the village. Luckily, the church was at the edge of the small cluster of cottages. She rode around to the private garden and dismounted, tying her mare securely to the fence. Entering through Father McCloud's kitchen, she waited and listened.

She heard Andrew's voice, the tone telling her he was unhappy, then Donald's. His harsh words struck a chord in her, bringing forth an anger already simmering inside her. Now it raged full force when Andrew's crying hit her. Kolyn entered the chapel, each step barely controlled as she fought the urge to run and grab her son from that horrible man. She recalled how he treated his animal, and blanched as she prayed he had not been so cruel to Andrew.

Donald's hand was raised to slap Andrew, his sneering face ugly with anger. "I'll only ask once." Kolyn's voice was even, unlike the turmoil that churned inside her breast. "Do not strike my son."

The hideous man turned to Kolyn and, to her amazement, sneered even more. She would not have thought he could twist his face into so many contortions.

"You are late," he shouted, his hand still wrapped about Andrew's wrist. The little boy's eyes rounded with joy at the sight of her, and he struggled to free himself.

"Let Drew go."

Donald didn't look like he was going to, but then with a grunt he let Andrew go. Andrew ran to Kolyn. She knelt down to scoop him into her outstretched arms. Tears overwhelmed her.

"My sweet Drew," she cried, hugging him as tight as she could. "My Drew."

Ainsley stood in the shadows, well hidden from view, but able to see the scene in the chapel. Tears wet her lashes as she began to understand Kolyn's questions of the night before. Kolyn had a son. She must get Ian.

"'Tis time t' go, lad," Donald said.

Andrew looked up at Kolyn, frightened, and hugged her even tighter. Donald tried to pull him free, but failed. The harder he pulled, the more Andrew screamed.

"Give us a moment more," Kolyn begged, trying to settle her son's fear. Donald ignored her pleas and kept pulling at Andrew. Finally, Andrew's grip broke, and Donald jerked him away. Andrew kicked out, his tiny foot landing a hard blow to Donald's shin. He hollered, then struck Andrew full across the face, causing him to fall back onto the floor.

Kolyn was enraged. She pulled the knife from her skirt where she had it hidden. "I said I'd tell you only once." She crossed the short distance between herself and her son in a flash. Donald turned, his arm raised in defense. The blade cut deep into the flesh of his forearm, his scream of pain mingled with anger.

Donald knocked Kolyn aside with his good arm, the blade still stuck in his other arm. Kolyn fell against a pew and hit her head, the stars she saw obscuring her vision of Andrew before she passed out.

Kolyn heard Father McCloud's voice calling to her. Slowly, she opened her eyes. Panic seized her at the quiet that permeated the church. She tried to sit up. Pain throbbed in her head, and she moaned from the effort. Father McCloud's sniffling forced her to ignore her own discomfort as she looked about for her son. She did not find him anywhere. She saw only Donald's body and the odd angle of his neck as he lay dead on the floor. Something had happened after she had blacked out—her

413

wound to his arm had not been the force that killed him. She made herself remain calm until she knew what had gone on.

"Where's Drew?"

Father McCloud's face was grim and her heart sank. Gently she touched his blackened eye, and knew without asking that he had not given Andrew to Donald willingly. Her gaze returned to Donald's body. She was confused. She looked back at Father McCloud.

"Who killed Donald, Father?" Her eyes widened with shock as she considered the good father killing Donald to protect her and Andrew. "You didn't . . ." She couldn't finish her question.

"No, lass. Was Dwight."

"Dwight?"

"Aye." Father McCloud looked about him nervously. "He said if you wanted to see the lad again, you were to go to the place where your father died."

Her heart sank. "Dwight wouldn't harm Drew, would he, Father? He's been uncle to the lad since . . ." Kolyn lost her voice as she choked on her dread.

"What does he want from you, Kolyn? He's no longer the man I've known all these years. Something has changed him."

Kolyn swallowed hard and closed her eyes, shame scorching her mind. "He thinks he loves me, but I believe he has confused me with my mother. 'Tis something that has festered for too many years and turned into a sickness of his mind. He is obsessed with the idea that I will be his wife."

"Surely you cannot mean this. He is your uncle. This cannot be." The shock on the good father's face showed Kolyn his feelings.

"I don't think that matters to him anymore. He has sworn to have me as his own, and now he is using Drew to force me to comply."

"We shall think of something else, my child."

"I have no choice, Father." Kolyn stood, steadying herself on the same pew she had struck her head against. "I must go to him."

"I cannot allow this abomination."

She looked at Father McCloud. How could he deal with the wickedness she must battle? "I was committed to killing the man I love to save my child from Emmett's madness. Father, can complying with Dwight's demands be any less of a sin than murder?"

He had no answer for her. Kolyn gave him a hug and kissed his weathered cheek. "Forgive me my sins, Father, but I will do what I must to keep Drew safe."

"You've had more than your share of grief, child. I had hoped it would be over with the death of your father. Never did I imagine such evil."

Kolyn felt the cut on her forehead, her blood warm and sticky.

"You're bleeding, Kolyn. Let me tend it." He took her hand and started to guide her toward the back.

"No, I cannot take the time." She smiled, though her mind cried out with sadness. "Good-bye, Father." Kolyn wondered if she would ever see this good-hearted man again.

Tears filled Father McCloud's eyes, and he wrung his hands in distress. "God bless you, my child, and may he watch over you in this time of your need."

Ian thought he would go mad before his mother rode up. When she tore into the courtyard he experienced a surge of raw emotion long before she began to tell what she had witnessed.

Outwardly, he remained calm, but inside he was in hell. Still, one thing confused him. Kolyn had a son. This was an impossibility, but it wasn't the main issue at that moment.

"I'm going back with you, Ian."

Ian turned to his mother and frowned. "It's best if you stay here, Mother."

Ainsley lifted her chin stubbornly. "I think not."

He knew that look and didn't want to argue. It wasted time. "Do as you wish."

Ian arrived at the church first, Geoffrey having slowed his horse's pace to match that of Ainsley's mare. Ian jumped from his mount and all but ran into the chapel.

"Kolyn," he yelled, bringing only the priest from the back.

"She's no longer here, my son."

It wasn't what he wanted to hear. "I think 'tis time you told me everything. I've little time, and my need to know what is going on is great." Ian sat and waited for Father McCloud to speak. Ainsley and Geoffrey joined him, all eyes on the holy man.

"'Tis difficult to know where to start."

Ainsley helped him. "Tell us about Drew."

Ian turned to his mother. "Who is Drew?" An intense pain made him draw in his breath sharply. He had hoped he'd tempered his jealousy, but he had obviously failed to do so. He tried to bring it under control.

His mother seemed confused by his question. "Why, her son, Ian."

Suddenly, Ian understood and he laughed. Kolyn's words came back to him, but this time the jealousy and hurt was gone. *I love you, Ian. But I love another more.* "She could not bear to lose her son!" His laughter stilled when he recalled their lovemaking the first night. It was impossible.

"It cannot be her son," Ian said stubbornly.

Father McCloud looked startled, then slowly realized what Ian meant. He blushed at the thought, but offered an explanation. "'Tis true, Andrew is not her natural son."

"Then whose, Father?" Ainsley asked.

"Kolyn took Andrew as her own to raise when

417

Fela Dawson Scott

she was but fifteen years of age. Almost a child herself. She has loved him and nurtured him no less than if she had given birth to him herself."

Ian watched Father McCloud, nervousness making him fidget. "You haven't told us whose child Drew truly is."

Father McCloud hesitated, uncertain what to say. He looked from one to the other, then made his decision. "'Tis Blair's son. Your son, Ian Blackstone, by birthright."

Ian wasn't prepared for this declaration. Even his mother was left speechless. Finally, he managed to speak. "Andrew is my son? I was told he died, that he had not even lived an hour. How can this be?"

Ainsley speculated. "Blair must not have wanted you to know of your son, Ian. Who could ever understand Blair and the reasons she did things."

It did not appease Ian. "Why didn't Kolyn just tell me I had a son? Why did she keep the truth from me?"

"Kolyn feared your finding out the truth. She knew only what Blair had told her, that you had rejected your child and you wanted nothing that was a part of Blair and her betrayal."

Ian was stunned. "And she believed this of me?"

Father McCloud felt sympathy for the man, but he held back no longer. "Kolyn knew nothing of you except the legacy of hatred left by her family. The clan feud has left her totally alone in the world, except for a brother who lies insane with rage and crippled in his bed. Wild tales that you are the Devil and turn into an animal only confused her more. Her father made her promise upon his sword before his men to avenge the family honor."

It all ran across Ian's mind, the horror of it leaving him numb. Yet it clarified so much. "Her father made her swear such a thing?" He still couldn't believe it of the MacGregor, that he had been so heartless and cruel.

"Aye." Father McCloud shook his head to confirm his answer. "It has haunted her every moment. Kolyn has always been a gentle child with a heart of pure gold. She was the only person who did not turn from Blair in her despair. Kolyn delivered Andrew; he has known no other mother but her, and Kolyn knows the child only as her own. 'Tis her brother's madness that has forced her hand."

"What has her brother to do with this?"

Father McCloud spoke of Emmett's insanity and his evil plan to force Kolyn to kill Ian to protect the life of her child and that of the child she now carried. He finished by telling of Dwight's obsession and that Kolyn had gone to him.

A deathly quiet descended on them.

Ainsley was the one to break the silence. "The poor child."

"Aye," Father McCloud agreed. "Only God can help her now."

Ian rose, his great height towering above them all. "Only God and the strength of my sword."

Hate coursed through Ian, each beat of his heart sending strength and determination to his body and brain.

"You stay here with Father McCloud." This time, when he spoke to his mother, she did as he said.

"Don't worry, Mother." His voice had softened, worry so clear on her face. "I'll bring *both* your grandchildren home. I promise."

Kolyn waited at the stone cottage. Neither Dwight nor Andrew were anywhere to be found. Her nerves were strained to the limit, but she waited, afraid to do otherwise. Finally, she heard a horse approach. She looked out the door that hung loose on its leather hinges. It was Dwight. He had Andrew with him.

Dwight's mood was black, his face frightening her. He let Andrew run to her.

"We must go t' the castle," Dwight said.

Panic touched Kolyn. "We can't, Dwight. Emmett will be angry that you killed Donald."

He looked at her, but it was as if he really didn't see her. "Do you think I care what Emmett thinks?"

"'Tis dangerous," she argued.

Dwight merely laughed. "'Tis no man I cannot take, Kolyn. And your brother lies abed with only his tongue as his weapon."

"He's mad and dangerous."

"Aye, he is mad. All that hate has turned inside him, eating his soul away."

Kolyn made her decision and took her chance. "I'll not risk taking Drew there. He must go back to Father McCloud's."

A growl erupted from Dwight, and he jumped at her, grabbing her hair. He pulled her to him cruelly, his eyes no longer showing any tenderness toward her. "You'll do as I say, or the lad will suffer. Makes no difference t' me if we take him with us or not."

"You loved Andrew once. What has taken the love from your heart, Dwight?"

"You have, lass. I no longer feel anything."

A shudder ran over her flesh, and she closed her eyes against the vision of hate she saw in his eyes. "I'm sorry, Dwight. I did not mean to hurt you. I only did what I had to."

"You've taken me heart and killed it. But I'll have you, lass, with or without your love in turn."

She placed a hand on his cheek. "If you leave Drew unharmed, I'll love you, Dwight. I promise."

Dwight shoved her from him, and she fell to the dirt floor. "You are lying," he yelled, punctuating his words with a kick to her side.

Kolyn scrambled away from him. Andrew

421

ran forward to stop Dwight, hitting at his legs ineffectively. Dwight tried to grab him, but Andrew bit his finger. The older man growled menacingly, then raised his hand to strike. Kolyn screamed, stopping him.

"Do not hit him, Dwight. I'll do whatever you want, just don't hit him."

Dwight lowered his hand, but the expression in his eyes remained. He did not try to stop Andrew when he ran back to Kolyn. She hugged him to her fiercely, whispering comforting things in his ear. He no longer cried, but she could feel him trembling. Kolyn felt helpless to protect him, to keep him safe.

"God help us," she mumbled.

"We must go," Dwight demanded, jerking her up from the floor. He tried to take Andrew from her, but Andrew's grip was so tight about her neck Dwight couldn't budge him. Dwight gave up and let her carry the boy.

"Why are we going to see Emmett?"

Dwight glanced back at her, his eyes dark and troubled. "'Tis not Emmett I wish t' see."

"Then who?" she persisted, needing to know. Even more, needing to prepare for what lay ahead.

"'Tis the witch-woman I seek."

The fear that clutched her made her heart stop, then rush ahead painfully. "W . . . why the witch-woman, Dwight?"

This time, he turned to look her straight in the eyes. "T' rid you of the bastard you carry,

Kolyn. I cannot have you heavy with his child while you sleep in my bed."

Panic seized her, squeezing all calmness from her with the air in her lungs. She bolted. Dwight was only one step behind her. In seconds, he had her firmly in hand.

Kolyn still held Andrew and couldn't fight him off, but when he lifted her from the ground to carry her back to her mare, she kicked with every ounce of strength she had left.

"Damn it, Kolyn, be still."

She did not heed his warning, and Dwight struck her with his fist across her jaw. Blackness engulfed her for the second time that day.

When Ian arrived at the cottage, it was empty, looking as if no one had been there for a long time. Yet as he walked about the dingy single room, he caught signs that someone had been there recently. Fresh footprints marked the dirt floor, and scuffed places showed there had been a struggle. His heart contracted as he thought of Kolyn having to fight the big man.

"I've found some fresh tracks, Ian."

Ian went back out at Geoffrey's call and examined them himself. "Aye, they're headed to the village."

"Makes no sense," Geoffrey said, his own features heavy with worry. "Dwight's been banished. Why would he risk takin' her there?"

"Why indeed," Ian mumbled. Instinct told him there was no time to waste.

423

Chapter Twenty-nine

Kolyn heard talking, and despite the pain, despite the desire to hide away from the horror, she pulled herself from the blackness that surrounded her. Slowly and sluggishly, the meaning of the words began to form in her mind. She bolted awake. She was at Gregor Castle, in Emmett's room. Immediately, she searched for Andrew. He pulled away from his uncle and ran to her open arms. She hugged him tightly.

"It seems my sister has joined us." Emmett looked from her to Dwight, who stood near his bed. "I still am not quite certain I understand what it is you want."

"The witch-woman," Dwight ground out between clenched teeth. "I want the witch-woman."

"What makes you think she is here?" Emmett pretended to examine his fingernails, looking undisturbed by Dwight's sudden intrusion.

Kolyn could see his irritation, though she was sure Dwight was beyond observing it. Dwight seemed too engulfed by his own emotions to interpret others' deception or intent.

"I left word that you wanted t' see her." Dwight's words held a steely edge.

A muscle in Emmett's jaw twitched. Kolyn knew he was angry. She had fought with him enough over the last months to read the subtle hints of his moods. Still, he merely smiled, then laughed.

"Now, Dwight," he mewed, almost too obviously. "I don't know if she will come, but we can wait if you'd like."

"We'll wait."

Kolyn prayed she would be a long time coming, but it wasn't but a few minutes until Jacob brought Juanita to Emmett's room.

Emmett waved his hand in the air. "You can go, Jacob. And see that we are not disturbed."

As soon as the door closed behind Jacob, Dwight grabbed the witch-woman and pulled her over to Kolyn.

"Get rid of it," Dwight spat at her, the fear that sprang to Juanita's eyes real. "If you don't, I'll kill you, lass."

Dark eyes turned to Kolyn, but she could no longer read them. "'Tis my pleasure, Dwight MacDougal."

"Don't touch me," Kolyn warned. "Harm my baby, and you'll have worse to fear than Dwight."

Juanita stopped. "What do you mean?"

"'Tis Ian Blackstone's baby. He'll kill anyone who harms me or the child."

Dwight twisted Juanita's black hair about his hand and pulled her head back painfully. "But you'll be dead if you don't. Do what I ask and you can go away, far away. I'm taking Kolyn with me, and that son of a bitch will never know what happened t' his bastard."

"Don't listen to him." Kolyn drew his angry gaze to her, but she didn't back down. "He's lying to you. He knows Ian won't rest until he's found me."

Dwight exploded and all but threw Juanita across the room. "He cares nothing for you! He only cares for the brat you carry."

"No, Ian loves me, Dwight. Unlike you, he doesn't want to hurt me or my child."

The stain of red crawled up his face, and Kolyn began to think he would burst from all that blood in his head.

"No one loves you more than I." His voice trembled, the shouting having subsided to a bare whisper. "No one."

"You don't love me," Kolyn said with every bit of hate she could muster. "You loved my mother. I am not"—she stressed each word with the strength she had left—"my mother!"

"Aye, I loved Katey." Dwight looked confused. "But I love you as much. You've her hair, her skin, her eyes made of emeralds. I've longed for you all these years, and now you'll be mine. I'll not let that bastard devil have you. Not my Kolyn."

"I'm not yours Dwight," Kolyn screamed, her own anger and hate consuming her. "I am Ian Blackstone's wife, the mother of his child. You'll not destroy the good I have found in the midst of so much that is ugly and sick."

Emmett's laughter filtered in through the haze of fury that engulfed her. She turned to him.

"You love him, don't you, sister?"

"Aye," she confessed, no longer wanting to keep it from them. "I love the Black Wolf, and neither of you will ever see him dead. He's too strong for you."

This hit her brother hard, his smile fading into a look of pure violence. "Kill that bitch that calls herself my sister. No MacGregor would speak so traitorously!"

"She's mine, Emmett. You gave her to me, and I'll take what is mine," Dwight declared.

Emmett looked disgusted. "You want the bitch? Even after she's spread her legs for him? You can rid her of his brat, but you'll never be rid of the stench of him on her."

"Shut up, Emmett." Dwight's voice was strained. "Shut up or I'll kill you."

This brought a look of arrogant pride to

Emmett's face. "You dare to speak to me this way." He puffed up, pulling his upper body up a far as he could. "You are nothing, Dwight MacDougal. You are nothing but the bastard child of this family, here only at the will of my mercy. Get out of my home, or I'll have *you* killed."

Emmett reached for the cord to ring for Jacob, but Dwight's hand stopped him. The surprise on Emmett's face was obvious, but it intensified when Dwight put a hand to his throat. Emmett twisted from Dwight and brought his fist up hard into his stomach. Though he had no use of his legs, Emmett's upper body was still strong.

Kolyn did not hesitate a moment longer. She gathered Andrew into her arms and ran from the room without looking back. Carefully, Kolyn made her way from the castle. She went down the back hallways as quickly as she could carrying Andrew.

She turned a corner and was stopped. Startled, she began to flee, but Nellie was the one who stood in her way. Kolyn had never been so happy to see anyone in all her life.

Quickly, she handed Andrew to her. "Nellie, take him to Father McCloud's. Do not let anyone, I mean anyone, stop you." Tears filled her eyes. "Keep my son safe, Nellie. Promise me."

"What's goin' on, my lady?"

"I've no time to explain. Please, Nellie, I beg

you. Do not delay." Kolyn ran down the hall from Nellie.

"I promise, my lady," Nellie called out after her.

Kolyn worked her way back to the front of the manor. Dwight saw her, and she fled down the stairs and to the entry. She managed to open the massive door before he reached her. She darted outside. A cry went up instantly, a villager spotting her. Kolyn understood that no one here would help her.

"Get her," Jacob cried as he ran out the door. "Kolyn's murdered her brother as he lay helpless in his bed."

Kolyn didn't have time to refute his lies. She barely escaped into the alleyways as many of the villagers rushed after her, including Jacob. She didn't know where Dwight had disappeared to. The outcries of the people were ugly, their calls of *witch* sending chills down her spine. She ran as fast as she could, but found her way blocked many times. Kolyn felt trapped, unable to escape the village where she had grown up, the very people she had once loved.

Jacob was the one who finally caught her, his hands brutal as he dragged her out into the street. A rock struck her on the arm, then another pelted her back.

"She's given herself to the Devil Blackstone."

"Traitor!"

Jacob held up his hand to stop their outcries.

The crowd stilled, but inched in closer, their looks threatening, hostile.

"This woman has betrayed us all with her wanton desire for the Devil Blackstone."

He held their attention, and when he looked down at Kolyn she plainly saw the hatred he had always disguised beneath his stony features. He placed his hand upon her rounded stomach.

"She carries his child with no regret. She has even declared that she loves this wolf-man, his evil now nurturing within her."

This brought a renewed outcry, the villagers' threats brutal and ugly. "Fire!" many called. "'Tis the only means of purification! She must burn in fire!"

"Fire," Jacob whispered into her ear. "They want to burn you, Kolyn MacGregor."

Kolyn wanted to say something, anything, but words failed her. Terror struck her with such ferocity she thought she might die from it. She prayed for instant death. It would be better than burning. Her knees weakened, and she slumped against Jacob.

"Do not pass out, witch. I want you to know what we are about."

He slapped her face, bringing her from her stupor.

"I want you to feel the flames tearing your flesh from your bones."

Jacob allowed the villagers to carry her across the meadow to the forest's edge, then

Fela Dawson Scott

tie and bind her to a tree. Kolyn cried out, but no one listened as they gathered brush and piled it at her feet.

Ian and Geoffrey entered the village, the tracks having led them back where they had begun. Frustration overwhelmed Ian. Suddenly, he saw Kolyn's servant woman, carrying a child—his son. Slowly, he recognized the dark head as that of the child he had seen in the forest so long ago. Then he remembered the name called out . . . Drew.

"Where do you go with the child?" Ian asked, stopping her as he put his war-horse between her and her destination. She looked frightened, but determined.

"None of your affair, my lord." She attempted to go around him.

Gently, Ian moved into her path again.

"I'll not ask again." He gentled his voice, but made his point clear. "Where are you going with the lad?"

Nellie looked about her, obviously confused. Ian saw terror on her face as cries and noises drifted from the village to them.

"I go to Father McCloud's," she finally managed to say. "My mistress has bade me not let anyone take this child from me but the good father."

"Is your mistress Kolyn?"

"Aye." Nellie looked up, tears streaking her face. "My mistress is in trouble, I fear."

Ian turned to Geoffrey. "Make sure this woman gets to Father McCloud unharmed."

Geoffrey started to object, but Ian's look stopped him. "Protect my son with your life, my friend."

"Aye." Geoffrey followed the servant to the church.

Ian immediately headed in the direction the noises came from. He found the streets unusually empty, setting off an alarm in his head. He twisted about, searching the village, but saw nothing, no one. When he spotted an old man scurrying past him, he stopped him.

"Where is everyone?"

The aged man straightened, and he held his hand to shade his eyes. Still, he could not see well. "They be burnin' a witch. You'd best hurry if you want t' see it."

He toddled off, his short, bent legs carrying him from town. Ian followed.

Kolyn watched in horror as Jacob set a torch to the dry wood, sparking it into a blaze. Suddenly, Dwight plowed through the ring of villagers. He knocked Jacob aside and put the flame out with his booted foot.

An animal-like growl erupted from Dwight as rage filled him, spurring many to move out of his striking range. He trampled the smoldering brush and cut Kolyn free.

"Leave her be," Dwight cried, slashing the air menacingly with his dirk. "She's mine!"

Before Kolyn was free of the ropes that bound her, Dwight grabbed her about the waist and pulled her to him. "She's mine and I'll kill any man who dares keep me from taking her with me."

The crowd hushed, Dwight's fierceness keeping them at bay. Kolyn kicked at his shin and twisted free. She stepped away, but the wood beneath her feet shifted and she lost her balance. She fell to her knees. Just as Dwight reached for her, a black wolf leaped between them, giving Kolyn time to scramble out of reach. The blade of Dwight's knife sank deep into the animal's neck.

Still, the wolf slashed at Dwight with his vicious teeth, his bite doing damage before the big man flung him away. The wolf hit the ground with a yelp, then lay silent and still.

Ian saw the crowd at the meadow's edge. He spurred his mount into a gallop, covering the distance in a matter of seconds.

People jumped from his path, the giant horse's hooves guaranteeing passage through the tight-knit crowd. A cry went up when they recognized who interfered, many fleeing in fear.

Ian spotted Kolyn, and jumped from his horse.

Kolyn put herself between Dwight and Ian. "It's over, Dwight."

"'Tis not over till he dies."

Ian moved forward, ready, waiting.

"Hasn't there been enough death? Enough killing?" She begged.

"You swore an oath, Kolyn MacGregor, before God and your father's men. What of it? What of the honor of the clan? Care you so little for the way of Scotsmen?"

Ian looked at Kolyn and saw the pain on her face.

"Are you a loyal MacGregor? Prove it," Dwight urged her. "Kill the Black Wolf."

Kolyn did not move. Ian took his own dagger and placed it in her hands. Once and for all, he had to be sure what she would do. "Do you want to kill me, Kolyn?"

She did not move. She merely stared at the knife.

"Kill me now. Take the dagger and plunge it into my heart. Now's your chance to fulfill your promise."

Kolyn still did not move, so he took her hand and placed the tip of the blade to his heart, his hand still over hers. She pulled away. Everyone waited. Everyone watched.

"No," she cried out in anguish. "I cannot kill the man I love, the father of my children."

She turned to look at Dwight. "If you truly loved me, you'd walk away, Dwight. I beg you, walk away and leave us in peace."

"I cannot, lass." He pulled his sword from its scabbard. "I love you more than life itself. I plan to kill your husband and take you with me, lass. It cannot be any other way."

435

"You're a fool, Uncle."

Dwight's cry of outrage warned Ian, and Ian pulled his sword in defense. The crowd scattered as the men fought, swords whistling as they cut air, swords clashing as they came together, edge against edge. Kolyn could do nothing but watch. And pray.

They were nearly matched in size, Dwight only an inch or two shorter in height. Ian's superior strength was matched by Dwight's years of experience. Each maneuver was outmaneuvered, each stroke countered. Time moved with aching slowness, and Kolyn thought her heart would burst inside her chest. To interfere would distract Ian, so she remained deathly still. With each drop of blood Dwight's sword drew, she screamed silently.

Ian grew tired, his sword weighing heavy in his hands, his only consolation the weariness in Dwight's stroke as well. Finally, Dwight let out a Highlander's cry and with his last bit of strength, swung at Ian. The tip of the sword skidded across his stomach as Ian drew back, then Ian stepped forward again and drove home his own blade. It sunk deep into Dwight's middle, stilling the cry in his throat. Dwight dropped to his knees, surprise still showing on his face. He looked to Kolyn, his eyes seeking hers.

Ian saw the grief on her face as she turned away from Dwight's hate-filled gaze. Dwight fell backward, no longer a threat to himself or his family. Ian went to Kolyn, put his arms about her.

Someone shouted out, "'Tis the Devil, Kolyn. You must walk away from such evil."

Kolyn looked up to Ian and said softly, "This man is not evil . . . he is kind and gentle."

Father McCloud moved through the crowd to stand by Kolyn and Ian. He turned to the angry mob and spoke. "Ian Blackstone is no more the Devil than you or I. He is but a man who has met the trials of God as best he could."

He turned loving eyes to Kolyn, then to Ian. "He is but a man who loves a woman enough to put his life into her hands, trusting her own love is as great as his."

"What of the wolf, Father? 'Tis the Devil's work I see."

"I saw a devoted friend, not the Devil," Kolyn argued.

Ian looked at Kolyn and offered his explanation, caring little what they thought, but wanting Kolyn to understand. "I found him caught in a trap many years ago. I nursed him back to health, and he has been my faithful companion when I go into the forest. He was but an animal, not the Devil."

Timidly, Kolyn moved to stand by the wolf, then knelt beside the dead animal. She mourned his death. He had been a friend to Ian, and to herself. She stroked his fur and said a silent good-bye.

"I never believed you could become the wolf."

She stood and faced the violent, hateful people of her clan.

"My father forced an oath from me I cannot keep," she went on. "I am shamed by the hatred and lies he perpetuated, the legacy he has left behind for his children and grandchildren. I was afraid to follow my heart." Her gaze moved to Father McCloud. "In my heart I had discovered a love so great I failed in my attempts to fulfill my promise."

Kolyn felt tears on her cheeks. "God blessed me by giving me Andrew, and now he has blessed me with a child of my own. Ian Blackstone has fathered both of these children . . . how can that be evil?"

"You dishonor your clan," another shouted.

"Dishonor?" Kolyn cried. "Is hatred and killing honorable? If that is honor, I'll have no part of its ugliness!"

Father McCloud came to stand beside her. "My good people, the MacGregor has not dishonored her clan. The promise has been fulfilled. The Black Wolf is dead." He pointed to the dead animal. "Let the legend die with the wolf."

"She killed her brother!"

"No." Juanita drew everyone's attention to her as she stepped forward to be heard. "It was Dwight who killed Emmett. Not the MacGregor. Jacob has lied to you."

A murmur went up and everyone looked

about for Jacob. He was gone, his disappearance more convincing than Juanita's words.

"'Tis time for us to go home." Juanita turned and left.

Slowly, the people drifted off. Ian pulled Kolyn into his arms and she hugged him tightly. She wondered at the strangeness in life—why Juanita had told the truth. Kolyn would never know.

Geoffrey rode up with Andrew, Ainsley right behind.

Kolyn took Andrew into her arms and with pride turned to Ian. "Ian, meet Andrew, your son."

Ian took Andrew from her, both of them timid as they eyed one another. Andrew finally laughed and hugged Ian with his chubby arms. When Ian turned back to Kolyn, she saw tears glistening in the dark gold of his eyes.

"'Tis a fine boy, Kolyn." Ian's look was proud, grateful.

"Aye." She put her arm through his. "Let us bury the wolf, Ian, in a place where his spirit can watch over our children as they grow. He was a true and courageous friend."

"I love you, Kolyn."

She smiled. "I love you, Ian Blackstone. Now and forever."

THE TIGER SLEEPS

FETA DAWSON SCOTT

Bestselling author of *Ghost Dancer*

In India she roamed wild, a seductive creature as exotic as any jungle cat. Now, tangled in the snares of London society, Ariel Lockwood is betrothed to a ruthless predator who will ruin her family should she refuse to become his prize trophy.

A tawny minx not a proper English lady once aroused Dylan Christianson's burning desire. Years later, Ariel's image still lingers in the Earl of Crestwood's dreams. The only man who can save Ariel, he will forfeit all he has to awaken her sleeping passion and savor the sweet fury of her love.

_3529-4 $4.50 US/$5.50 CAN

Top-selling Historical Romance
By Leisure's Leading Ladies of Love!

Savage Embers by Cassie Edwards. Before him in the silvery moonlight, she appears as if in a vision. And from that moment, a love like wildfire rushes through the warrior's blood. Not one to be denied, the mighty Arapaho chieftain will claim the woman. Yet even as Falcon Hawk shelters Maggie in his heated embrace, an enemy waits to smother their searing ecstasy, to leave them nothing but the embers of the love that might have been.

_3568-5 $4.99 US/$5.99 CAN

Winds Across Texas by Susan Tanner. Once the captive of a great warrior, Katherine Bellamy finds herself shunned by decent society, yet unable to return to the Indians who have accepted her as their own. Bitter over the murder of his wife and son, Slade will use anyone to get revenge. Both Katherine and Slade see in the other a means to escape misery—and nothing more. But as the sultry desert breezes caress their yearning bodies, neither can deny the sweet, soaring ecstasy of unexpected love.

_3582-0 $4.99 US/$5.99 CAN

LEISURE BOOKS
ATTN: Order Department
276 5th Avenue, New York, NY 10001

Please add $1.50 for shipping and handling for the first book and $.35 for each book thereafter. PA., N.Y.S. and N.Y.C. residents, please add appropriate sales tax. No cash, stamps, or C.O.D.s. All orders shipped within 6 weeks via postal service book rate. Canadian orders require $2.00 extra postage and must be paid in U.S. dollars through a U.S. banking facility.

Name_____

Address_____

City _____ State_____Zip_____

I have enclosed $_____in payment for the checked book(s).

Payment <u>must</u> accompany all orders.☐ Please send a free catalog.

Discover the real world of romance in these passionate historicals by Leisure's Leading Ladies of Love!

Apache Conquest by Theresa Scott. Sent to the New World to wed a stranger, beautiful young Carmen is prepared to love the man chosen for her—until a recklessly virile half-breed sets her blood afire.

__3471-9 $4.99 US/$5.99 CAN

Song of the Willow by Charlotte McPherren. When tomboy Willie Vaughn meets handsome Rider Sinclair, she vows to hang up her britches and Colt .45 and teach the mysterious lawman a thing or two about real ladies.

__3483-2 $4.50 US/$5.50 CAN

Elfking's Lady by Hannah Howell. When Parlan MacGuin takes lovely young Aimil captive, the fierce Highland leader means to possess both the beauty and her magnificent white stallion Elfking. But only love will tame Elfking's lady.

__3475-1 $4.99 US/$5.99 CAN